RAVENWOOD

NWOOD

ANDREW PETERS

Chicken House

SCHOLASTIC INC. / NEW YORK

Excerpt from *Wandering* by Hermann Hesse (Picador, 1972),
copyright © Hermann Hesse

Library of Congress Cataloging-in-Publication Data

Peters, Andrew, 1965–
Ravenwood / Andrew Peters.
p. cm.
Summary: On Arborium, the last forested island in the future,
fourteen-year-old Ark, who lives in a mile-high city set in the
treetops, overhears a plot to rob Arborium of its wood,
a natural resource more precious than gold.

ISBN 978-0-545-30550-1

[1. Fantasy. 2. Adventure and adventurers—Fiction. 3. Trees—Fiction.
4. Conservation of natural resources—Fiction.] I. Title.
PZ7.P4415466Rav 2011
[Fic]—dc22
2010044484

10 9 8 7 6 5 4 3 2 1   11 12 13 14 15
Printed in the U.S.A.   23

First American edition, August 2011

The text type was set in Centaur.
The display type was set in FLLW Terracotta by P22 and Serlio.
Book design by Whitney Lyle

To my wife, Polly, who helped so much with structuring, editing, and creating the world and who has been my constant companion in traveling deeper; to my lovely children, Roz and Asa, who were my first readers; to Eugene, who kept me going when I was ready to give up; to Uli for fighting the good fight; to Rachel Hawes, who gave me so much helpful advice about clothes up in the trees; to Barry, who had faith in me and the work and who took the risk; to the team at Chicken House who backed this to the hilt; and finally to Imogen, my brilliant editor.

TABLE OF CONTENTS

1   The Chase 1

2   One Hour Earlier 9

3   One Minute Before Ark's Jump 19

4   An Unexpected Meeting 24

5   Dead and Alive 31

6   Poison Gas 39

7   The Journey Begins 49

8   A Fall from Grace 58

9   Time to Act 68

10   Danger in the North 76

11   Sewers Are a Boy's Best Friend 85

12   Confrontation 94

13   The Slippery Truth 99

14   Going Down 107

15   Bribery or Execution 114

16   Finding Your Roots 122

17   Diving Deeper 130

18   A Cunning Way Through 136

19   Deep Down 143

20   A Meeting of the Minds 149

21   Infant Terrorism 157

22   Flight and Fight 166

23   A Friend in Need 174

24   Bait 182

25 Only a Boy 188

26 The Ravenwood 195

27 Curiosity Kills 201

28 A Sudden Discovery 206

29 Acting Scared 217

30 A Really Boaring Lesson 223

31 Hunger to Live 230

32 Dungeon Delight 238

33 The Miracle of Technology 245

34 Escape and Betrayal 253

35 An Old Friend 259

36 Deadly Training 264

37 Reunion 270

38 Practice Makes Perfect 277

39 Communion 282

40 Preparation Is the Key 286

41 All the King's Men 296

42 Payback 302

43 To Battle 309

44 Death of a Rootshooter 316

45 A Sudden Turn 328

46 The Last Grasp 335

47 An Unexpected Visitor 342

    About the Author 353

RAVENWOOD

"Trees are shrines. He who knows how to speak with them,

who knows how to listen to them, experiences truth. They

preach no catechism or recipe, they preach original law."

HERMANN HESSE

1 · THE CHASE

🌿

Stay on the wood, it's as it should.
Step off the tree: end of thee.
—Dendran proverb

The forested island of Arborium
October 5, early evening, one week before the Harvest Festival

The arrow flew over his shoulder and thudded straight into a wooden post. Too close! If he hadn't stumbled out of the way, the shaft would now be buried somewhere near his heart. He imagined the blood blooming like a flower across his shirt, his body tripping over the edge of the branch to fall lifeless to the earth, a mile below.

Ark was exhausted. Sweat coursed down his back, and his calf muscles ached. He whipped his head around: They were only a hundred yards behind. This part of the highway was wide and straight. Not only had the original, huge branch been carved flat, like all the smaller branch roads, but also it had been extended widthways with beams and scaffolding. Now it was twenty feet across at the passing places. At this time of the afternoon, before brush hour, the way was deserted. Ark ran lightly, feeling each knot and dip in the wood.

Somewhere hidden up above, dark clouds squeezed out their downpour, filling the forest with echoing drips. The constant drumming urged him on and Ark ran for his life through a mass of shifting shadows. His plumbing belt was weighing him down. Wrenches against crossbows? Forget it. But there was no time to get rid of it, either. Another arrow whistled past and vanished harmlessly into the leafy green depths.

His pursuer paused, wiping rain from his eyes, taking careful aim for another shot. The escaping boy's drenched clothes, from the brown leather skullcap and grotty tanned jerkin to the tight britches and worn stockings, showed him up to be just a sewer worker. In fact, his prey resembled one big turdy stain on the treescape. The guard tried to keep up, straining his eyes through the downpour. The boy streaked ahead in his rubber-soled creepers, standard wear this high up. No one wanted to slip off the edge, especially in this weather. As for killing a fourteen-year-old? It wasn't a problem but the solution.

Straight ahead, the highway ran toward a huge, hollow tree trunk. Ark bolted into the center and hesitated, catching his breath. A bird shrieked in the distance, and a rustling sound echoed around the wood, causing Ark to glance up into the shadows above. The dead tree was a crossroads. Its massive trunk supported the junction with branch lines leading off in three directions through carved archways. He looked toward each in turn. In a dark corner, ancient moss-covered steps led down into the hollow depths. He was desperate, but going earthward? He shuddered even to think of it. Which way?

Ark's head replayed the day. *Just another clogged drain,* his boss had said, not wanting to dirty his clean white hands. *You can sort it out, Arktorious Malikum. It's a job. In fact, it's a "big" job! And, let's face it, you're brown already—so sticking your hand in a great fat pile of it won't make much difference!* The man laughed at his own joke. He always did. But this was no laughing matter.

Right in front of him, a red squirrel squatted on the wood-way, nibbling at a hazelnut. It stared at Ark briefly before diving down the stairs.

"This way . . ."

Ark looked around. The voice was so soft he wondered if he was imagining things. Talking squirrels? He was going nutty! Without thinking, Ark followed the animal, darting into the archway to be swallowed by the enveloping blackness. For a moment, he could catch his breath out of sight of the guards. He had to make the most of it.

A snorting sound ahead startled him. Moving slowly toward him out of the gloom was a laundry cart piled high with clean clothing, being pulled by a small mottled brown pony. As the cart passed him, its wooden wheels hit a knot in the deeply carved ruts and the brass harness jangled, sending strange harmonies into the leaves. It meant *move out of the way*, as these unaccompanied pack ponies didn't change their pace for anyone.

A gift horse! Ark smiled grimly and sprinted to the back of the cart. He scrambled up the tailgate and dived under the waterproof treepaulin into the carefully sorted mounds. He wriggled under, pulling clean petticoats over him, and crossed his fingers, praying to Diana for safety.

"Where's the little sliver gone?"

"He was 'ere a second ago. . . ."

The voices were muffled as they drew closer.

"I reckon we nearly got 'im!"

Ark held his breath, waiting for pressed shifts and undergarments to be stripped away. His mother had always warned him about going out alone in the wood, else the ravens could snatch his body and suck out his soul. This was far more dangerous.

"'Ave a look from up there." The cart shuddered as feet

clambered to the top of the laundry pile. The full adult weight of a hulking guard crushed down on Ark, squeezing out the remaining air in his lungs. They'd either hear his ribs cracking or his heart hammering like a woodpecker's beak.

A phrase from childhood came into Ark's head:

> *Hold the feather, grab the weather,*
> *Woe betide me, Lady hide me!*

It was a nonsense chant spouted by old crones and repeated with glee in the nursery. But he was happy to believe in anything at this moment.

"Buddy holly!" the guard swore. "Can't see 'im anywhere! Maybe the slippery twig fooled us into thinking 'e turned left."

"Grasp'll kill us if we don't find the boy!" hissed the other one. "Let's split. He can't 'ave got far. . . ."

The weight on Ark's chest lifted and the voices faded away. Had the old chant worked? Ark breathed deeply, filling his lungs, and counted to two hundred, even though his legs were itching to take off. Maybe he could stay in the cart and wait until it delivered its load? He was almost lulled by the gentle rocking motion. No! He shook himself. He had heard too much. Grasp would put the word out. As of now, he was dead wood.

First, he had to put some distance between himself and the High Councillor's thugs. He carefully pulled back a pair of hose stockings and several layers of leather codpieces to make a peephole, trying not to think of where those items of clothing had nestled. He peered out. All clear. Ark slid backward and slipped cautiously off the end of the cart, wishing he had an apple to offer the steadily plodding pony.

"Thanks, old fellow!" he whispered. "I owe you one!" The pony's blinkered eyes flicked toward him as if in acknowledgment, and the cart moved off, leaving Ark alone on the highway.

He looked warily around at his world with new eyes. All that he'd taken for granted: no longer safe. A humid mist blurred the edges of the huge leaves, each one the size of a fully grown man. Above, below, behind, and in front, branch lines and highways were woven and cantilevered together with rope, scaffolding, and a million wooden nails. Trunks of massive girth, large enough to support the hundreds of houses, businesses, and hostelries carved into the hollow depths, punctuated the sprawling treescape. Ark had always believed that, despite its turbulent history, this vast island of Arborium was the safest place on earth, lifted up and spread out as it was through the canopy of trees, a mile above the dirty ground. Not anymore.

"Oi!" The shout cut sharply into his thoughts. There! Only yards away, one of his pursuers was hurtling straight toward him. The branded emblem on his tabard gave him away: the cruel-beaked hawk of the Councillor's household. Of course, the guards weren't that stupid. Wait long enough and every mouse pops out of its hole.

Ark cursed himself as the man lunged and made a grab for his wrist. Ark jumped back and twisted away, but not quickly enough. The man's grip landed and tightened. Although he was almost as skinny as Ark, his muscles were strong as oak.

"Let me go!" screamed Ark.

"Don't think so, squit-features." Viselike fingers squeezed closer, forcing tears of pain from Ark's eyes. "You're a month's bonus, you are!" He smiled menacingly, revealing a set of teeth like rotting fungus, with breath to match.

Ark stopped struggling as cold fury overtook him. What right did they have? His father had always told him he could think his way out of any situation. But what good was thought against brute strength? As his mind tried to focus, pure instinct kicked in—after flight comes fight. It was like watching himself from outside his body . . . his right hand was still free. In one perfect curve of movement, Ark reached down, slipped the heavy wrench from the plumbing belt, and swung it up and around with all his might.

The guard was expecting a cowering youth. What he got was a well-aimed weapon and a sickening crunch for a punch line. The man's eyes went wide and he slowly folded to the ground.

Ark didn't pause. He was off even before the thump of body falling on wood. His pursuer's scream would have been as good as an alarm bell, and where there was one guard, more were sure to follow. At least, Ark thought, tasting the adrenaline of escape, he'd bought himself some time. But the branch line he was following was long and straight and seemed to keep going forever. He knew that the next turnoff was nearly a quarter of a mile away, and his thin legs were beginning to cramp with the effort of the chase.

He scanned the way ahead and skidded to a sudden halt on the treacherous woodway. His worst fears were already advancing in the distance: another guard, twice the size of the first, footsteps creaking toward Ark. The man's stiletto was drawn purposefully, its sharp blade shimmering in the rain. Ark could make out a rough scar zigzagging across the man's shaved head like a bolt of lightning.

Ark spun around. He'd have to double back. How far to the next branch crossing and, even if he got there, where next? He looked over his shoulder and saw that the guard had broken into a run and was shouting and pointing. As he turned again, he saw why. Farther along, the first guard—the one he thought he'd knocked out cold—was already sitting up. Could things get any worse? This time, there was no welcoming crossroads, no alternative route, nothing. Ark was trapped.

The rain soaked into the forest, thickening the mist that now hung in drifting patches. The highway was plunged into shadow and the two guards could hardly make out the figure of the boy, already neatly camouflaged in his stained brown clothes. No matter. Where could he go? They came at him slowly, sure of their prey, sure of the outcome. No need to hurry: It was over.

The boy appeared to kneel down as if praying. Then he stood up, looked over the edge, and took a single step back. Before the men could do anything, the boy leapt from the highway, breaking the great unwritten law of the Dendrans:

Stay on the wood, it's as it should.
Step off the tree: end of thee.

As the boy flew into space, the lead guard shuddered. To jump willingly, away from all that was known, down to the foul, poisoned earth so far below . . . it was madness!

They ran as fast as they could through the mist, but it was too late. By the time the guards finally converged on the spot, the boy had vanished. One of them crawled to the edge of the branchway and lifted the safety ropes to peer nervously over the edge. But even though he strained his eyes down and down, all he could spy was the lad's plumbing belt, caught on an old bit of scaffolding on a dead trunk a hundred feet below.

"Nothing would survive that fall," the other guard muttered,

behind him. From his perch on the branchway's edge, his part-
ner pointed out the plumbing belt. That was that, then.

After a brief discussion, the older guard cleared his throat
and launched a nice fat gob over the edge. Gravity did its job
and it fell, just like the boy.

"Good riddance!"

"It's peeing down. Let's get out of here." If the boy was dead,
their problems were solved. Even better, their master might just
be persuaded to give them a bonus and a barrel of beer.

"How's your head, Alnus?"

"Do you really care?" The smaller guard clenched his fists.

"Knocked out by a mere kid! That takes talent, that does."
There was a nasty glint in Salix's eye. He was thoroughly enjoying himself.

"Yeah, well at least I caught him in the first place!" They'd
be ribbing him for months now.

". . . and let 'im go! You must have the thickest skull in the
business, plank-for-brains!"

"Oh, cheers, Salix. I appreciate your concern. . . ." He could
feel the bump already rising. Why couldn't he have been the
one to push the boy off? The stupid squit had deprived him of
revenge. Still, at least it was taken care of now, and once they
were dried and warmed up, a good night of drinking might just
take care of the throbbing between his ears.

2 · ONE HOUR EARLIER

Petronio was desperate for a crafty smoke. At the School For Surgeons, the masters had of course lectured on and on about the dangers of tobacco. Ha! What did a bunch of crusty, dried-up old men know? After all, he thought impatiently, he and his fellow students were *still* being asked to dissect pathetic little squirrels. For Diana's sake! When would the masters give him a chance to cut open a real corpse? However, now that lessons were over for the day, he was free to ignore the dire warnings and indulge in a little petty pilfering to satisfy his craving. He stopped to listen carefully before slowly opening the door to his father's study. Councillor Grasp was busy entertaining downstairs and there was no one else around.

Petronio's gaze wandered around the room. The desk was neat and tidy, with folders stacked in a perfect line against the right-hand edge. Tapestries covered the walls, depicting his father single-handedly defeating pine wolves and whole packs of wild boar. A smile dimpled Petronio's face as he stroked his fake-beard extensions. The closest his father had ever got to killing a wild animal was spearing it . . . with his fork as it lay on a gold plate handed to him by a crawling servant. Still, it impressed those who came to do business with the Councillor, and "business" was what gave them this luxury house in the very crown of the tree.

Large floor-to-ceiling windows kept out the driving rain. Beyond lay a balcony where visitors could stand on pleasant days and be suitably awed as they looked out across the treetops, all the way to Barkingham Palace, the residence of King Quercus ten or so miles away. Why did the people of Arborium still love their ruler? Giving out coins to the poor on Diana's Day was hardly going to change the whole wide-wood. Petronio's father was right about how out of touch the King was.

But Petronio wasn't interested in the views, political or otherwise. He moved soundlessly toward the desk, knelt, and slid open the bottom drawer. He lifted out a carved wooden box. Surely his father wouldn't miss just one?

As he stood up, he caught his reflection in the mirror. A well-built young man stared back at him. Others might have snickered *fatso* behind his back, but he carried the weight with ease. His curly black hair was oiled and perfumed, his hazel eyes filled with false friendliness. A decent chunk of shiny hematite mined by the Rootshooters from the depths of the trees dangled from his left ear. White was the latest rage in court, but this meant his shift had to be repeatedly dipped in urine and left to bleach in the sun. The price was a slight whiff, but the dazzling result was worth it, topped off by a decent sun yellow silk doublet, puffed-up red britches held down by crossgarters wrapped around his knees, the whole lot finished off with an oversize codpiece. The mirror approved him. It was a good look.

A few seconds later, he was out of the study and slipping down the servants' corridor toward the utility room. Once inside, he breathed a sigh of relief. The cleaners had been and gone. He was safe.

The cramped, enclosed room was a jumble of gas pipes, waste chutes, and laundry tubs. It was nearly dark, apart from the flare of the single gas lamp. He carefully sidestepped a collection of dustpans and mops and made his way to the central flue, lighting the cigar with a match as he went. He swung open a small vent door and dragged deep, savoring the smooth taste, before leaning forward to blow the smoke right into the flue cylinder, letting the smoke wind its way up and out of the chimney system high above.

There was a sudden sound of footsteps. Fast and purposeful, they stopped abruptly on the other side of the door.

"Woodrot!" Petronio stubbed out the cigar and threw it down the flue. What a waste! As the door to the utility room swung inward and light spilled in, he stepped quickly into the far corner behind a pile of boxes and drew back.

Whoever it was who'd just entered didn't seem to notice the smoky scent. The intruder was humming a tune, badly. The hum came to a stop, followed by a moment's silence and then clanking noises accompanied by an interesting variety of muttered swear words.

A disgusting and all too familiar smell of sewage slowly filled the room. There was more muttering followed by a sigh and "Gotcha!"

Of course! Petronio's father had been complaining about the drains for weeks. Being rich made no difference—plumbers were always booked up. However, it appeared that one of their species had finally bothered to turn up. Bad timing, nothing more. Petronio thought about stepping out and startling the worker. It would serve him right for spoiling his smoke. But he wondered what a lowly plumber would make of the High Councillor's son lurking in the utility room. No, that wouldn't do at all.

He leaned back and nearly collapsed against the boxes when the unmistakable voice of his father suddenly echoed around the room. What the holly was his father doing in the utility room, talking to someone up to their elbows in the brown and nasty?

"We must move cautiously. Quercus is old, but not stupid." The voice sounded muffled and slightly distorted.

Petronio was confused. Only one person had come into the utility room.

Another voice, sharper and more feminine, answered. "*We?* Do not presume to speak of *us*, Councillor!"

"Naturally, my lady. A slip of the tongue. I beg you, accept my apologies. . . ."

Petronio forced himself to breathe slowly as he twigged the truth. No wonder the speakers sounded odd: They were distant. The plumber must have opened up one of the air-conditioning pipes and the voices were being carried up from the vent in the drawing room downstairs.

The woman continued as if his father hadn't even spoken. Petronio could detect a strange accent, her pronunciation of the Dendran language sounding stilted and formal.

"We pay you for information. As I have explained, the Empire of Maw is running out of space and raw materials. It is amazing to us that your puny little forest kingdom has managed to deflect all inquiry and communication for thousands of years: Arborium is truly the last potential frontier. The gas your trees exude to deter unwanted visitors was a clever evolutionary trick."

"Yes," mused Grasp's voice. "Nature is rather ingenious. However, as you are standing here, I presume that your empire's science has afforded you some protection?"

There was no answer. Petronio wondered if the woman was nodding or ignoring his father. And who the bark was she?

Councillor Grasp filled the silence. "We keep ourselves to

ourselves. But I fervently believe that the time will soon be right for our little country to serve a greater need. My lady, I stand at your service."

The sound of a chair being scraped back along the floor rose up the air shaft.

"Oh, do sit down, you stupid little man."

Petronio felt a surge of anger. Nobody called his father stupid and got away with it! Businessmen who stood in the High Councillor's way had a habit of vanishing over the edge in sad but unforeseen accidents.

The woman continued, "In our country, the amount of wood in this room alone would make one a billionaire! This island will be a farm unlike any other, and your people will make excellent workers! Of course, once we have cleared sufficient trees and revived our economy with controlled stocks of precious timber, we shall be able to tap your huge reserves of underground natural gas . . . and clearly, you will of course be wanting a *handsome* cut!" Petronio smiled. Whoever she was, she had certainly got the measure of his father.

Grasp's tone became wheedling. "Well, my lady . . . a small pecuniary deposit will simply help to smooth the machinery of change. And . . . I do believe you mentioned the job of President of Arborium for someone who stays, ah, loyal to the end?"

"You want more, and yet more again. I think we understand each other well, Councillor. Our plans are progressing, but time is short. In seven days, I believe you hold a quaint celebration called the Harvest Festival."

"Yes. What about it?"

"This shall be the moment we act!"

Petronio's mind darted off. What was his father up to? President? Petronio tried the phrase out in his head: *My father,*

President of Arborium. It sounded good—more than good. His duty was to report traitors, but duty be hanged! And what did she mean about the festival held on the first full moon of autumn? It was a waste of time, a bunch of poor plebs cluttering the capital with their stupid lanterns, gossiping about the weather! What was she on about?

His musings were interrupted by a sneeze. Petronio was startled. How could he have forgotten the presence of the plumber? More to the point, he now knew he wasn't the only witness to the high treason unfolding below.

"What was that?" came the woman's voice, sharp and alert.

There was a short, shocked silence. Petronio could almost hear the conspirators thinking.

When Grasp spoke, his voice was flustered. "The house creaks and groans. It is the nature of wood, unlike your . . . er . . . cities of glass and steel."

"Are you as stupid as you look, Councillor?" hissed the woman. "Ceilings . . . don't . . . sneeze!"

Petronio could hear the tension in her voice.

"Yes . . . of course. I think . . . it's possible . . . a spy!" deduced Grasp.

"Do you have any idea what that means? *Do* something about it. Now!"

Somewhere in the house, a bell immediately sounded, summoning security.

In the utility room, Petronio plunged his hand inside his jacket. Damn and Diana! His trusty knife was currently lying under the mattress in his bedroom. Totally useless! Maybe it would be better to wait for the professionals. He wasn't sure how to go about tackling a fully grown man, especially one who would be armed with both muscle and an array of heavy wrenches, but he could try. After all, he was well known for his *ungentlemanly* successes in combat class. He'd use the element of surprise.

He took a deep breath and jumped from his hiding place with a screeching yell. The plumber spun around toward him, an ugly-looking iron wrench poised in midair. But it was a slight brown face with high cheekbones that hovered behind, topped by the customary leather skullcap. And the eyes that stared wide with alarm were a vivid, almost jewel green. This was not the sort of surprise Petronio had intended.

"You!" Petronio shouted.

The face stared back with instant recognition. In Arborium, children from all backgrounds attended nursery and acorn school together until the age of seven; rich and poor mixed together like compost. After that, education cost; only those with means could afford it. The King enjoyed using words such as *equality* but the reality was far different. Ensconced within his palace walls, the old man had no idea that the compost was rotten to the core.

Once Petronio had moved on and become aware that his former playmate, Ark Malikum, was the son of a sewage worker, he'd wrinkled his nose and quickly joined the other children in looking down on him. Ark had always been skinny and faintly smelly: easy prey. Petronio remembered how his embarrassment at the association had given way to casual threats and intimidation whenever he and his new friends crossed paths with the unfortunate Ark. Their lives had gone in very separate ways, as birth intended—until now.

This momentary shock delayed Petronio for a split second too long.

In that instant, Ark dived for the door, knocking a pile of

boxes sideways. Anything he lacked in strength, he made up for in speed. Flight had always been his best way out of trouble and he was nearest the door.

By the time Petronio recovered his senses to scramble over the boxes and lunge out through the open doorway, he was greeted and grabbed by two sets of powerful arms.

"What 'ave we 'ere? A chubby mole in a hole!"

"You've got the wrong person!" Petronio shrieked, only too aware of the consequences of this mistake. "Quick, he's getting away!"

"Oh dear, oh dear, oh dear! Always innocent, aren't they?" The guards were obviously newly appointed, and what was more, they were smiling a bit too eagerly as the sturdy youth tried to struggle free.

"Don't you know who I am?" Petronio demanded. He wondered whether to try attacking at least one of them, but instantly decided against it. One was slender and sinewy, and the other had a scar on his head like a warning sign: *Don't mess with me!* Petronio was in enough trouble already, but he still protested. "You'll be shoveling squit by tomorrow for treating me like this!"

"Ooh! Hark at him, all high and mighty, considering we caught him in the act! Wot you think, Salix?"

"A fancy bit of lip, that! I think we got a right smart-arse 'ere, Alnus!" The guards were taking no chances. The larger one held the intruder in a neck lock as they hauled him downstairs.

"Here's your spy, sir! Perhaps if he'd been on a diet, he might 'ave slipped away. Thank Diana fer too many goat pies!" said Salix, shoving him into the room, before standing back.

Petronio stumbled forward and found himself looking up into a pair of strange, almost violet eyes.

The woman stared at him, then turned to read the explosive expression on Councillor Grasp's face. She raised an eyebrow. "Ah, let me guess. The family resemblance gives it away. Your son? Yes?" She circled Petronio slowly. He was transfixed.

Admittedly, Dendrans came in all shapes, sizes, and colors. The only trait that marked them out was the extra length of their fingers, all the better to grasp at branch or twig. But this woman was unlike any Dendran he'd ever seen. Her eyebrows were sculpted into twin crescent moons, her lips were painted red as rowanberries, and her black hair was pulled tightly into a woven bun. Her robe was like that of a Holly Woodsman, hood pulled back—though women priests were unheard of these days.

"*What* is the meaning of this?" thundered Councillor Grasp, addressing both his son and the now uncomfortable guards.

"Father. I humbly apologize." Petronio spoke quickly, trying to gauge how much time had already been lost. "But please listen. There was someone else in the utility room. A boy. Arktorious Malikum." He felt sweat gather under his armpits as he tried not to breathe in his father's general direction. Being caught out smoking would sidetrack the situation.

"The plumber boy?"

"Yes. And he'll be out of the house by now!"

"What?" Grasp was shaking with rage. "You mean you let him escape!" The Councillor smacked his forehead with the palm of his hand. "Don't they teach you the buddy obvious in school?"

Petronio was shocked. It was the guards' fault! If only they hadn't got in the way. As for the insults, he'd get his own back later.

His father lowered his voice. "Did you hear *everything*?"

Petronio was a born liar. *Like father, like son.* But for this once, he would make an exception. He nodded and mumbled, "Both of us . . . heard." He was digging himself deeper with every word.

"Let me assure you, boy, that if you breathe a word of this to anyone, I will not treat you like a son, but a traitor. Do you understand? The last fifteen minutes of your life never happened. Now leave us!" Grasp flicked his hand, dismissing Petronio as if he were a speck of dandruff. He turned to the guards. "So, it looks like we have more than one plumbing leak. There's another little drip that needs to be stopped— permanently! Don't prove as incompetent as my so-called son! And report straight back to me as soon as it's dealt with," Grasp snarled. "Do what you have to do. The sewage worker you let in earlier is a liability. Now move it!"

The guards did as they were told, pounding out of the house and onto the highway. The chase was on.

3 · ONE MINUTE BEFORE ARK'S JUMP

The mist had done Ark a huge favor. At this level, a few hundred yards below the treetops, the forest transformed into a backdrop of blurred shapes. He was now no more than an outline crouched between the advancing guards. Ark only had seconds.

His mind raced. What he'd overheard in the utility room was a death sentence. He had to do something, but what? He looked desperately at his plumbing belt: wrenches, screwdrivers, pliers, ratchets, and rope, thin but strong, for crawling through dark, stinking pipes . . . Rope! That was it!

The leaves shivered in the gloom, whispering amongst themselves, as Ark peered briefly over the safety posts at the edge of the highway. Why wait to be pushed? All he needed to do was unhook the rope from his belt, loop it around one of the posts, and then tie the ends tightly around one wrist. Crouching down for just a moment, he fastened the rope with nervous fingers.

It was now or never. All he had in his mind was blind faith. If the post was rotten, then . . . *snap!* Ark would truly plummet down: a wingless bird. Dead.

He stood up and took a running leap straight over the edge.

Every instinct screamed at him to stop. Too late. He flew out into space in a great arc. The rope unraveled, then pulled taut. The wrench was so sudden, he thought his shoulder might have dislocated. But underneath the branch line where he now swung wildly, he was still breathing, still alive. The earth had not claimed him — yet.

Quickly, with his free hand he undid his plumbing belt, which had been handed down from father to son for generations. His father had given it to him only last year when he had grown too ill to work. But Ark had no choice. He spotted his target, a broken bit of scaffolding sticking up from a withered old trunk, and threw the belt down toward it. He was a good shot. Even before it landed, Ark began climbing back up the doubled rope. He was as deft as a spider, soon reaching the underbelly of the scaffolding.

Beneath all the branch lines and highways, higgledy-twiggledy structures of wooden scaffolding supported the infrastructure of Arborium. There were mail tubes and gas pipes, and mini aqueducts that carried the supplies of water pumped up by the tree roots from deep beneath the soil. Ark had to keep moving fast through this tangle. He scrambled up until he found a perch directly under the branch line. He undid the rope from his wrist and pulled hard. It slithered back around the safety post and was swiftly coiled.

Just as the rope slipped finally into his hands, footsteps reverberated along the planks above him and cries of alarm were lost in the leaves. The steps finally came to a halt. There was a scraping sound, followed by a curse. So close.

Ark hugged his knees, trying to shrink into himself, and made his breathing shallow. Could they have spotted the thin strand of rope in the deepening dusk? If they had, it was over. He waited for a face to be thrust right over the edge, to stare straight underneath at him or for the thud of a close-range crossbow bolt.

"Nothing would survive that fall," muttered a voice that could only be a few feet away.

"Not quite 'nothin'.' What's that?" Another voice, even closer.

"Where?"

"Down there! Plumbing tools?"

Silence.

Ark counted to three. Would it be better to be caught or to actually jump?

"Ha!" A short, hard laugh. "Gives a new meaning to *belt up*, that does, doesn't it!"

"Almost makes you feel sorry for 'im!" There was more grim laughter, followed by coughing and then the rumble of a gob of spit being dredged from creaking lungs. "Pah! Good riddance!"

That was that! The plan had actually worked. The half-witted guards had seen what he wanted them to see. Now, according to the fading sounds of mockery up above, he was dead, off to the River Sticks to join the other sorry souls who had killed themselves.

He heard a far-off rumble of thunder, but the drum of drips on the woodway above had finally stopped. A pigeon warbled softly somewhere to his left. The men must have gone. But Ark still didn't move, curled up among the jumble of pipes and tubes. He wasn't sure that he could and he felt no satisfaction in having fooled his pursuers. After all, from now on, he might just as well be dead. His throat was dry and he felt like he'd been turned inside out.

If anyone had been watching, they would have seen what looked like a bundle of rags wrapped tightly around the scaffolding. Ten slow minutes passed before the bundle gradually began to separate into moving limbs. Ark unfolded and shakily pulled himself upright. He had to bend sideways to avoid knocking his head on any pipes. At waist height, a zinc-lined aqueduct ran either side of him on the underside of the branch. Water. He climbed closer, scooped his hands into the clear liquid and lifted it to his lips. As he straightened up, two pairs of identical eyes stared back at him.

Flippin' fungus! he cursed silently. Just what he needed!

Admittedly, it was the perfect spot: tucked out of the way with a plentiful supply of refreshment, the woodway above a convenient waterproof roof. He should have noticed that what looked like a haphazard pile of twigs was, in fact, artfully woven around the pipes, but his mind *had* been on other matters.

The two baby ravens continued staring at Ark as they opened their beaks and screeched. But the word *baby* in no way described these creatures, their claws already able to slice to the bone with one swipe, and beaks capable of cracking a puny Dendran skull like a walnut. Each of the fledglings was half as big as Ark and if these were the tiddlers . . . he shuddered to think about their parents.

Ark checked his arm. The rope burn all the way up the skin of his upper arm had begun to weep. There was a small beading of blood: all that was needed as scent to draw a keen hunter. Very bad. He looked and smelled like dinner on a twig.

"Hello, little birdies," Ark murmured. "No need to cry."

But to them he knew he was simply edible-looking prey, just feet away from their nest. They didn't want soothing words, they wanted Mommy. Now! Especially as Mommy could turn this intruder into din-din!

"Hush there!" Ark tried, but he might as well have told the sun not to get up that morning. Frantically, he attempted to lick the blood from his arm while looking for a way back up onto the branch line. Could he risk it? Did he have any choice? The ravens' screeching was getting louder and they'd begun flapping excitedly. Once they'd got the scent of injury and weakness, it was almost pointless even thinking about escape.

Ark heard the beating of wings before he could see anything. He was in just about the worst place possible. He knew that female ravens would do anything to protect their young. Out of the shadows of the underforest, a darker shadow blotted out his vision. As he shrank down instinctively, he forced himself to look up and saw the huge, dark eyes swallowing him, the claws—each the size of a sword—advancing to rip him up for supper, and the vast wings about to settle and draw a cloak over all his days.

At the same moment, the mist suddenly parted and the last of the evening sun shot a rare beam of light right down through the gloom. It pierced his retinas and he screeched in pain, a noise echoed by the raven's cry. *This is it!* he thought, closing his eyes. His mind filled up with home: his father curled like an arthritic leaf by the fire, his mother humming soft tunes to herself as she stirred the pot, his sister, Shiv, making tiny, complete worlds out of twigs and nutshells, the curve of the branches that held them up high. Each image slipped away until there was only the imprint of a black sun rising between his ears. All gone. All . . .

4 · AN UNEXPECTED MEETING

The blinding pain disappeared as quickly as it had come, and the cry faded from Ark's lips. He hesitantly risked a glance, then opened both eyes wide in surprise. The baby ravens still stared at him but were mute. Their mother, with her ravening claws, was nowhere to be seen.

Ten seconds ago, he'd been a meaty morsel in the making. Now he wasn't even frightened of the fledglings. What the bark had happened? Nothing made sense. He felt queasy. The raven of myth and story had veered away from him instead of swallowing him up. Two lives down. How many left?

But when he was calm, cold fury took over. It wasn't *his* fault that he'd overhead talk of a revolution and threats to Arborium! He was just a simple plumber's boy. The job was squitty, but it was a life. Ark felt the tears prickling his eyes. All that he loved in the whole wide-wood could be snatched away.

When his father had first fallen ill, Ark found himself one evening punching the thin wooden roof above his bed so hard that his knuckles had begun to bleed. School was for little children or for rich kids. He was neither. That was the way of Arborium. He was an apprentice and now he would have to be the head of the house, too. He remembered how scared he'd been to pick up his father's tools and his first day at work, filling his father's place, and all the jibes and jeers. How would he survive in the dark sewers, away from the sunlight that sank through the leaves, and the rain that battered the branches?

Somehow, he'd got through, even though the boss had made

sure that the newbie got all the dirtiest tasks. He'd survived, kept up to his targets, and even gained the grudging respect from workers twice his size. Now it could all have been for nothing.

It was time to go. Ark glanced one last time at the baby ravens. They didn't move but simply stared back at him. A strange instinct made him want to reach out and stroke their plumage. These were birds of myth and legend. He'd never been within touching distance before. *Forget that!* He levered his way out from under the scaffolding, shinned his way up various supporting poles, and peered over the edge of the branch line.

In all the activity, he hadn't heard the clocking-off bells. The empty highway was beginning to throng with tired day workers streaming away from court and the businesses that surrounded the seat of King Quercus. Ark chose a particularly dense, shaded spot a few feet away and, at the perfect moment, slipped up and over the edge. The storm had gone and taken the mist with it, leaving the trunks shining as if polished.

No one even noticed the dirty plumber's boy climbing out from under their boots and he allowed the crowds to sweep him along the branch line toward the nearest trunk. That was the thing about Arborium—it was a country that was never still. Buildings creaked, floors vibrated, wooden highways arched and flexed with wind and weight.

Amazing to think that the city of Hellebore, with the palace at its center, was almost all that remained of the great Arborian counties, before the ancient choleric plagues reduced the population to a sliver of what went before. The great forest truly was a place of abandoned echoes.

The trunk gates were wide open. Inside, beyond the through way, cavernous stairs wound left, going up, and right, going down. They were carved around the central, living core of the tree and worn with the footsteps of generations of plodding Dendrans. The smell of hot pies wafted up the nearside stairwell, reminding Ark he hadn't eaten all day. Of course, now he could hardly go back to his job and ask for his wages. Ghosts didn't usually get paid, as far as he knew. Anyway, he consoled himself that he'd always doubted that the advertised *one-hundred-percent-pure-goat* pie contents was strictly honest. Fifty percent dog and other unsavory leftovers was far more likely.

He ignored the fast-food stall, shoehorned into a dark alcove of the trunk, and wearily trudged on down the steps toward the lower levels. This way took him past the inner doors and windows of apartments hollowed out into the heartwood: prime property for the rich, but far out of reach of a plumber's income. The steps continued, winding down and down the central trunk, and the crowds eventually began to thin as he descended to the lower levels. Finally, a poorly patched-up gate swung open, revealing his local branch line. He stepped out into a land of shadows. The twilight had problems reaching this far. Night came earlier for the poor. But in the darkness Ark felt safe for the first time that day. *Home* was the only thought in his head. In the distance, he could see the gaslighter reaching up with his flare pole to spark the first evening lamps.

"Wot are *you* doin' 'ere?" The voice boomed in his ear as a meaty pair of hands grabbed him in a viselike headlock.

Ark's heart faltered. So close to home and he'd been found. Why had he come back? Of course they'd look for him here.

"Get off!"

And amazingly, instead of strangling him, the hands did as he asked and let go. Then, before he turned around, it hit him.

The voice. "Mucum, you big overgrown lump!" Ark hissed as he faced his workmate.

The boy he confronted fit the description perfectly, his tatty sheepskin waistcote barely able to contain a thick trunk, legs, and arms solid as oak as they almost sprouted out of his mud-colored hose stockings. The eyes, under a bright orange fuzz, stared at him amused.

"And keep your voice down. I'm supposed to be dead!"

"Yeah, right. That toilet must have been a real killer, huh? Looks like you fell in it! Yer soakin'! Didn't drown, did yer?"

Ark looked around frantically. "It's no joke. I'm in danger. I can't go home, can't go back to work, can't do anything." At that moment, Ark burst into tears, the tension of the last hour finally spilling out.

"Don't be such a girl!" said Mucum.

Ark wanted to kick Mucum, but all he could do was sob.

"Here . . ." Mucum pulled out a handkerchief that looked like it was stained with moss. He pushed it in Ark's direction.

Ark shuddered. "Thanks, but no, thanks." He wiped his tears away with a grubby hand.

"Suit yourself."

Ark wondered if he could trust Mucum. Working in the same sewage station didn't exactly make them best of buds. In fact, he hardly knew the boy, except to make the odd comment about the weather. After a second's indecision, he pulled at Mucum's sleeve and dragged him off the main thoroughfare, away from any possible listening ears. "Here! Sit! Be quiet . . . please!" He pointed at a gap between two piles of pine pallets ready for recycling.

Mucum wasn't used to being ordered around. He frowned. He could either sit on Ark and squash him or squat like a good boy on a pile of rubbish. He shrugged. "I'm all ears. But let me tell you that if you managed to flood Mister High-and-Mighty Grasp's basement with squit and are now sitting on the pity potty, I don't wanna know!"

"It's worse than that!" said Ark, scanning the walkway uneasily. "Much worse." He squeezed in alongside Mucum and finally filled him in on the events that had begun when he'd tried to unblock a toilet.

When Ark had finished, Mucum shook his head in wonder. "That's the longest speech I've ever 'eard from you!" He stared back at the normally quiet plumber's boy. "Either you've totally gone off your tree and made up the whole thing, or—"

"Since when have I been an expert liar? That's your department."

Mucum smiled. It was true. His excuses for being late for work had a legendary quality about them. The only reason their boss, Jobby Jones, tolerated him was that, occasionally, plumbing problems could be solved with brute force only. And when it came to bolts that refused to budge, or pipes that were heavy enough to squash mere mortal Dendrans, Mucum was the one for the task. "Okay. I always thought that Grasp was a bit too big for his boots, strutting around the place with his thugs as if he owned every buddy woodway! But from moron to traitor—that's a holly big leap! You dead sure about this?"

"I heard what I heard," said Ark.

"Maw coming here to nick the whole lot?"

Ark nodded. The place sounded like a far tale. A land without trees? Now, that really was a Holly Woodsman's version of hell. Towering palaces of mirrored glass and metal machines that flew. To most Dendrans, the distant empire was something of a rumor, a story that lurked at the back of their dreams. Now those dreams, those nightmares, were about to come to life. From what he'd heard today, Maw was rightly named, a greedy mouth keen to chew up their little island and spit out the pieces.

Mucum grabbed a small broken twig and began chewing it. He paused suddenly. "Every splinter worth its weight in gold to that lot? Makes yer think . . ." He looked around at the branches deepening into shadow, as the last of the stragglers from work made their way home and gaslights came on.

"Maybe they're right. This place is precious," muttered Ark, shivering at the thought of the future.

Mucum was already bored with talking about the end of the wood. "And they really shot at you with their crossbows?"

Ark nodded glumly.

"And you smacked one with yer wrench! Even I 'ave to admit that's dead impressive."

Ark tried not to smile, but actually, escaping killer guards was quite an achievement.

"That's better. You're cheerin' up now. As for pretending to kill yourself—buddy marvelous! Who'd have thought that our mousy little apprentice had it in him?" Mucum paused for a second. "Wot about them ravens?" The boy shuddered at the thought. He'd fight anyone. But the ravens? "Stuff of nightmares, they are, not that I'm scared or nothing, right?"

Ark knew it was a good idea to nod his head in agreement.

"But since when did they let a free meal go asking? And that close to the nest. You might as well 'ave had a target painted on yer 'ead! Am I missing something 'ere?"

"No. I don't understand it either. It's strange." Even stranger that he wanted to stroke the raven chicks.

"Anyways. Your problems are bigger than a bunch of monster babies."

"Thanks, Mucum. That really helps." Ark suddenly felt heavy all over, exhausted from running, from everything. He could just curl up in these boxes and let everything else fall away.

"Oi, sleepyhead. Go home. Take advantage of being dead! It's an asset, right? They're hardly gonna be looking for yer!" Despite appearances, Mucum was not as thick as a plank.

"Yes. Of course, you're right."

"I'm always right, me. When did yer say it was all kickin' off?"

Ark tried to remember what the woman had said. "Harvest Festival."

"Spot on. We got seven days. You can save Arborium when yer head's clearer. I've gotta get home for tea or me dad will kill me. Meet us outside work. I'll find an excuse and get out an hour before lunch. We'll think up a plan. And I promise if I see that Petronio, he'll be sorted." Mucum thumped Ark on the shoulder, almost knocking him over, then stalked off, his massive feet making the whole woodway vibrate.

It was time for Ark to go home.

5 · DEAD AND ALIVE

Despite himself, Ark managed a smile. At least he wasn't alone, though describing Mucum as a friend might be stretching it.

He was nearly back. Down here, between the branches, a thousand shanty homes had been erected, built from uppercanopian leftovers. There were trunnels, bark boards, and treepaulin, and pieces of cheap sheet resin for windows. Reworked iron sprouted and supported a thousand chimneys, now smoking away as if each house were secretly puffing on a cheroot. The twinkling subsettlement on the outskirts of Hellebore was strung on a precarious network of fraying ropes and vines. Ugly to some, but in his eyes, the dusklight revealed a winking, flickering necklace of beauty. Who needed stars in the sky when you could have this?

Ark trudged along the branch, trying to work out what on earth he could possibly tell his parents. The truth? Right— so he'd overheard a plot that would destroy their home and country, had nearly been murdered, then almost eaten by a bird straight out of the Ravenwood, was now believed to be dead . . . oh and, by the way, he'd brought no money home for food or rent and wouldn't be able to earn any more for the foreseeable future. Yes, that story would go down a treat.

He wove his way down a wood-alleyway between the densely crowded homes. Smoke swirled around the branches, its aroma mingling with the verdant leaves and resinous bark. Ark breathed in the smell of home.

"Whoa!" His foot paused midair. There in the middle of the woodway stood a bunch of bristles. The tiny hedgehog curled into a spiky ball, determined to defend its territory. As Ark stepped carefully around the creature, he frowned. If the empire had its way, the animals of Arborium would be no more than pests to be dealt with.

A minute later, he rounded the corner and his heart lit up. A tethered, somewhat grubby, curly-haired child played with a pile of twigs, dropping one, then another, over the edge of the branch. She had a look of rapt wonder on her face as the sticks spun down into the fathomless dark. Though she was already four, her imagination still lived in the wild wood.

"Hello, Shiv!"

"Arky-Parky!" cried his little sister. Her smile was even bigger than his.

He bent to inspect her tether. "We don't want you slipping off the edge, eh? I fell off the branch today and I pretended I was dead!"

"Arky's not dead! I won't let you, ever!" She frowned.

"Good for you!" He lifted her in his arms and landed a big kiss on her forehead.

Shiv squealed with delight. "Throw me off the tree? Pleeeeease?"

Ark could feel the weight of her. "You, my beautiful girl, are growing up too quick." Ark still loved playing the old game of holding his sister over the safety rope, upside down, and pretending to drop her, but then thought better of it. Too close for comfort, and besides, it occurred to him he ought to get inside before he was seen by any passing neighbors. He placed her back down carefully on the branch. "Sorry, Shiv. Another time. I have to go in to see Dad."

Her bottom lip drooped and a cry threatened to erupt from her lips.

Ark tried to head off the sulky storm. "Later. I promise. Be good now."

"Humpph!" muttered Shiv and turned her back on him to tell off one of the sticks.

Ark took a deep breath. At least he was back. The dome-shaped family home nestled by itself in a cradle of rope, like a giant egg. He stepped off the branch line onto a thin, swaying walkway, and bounced lightly. The creak was familiar, welcoming.

"Anyone home?" Ark lifted the flap of the treepaulin, the stitched-together harvest-leaves that provided waterproofing and protection. As the leaves fell throughout autumn, Dendrans would haul in their nets strung between the trees. The leaves were a strong and flexible crop. Once tanned, they were far more durable than cow leather.

Ark ducked down out of the gloom. The round, single room was divided by thick, moth-munched blankets. Wall gaslights flickered in a breeze that made the whole house tremble in its fragile cradle of rope. Ark steadied himself as the fuggy heat warmed his damp body.

"Here, son," came a weak voice. His father lay curled up in a large cot-basket next to the wood burner. His filmy eyes gazed toward Ark. "Good day?"

"It was all right," Ark lied. He was wet, tired, and his whole world had been turned upside down. *All right* was nowhere near the truth.

"Your mother's out veg-haggling. Back in a bit."

Ark felt guilty. Their last coins would be gone on a few blighted spuds and wrinkled carrots. "Dad. I'm in trouble."

"Oh?"

But he had no chance to explain. They both turned at the sound of hobnailed boots clattering down the walkway. Ark looked wild-eyed at his father, who quick as a flash motioned his son down behind one of the partition sheets.

Before Mr. Malikum Senior could say *Enter*, the flap was roughly pulled aside, letting in the chill evening air.

"Who's there?" Mr. Malikum looked up to see two men dressed in leather tabards branded with the image of a peregrine falcon. The holstered knives in their belts were not there for ceremony. The larger one, with a scar that ran from side to side over his scalp, was also wearing a smirk that he was not quite able to hide.

"Are you Mr. Malikum, father of Arktorious, the plumber's boy?"

"Yes. I am. What is this about?" Ark's father tried to sit up in his cot to face the unwelcome visitors, but the effort proved too much and he collapsed back.

"We've come with some unfortunate news," said the first, as if he was reading from a script.

"It appears that your son has met with an accident," said the second.

"He tripped and . . . fell off the edge."

Mr. Malikum played his part well. "Oh my word. No! You mean he's . . . ?"

"I'm afraid so, *sir.*"

The *sir* was delivered with a curl of the guard's lip, and to add further insult, the other guard pulled out a few bronze coins and chucked them casually onto the bed.

"Naturally, there'll be an inquiry. Pretty straightforward, though. It appears that the stress of work became too much.

He jumped!" And to emphasize the point, the guard jumped suddenly on the spot, thumping down forcefully on the thin boards.

Mr. Malikum didn't disappoint. His shoulders shook as he huddled forward, scrabbling at the sheet covering his legs to wipe away nonexistent tears.

"Councillor Grasp is most sorry for your loss." Speech over, the guards swung around and marched straight out of the house without so much as a backward look at the whimpering man. Outside, they nearly tripped over a young girl playing with a stick figure made out of twigs. She had tied a bit of string to it and was pushing it along the edge of the branch.

"Wheee!" she said over and over again, pushing the figure off the edge and then pulling it back up again.

"Poor kid," said Alnus, the younger of the guards, as he rubbed his mustache.

"Squit me! Alnus going soppy over a sewer rat! Whatever next? We've got more serious matters to attend to."

"Like what?"

"Like drinking ourselves stupid!"

"Yeah. Suppose so."

"No 'suppose' about it. Come on! Let's leave this Diana-forsaken heap of hovels. Job done." The guards fell into step together and sauntered off into the gathering gloom.

"Father. I'm sorry." Ark rose slowly from behind the worn curtains.

"Sorry? Why? You're alive. That's what counts. Now get yourself changed and stick the kettle on. Once we're warmed up with a brew, you can tell me how you died!" There was a flicker of the old spirit in his father's eyes.

After putting on some dry clothes, Ark moved the kettle back to the hot plate on top of the iron woodstove and waited until it whistled. Tea was a rare pleasure, even when bought secondhand. Arborium wasn't completely cut off from the outside world. Its borders were as porous as a sieve when it came to supply and demand. The mud-pirates who lived in the twilight world a mile below at the bottom of the trees were only too happy to act as smugglers. They filtered through spices and coffee from Maw and delivered them to the dumb butlers that provided the only means of access to this country high aboveground. The two spoonfuls of the dried leaves now covered with steaming water had traveled far, just like the woman Ark had overheard. The difference was, a pot of tea didn't present an absolute threat to their way of life.

The roughly carved wooden cup warmed his hands and as Ark sank to the floor, he realized how tired he was. It was time for the truth. He told his story for the second time that day.

When Ark had finished, his father stayed silent for a while, studying the leaves at the bottom of his empty cup as if they might reveal the future.

"What now, son?"

"What do you mean, 'now'?" Ark was close to tears again as the despair closed in. "I can't go back to work. I can't earn any money. I can't feed you and Shiv and Mom. I might as well have been banished to the Ravenwood for all the good I can do this family."

"Hush. There's always something you can do." His father might be crippled, confined to his cot-basket, but there was a strong edge of certainty in his voice.

"What? The moment I walk out of here, there'll be a price on my head. I've failed you. I'm just a —"

"You're just a child. I know." His father shook his head, then gently pushed Ark's fringe of black hair aside to study the boy's face. "And yet, there was always something different about you. There was me climbing a branch to work out why twigs kept clogging a drain, while the wind tried to pluck me off the tree like a feather!"

Ark had heard the story a hundred times. Usually, it was reassuring. Now it filled him with unanswered questions.

"And there you both were, swaddled in a feather-lined nest and smiling up at me with your strange green eyes."

That whirlwind of an afternoon fourteen years ago, Mr. Malikum the plumber had gone out with a wrench and come back with two babies. His wife was shocked, then delighted. Who were they to refuse a gift of the trees?

"You were a miracle. Though why someone left you out there in the cold, Diana only knows. And your poor sister, Victoria, caught the fever. It took her so quick. . . ." He shook his head, remembering.

After a day of mourning and the blessing of Warden Goodwoody, they laid the body of the baby out on the branches, dressed in rags, sacrificial food for the ravens. Apparently, Ark had screamed through the whole ceremony, only falling silent when the first bird came tumbling from the sky. Instead of claiming its clot of flesh, it had snatched his sister's body and lifted off into the air, while its companions circled and cawed ferociously. Sometimes he tried to remember his last glimpse of his lost twin, but the picture in his mind was forever full of indistinct, swirling black feathers.

"You know we always loved you like our own?"

Ark nodded. Mr. and Mrs. Malikum were his dad and mom. And Shiv was his real, living sister. It was enough, almost. But

Dad was right. Who would abandon them in the middle of nowhere? The question had nagged him through all his short years. But the answer was obvious. It was someone who obviously didn't care. That was all he needed to know.

"We've always managed before and we will again. For tonight, there is nothing we can do except hand it over to Diana." He briefly closed his eyes. The subject was closed. "Now then, have you eaten today?"

Ark shook his head dumbly. The chase had done him in. He was starving.

6 · POISON GAS

Petronio had no difficulty keeping out of his father's way the following morning. He slipped out after breakfast and joined the busy branchways, his own head crowded with the events of the day before.

When the guards had brought back the news of Ark's death, Petronio had been mildly surprised by his own reaction. He looked for regret but could find none. In fact, he was significantly more upset at his treatment from the two new guards. To be dragged in front of his father like a naughty schoolboy was an affront to his pride. He would not forget that moment, that was for sure. When the time was right, he'd make them pay dearly.

Petronio shouldered his way through the throng, squeezing past several frustrated horsemen, a cart piled high with onions from the scaffields and a bleating flock of sheep stuck in the sea of faces. He was amazed that more people didn't tip over the edge as they scurried to work. The safety ropes helped, but council lane-widening programs didn't stop the sheer numbers using them.

Why couldn't some of these commoners move out of Hellebore and reinhabit the old plague settlements out in the wilds? The disease had long gone, apart from the odd isolated outbreak, but Dendrans were a superstitious bunch. And in the capital, there was work to be had, so they congregated like flies. Petronio gritted his teeth and pushed on through. If his father took over as president of a new republic, perhaps he might begin with a bit of forced population reduction.

Petronio looked up to see how little light was filtering through the leaves. The clouds were thick and gray today, threatening a repeat of yesterday's storm. Down here, several levels below the canopy, the lack of light turned the walkways and roads into a land of shadows that the hiss and flare of gas lamps did little to dispel.

The School For Surgeons was imposing in the distance. Vast windows shouted its importance and status. The wooden structure was six-sided, rearing up on an impressively engineered platform that was supported between four sturdy trunks. The operating theaters took over the top floor, skylights capturing the greater share of daylight. Trainees like him had to make do with the darker lecture halls on the ground floor. As he pulled open the outer door, the familiar smell of formaldehyde folded around him.

Inside, he nodded at a few faces as he took his place on the tiered seats rising in a semicircle around the main podium. If only he could tell his friends what he'd heard. They'd be more than impressed. But *friends* was really too strong a word. All the young men here were careful around Petronio, knowing full well his father's reputation. He would never admit it publicly, but he liked the way his fellow students treated him. Fear was a useful weapon.

This morning was General Studies and the elderly bald eagle of a lecturer was wittering on about a bunch of stuff that Petronio knew backward.

"The evolution of the forest and the Dendran society that depends on it bears examination," droned the lecturer in his dried-leaf voice. "We came from the trees and strangely, after many thousands of years, we have returned to them. For the explanation behind this new direction, we must thank our great philosopher Darewin." The teacher tapped a picture on his corkboard of a man doing something dull in a library.

Petronio didn't bother hiding his yawn.

"At that time, the earth was poisoned by those who went before. How could the trees and our ancestors live off water from rivers long dead and soil that was dirtied by cities? Desperate times bred both desperate measures and inspiration! Trees have always fought for their share of light. As Darewin put it, only the strongest triumph."

Petronio nodded. The old fuddy-buddy was making sense at last.

The lecturer paused, pointing to another picture of a sapling that would have looked insignificant but for the minute figure of a grown man next to it. "The superstitious say that the trees are conscious. They knew the earth was polluted and to survive they must dig deeper with their roots. As the rest of the world was turning into one huge city, something different was happening in Arborium."

The keener students were taking notes, but Petronio's mind wandered from the mention of growing ever higher to the notion of falling. He tried to imagine Ark's strange leap into the unknown. What split-second thoughts had propelled him over the edge? It was a long jump from being a pushed-around nobody to taking your own life. Or was it? Petronio's hands instinctively made the sign of the Woodsman Cross: *Earth Over, Sky Under, Leaves to East & West.* But then he stopped and determinedly folded his arms. What was the point in ancient, useless habits? Prayers were for the weak. He had his future to consider now.

"The philosopher called it 'evolution,' a fascinating process wherein the trees that developed deeper roots and taller trunks survived, as did the Dendrans by removing themselves from the foul earth into this cradle of branch and twig. We could almost say, if you'll permit me a pun on Darewin's behalf, Trees Who Dare, Win!"

There were a few groans, but no one laughed.

The lecturer carried on regardless. "The religionists tell other stories, clothing facts in a fantasy of goddesses and trees that think for themselves. And some families still follow the old superstitions. It is pure barbarism, sacrificing a boar to appease the Raven Queen! Those ravens really are not 'birds of death,' merely by-products of nature!" His smirk was at last rewarded with a few intellectual guffaws from his audience. "Precisely. Dendrans can believe what they wish, but my task is to deal with *reality*. So, whatever your take on the origin of species, one remarkable change emerged. It was as if this new genus of tree had a built-in code for self-protection. The skunk emits a revolting odor from a gland near its back passage to ward off predators, yes?"

This raised a few titters from the more loutish lads in the audience.

"And the hedgehog becomes an impenetrable phalanx of spears. So it is with our hybrid trees. As they grew ever taller and the original humans abandoned their old, ground-dwelling ways, it was noticed that travelers to the shores of Arborium would immediately fall ill as they set foot upon land. And why was that?" He pointed his marker pen directly at Petronio.

Every student's face swiveled around, expecting the usual sarcastic, clever response.

"Gas . . . *sir*." The manner in which Petronio addressed his lecturer did not hide his contempt. And he would get away with it. No one gave the High Councillor's son a detention.

"Exactly, young Grasp. The roots of these new species delved deeper into the earth's crust, burrowing beneath our ancestors' dirty landfills, searching for clean sources of water and minerals. But the roots, almost with minds of their own, made another discovery. They finally pierced reserves of undiscovered gas. For the tree dwellers, it was a defining moment with infinite possibility. The trees themselves had no use for it, but for the human parasites who populated the canopy, it was the leverage needed to get off the ground: a free source of heat and power! The trees provided warmth, habitat, and clean water for all the creatures emerging to live high up in the canopy. In turn, we newly evolving Dendrans could defend the forest from outside interference. Give-and-take. Nature truly is remarkable, though we can safely leave the realm of talking trees to children's tales."

The old man smiled and scratched at a scab on his shiny head. "But the cleverest piece of the puzzle was yet to come. Somewhere in the trees' biological makeup, the roots that tapped the gas also instituted a filtering process. The gas was cleaned up, so to speak, the waste siphoned out and released as a harmless odor by the leaves. Harmless to Dendrans and other tree dwellers, that is. And so, this relationship has worked well for generations and those from outside who seek to infiltrate our country now pay the ultimate price of . . . asphyxiation!"

A few of the boys made deliberate strangling noises as they clutched their own necks.

"Yes, yes. Very amusing, I'm sure. But perhaps you wouldn't find my words so hilarious if our little nation was under attack, hmm?"

If only the lecturer knew the half of it, mused Petronio.

A bell sounded and everyone started packing up their books.

"Your essays by tomorrow, please," the professor called over the hubbub. "Remember, you are supposed to debate the difference between the so-called religious creation myths of Diana and her dark consort, Corwenna, compared to the hard facts of evolutionary dendra-chronology."

The pupils ignored their teacher, pouring out of the hall for break. One of the other students offered Petronio a cheroot. He had no objections to a bit of false friendship, especially if it involved a free smoke. He joined the small group of boys in their secretive puffing outside and drifted along with them when they headed to the corner of a public square. Tables were laid out along one side in preparation for the lunchtime trade. A waiter sweeping the floor free of pigeon droppings and twigs scowled at the students, making it plain that it was not *their* custom he was after.

Petronio leaned back against a support column, not joining in with the banter. He watched the ever-moving flow of Dendrans pouring across the boarded platform and carefully stubbed out the cheroot. Starting a forest fire was in no one's best interests. Petronio debated whether he could be bothered to hang around any longer when a figure caught his eye. It was a Holly Woodsman with hood up and trailing cloak, purposefully crossing the square. Nothing unusual about that — except there was something in the way the Woodsman moved, appearing almost to glide, rather than stride. Then Petronio's eyes traveled down to see not rough sandals but expensive, neat, fur-lined boots.

"Excuse me, lads. Gotta go." Petronio didn't bother to say thanks. He never did. The figure had already vanished from view. He ran across the square, not knowing quite why he wanted to follow. It was just instinct. Around a corner, the branch split. Left or right? Petronio sniffed the air like a hunter. A scent hung there. It seemed familiar. He veered right and followed the twisting branchway, trying not to run. Up ahead, the Woodsman came back into view, moving with the same intent pace. At each turning, the Woodsman took the fork that seemed to lead ever farther off the beaten track until even Petronio began to wonder where they were.

An old, weather-beaten sign warned that the way ahead was closed for repairs. The Woodsman ignored it, climbed nimbly over, and continued down the disused branch line. Petronio paused, his eyes nervously scanning the treescape. If he kept following now, it would be more than obvious. Up above, a couple of wild timber goats were perched on high branches that looked like they wouldn't support a sparrow, let alone a cloven-hoofed mammal. The goats didn't even bother looking at the stranger below, too busy grazing on the fungus blossom that covered the bark.

A sudden cry from farther along interrupted Petronio's indecision, followed by a thud. Robbers? He doubted it. His father ran the protection rackets with an iron fist. Criminal free enterprise had been stamped out. Maybe it was the ravens. But whoever heard of a raven attacking a priest?

There was another cry, closer now. "Help!"

Instinct again. Petronio leapt over the warning sign and ran wildly down the line. The figure had collapsed. A horrible rattling sound was bubbling from the Woodsman's throat. Only as Petronio drew closer did he remember where he'd first come across that scent.

"My . . . lady?"

"Help . . . need . . ." The fine, thin fingers with bright

red nails were scrabbling toward a leather bag at her side.

The hood had fallen back, and he could see the woman's face covered in a light sheen of sweat as her other hand clutched at her throat.

"What? I don't understand what you—" But Petronio grabbed up the bag anyway.

"Quick . . . gas . . ."

Of course! Maybe this morning's lecture hadn't been so irrelevant after all. Petronio quickly emptied the bag. Various odd-shaped metal objects cascaded out. To a trainee surgeon, one of them was well known, though much smaller and finely worked than its Dendran version: a hypodermic syringe.

Time was running out; the woman could barely draw breath, let alone speak. With her remaining strength, she pointed weakly toward her upper arm.

His first real emergency! Petronio grabbed the syringe and quickly pushed up the rough woolen sleeve, revealing a smooth, hairless arm. The touch of her skin made him shiver. Clinically, his fingers felt for the right spot. He uncapped the needle and pushed it in deep, slowly depressing the plunger.

The woman's eyes rolled back and her arms flailed once, then flopped to her sides. She was dead! He'd killed her! But his hands worked of their own accord, doing what they'd been taught to do—grabbing her wrist and feeling for a pulse.

Nothing. No. Wait. He felt something, faint as a breeze through leaves. The relief was enormous. Petronio took the leather bag and placed it under her head. Then he folded her body to one side, in the recovery position. All he could do now was to wait and see if whatever was in the syringe would do its work.

A few minutes passed. The forest was unusually silent. No

birdcalls. No scampering of squirrels. It was as if the trees were holding their breath to see if evolution could so easily be tricked. The woman's eyelids began to flutter. Petronio bent over her and checked her vital signs again. Some moments later she opened her eyes, resting them on her rescuer. Even though the woman had nearly died, a thin smile creased her lips.

"You saved my life."

Petronio turned bright red. He was surprised by his own actions. "Happy to be of . . . er . . . service."

"Yes. I think you are. Here . . ." She tried sitting up.

He leaned forward to help, grasping her wrists to pull her up. He became aware of her scent again, her too-smooth skin, her *differentness.*

"Your clever trees have tried to kill me. I am looking forward to returning the favor one day!"

Petronio felt suddenly too close for comfort. He stood up, unsure of what to do, or say. "I'm, um, studying to be a surgeon." He held up the syringe. "This must be some kind of fast-acting antidote?"

"Good boy. They teach you well." That smile again. It almost knocked him out.

He nodded.

"I have a daughter your age. Randall." For a moment, her tone was distant. "We used to get on well."

Petronio wondered what life was like in Maw. The thought of it sounded exciting, full of potential.

Hidden among the leaves above, a pigeon cooed. As if it was a signal, the woman recovered herself. She turned slowly to study him, her raven-black eyes like slivers of glass poking deep into every secret cranny of his soul. "I think, son of Councillor Grasp, you could be very useful to me. I might have a task for you, if you were willing. It's dangerous, but there would be . . . rewards. What do you say?"

A few minutes ago, the woman was nearly dead. Now she was asking him to join her. Excitement ran like chlorophyll through his veins.

"My name, ma'am, is Petronio. Whatever you ask, I shall do!"

She laughed. "How very gallant! And I am Lady Fenestra, secret envoy of Maw. I am glad we are properly introduced. A bright future awaits us. All we have to do is *take* it!"

7 · THE JOURNEY BEGINS

Ark slept fitfully, his dreams punctured by huge ravens swooping toward him. Through the night, every little creak and cry saw his eyes shoot open, convinced the guards had worked out that he was still very much alive and in possession of dangerous information.

That dawn, like any other dawn, his mother held him close and gave him a kiss that he'd usually find embarrassing. Only this time, she wouldn't let him go.

"I know it's the only way," she said. "You're right that the King must be warned and soon, before the coming festival. If he is overthrown, chaos will rule and Maw will already have won. He needs to see that his councillors have driven a rusty nail into the heart of this good wood. But I hate to think of you facing danger. Maybe your friend can help."

"He's not a friend!" Ark protested. "I hardly know him." Mucum was someone to get out of the way of at work.

"He's on your side — we think you should trust him. Anyway, Father and I spent hours discussing it. You'll have to be the one to go. You can see, he's not up to the journey today." His father sat in his cot-bed staring at the fire.

Nor any day, thought Ark. He looked at his mother's face. The red rowanberry hair dye did its best to disguise her gray roots, but the years had eaten away at her youth, leaving furrows that lined her forehead, deeper than a scaffield plow could cut. Her dress was moth-eaten, second- or probably even thirdhand.

How could they afford new cloth on his tiny wages? And now, even they were gone.

"And they won't listen to me, a mere woman."

"How can you say that? You're stronger than any of them!"

His mother shook her head. "That's the way of the wood these days. But bless your heart for believing it. Now let's have a look at you!" Ark's britches were scraped from climbing over the woodway. At least she had managed to sew up the rips in his stockings. "It'll have to do."

"It's not a dress-up party, Mother." Ark wished she'd stop fussing.

"There's nothing wrong with a plumber's uniform, dearest, but you should look your best for the King!" She pushed a packet of food into a leather bag. "May Diana put wings on your feet! Here's a coin for the shrine." She pressed a shiny copper into his palm.

"But, Mother, we can't afford it!" It was worth two loaves and half a dozen eggs, at least.

"*Afford?* What price prayer? Now go, before your old mother starts to cry. And take care." He had been found long ago, a gift of the trees. She didn't want to lose him now.

Ark pocketed the coin and quickly crept behind the curtain to snatch a last look at his sleeping sister. She held her stick figure tight and her thumb had fallen out of her mouth. It was almost too much. Ark came back into the main room and knelt down by his father's cot.

"Good-bye, son. Don't let the buzzards grind you down, eh?" Mr. Malikum tried to smile, but Ark could see his father's eyes watering.

Ark nodded and, before his face could betray his own emotion, walked off down the branchway. He stopped once and turned around. The forest filled with birdsong: robins, sparrows, blackbirds, and thrushes battling it out to greet the new day. Already, his home was lost among shifting shadows. No one waved good-bye. He felt a tightness in his chest, trying not to think of all those he was leaving.

He felt like a ghost as he drifted toward the local sewage station, lingering in the shadows to avoid the few Dendrans who were up this early. But they were unaware of him, hurrying about their business. What was *his* purpose? He had to get to the King and quickly, but how? Maybe Mucum would come up with an idea.

Ark set off down the inside of one of the nearby trunks, his footsteps echoing into the hollow depths. After a few minutes, he reached a landing with two exits. The branchway heading to the meeting spot was on his left. He paused, thinking about the coin in his pocket. The early service would have ended already and there would be no one around. What did he have to lose? He took a right instead and ten minutes later, the path led him to his destination.

The great tree he approached from a thin, swaying gangway was different from all the others in one respect. The smooth bark was studded with portholes of stained glass, topped by a roof of thatch that clung around the edges of the massive hollowed-out trunk. Even in this gloom, way below the crown of the tree, light from the glass punctured the endless shades of green, making the surrounding leaves look like they'd been dyed for display in a dazzling market stall. This was the effect that kirk was supposed to have. The doorway, always open, could only lead out of this drab life. Beyond, lay a kingdom of color, the palace of Diana.

Ark paused before the entrance. A trickle of water spouted

from a hole in the bark and made its way into a gleaming copper bowl, forged into the shape of raven feathers and set into the trunk at waist height. Water was a gift from the roots deep down, sucked up by the tree itself to spill out into this sacred spring. Ark crossed his hands over his chest. *Earth Over, Sky Under, Leaves to East & West.* He said a quick prayer for the soul of his long-dead twin, then pulled the coin from his pocket and dropped it in, watching the ripples as it sank to join the other offerings. A near fortune of gold and silver shimmered a foot under the surface, enough to feed his family for years. But nobody, not even Councillor Grasp, stole from Diana.

There. He'd done as his mother had asked. Maybe he should leave now. But the open doorway beckoned to him, as it always did. Going inside meant there was a chance he might meet a Holly Woodsman. He'd have to take it. Before he could think about it, his feet carried him into the porchway where he gently pushed open the second inner door.

The main body of the kirk was a room about fifty feet around, with a carved and vaulted ceiling lost in the shadows high above. Many came to kneel in silence on the polished wooden floor. The air was thick with incense, an indoor fog of burned pine resin. Ark loved kirk, the way the light filtered through the stained glass, picking out the wooden statue of the Mother, cradling the first changed acorn. He fell for the mystery of the Holly Woodsmen, faces hidden in their hoods as they repeated words and phrases from a thousand years ago, raising their silvered acorn cup to sip of the tree's water and share it in communion with their flock. But he also felt cooped up, as if the strength of the trees lay not in this chamber of worship but in the outside, the whole wide-wood.

About twenty feet away, a figure, draped in a black cloak

and squatting on hands and knees, was laying flowers for the coming harvest: chrysanthemums, asters, and pansies.

The figure hummed to itself, and Ark hoped if he could creep past, the sound might cover his —

"I recognize those footsteps!" The voice echoed around the hallowed hall.

Ark stopped dead. He was discovered.

"Where do you think you're going, my Ark?" The figure shuffled around, revealing a face wrinkled like a winter-stored apple. The hair was tied back in a messy pigtail. Only the eyes, without pupils, seemed lost, their white expanses roaming aimlessly within their sockets.

Ark had no choice. "Warden Goodwoody." He bowed.

"I thought so. Delicately as you might move, my ears shall pick you out!" and the face was split in half with a grin as sweet as any winter-stored fruit.

Ark shuffled closer, nervously checking out the side chapels.

"Why the worry? What is it?" A hand reached out, sweeping the floor like a broom until the fingers found what they were looking for. The Warden used her elm staff to pull herself up, towering over Ark.

"Nothing. I came in. I wanted to . . ." He didn't know what he wanted, why he was here.

"Catch a cloud, eh? Well, don't mind me." She motioned her head to indicate a set of stairs at the back of the kirk, hidden in a dark recess. "Go on with you, then."

Ark wanted to stop and talk, but the urge was in him now. "Thank you," he said.

"And if you find the Goddess up there, send Her my love!" The woman sighed and bent back down to continue her arranging.

Ark paused by the stairs, suddenly feeling like he was being watched. He turned uncertainly. A pair of eyes stared out at him from the dark. Ark almost stumbled backward in fright.

"Dendrans ignore the Raven Queen at their peril!"

How could Goodwoody have noticed what he was looking at? The eyes appeared alive, staring out from a dusty stained-glass panel disguised by a jumble of old broken chairs and rolled-up rugs. The figure was dressed in black. Ark peered closer. No. Not dressed in black, but wearing a cloak of black feathers that billowed out over a shadowy throne.

"Our pious men have forgotten the old ways," the Warden continued, "but Corwenna is the true face of nature. Some say She is the other face of Diana. One cannot have light without dark. . . ."

Ark had no idea what she meant. Disturbed, he ran to the back stairs and leapt up them two at a time, drawn to his favorite spot. The way up was far narrower than any main trunk, the steps little more than horizontal slivers. There was no expensive glass up here, only the occasional knothole through the skin of the tree letting in wind and ever more light as he climbed the familiar route. Soon, he left the main body of the building far behind, squeezing his already thin body into an ever-decreasing spiral, the triangular steps now so small his toes could barely find purchase. The branch in which he climbed began to rock from side to side. Up here, he and the tree were the wind's playthings. This journey was never for the fainthearted. One strong gust and the wood could easily snap, with Ark, wrapped tight in this coffin of bark, tumbling down to certain death.

But Ark felt the opposite of fear. He was a foundling of the forest. The trees would not abandon him now. Sometimes, he wondered who his real mother was. How could she have left him and his sister out in the cold? Maybe he was the hidden son of a duke, and one day the knock at the door would come announcing his inheritance. He shook his head. Useless day-dreams. The closer he got to the sky, the more the events of the last day and night faded from him. The back-and-forth motion soothed his runaway mind. A few more steps and there it was: a tiny door, set like a stone in a ring. He pushed and with that one movement left behind a world of gloom.

The view, from this tiny circular platform high above the crown of the tree, was immense. The forest that contained the country of Arborium spread away from him in every direc-tion. It was an unending and undulating green blanket, rippling with leaves and hidden life. This rickety nest that now only children could reach was ancient, its original use lost over the centuries. Ark imagined it as a lookout post in a battle from long ago, or perhaps the site of offerings to Diana. The kirk services were all right, but it was here, where the only vaulted roof was carved out of cloud and air, that he felt as if he slotted into place.

Not far to the west Ark saw the great palace of Quercus rearing up out of the trees. It was still a few miles away, its bat-tlements gleaming with beaten and polished copper. He'd never had business there, although he'd been on the grounds along with all the common folk for the yearly Harvest Festival. But the son of a plumber was hardly welcome at court. Those snobs would thumb their noses while the whole country went up in the fires of treachery.

The sense of well-being that normally met him up here was missing today. He was no longer soothed as he swung back and forth high above the world. His head filled with family; the look of surprise on Petronio's face; the chase that had ended in his so-called death; the image of Arborium chopped down and burned. The weather sensed his mood, the sharp wind pulling at his clothes, making his eyes water with its promise of winter. The sun lay low, hidden behind the clouds, as if ashamed at the treachery soon to take place far below. Ark circled the platform, carefully holding on to a waist-height rail that banded the trunk. This was stupid. He needed to get going, meet Mucum, work out a—

A black flash caught his eye. For a brief moment, the clouds parted and the sun caught a reflection off the lip of the platform. "What's that?" Ark muttered to himself. The lip of the platform was ridiculously low. As he leaned out over the edge, he tried not to look down. This platform reared out of the woods like a single, slightly crooked finger. He was hundreds of feet above Arborium. Normally, he felt at home in the trees, but they might not feel the same for him. The glint caught his eye again, resting in the crook of a branch, just out of reach.

Ark tried to hook his feet around the door frame and lean over the edge of the platform, trusting that ancient carpentry would hold his weight. Infuriating! His fingers brushed the edge of the object. With the wind now blowing so hard, his eyes filled like cruck wells and he could hardly make out what lay in front of him. Just one more stretch. One more and . . .

As Ark reached toward what resembled shining black treasure, as he leaned out over the edge of the platform, the wooden door frame began to creak and groan. The wind joined in, howling with invisible strength as it bent the branch forward until Ark was no longer horizontal but facing almost straight down.

A voice called out, "Ark!"

His head whipped around. No one. A trick of the screeching wind.

"Oh . . . dear," said Ark. The frame, devoured by centuries of woodworm, cracked and splintered, unhooking Ark's feet and toppling him over the edge to plunge headfirst toward the forest like a stone.

8 · A FALL FROM GRACE

This time there was no rope, no backup plan. As Ark plummeted toward the forest, he wondered vaguely what would happen first. If he was lucky, his neck might be snapped by a passing branch. If he hit a woodway, every brittle bone in his body would be crushed. The thought should have terrified him and yet he felt strangely calm as the ever-nearing woods spread their green arms ready to envelop him.

The acceleration was terrific. His cheeks pulled back like rubber and his eyes streamed like a cruck spring in full flow. He felt invisible fingers trying to rip off his clothes as he sped earthward faster and faster. Maybe this was what it was like for a raven, pulling in its wings and plunging straight down through nothing but air, a feathered arrow flying for no more reason than the sheer joy of the hunt. Ark was no raven, though. Wingless and out of control, he was not the hunter but the victim as death stalked him, about to claim the prize.

Ark closed his eyes as the thatched roof of the kirk reared up to meet him. *So this is how it ends.*

WHOOOF! There was an almighty thump and Ark felt the breath punch out of his body. Milliseconds later, this was followed by an earsplitting crack. Ark briefly smelled a whiff of some strange perfume and then everything went black.

All was well. Ark drifted, feeling a wonderful warmth cover and fold around him. The sensation soaked into him. If this was death, why were Dendrans so worked up about it? He remembered falling from the clouds, something about a king. It wasn't important now. He could just float here forever. The Holly Woodsmen were spot on. His spirit was definitely making its way down the River Sticks. Eventually, Ark would cross to the other side and walk the woodways of the Far Country. Now *that* was a journey worth making. He tried to open his eyes, but they were gummed closed. No matter. The blackness was welcoming. He sniffed. A wonderful smell filled his nostrils. Wasn't that incense?

"My Ark. My fallen angel!" The voice was tinged with hysteria. "Come back. By Diana, by Corwenna, by all that is holly and righteous, come back!"

"Ow!" The voice coincided with a sudden shooting pain in his backside. Hang on a second, the dead weren't supposed to have sore butts. "Ow!" he repeated. It felt like a little fire devil was stabbing him in the nether regions with a pitchfork. •

"Praise the Mother! You're alive!"

Ark recognized the voice. He groaned in pain as he finally managed to push open his eyelids. A familiar figure filled his vision. "Yes. I am. I think," he finally muttered.

"But where did you come from? I heard a crash that sounded like the kirk was under attack and then something landed on the floor."

"Uh. Warden Goodwoody. That something was . . . me." Ark looked up and could see the hole in the roof that was his point of entry. But that didn't explain why he was still breathing.

"Oh!" she said, her fingers feeling around Ark's body. "Can you move?"

It hadn't occurred to him that surviving the fall might mean broken bones. He quickly flexed his arms and legs. "I think I'm all right."

"This is a miracle!" The Warden sighed. Her fingers came away with a handful of dry reeds.

Ark wasn't too sure about the miracle side of things. He looked around and saw that he'd landed in the middle of a straw cradle. As he'd punched through the roof, the thatch had also come away, cushioning his fall. "I was trying to grab . . ." It was coming back to him now. His left hand uncurled to reveal an object shining black in the candlelight. A feather. A raven feather, its quill viciously sharp.

"What?" said the Warden.

"Nothing." How could Ark explain that a feather nearly killed him? It didn't make sense. *Hold the feather, grab the weather, woe betide me, Lady hide me.* The chant came back to him. That's what he was doing. Holding a feather.

Before he could hide it away, the Warden's hand shot out, fingers touching the vane.

"Sky preserve us!" she shuddered, her fingertips recoiling in shock. "This is not possible."

"What?" said Ark.

"A gift. And there was I beginning to lose all faith. But this is a dark matter indeed." A frown carved itself into the reverend's brow. "There is danger and death folded within its softness."

Ark felt the feather. The quill was sharp, but it wasn't exactly going to kill him! "If it's a gift, who did it come from?"

The reverend ignored the question and fell silent, her blind orbs of white trying to see something beyond her vision. "As you are invisible to me, when the time comes, darkness will help to hide you."

"Right . . . ," said Ark, his head aching. Goodwoody was spouting riddles again.

"Are you in trouble, my boy?"

Ark noticed the lining of bright red silk peeking out from inside the Warden's cloak. For the Holly Woodsmen, such bold color worn inside the kirk was almost heretical. But who else would keep the shrines spotless, the figurines waxed and polished, the candles trimmed and lit? What could he say to her? He'd already told Mucum and put him in danger. "I'm fine," he lied, continuing quickly, "apart from a few bruises. I guess I'll be a bit stiff in the morning." It was the best he could do. "Please. You haven't spoken with me. I can't explain now."

The reverend smiled sadly. "But the feather has spoken to me! You must trust in your instincts. And know now that you are not alone."

That was no answer. He slid the feather silently into his bag, feeling frustrated. "I'm afraid there's a hole in your roof. You'll be in trouble."

"Never! I shall simply say a bird . . . maybe a *raven* . . . dropped a nut in an effort to crack it. A rather big nut that went to feed the poor at harvesttime." The Warden smiled at her rather inventive lie. "Now, if you are still among the land of the living, fetch a broom and help me clear up!"

This was nuts! A minute ago, Ark was about to die, and now he was hobbling toward the broom closet to help sweep a heap of straw away. He winced as the little devil gave him a few more stabs in his backside for good measure.

Ark returned and began brushing up the straw, feeling a downdraft of cold air from the hole in the roof.

Warden Goodwoody leaned on her staff, stubborn as a statue, urging Ark to talk.

He had to give her something. "I was already supposed to be dead. You'll hear the news. It's somewhat exaggerated."

"I'm glad to hear it!" The Warden's face crinkled up with delight. "Your company would be most missed. Oh, don't get me wrong. I love the hymns and prayers, but the thought of you scampering up to the sky always cheers me up. I sometimes think you are closer to the spirit of the woods than my most esteemed colleagues. This gift of yours confirms it."

A distant clock chimed and Ark suddenly realized he was late. "I have to go. Sorry." He quickly pushed the straw into a corner. "My family . . . I can't go home for a while." He wrung his hands, hating himself for asking. "Please, would you visit them if you have any spare food?"

"That's what harvest is for." Warden Goodwoody spread her arms to indicate shelves burgeoning with apples, pumpkins, and squash, all scaffield-grown. "Now go." But before he could, the Warden grabbed his face in her large hands and swooped to kiss the top of his head.

As Ark was leaving, a rare beam of sunlight found its way through the roof and onto Warden Goodwoody's upturned face. The boy was in her prayers. What more could an old blind woman do?

Ark nearly ran straight into a queue of Holly Woodsmen, faces lost deep inside their hoods, bodies cloaked in raven-black cloth as they shuffled in a long, swaying line, murmuring their prayers of protection. The sound they made was like the buzz of bees, haunting and hypnotic.

Ark quickly pulled his hat down over his face, bowing quickly as the priests swept past him and through the doorway. No one looked up. No one was interested. He hoped the Warden would get away with her story.

Ark ran, aware of the time, his fall from the platform retreating behind him as he descended endless sets of steps into the forest gloom. Maybe he'd imagined it. How could he fall that far and escape only with bruises? But the feather was real enough. As he sprinted along the woodways, it wormed its way through the stitching of the bag to scratch at his skin.

He finally reached the meeting spot out of breath, tucking the feather back inside his bag. The day before, they'd agreed to rendezvous at this quiet corner off the main woodway. He was late, but Mucum as ever was even later. Their workplace lay cradled among the leaves barely one hundred yards away.

This local sewage station was one of many dotted around the country. They were the underbelly of Arborium, hidden deep down in the undercanopy, like dirty washing at the bottom of a basket. *Where there's Dendrans, there's squit, and where there's squit, there's business!* went the company motto. The profits obviously hadn't been spent on this long, misshapen shed and the platform it balanced on. The building was made up of leftover planks and iron, cobbled together and hugging the side of the trunk. Raw sewage, channeled by gravity from all over the neighborhood, poured into the station via various pipes and wooden channels. Being so badly built gave it at least one advantage. The wind that whistled into every corner provided much-needed ventilation and carried off the worst of the smells. Not that Ark even noticed the stink anymore. You get used to anything, given time.

"Pssst!"

Ark nearly fell off the edge. "That's not funny. Do you always creep up on people like that?"

"Only the dead ones! Who'd ever thought I could scare a ghost?" Despite his bulk, Mucum could move as silently as a timber goat. "How'd yer sleep?"

"What do you think?" Ark kept silent about his trip to kirk. Mucum had no time for the mumbo jumbo of Holly Woodsmen. And if he saw the raven feather, he'd probably run a mile. "We need to see the King."

"Spot on, mate. I already thought of that." Mucum scanned the treescape nervously.

"And stop acting like a villain!"

"But I am!" protested Mucum.

"Fine. Can you steal me some tools, then? I lost mine, remember?" Ark without his gear was like a raven without a beak. Unnatural.

"Yeah. Anyways, Jobby Jones is out for the count. Come and get some yerself." Their boss, Mr. Jones, was always asleep. It was one of the perks of the job.

Ark followed Mucum across a perilously swaying rope bridge.

Mucum briefly looked back. "You look a bit shaky to me. Sure you're oakey-doakey?"

"The bridge is moving. So am I!" Ark winced. As they reached the other end, Mucum put his fingers to his lips. Even from outside the door, they could hear the snoring. A sign, etched in stark brown and white into the grain, said:

EFFLUENT EXECUTIVE STATION
EMPLOYEES ONLY BEYOND THIS POINT.

Underneath, someone had scribbled, *Wot is the point? It's all a load of . . .* The last word had been crisscrossed out with a knife.

Ark frowned. "Are you sure about this? Why don't you go in?"

"You worry too much, mate! The patter of little footsteps won't wake the old man, I promise."

Mucum eased the handle and they crept in. The room spread before them resembled an enormous and rather smelly kitchen, though it wasn't food that was on the menu here. Various pipes and mini aqueducts wound their way through the roofs and walls to discharge into two huge troughs that ran the length of the shed. These bubbled away, releasing their noxious gases in the first stage of composting. Large wooden paddles turned the muck slowly, worked by winches and a series of cogs and chains that ran all the way up to sails far above the crown of the tree.

The troughs had color-coded depth levels marked up the side. If the level went too high, for instance when a bout of diarrhea hit, an alarm went off. Jobby Jones, their line manager, would then run about screaming: "Incoming! Incoming!" and happily leave it to the plumbers to bail out the troughs into what was called "overflow" — a big hole in the floor. The rest of it, once composted, was sent along pipes through the forest all the way up to the high scaffields for the crops that Dendrans relied on.

It wasn't the best system in the world, but it worked and it gave them all a living of sorts. Jobby Jones ruled this under-crown empire with a fist of oak, when he could be bothered. Today, at least, his bulbous body was happily ensconced on the daybed in the corner, his twitching nose no doubt dreaming of perfume that only the richest could afford.

Little Squirt was curled up on the floor next to the nearest trough, grabbing a moment's peace. It was his task to remove any blockages and help the general flow. Being a squit stirrer wasn't the best job in the world, but someone had to do it.

"Hey!" whispered Mucum. "Over here!" He motioned to the tool closet, but Ark was drawn to an old bird's-eye map pinned up on the wall and covered in familiar stains.

The castle of King Quercus lay at the center, an ornate *H* signifying the capital, Hellebore. But his eyes veered off east, west, north, and south, picking out the few still inhabited settlements scattered far from the capital: the carting unions of Cowley, the armories of Moss-side, the bakers of Pudding Lane. And between these carefully illustrated hives of activity, the map had only printed names to denote towns and villages long gone, leaving only rotting woodways and cobwebbed hollows—Ulm, Backwater, Gall, Canker, and the plague towns of the North. These were places no Dendrans willingly went. Who would want to rub shoulders with their ghostly ancestors?

Ark traced his finger to the left, to the west and the ring of mountains beyond which was supposed to lie a forest undisturbed: the Ravenwood—empty trees, devoid of Dendrans, green holes filled with unlit ways and stories about what happened *if you go down to the wood today.* What had Goodwoody meant about the feather being a gift from Her? Surely the Ravenwood, with its dark queen feasting on the innards of any Dendrans stupid enough to be caught, was a myth?

Mucum shoved a plumbing belt into Ark's hands. "What's with the daydream? Come on, let's get out of this squithole before it's too late," he hissed, grabbing his friend by the hand and pushing him toward the door.

Mucum was right. What was up with him? He began buckling up the new belt. But his fingers fumbled and the whole lot clattered noisily to the floor. Disaster!

Jobby Jones's nose did more than twitch as two pairs of beady eyes shot open and swiveled around. Jones was awake. What was more, he was staring directly at the two boys.

"Elms bells! If you weren't dead before, you will be now!" whispered Mucum.

9 · TIME TO ACT

❧

Jobby Jones was trying to come to grips with what his eyes were telling him. Just this morning, they'd gathered a paltry collection of coins for the Malikum family. So what was this?

Ark and Mucum froze. How could it be explained away? The boy who was dead was alive. No doubt their greasy boss would sniff out any potential reward for informing Grasp's guards of this fascinating fact. Jones's bed lay near the door and he was already rising off it, blocking their escape.

Mucum had a sudden brain wave. "Start groaning!" he hissed out of the side of his mouth.

Not only was Ark trapped, but his best bud had gone barking mad. "You what?"

Mucum mouthed a single word: *Dead!*

A split second of hesitation and then Ark twigged. Though he'd never been known for his acting skills, what did he have to lose? Ark raised his arms up and groaned loudly. "Erghhhh!" For more effect, he let his tongue hang out and crisscrossed his eyes.

Mucum joined in with a quavering voice. "Ooooh Diana! It's Ark's . . . ghost! He's come to haunt us for treatin' him bad!"

Their boss's eyes bulged out. Nothing made sense, so it couldn't be real. His high-pitched voice squeaked, "Stop being stupid and get back to . . ."

Ark wasn't going to give up the ghost so easily. He stomped slowly toward his hated bully of a boss. The limp from his earlier fall was suddenly an advantage. "Jobby Jo-ones!

Jobby Jo-ones!" he wailed. "I have come from the Copse of the Slumbering Dead, crossing the River Sticks to take my revenge on yooooooou!" Ark added a final, throat-rattling "warghhhhhhhh!" for effect.

By this point Little Squirt was sitting up on the floor, sucking an unsavory-looking thumb, watching the entertainment unfold. He wasn't too sure if the stinky fumes were making him hallucinate.

As Ark let a string of saliva dribble from his lips, the dumber part of Jobby Jones's brain made a decision. Shutdown time. Their boss fainted, collapsing none too gracefully in a heap on the floor.

Mucum and Ark made a run for the door. "Squirt! I'll explain later! Do us a favor and tell Jobby he imagined the 'ole thing." Mucum shouted as they dived out to freedom.

As they sprinted away from the sewage station, Ark couldn't get rid of the smile on his face. "That was—"

"Brilliant! Forget plumbing, you should be onstage! You'd slay them . . . every time!"

"His eyes nearly popped out!" Ark could feel giggles bubbling up. It beat plunging through the roof of the kirk any day. "Warghhhh!" he wailed again, not caring who heard, for a second not caring about anything. He suddenly came to a skidding halt. "Do you think we got away with it?"

"Listen, Malikum. Old Jonesy ain't gonna report a ghost, is he? He'd be laughed out of town. And Little Squirt will spin 'im a good tale. Let's move it!"

"I suppose so."

"By the way, what's with the limp?"

"I don't know what you mean," he said, though his butt throbbed as if it had a life of its own. Not surprising after a fall of over three hundred feet. Maybe Warden Goodwoody was right about miracles, and Ark wasn't just clutching at straws. "Wait a second." Ark deftly changed the subject. "You'd better have this." Ark took his hat off and passed it over.

"Look, I know you wanna say thanks for gettin' you out of trouble, but . . ." Mucum inspected the greasy, stain-ridden cap.

Ark rolled his eyes. "Your hair stands out like poppies on a pile of poo. Put it on."

"Right you are!" As Mucum covered up his orange fuzz, he transformed from being a tall, lumbering brute who could be seen a mile away, to a tall, lumbering brute. "So, will I do for an audience with the King?"

Twenty minutes later, and after several sets of trunk stairs, they stood before a single rickety door, which was framed with light and surrounded by a high, planked wall that stretched off in both directions.

Mucum bent over to study the lock. "Got a key?"

"No."

"Thought not. I'll have to use me other skills."

"What? You're going to pick it?" Mucum and delicate, bent wires somehow didn't go together.

"No, stupid. Diana give me this body for a reason, right?" He turned around until his backside was up against the door and shoved, hard. The rusty lock was no match and the door burst open.

Ark looked around, wild-eyed. "You could get arrested for that!"

"What, having a butt that could shoot for Arborium? It's the least of our troubles, mate!" If he didn't make it home tonight, his dad would be up worrying. But what could he do? As

Mucum pulled Ark through the doorway, they were finally free of the gloom of the undercanopy. Instead of wood underfoot, there was grass. Ark quickly closed the door behind him, then turned to take in the view. The clouds had also given up the ghost, drifting away to bother some other part of Arborium. He'd forgotten that the sun still shone above the treetops. At least the place was empty. They were safe, for now, but the closer they came to the castle, the more nervous Ark became.

"Bit of all right, this is!" Mucum walked away from the wall and slid down to rest his back against an apple tree bursting with ripe fruit. The orchard fringed the edge of a single huge scaffield, one of many that ringed the agricultural areas, their acres of crops suspended high above the earth. These enormous, walled-in platforms leaned at a slight angle to catch the sun, and were planted with wheat, barley, and corn. Ark always marveled at the stupendous engineering required to support the weight of the soil, piled at least ten feet deep on top of the platforms.

The harvest was already in, leaving a field of stubble like the beginning of a giant's beard. In less than a week, Dendrans would gather by the palace to celebrate the year's produce, the merriment of festival fireworks covering up the treachery growing deep down.

Mucum grabbed an apple and bit into it. "Can't beat the taste of a Mary Pippins!"

"You shouldn't steal." Ark frowned disapprovingly.

"Oh, for Diana's sake. You're startin' to sound like my mother. Give it a rest. Hey!" Mucum perked up. "The look on the old man's face! Priceless!"

Ark crumbled some soil between his fingers. A few sheep dotted the grass. In the distance, golden heads of barley bowed to a light breeze. "You don't get it, do you? It's more than skiving off. All this is going to be chopped down, gone!"

"Whoa there! Just because we had a laugh, it don't mean I ain't thinkin' about it."

"I have to speak to the King. We're running out of time."

"Oh, right. *Arktorious Malikum, fourteen-year-old sewage worker, here to uncover a secret plot to a-sausage-mate . . . a-sissy-mate . . .* err." Mucum bunched his lips tight in concentration. "Got it! *to . . . kill the King! Take me to your leader!* It's really going to work, that is!"

"I'm glad you're so amused. Have you got any better ideas?"

"Actually, I have. You'd be surprised what's lurkin' up 'ere!" Mucum tapped the side of his head as if the wisdom of ages lay within.

"Well, I hope it's better than your spelling."

"Give us some of that cheese and I might let you in on my brilliant plan."

By the time they finally approached the edge of the court, the October sun was falling over the far forest. The platform that supported the home of King Quercus was the biggest in the country. Some of the beams that underpinned the foundations were a hundred feet thick and over a thousand yards long. Barkingham Palace itself was massive, a magnified log cabin with battlements.

At this time of evening, the landscaped pleasure gardens were full of courting couples. The scent of honeysuckle hung in the air, and noble families gathered for supper picnics in the grass, under ornamental cherry trees planted in raised beds sunk into the boardwalk. Happy families. Ark longed to be part of it, chewing on a chicken leg and making small talk into the twilight with not a worry in the world. Despite the unjustness of it, it was still his country, still worth saving. Maybe one day, all would be welcome. A mad dream.

"This is how the other 'alf live, eh?" muttered Mucum. "Anyways, we're 'ere to do a job. Do yer see it?"

Ark's eyes focused. A bog-standard manhole cover was set within the planking, just a few feet from the outer wall. He'd seen a thousand in his short life. This one might be their ticket.

"Now, remember what I said. I'll see you in a minute." Mucum sauntered casually toward the manhole. Ark studied the scene. Luckily, all the couples had eyes only for each other, and the plump children of the court were too busy stuffing their faces. A plumber going about his legitimate business wasn't a cause for concern. The guard was another matter. The thought of it made Ark's forehead prickle.

He had no choice. Time to move. The steps at the front of the castle were wide and burnished with gold. The risers were embossed with stags, boars, eagles, and ravens, all bowing before their king. At the top, a pair of huge oak doors reared up into the sky. The sun, now orange as it sank toward the horizon, lit up the flag of Arborium high above: an oak leaf twisted into the shape of a crown.

The studded doors were firmly shut. The guard who stood on sentry duty, with his ceremonial hat in the shape of an outsize acorn, frowned at the sight of a boy messing up his newly polished metalwork.

"Yeah?" said the guard menacingly. The man might once have been a mountain of muscle, but his features now sagged downward, thanks to an excess of pies and too much standing around, bored out of his skull.

Ark was on his own. "I'd like to . . . that is . . . the King.

Well . . ." So much for speeches. "He's in danger! I've overheard a plot, you see —"

His words were cut short. "Yeah. I do see. And what I see is a little oik!"

Good. The man was distracted. Out of the corner of his eye, Ark saw Mucum working the first bolt of the manhole. The plumber was in plain sight. Ark gulped down his fear.

"Did yer mates set you up for this as a dare?"

The guard leaned down and Ark caught a whiff of stale beer.

"No!" It wasn't a dare. It was a plan. A dumb, impossible plan. If the guard would just turn a couple of inches . . .

"Well, I don't see no plot here, unless you've been sent to assassinate our beloved leader?" The guard leaned back and his shoulders bobbed with laughter at his own joke. But then he lunged suddenly, grabbed Ark hard, and lifted him up until they were both at eye level. "We've had a bit of fun, you and me. Now go back to whatever miserable little squithole you crept from and leave me to do my job, guarding the King from real danger, eh?" He let go and Ark dropped in a heap on the floor.

Ark allowed himself to slide his eyes quickly toward his friend, struggling with the final bolt. Ark knew this one was going to screech. Plumber's instinct. Rust was never silent. He had to do something!

Ark jumped up and screamed as loudly as he could at the guard. "You'll see! Trouble's coming!"

Instead of running toward the sound of the bolt giving way, the guard put one hand on the hilt of his sword. "It will be if you don't clear off, you nutter!" he hissed.

Ark's heart pounded as he retreated down the stairs just in time to see Mucum's head vanish beneath the walkway. He was in! It worked! Now his only problem was how to also vanish as the guard's eyes tracked his every movement.

"Cooeee!" Ark and the guard turned their heads at the sound. It was an invasion that couldn't have been timed better. One moment, the guard was glaring at the boy who was clearly off his tree, and the next, he was surrounded by a gaggle of gossiping girls, desperate for his autograph.

I owe you one, Diana! Not the best prayer in Arborium, but Ark was truly grateful. He ran for the hole, slipping his legs over the edge.

"We haven't got all night!" said Mucum from the darkness below.

"Give me a chance! Our *friend* is too busy being adored by some tourists of the female variety." If Ark wasn't so terrified, he would have laughed. They were in. Next stop, the King.

Just as Ark was about to pull the manhole cover over his head, a voice stopped him dead.

"Oi! What do you think you're doing?"

He froze. They were so close. It was over.

10 · DANGER IN THE NORTH

Once again, Petronio felt he was in the wrong place at the wrong time.

"What is the boy doing here?" Grasp wouldn't even refer to him by name. The High Councillor paced the rug-strewn floor, clearly ill at ease.

"Calm yourself. Isn't it better than having him hidden in the utility room?" Lady Fenestra sat by the fireplace in a high oak chair, staring at her fingernails. Her lips curled upward in amusement.

"Is this your idea of a joke?" Grasp briefly stared at his errant son.

Petronio shrank back toward the door. It had been the lady's suggestion to have him present at the meeting, but now he wasn't so sure.

"The boy is . . . special."

"In what way? Other than *specially* capable of letting go of a spy and making my men take part in a wild-goat chase? Lucky for him, the plumber's boy decided to end it all." He turned to Fenestra. "Aside from that *little* failing, maybe you've discovered talents that I have yet to see. I will concede that he has a general ruthlessness that is unusual in a mere youth." Even his compliments were barbed.

"I'm glad you understand. Now, to the point." Fenestra's voice took on an edge that demanded total attention. "In a few short days, I need to know that your associates will follow you and rise against the King."

"Of course they will! The man is weak-willed and Arborium is rotten. He began with strength and resolve, but they have leached away, leaving only a dry husk of the leader that he was. It is time to cut that particular tree down to size." Grasp was making speeches again. "But I don't have the necessary manpower!"

Petronio saw the spittle flecking his father's beard and he realized that the High Councillor was, after all, only a little man. He also knew for the first time that after years of public put-downs and not so public beatings, he despised his father.

"Our great empire has armies that would swamp this little backwater"—she snapped her fingers as if that were all it would take—"but unfortunately, there is the problem of a certain deadly gas." She looked meaningfully at Petronio. Strange to think that mere hours ago, she had been on the brink of death herself.

"We have managed to produce a tiny amount of vaccine, but not enough to equip an invasion," she continued. "Thus, the necessary use of force must come from elsewhere. *Inside.* I propose that we utilize your son to go on a little errand, up north to your armories. There is a certain commander there who may be, shall we say, sympathetic to our cause."

Petronio's heart beat faster. So this was what she had in mind!

"That is preposterous! The boy going by himself to Mossside! They'll turn him into mincemeat!" It wouldn't be the injuries that were a problem, more the damage to the High Councillor's reputation.

"Oh, do I have to explain everything? Your well-known presence may raise suspicion up there, do you not agree? Whereas a boy can travel like a ghost, and the message he carries slip through with ease. I also have faith that this young man is more than capable of looking after himself."

If Petronio could have purred, he would.

"Why can't you go?" demanded Grasp. "You seem to be able to crawl around our kingdom without being seen!"

"What? A woman in the world of swords, crossbows, and the other backward weapons your culture is so fond of? I would stand out like, in your language, a blossom in winter!"

Grasp wasn't convinced. He shook his head, his mind filled with all that could go wrong.

Lady Fenestra had no doubt. "Come, young Petronio. I am sure your father can spare his best horse?"

Petronio found himself enjoying the emerging battle of wills, especially as his father was the loser. The Councillor looked ready to explode, but thought better of it. There was a tight silence.

"Talk to my groom in the stables. He can take Mercury. I shall have to make do with one of the old plodders." He pulled open the balcony doors violently, as if fresh air could blow away such madness. In the west, the sun was beginning to sink on the old country. When it rose again, what would they have set in motion? "I shortly have a meeting with Quercus concerning security arrangements for the Harvest Festival," Grasp continued, his jawline rigid. "I shall play my part and reassure our wise king that all is well." Then he walked out onto the balcony. As far as he was concerned, they were both dismissed.

Lady Fenestra smiled slyly at Petronio. "That's settled. There is much to do and little time. Follow me!"

"Err . . . yes."

As Petronio left his father sulking in his study, Lady Fenestra pulled back into the shadows of the hallway and hissed at him.

"Wait! The guards can be trusted, but my face will cause gossip if seen by other servants. Listen carefully. The man you are looking for has the name of Flint."

"Julius Flint?" Petronio looked suitably awed. Who hadn't heard of him?

Lady Fenestra arched her eyebrows. "I was right about you."

Petronio was desperate to impress her. "When I was younger and ready for bed, my nurse used to tell me to close my eyes or Flint would pluck them out. I always thought it was a far tale until my father told me how Julius Flint, a young second-in-command of the armories in his twenties, put down a civil uprising when Quercus was challenged for the throne."

"Yes?"

"Once the protesters were rounded up, he grabbed one of them out of the crowd and dangled him over the edge of the branch, offering to drop him unless he informed Flint who the ringleaders were. The man was only too happy to oblige. In thanks, Flint let go."

"Brutal but effective!" commented Lady Fenestra.

Petronio was on a roll now. The story beat any far tale. "That's only the half of it," he continued. "The leaders were dispatched in the same way, one by one. The rest of the crowd awaited their punishment, thinking about docked wages, fines maybe. Guess what he did?"

"It's hardly difficult."

"Ordered his men to push the whole lot off, saying later that every one of them—men, women, and children—had been resisting arrest and the result was truly unfortunate. Apparently, Quercus was so angry about what had been done in his name and without his agreement that he sent the lot of them up north. Out of sight, out of mind. But in fact, it's said that in the end, the crushing of the revolt brought lasting peace to Arborium. That was the last-ever uprising. Every Dendran knows the story. After old Ponticus had his heart attack, Flint was named commander in chief—" Petronio suddenly blanched. "And this is the man you want me to find?"

"Precisely!" She reached within the folds of her habit and pulled out a purse that jingled as she handed it over. "The old ways are the best when it comes to persuasion. And from what you say about your king, it might be easier to deal with him than I thought. Now, I want you to deliver this message and emphasize that we have only a few days to prepare." When Lady Fenestra had finished whispering her precise instructions, she turned away and disappeared through a side door.

Petronio was on his own. Only this morning, he had been bored to tears in a stuffy lecture hall. This was more like it! A mission. The trust of someone powerful. He ordered the groom to saddle up and took off down the branch line, the rubber-shod hooves gripping the wood as he cantered away into the twilight.

Five minutes later, his father was also on the move, flanked by his two bodyguards. He was heading toward the Court of Quercus. The old shire horse he rode could barely keep up with the two guards. Grasp cursed Maw, Lady Fenestra, and especially his son as the horse ambled unhurriedly along the byways. At this rate, it would be midnight by the time they arrived.

Petronio's passage was quicker. Mercury, a silver-gray stallion, was true to his name. They flew along the broad branch lines, beating out a muffled rhythm as the sun slowly sank from the sky, and the woods filled with lengthening shadow. Petronio didn't bother with the niceties of the Highway Code. Dendran pedestrians were a nuisance. Luckily, most heard the horse before he was upon them and they jumped out of the way, offering the rider various gestures with arms and fingers that certainly weren't polite. The populated areas were soon left behind and Petronio was by himself, heading north into unknown territory.

He'd never been this far before, never seen for himself how the whole country truly was one big, intersecting treescape. He paused momentarily to let the horse drink from a wooden trough set against an old abandoned trunk. Either side of the deserted highway, the trees gave into darkness. His mind wandered, fixing briefly on a weathered wooden figure of a raven covered in tattered black ribbons. The old wayside shrine was almost hidden in the ivy, but it gave Petronio the shivers. The lonely byways were still dotted with these symbols of the old religion.

As a child, when he woke calling for a mother who was no longer there, his nurse conjured tales out of the shadows of his bedroom. Her main intent seemed to have been less about comfort and more about scaring him half to death. One of her favorites was the story about Little Red Ride In The Wood, who strayed too far from the safety of home, until the Raven Queen, disguised as an old granny, invited her into a little cottage deep in the middle of nowhere. A delicious-smelling cauldron was on the boil, and it only needed one more ingredient. . . .

His nurse would always grab him at this point and shout:

> *Into the pot with you! Corwenna's having a do.*
> *Sugar and spice, gristle is nice,*
> *Two legs and a head and soon you'll be dead.*
> *It's time to serve up a stew, ooh!*

Woodrot! A bunch of old wives' tales. He gathered his cloak about him and pulled the bridle hard, jamming the bit back into Mercury's mouth.

"That's enough. You're not a buddy water bottle, eh?" He dug in his heels and galloped off along the track. Roosting rooks squawked into flight, disturbed by the thundering hooves. Gray light pouring from a half-formed moon turned the forest around the highway into hills and valleys. The main north-south route was relatively straight. Under the highest leaves it swept along the massive, flattened branches with braced bridges joining to each next branch. As the highway spanned the gap between the distant trees, scaffolding flared out to hug their giant, curved trunks. Petronio sped around these lonely round-abouts, urging his steed onward to the sound of wind hissing in the leaves.

As he rode, Petronio thought about Fenestra. She was so alien, so different, especially against the dull fellows of col-lege. And what was Maw like? The woman made it sound so exotic. As he had helped Fenestra to her feet after her dramatic near-death and they had walked back that afternoon, she told him about wonders he could only imagine. Cities of glass and metal that dazzled the eye, flying machines and cloud-piercing towers where a hundred thousand people lived! He didn't know it, but his mind was thirsty. His life so far had been bark-bound. But now, what this foreigner offered . . .

Petronio nodded off. Or at least, he thought he had. Had hours or minutes gone by? All he knew was the difference in the rhythm. His eyes shot open and he was instantly aware. It was colder, for a start, as if he'd ridden into the next season. An early autumn mist had suddenly descended, softening the edges of his view, cutting distance down to only twenty yards. His riding cloak was already clammy with dew. The road looked no different, a bit rougher, maybe. Then he realized what had changed. The way ahead was lined with gas lamps, creating halos in the fog. But most of them had been smashed so that only about one in ten flickered feebly. Also, the sides of the branch were littered with trash — bits of old food, discarded clothing, twisted wicker shopping baskets. Why hadn't a rubbishman swept them over the edge? The trees themselves were carved and gouged with strange markings that looked like doodles. As he peered closer, he realized that some of the inscriptions contained swear words that even he hadn't come across. The place was a mess.

As he took in the new surroundings, Petronio began to realize that some of the gloomy hollows lurking at the sides of the branch line weren't in fact shadows. He pulled on the reins, and the horse went from canter to trot to a standstill. He twisted around in the saddle. Behind him now, figures detached themselves from the thick darkness and began to move toward him. At the same time, in front of him, he could see someone else moving to lean against one of the unbroken lamps, picking at the nails of his left hand with a knife as if hoping he'd discover some treasure under the grime. The boy's head was shaved, except for three straggly braids of hair at the back, woven in with silver bells. This marked him out from the other dozen or so total baldies who now surrounded Mercury.

The boy looked up lazily. "All right?" he drawled.

Petronio tried to stay calm. "Yeah. All right." That is, as much as he could be, surrounded by a bunch of knife-wielding thugs. They were all dressed in loose-fitting clothes that matched their messy surroundings: cotes too big, with lots of pockets, ill-fitting cloaks, and floppy boots, all in black.

The boy unglued himself from the lamppost and pointed the knife at Petronio. "Doesn't look like your manor, does it? Not lost, are you?"

"No," said Petronio, looking around, "I think I'm in the right place." But as the gang closed in, he wondered, remembering his father's warning words about *mincemeat*.

11 · SEWERS ARE A BOY'S BEST FRIEND

※

"Oi! What do you think you're doing?" the voice shouted again.

Ark hurriedly slid the iron manhole cover back into place. He could feel the boards vibrating. Any moment now, the cover would be ripped from his fingers and he'd be skewered by the guard's sword.

The voice was closer now, spitting with anger. "You're in serious trouble!"

Even Mucum, who would happily take on a killer hornet with nothing more than a crosshead screwdriver, was trembling in the darkness.

Suddenly, the pounding on the boards veered away from them. "Get out of those branches, you little twig! Those cherries belong to the King!"

A second, feminine voice piped up. "I say, Gerald, do as the gentleman asks." There was a pause. "I do apologize for my wayward progeny, Officer."

"Yeah. Well. Just keep an eye out, madam. Or I could get in trouble."

"Of course! Gerald, come and make a gesture of contrition to the smart young man!"

"Do I have toooqoo?" another voice whined.

Mucum could easily picture the snotty-nosed brat. At any other time, he'd give him a good slap. But as far as he was currently concerned, the boy was their best friend in the whole of Arborium.

The mother was doing *her* best to reason with the child. "Yes, or Mommykins will be most upset!"

There was a shuffling of feet and then an unconvincing "Sorreee . . ."

Not far below, Mucum snorted with disbelief. "Thank Diana for rich, spoiled brats!" he muttered as he descended into the darkness, followed by Ark, whose trembling fingers nearly slipped off the rungs.

Within a few yards the vertical shaft hit the main artery serving the castle. Luckily, the engineers who built this underworld had as little desire as the two boys did to splodge through the river of muck. On either side of the lead-lined tunnel, a raised platform provided access as the human waste poured by below. Low-level guide lamps were strung between pools of shadow, fed by natural methane.

"I say!" Mucum drawled, doing his best to imitate the mother's voice. "Would you think, perhaps, that if we take another left, we might find ourselves under the inner walls of the castle, what, what?"

"Rather!" said Ark, joining in. "I do believe the old fellow might be jolly well right!" Then it would be a simple matter of locating the nearest access hatch. Ark grinned. Despite the fear, he was enjoying himself. They'd come to see the King. Nothing would get in their way!

"What's that?" Mucum stopped dead and Ark walked straight into him.

Ark could hear the constant drip of stalactites from the ceiling and the occasional blurping noise that the sludge made as it released yet more noxious gases. And then, in the tunnel ahead of them, a scurrying sound. It wasn't receding, but approaching, fast.

"Oh!" said Ark. "That—"

Three pairs of red eyes filled the darkness. The eyes approached slowly, fearless. The color of the creatures' mangy fur was mottled brown. They resembled what they fed on.

One by itself would be no problem. And between Mucum and himself, they could, if they were lucky, face down a pair of them. But the stories at work hadn't yet explained how to survive an attack by three peckish sewer rats, each the size of a fully grown wolfhound. Their teeth, used to dealing with dead pets that got flushed into the system, would have no problem snapping the odd leg bone.

"Jobby Jones got it right for once," said Mucum.

"How?"

"All that health and safety malarkey about carrying a crossbow every time you go below. Wish I'd listened."

"Thanks, Mucum. Really helpful."

The rats sensed their fear, edging forward. Mucum responded by shuffling backward one step at a time, Ark cowering behind him. A slow-motion dance toward certain death.

"You know that fing you did with the ravens? Now would be a good time to pull it off again. What do yer think?" Mucum being polite was not a good sign.

Ark waited for the blinding flash. But whatever he had was gone. The raven mother veering off was dumb luck. He was only a sewer boy, back where he belonged, the slime soaking into his shoulders as he slid along the wall. He wondered briefly about the feather in his bag. There had to be a reason for it. Was there magic hidden within its blackness? At this moment, he doubted it. Maybe he could stab one of them with the quill. He looked again. Rat hide was thicker than bark. Stupid idea.

The rats brought with them a stench that made the boys almost gag, as if the whole sewer system was concentrated into these three scavenging machines. Their intent washed over Ark. It was time for a feast!

"Head for the ladder!" he cried, about to turn tail and run. Rats were renowned for their intelligence, but evolution hadn't yet taught them to climb a set of vertical iron rungs. He hoped.

"No time!" said Mucum. Any second now, these scabby monsters would pounce. He thought about jumping in the river of squit that flowed past their feet, pulling his scared companion behind him. Maybe not. Rats were born to swim. A bath of Dendran doo-doos was their equivalent of paradise.

"You know, Ratty," Mucum announced suddenly, stopping still, "I've 'ad enough!" At the sound of his raised voice echoing around the circular walls, the rats paused in their advance.

Mucum aimed his words at the biggest and meanest of the creatures, fixing it with a stare. "I mean, fair's fair. You spend all this time wandering around in darkness, dining on Diana knows what, when along comes lunch on legs, eh?" As he spoke, Mucum ignored his instincts and reversed his direction, walking slowly, ever so slowly, toward the apparent leader of the beasts.

The rats were fascinated. Prey normally ran away, fast.

"What are you doing?" Ark whispered, horrified as he hovered behind Mucum's bulk.

"Shut up and hand me yer hammer!" Mucum hissed.

Ark had no idea what one tiny tool would do against a hundred pounds of muscle, claw, and tooth. Anything was better than becoming dinner, though. As Mucum continued speaking, Ark slid his hand to his side and eased out the hammer from the folds of the plumbing pouch before passing it over to a held-out hand.

The talking went on, the river of words confusing the rats. "We've got more important fings to do than bein' eaten, yeah? Like savin' the country, for starters." Still Mucum came on, until he was within a yard of the leader and leaning down, almost face-to-face. "That's the be all and end all of it. I don't 'ave no choice. Old Mucum ain't known for running away. Anyways, I'm doin' you lot a favor. If Maw gets ahold of these trees, trust me, there won't be no nice sewers to play in no more. So . . ." Mucum launched himself forward, bringing his arm up and heaving it down in one smooth motion.

Before the lead rat could even move, the end of the hammer made a perfect landing right on the crown of its matted head. As the rat finally reacted, trying to reach up its claws to rip out the throat of this interloper, the hammer smashed through its thin skull and straight into its brain. There was a dreadful squelching noise and the rat toppled over dead, the contents of its skull oozing out on the platform.

The other two rats stood stock-still, glittering revenge in their beady eyes. A moment later, there was a sudden screech as the furry fiends took flight, accelerating straight toward them in a frenzied blur.

Mucum stood his ground as Ark prayed the end would be quick.

However, instead of sinking their claws into soft Dendran skin, the rats made a split-second decision. The spirit of the pack was already broken. Instead of pouncing, they brushed right past and vanished into the tunnel's depths, hoping to find a dinner that didn't fight back quite so ferociously.

"All in a day's work!" said Mucum with a ridiculously cheerful look on his face. He wiped the bloodied hammer on his leg and passed it back. "Wish me mates could've seen that. It would've been free drinks all around, I reckon. Gimme a hand with this." Mucum put his palm against the still-warm body of the rat and pushed.

"Do I have to?"

"Yer not getting squeamish on me, are yer?"

Ark sighed. Clogged toilets were one thing, but greasy, bloodstained fur and the airborne army of fleas leaping off the corpse to sample his own skin were not his idea of fun. They finally heaved the dead rat to the edge of the platform. One last shove and the body fell off the lip with a *plop* and was carried away by the current.

Mucum gave a bow. "I took a leaf out of your book, little Ark. If a tiny apprentice can take on a guard with a wrench, then what's stopping old Mucum sorting out a coupla vermin? Never thought I'd be grateful for some squitty old plumbin' tools!"

"You saved my life." Ark looked at Mucum in a new way. Up to yesterday, this overgrown hulk would barely have grunted at him as they passed each other in the sewage station. It felt strange, and comforting. No one normally looked out for him.

Mucum floundered for a second. Confronting rabid creatures was one thing, but a compliment? "If you get all mushy on me, I'll have to kill you. Before I do, though, could you 'and over some of that nosh. Murder makes me 'ungry."

Ark undid the buckles on his bag, his legs still trembling as he sat down. "There's dried goat sausage or —"

"Dried goat sausage," interrupted Mucum. "Hard choice, that."

As Mucum munched away, Ark took a swig from the

bottle his mother had given him. Blackberry cordial, its sweet-
ness cutting through the foul smell that filled the tunnel. He
passed the drink over. "It's time for me to go see the King."

"Wot you mean?" Mucum spluttered. "We're in this
together!"

"Listen. No one knows about your involvement yet. You and
your family are safe. It's up to me now." Ark's lips were set
straighter than a sawn plank.

"Arktorious Malikum, the great warrior?"

"I don't need to be. I've worked out where we are and it's only
a couple of hundred yards from the King's quarters."

"Have you gone psychic on me?" Mucum squinted at his
friend.

"No, silly. Look!" A small drain opening by their feet had a
rather grubby royal crest emblazoned on the edge of the pipe.

Mucum wiped his lips as he gave the bottle back. He stood
up and walked on a few yards. Sure enough, the next drain had
no crest. "Oh. Very clever, that is."

Ark was proud of his detective work. "This outflow is com-
posed of nothing but the finest royal produce!"

Mucum sniffed. "Yeah. Well, it smells the same."

"I'll follow the pipework and take myself straight into his
private residence, explain what's going on. The King will have
Grasp arrested and—"

"You make it sound dead easy," Mucum grumbled. "But I
don't see why I can't do the bodyguard thing."

Ark was desperate not to get his friend into any more trouble.
"Mucum, if it goes wrong, if I get caught, who's going to get the
word out? We need a Plan B."

"You've got a point, I suppose. What is Plan B, by the way?"

"No idea. I'll see you later. Go home."

Mucum folded his arms. "No way. I'm not havin' that. Find Quercus. Sort it out. But I promise I ain't going nowhere 'til I know you're all right. I'll give you an hour and then I'm comin' in after you!" He stood there as if he was putting down roots. "And leave the rest of those sausages behind. A man's gotta eat."

Ark mostly kept to himself at work. He wasn't the sort to have a best bud. He felt tears bubbling at the edge of his eyes and turned away, not wanting Mucum to see his face. "Thanks . . . for everything."

Five minutes later, Ark was sure he was right under the royal chamber. He quickly located a maintenance hatch off a side tunnel. He climbed the ladder and pressed his ear up against the floor hatch, listening for footsteps. All clear. He undid the double-sided latch and swung it open.

The corridor he tiptoed into easily outdid Grasp's house in opulence and finery. All the walls were painted with murals cunningly hiding the door frames in archways of golden leaves. The gas lamps were polished silver, their flames giving off perfumed scents, and the floorboards were covered in silk rugs.

Hope flared like a gas lamp in his heart for the first time since it all began. Was it really only the day before? One day ago, he was Arktorious Malikum, tired, broke, and hungry. And now, he was still tired, poor, and hungry, but somehow at the center of unfolding events. He would find the King and warn him.

It's going to be all right! he thought as he walked right into the armed guards outside the King's rooms.

The soldiers' eyes went wide. Who the holly was this blood-spattered runt of a boy with crazed eyes? Even worse, how had he managed to break through all security and get within feet of the King?

Ark was dumbfounded. If only he'd chosen the next hatch. Being out by a few yards could be a fatal mistake. He was so close! What could he do? If they weren't Grasp's men, they might listen to reason. Maybe . . . "Thank Diana I've found someone!" he announced. "The King is in grave danger. He's going to be betrayed at the Harvest Festival! Councillor—"

Before he could say another word, a punch snapped Ark's head backward. He crumpled to the ground before being heaved over the second soldier's shoulder like a carpet and carted off.

12 · CONFRONTATION

Petronio took stock of the situation. He was alone, apart from his father's horse, in unfamiliar territory in the middle of the night, surrounded by a gang of yobs with knives. The purse he carried was the perfect motive for murder. It wasn't a good starting point.

"Which one of you would like to be the first to be trampled to death under my horse's hooves?" Petronio held his gaze steady as he looked around the assembled thugs.

The leader spoke. "You're havin' a bit of a laugh there, mate. That's proper good, that is!" He smiled and this gave permission for the rest of the gang to join in the snickering. "In fact I've never been so scared in my life!" Catcalls followed the sarcasm.

Petronio responded by suddenly jerking hard on the reins and leaning back with all his considerable weight. He'd seen his father do it once and had no idea if Mercury would comply. Quick as a flash, the mighty stallion reared up onto two legs, his front hooves pawing the air and missing the leader by inches.

Unless he wanted his head mashed to a pulp, the boy had no choice. He fell back, out of the glow of the flickering gas lamp, the bells on his hair braids jingling in the darkness, a scowl on his face trying to hide the fear.

The horse crashed his hooves back onto the branch, making the whole road vibrate and the leaves rustle in agitation. The obvious next move would have been to gallop away, smashing the gang members to left and right. The horse snorted, his hooves pawing the ground in anticipation.

Petronio licked his lips. The fog had thickened around them, like a damp blanket. If he dug in his spurs and Mercury took off down the woodway, they might not see the route clearly in the sputtering arc of the lamps, nor the swinging of the low safety rope, before it was too late. The boy, Malikum, was welcome to his suicide. But for Petronio, a leap over the edge into eternity was not an option.

He held the reins tight, stroking the horse's neck. "Steady, boy. Steady!" he whispered. They were back to square one. Stalemate.

The leader recovered himself, stepped back into the lamplight. "I'm doin' a bit of countin' 'ere. Twelve of us. One of you and a nutter for a horse." He pointed the knife. "Though when my lads are finished, your little pet won't be good for anything but steak pie. And you, softy southerner, we'll be 'appy to shave a few pounds off, if you get my drift!"

Petronio did. He swung one leg out of its stirrup and over the saddle, slipping off the horse and landing easily on the ground. He continued holding the leader's stare, not letting his eyes drop for one second. It was a game he was playing, with the highest stakes.

"I've an idea about you," Petronio answered. "Without this lot as backup, you'd be squitting yourself right now." He turned to address the rest of the gang. "Isn't that what cowards do? Surround themselves with fawning acolytes?"

The words went over their heads, but the gist was more than clear. The leader didn't like it. A stranger giving him lip, showing him up in front of his mates. He couldn't have that, could he? He'd be laughed at all the way through Moss-side. Carving obscenities in wood was one thing. But now it was time to carve his name into the pompous prat's face.

"Go on, Flinty!"

"Have him good!"

"Stick him!"

The crowd was eager for their leader to put the stranger firmly in his place.

With a howl of anger, the boy came for Petronio, knife hand slicing through the air.

It was exactly what the surgeon's apprentice expected. After all, he was his father's son. Scalpels weren't his only specialty. Instead of toys, his father's thugs had given him miniature knives to play with from an early age, teaching him all the classic street moves: feint, parry, double bluff. It was like a poker game, really, only a shade more physical. Make the other side think you've got a weak hand. Then, *Bam!*

Instinct kicked in. As the knife came toward him, held in his enemy's left hand, Petronio noticed and instantly analyzed his opponent's classic mistake.

The other boy was so keen to attack, he'd forgotten that extending one side of his body left the other totally vulnerable.

As the boy overextended himself, nearly losing his balance, Petronio easily swerved out of the way, then pushed up hard with his haunches. Impact was instant, completely throwing his attacker off balance.

"What?" squawked the leader in shock, as his own knife clattered harmlessly off the edge of the branch.

Even as the word left his mouth, Petronio completed the maneuver, pulling the boy's hair savagely so that his head was forced back, exposing his neck to the short but lethal blade that now zoomed like an arrow straight toward the soft flesh.

Somewhere nearby, a gas lamp flickered and went out. No one dared to breathe, waiting for the blood to spill. The pack mentality was already kicking in. The stranger could kill one of them, but once the rest of them piled in, he didn't stand a chance. A couple of the older lads were already working out who would take over, who would be next top man. King Flinty was about to die. Long live the king.

Petronio was no fool. Killing the boy was the equivalent of committing suicide. The knife came to a sudden halt, pricking the underside of the boy's chin.

"Well! Well! Well!" announced Petronio to astounded silence. "Who's the softy now, *Flinty*?"

The leader wasn't entirely stupid. "You've made your point, pretty boy. Wotchu want?"

And that's when Petronio pulled off the biggest surprise of all. He let the boy go and put away his knife. "I've come to see your father. So let's get on with it."

Flinty's eyes went wide. "How d'ya know 'oo my old man is?"

"Oh, please. Work it out. Your colleagues here call you *Flinty*."

Flinty paused. He didn't like the sound of it. "And wot's my dad gotta do wiv this?"

Petronio took hold of Mercury's reins. "Plenty. Shall we go?"

He could see that Flinty thought he was mad. One second, the stranger was about to kill him, and the next, he wanted to see his old man. With the knife out of the way, all it would take was one look for the rest of the gang to do him.

"And I have a feeling that if I turn up damaged in any way, your father, Julius Flint, Commander of the Arborian Armories, won't be pleased." Petronio's words were sharper than any knife.

"Why didn't you say before?" Flinty muttered.

"Like you said," Petronio answered reasonably, "they're soft as squit down south. Now, I've been riding for hours and would like a drink. . . ."

Flinty pulled out a flask from inside his cote and handed it over. "Get that down your neck!" he sneered. The fiery, forty-proof, home-brewed hooch would soon have the boy spewing his guts.

Instead, Petronio glugged away merrily. "Not much flavor, though it hits the spot. Brewed from scaffield potatoes, I believe?" He wiped his lips in satisfaction.

"Suppose . . . ," muttered Flinty. Even this small victory was denied him.

"Lead on!" said Petronio, pointing into the mist.

13 · THE SLIPPERY TRUTH

Five minutes later, Ark came to, his head throbbing with an all-too-real headache this time. He'd blown it. Did it look like he was capable of killing a king? They obviously thought he did. He should have brought Mucum with him. Ark tried not to open his eyes. He was aware that he was sprawled on the ground, but where, he had no idea. He could smell . . . ammonia. Better to pretend for a while longer.

"By all that's green, we're gonna be in big trouble." The soldier who spoke poked at Ark with his foot as if he were no more than a sewer rat.

Ark wanted to try and explain. But whatever he said, they wouldn't believe.

"Look, we didn't let him in. It won't be us losing our jobs. Leave it to the head of security. He's in with the old canker right now."

"If the King heard you calling him that, you'd be chopped."

"Nah! Not him. He's soft as fungus. But I wouldn't want to cross the other one. He can do the interrogation. Councillor Grasp is well known for his methods of extracting information!"

They'd decided. A door swung open and slammed shut, a key grinding in the lock.

At the mention of Grasp's name, all the hope in Ark's heart died. He really was too late.

He tried to study his surroundings. His right eye had already swollen up so badly that he could hardly see through it. With the other one, he made an inventory: a bucket full of ammonia;

several mops; a gas boiler; a servant's toilet bowl that was shockingly dirty; and a door that looked solid enough to withstand a siege. Obviously, it was the first place the guards had found with a lock. It was a never-ending circle. It had all started in a utility room not unlike this. That first time, he'd been able to run out. Now what? If the Councillor found him, he'd be shut up, permanently, and the King would be no wiser. Even Mucum couldn't help him now.

Something sharp dug into his ribs. That stupid feather again, nestled among the loose tools that didn't fit into his plumber's belt. Hang on a second. . . . He still had his tools! He gave a little prayer of thanks to Diana and crawled over to the toilet. He never thought he'd actually feel affection for a place where you did your ablutions, but he could almost have kissed the seat. Warning the King would have to wait; living through the next ten minutes was a priority.

It was an everyday job for a sewage worker. He quickly shut off the water, pulled the handle to drain the remaining liquid, and then proceeded to undo the bolt surrounding the base. In a flash, the toilet bowl was pushed aside, revealing a welcoming hole in the floor. It was small, but then, so was he. Ignoring the rising stink, he put his feet over the edge just as he heard footsteps pausing outside the door and a voice drifting through.

"And you caught him where?"

It was now or never. He put his hands high over his head and let go. His feet and legs vanished downward but the ragged lip caught at his belt, halting his descent. He was stuck fast!

The key began to turn. *No!* Ark fumbled with his belt, trying to undo the buckle, his fingers slipping in panic as his legs wiggled free beneath him like worms.

The door swung open to reveal not just the two soldiers but an overweight figure dressed in gaudy colors like a bloated parrot. The man whose voice he'd heard plotting treachery only the day before. Grasp! And on either side of the Councillor, two guards whose faces he knew only too well.

"What?" Salix's eyes almost popped out. "But you're dead!"

Ark would be if he didn't get a move on.

Alnus instinctively rubbed his head where a nice lump had formed thanks to the application of a certain wrench belonging to the very much alive boy in front of him. "Why, you little...!" The fruity insult was lost under the sound of Salix's hobnailed boots pounding toward the center of the room, his whole body eager to rip the little spy into even littler pieces. But just as his meaty fingers reached forward to pull Ark out like a snail from its shell, the belt finally gave way. With a slurping sound and a wail of fear, Ark slipped suddenly from sight.

Salix leaned over the edge and peered into the darkness, trying not to breathe the stench in through his nose, shaking his fists in frustration. The boy had got away, again, down a hole that no grown-up ever had a chance of entering.

Grasp was beside himself. "Twice you've lost him! What do I pay you for?" he fumed. "Find out where the soil pipe leads, you fools. Get some men and search the sewers." He turned to the soldiers as Salix and Alnus ran down the corridor. "And as for you two, if you value your livelihoods and reputations, don't, I repeat, *don't*," he snarled, "disturb the King with the news that you very nearly allowed him to be assassinated! Get back to your station outside the doors and do what you're supposed to do. GUARD THEM!" he screamed. "We shall deal with the would-be killer and let His Majesty focus his great mind on more important matters."

Both soldiers stood at attention. "Yes, sir! Whatever you say, sir!"

"I do say. Now leave me. Your incompetence has made me weary."

The soldiers marched away, glad they would still have wages at the end of the week. But Grasp was worried. Could a mere boy come between him and power? Of course not. There were only so many places a sewer could lead. His men would not, could not, fail.

It was time to return to the late-night meeting with Quercus. The Harvest Festival was only six days away and the King wanted every boring detail gone over, as if it hadn't been the same for year upon year. It really was time the ineffectual sap was cut down to size so those with ambition could rise up in his place. That was one part of the celebration plans that Grasp would keep secret. His Majesty's sudden and inexplicable death.

Ark had only a split second to take in the astounded look on the guard's face before he was sliding straight down a pipe that was more used to effluent than half-size Dendrans.

I really am in the squit now! How long before Grasp's men found him? Mucum wouldn't stand a chance. And then what? Falling through emptiness was turning into a dangerous habit. His feet scrabbled to get purchase on the smooth, near vertical walls, but there was nothing to hold on to. He was sliding faster and faster, with no choice but to point his toes and keep his arms up together above his head like an arrow, say his prayers, and go with the flow. He remembered a book his mother used to read to him when he was little, about a girl who fell down a hollow trunk into a magical otherworld: *Alice in Underland.* He thought it was stuff and nonsense. Now he wasn't so sure.

He reached out his fingers to try and get purchase on the sides of the soil pipe but it was impossible. The pipe suddenly zigzagged, tumbling him around until he had no idea which way was up, though the wind whistling past his ears told him that he was moving way too fast.

The soil pipe suddenly widened and before he could even think, there was a splash, his fall cushioned in a way he could hardly bear to think about. This was no comforting cradle of straw. Nor did his head fill with the scent of incense. His head briefly went under. With a push of desperation, he surfaced again, wiping a film of indescribable liquid from his face and eyes, just glad to be alive. The river of so-called royal muck he flailed about in had just saved his life. The Holly Woodsmen said that the Goddess moved in mysterious ways. This really had to be one of them.

He let the current take him, doing the loggy paddle that every sewer worker learned for their Basic Safety Certificate. Any second, he expected to hear the scraping back of an inspection hatch and the pounding of boots. The guards might be reluctant to get their hands dirty, but he was a bobbing target. An arrow would save them the bother and then Ark would end up as another bit of compost, his bones fertilizing the scaffields.

"There are better places to take up swimming!"

"Mucum!" Ark gasped, ecstatic to see a familiar and friendly face.

"Do you want a hand?" Mucum leaned over the edge and grabbed hold of Ark's forearm. "Yeurghhh!" His hand slipped and Ark briefly went under. "Ark!"

A bespattered head rose above the surface. "Not . . . dead . . . yet!" Ark spat out.

This time, as Ark paddled closer, Mucum knelt down and reached out both arms to grab hold of Ark's body. The slurpy stuff wasn't willing to give up its guest so easily. It was like pulling a stubborn carrot out of soil, but finally, with one last *glop*, Ark was heaved out onto the side.

"Eye, eye, what's goin' on 'ere, then?" Mucum peered at Ark's swollen eye.

"Very funny," Ark said, trying to catch his breath.

"I take it you weren't successful in yer mission?" Mucum wiped his hands down his britches as if that would take away the smell.

Ark began shivering all over. "Worse than that. We're really in the squit now. The guards are on their way. We have to run!"

"What? We only got 'ere 'alf an hour ago and now you wanna leave? Wot's a coupla guards? I can sort them, easy." Mucum cracked his knuckles to show he meant business.

"Mucum, stop being thick! It's not a few rats we've got to face but the whole of the King's bodyguard, armed with swords."

Mucum's face went red. Nobody called him stupid, least of all this stinking stick insect. He should have known the boy was trouble the moment Ark started weeping all over him. Without thinking, his fist shot out, ready to black Ark's other eye.

"Don't!" Ark squealed as he ducked down.

"Blood and Diana!" swore Mucum as his punch impacted on a very solid wall. He hopped up and down, the agony in his hand finally bringing him to his senses. "Not thinking . . . ," he mumbled.

"Me, neither," Ark admitted. Arguing wouldn't save them. "Anyhow, forget it. We need to disappear." His thoughts flew around like a whirlwind. At this very moment, they were right where the guards expected, in the sewers under the castle. He had to confound them, make them lose the trail. Suddenly, his one good eye lit up like a sap-sozzled firefly. This under-land was the place where engineers put all the gubbins that made a building work — sewers, gas pipes, mail tubes, and . . . waterworks.

Ark shook himself off like a dog. "We need to find a door with a porthole!"

"Do you mind?" said Mucum, as he was covered in spray. Now he knew how the miniature trees in the local park felt, being endlessly visited by dogs desperate to go.

"Not at all!" Ark smiled. He ran, or rather squelched in his soaking wet creepers, down the tunnel in the direction of sewage flow, looking for evidence. Someone crafty had built this place — squeezed all the utilities through the same pipe but charged for them separately. He hoped he was right as he pounded along the iron mesh floor. Mucum's heavy footsteps followed behind. The tunnel twisted and turned as more sewage outflows transformed the fast-flowing stream into a roaring river. At least this time, there were no rats.

Ark slowed to a halt. Built into the side of the tunnel was a door with a porthole viewing panel and rotating locking wheel. He peered through with his left eye, unable to believe his luck. There was a small chamber followed by a second door. The double system was put in to prevent infection. Dendran effluent and drinking water did not make a good mix. But this was no time to worry about health and safety. He grabbed the wheel with both hands and tried to force it free. No good. It was stuck solid. He looked nervously up and down the passage as he tried again.

Mucum pushed him out of the way. "Think *I'm* thick, eh?" Mucum grabbed the wheel, braced his legs, and strained.

Ark could see the veins bulging along Mucum's arms. Of course! He'd been pushing clockwise, tightening the seal.

Mucum gave one last grunt and the wheel finally began to turn. "See?" he gasped. In a few seconds, the wheel spun around on its bearings. The seal was broken. With a hiss, the door gave way reluctantly, an all too loud screech echoing into the darkness.

Ark checked the tunnel. Clear. They both slipped in, Ark closing the door behind him and turning the locking wheel as fast as he could.

Their timing was spot on. As Ark leaned against the curved wall to get his breath, he felt the telltale tremors. Footsteps. Coming their way. They were trapped in a tiny capsule space between two doors, like spiders in a jar. It was too late to even think about turning the second locking wheel. The smell of his clothes, concentrated in this confined space, made him feel like retching. He pulled on Mucum's shoulders, motioning him to crouch down into the shadows. "Keep your head down!" he whispered.

"All right!" muttered Mucum. It wasn't Ark's plea but the thought of all those sharply honed swords that convinced him.

Seconds later, as Ark peered up, a face squashed itself against the glass, a face he recognized. Grasp's man. Surely, if Ark could see the guard, then the guard could see him? But what did eyesight need? Reflection. The moment Salix looked down, he'd see Ark staring back.

14 · GOING DOWN

Instantly, Ark closed his one good eye. It was like Shiv closing her eyes and pretending to be invisible. As if that would help! They were two foxes in a hole and Salix had hunted them down.

As he huddled into the corner, Ark thought back to earlier in the day. Goodwoody's words suddenly made sense. Maybe what had nearly killed him would now save them. It was worth a try.

Ark stealthily reached into his bag, his fingers fumbling as they searched. Where was it? His hands closed around something soft. Holly prickles ran up his forearms. What could a feather do? The Warden had talked about *darkness helping to hide*. Of course! Ravens cast a shade that beat all colors as they hid among the trees, still as statues. Instantly, his panic floated away like falling feathers. They were nothing, him and Mucum. That was what Jobby Jones thought of them as he bossed them around all day. Fine, then. That's what they would become at the very moment Salix's eyes pierced the dark like daggers.

"Ark! Ark!" The whispered voice should have shocked him. Ark turned, remembering what he thought was a trick of the wind on the treetop. No one. Again. But the voice lulled him like a lullaby. *Woe betide me, Lady hide me.*

In and out, Ark's breath grew as long as a strand of spider silk, the air expelled from his lungs a sleepy incense that wove its web, filling his every fiber. Mucum's head also felt heavy, his body a lump of bog oak as he sank soundlessly into the floor. They were smidgens of darkness, the blanket of black erasing them like a pair of candles pinched at the wick. Nothing becomes of nothing . . . nothing reflects nothing back.

From a great distance, Ark heard muffled voices. He waited calmly for the wheel to turn, their hidey-hole to be exposed. Instead, the footsteps finally moved off. All that remained was silence.

"I feel drunk!" came a woozy voice. "You sure that blackberry stuff had nuffin' in it?"

"Nothing," said Ark, heaving a sigh of relief. His fist was still clamped tight around the feather, but now he relaxed and retrieved his hand from the bag. The drink his mother had boiled and filtered from the wild brambles that encroached on the woodways hadn't saved them. He blinked his eyes, aware of the dim light of the sewer gas lamps filtering in, aware that by all rights, they were as visible as poppies in a scaffield of barley.

"Lucky he didn't spot us, eh?" Mucum jabbed Ark in the ribs.

"Maybe." Ark stood up.

"Hang on a sec! That wasn't a piece of hocus-crocus, was it?" Up to now, Mucum had thought that Ark's encounter with the ravens was somewhat exaggerated, no more than a lucky escape. Now he wasn't so sure.

Ark didn't answer, still dazed with their success. Was it the feather or had he done it himself? And how had the Warden known? He still couldn't believe it. Arktorious Malikum, foundling son of a sewage worker, briefly invisible!

"Weird . . . It's like I was curled up in me gran's lap, there." Mucum shook his head as if to get rid of any remaining soppiness. "Don't ever tell anyone I said that, right?"

"Whatever." Ark suddenly thought about his sister, Shiv, throwing sticks off the edge. The image of her little grubby smile was almost too much. Would he ever see her again? But her playful throwing game had given him an idea. There was only one place safe to hide. One place they'd never think of looking. Down. Ark stood up and squeezed past Mucum's bulk to reach the other porthole.

That single moment of quiet had filled Ark with certainty. He was already turning the wheel. This second valve was well greased and the door opened easily. The smell hit them first. It was the opposite of work—sweet, fresh, hinting at treetop meadows and the hundreds of cruck wells, natural hot baths, springs, and meandering branch tributaries that fed Dendran dwellings high in the canopy as well as filling the leaves with liquid life.

Mucum pushed in beside him to stare at the huge, dark shaft at least thirty feet across that vanished into the hollow depths of the trunk, lit by a string of feeble, flickering gas lamps. "You must be kidding, Malikum! This ain't no place for the likes of us!"

Below them, a series of rusty metal rungs descended into the gloom.

"We'll be fine. . . ."

"No, we won't!" Mucum unwittingly crossed himself. "It's another country down there!"

"Exactly. The guards will never follow us."

"Save us from acorn nutters! The guards won't follow us 'cos they fancy still being alive in the mornin', unlike you, Mr. Holly High 'n' Mighty!" Mucum craned his head up, trying to make out various outflows that ran off the main shaft, empty at this moment, waiting for the tide to turn.

"We've got plenty of time," said Ark. But the certainty was beginning to fade.

"Oh, so yer suddenly the expert, eh? I don't see yer tide tables!"

"I know what I'm doing."

"Like you did with the King? That little swim has left your brain full of doo-doos! You've forgotten yer basic trainin'! Turn on the tap and what do yer get? Water! Where's it come from?"

"The day that you teach me anything . . . ," said Ark as he grabbed hold of the first rung and swung his legs over the side.

Mucum flared up. "You don't get it, do yer? The roots are thirsty; they suck up water from way, way down and when this baby blows"—Mucum pointed at the shaft that Ark was climbing into—"it hits over a hundred in seconds flat. You'll be shot straight like a cork from a bottle. When your little stick body slams into that roof . . . *SPLAT!* I don't wanna be the one sweeping bits of yer insides into the sewers."

"Then don't," said Ark as he disappeared over the edge. "No one saw you. You're not in trouble. Go home."

"Why me, Diana?" implored Mucum, wondering if the Goddess even took notice of an insignificant sewage worker. "I had a nice little earner going, a job for life until Malikum came along and ruined it all! It's not fair!" he ranted. But despite the complaining, being confronted by homicidal rodents and chased by sword-swinging soldiers, if he was being honest, he was having the time of his life! Mucum reached for the top rung. "Wait for me!" he shouted, his voice echoing into the depths.

The rungs were solid enough, though crusty with oxide and slimy from the constant damp in the air. After the first few steps, Ark settled into the rhythm, ignoring the heavy breathing above him. If Mucum wanted to follow, that was his business.

"Yer not sulkin'?" Mucum gasped after a few minutes.

"No." Ark was secretly glad not to be alone, but he wasn't going to let on.

The echoes of their grunts bounced off the dripping, trickling walls.

Mucum found the going slow, worried any moment that the spindly rungs would snap under his weight. "Wait up, will yer?"

Ark was twenty feet below, scampering down the ladder like a spider. He paused and looked up, his eyes catching the dimming reflection of the gas lamps. "You were the one worried about the tide!"

"Don't get clever with me!"

Ark waited, allowing Mucum to catch up. There was a reason why he'd stopped. Stepping off into the shaft was bad enough, but at least they had light to see by. But now the shaft descended into a blankness, the ladder vanishing as if it were a drawing rubbed out at one end.

"Can't go on," said Ark. His arms and legs were soldered to the ladder. In Arborium, there was always light, whether it was moon, sun, gas, candle, or lamp. It was a world of shadows, constantly shifting and moving. This dark beneath them spread like an endless cruck pool.

"Yeah, you can!" Mucum's voice was surprisingly gentle. "Close yer eyes, mate, and jes' listen to me, right. It's one rung at a time. Think of Shiv. She'd be loving this!"

Ark kept his eyes tightly closed, picturing his sister's beaming smile. For her, this would be the best adventure in the whole wide-wood. His foot twitched, unfreezing.

Mucum breathed a sigh of relief. "That's the one. Your little sis is 'ere wiv you, right now, laughin' 'er 'ead off!" He followed Ark down as the light above him dwindled into a spot, then a pinprick, then . . . he shivered. His eyes were now useless. If he fell, it might be all the way to the center of the earth. "We're gettin' there, mate! Yer doin' all right." The trick was to fill this emptiness with words; otherwise the blackness would soak into his eyes, stuff up his lungs, and . . . "How yer doin'?"

Ark gave an invisible smile. "Fine. Legs ache a bit." Blood oozed from cuts on his fingers as the rusty metal bit into his skin. Hand, foot. Hand, foot. Ark's thoughts drifted as they descended farther from all they knew. What were they? Tiny insects drifting down a single water shaft, one among a million trees.

"How deep d'yer reckon this goes?" Goose bumps on Mucum's skin told him it was growing colder. His voice sounded different, as if the echo had been swallowed.

The voice brought Ark back. "A mile for the height of the tree, but the roots could go down much farther." His eyelids felt odd. Something forced them open. "Look!"

The word finally meant something. Mucum stared. His eyes, grown used to the endless beetle-blackness, were suddenly shocked. Light seeped up from beneath them. And the rungs had taken on a different quality. They were no longer rusty, but smooth and cool to the touch. "Told yer!" he said. The shaft had widened significantly. "Must be near the bottom!"

Visibility increased, though they couldn't see where the light came from. The walls were lined with a lush carpet of plant life that clicked and skittered with bleached white beetles.

"Look!" said Ark again.

Dotted amongst the ferns were millions of pairs of shiny black oval shells, which gave off a tangy smell that made Mucum's belly lurch with hunger.

Ark's silent prayer of thanks was interrupted by an ominous rumbling sound, followed by a rush of air that filled his lungs with the scent of the sky. As if in response, every single shell snapped open, revealing a yellowish, glowing pod plopped at the center. It was like watching a flock of lit-up butterflies unfolding their wings. *"Let there be light!"* he whispered. With one hand hooked on a rung and his legs anchored, Ark reached with his free hand through the fronds of a plant to touch one of the pods. It was soft and alive, quivering under his fingertips. The moment he removed his hand, the shell clicked shut.

"While you're playin' with your new pet, have you worked out what's goin' on yet?" The look on Mucum's face was pure terror.

"What?" said Ark, entranced.

The shaft now echoed with the sound of the shells sliding against each other.

Mucum's voice shook. "If these slimy creatures are opening up shop, it might be 'cos they're thirsty!"

"I don't understand." Ark's legs and arms throbbed with the effort of the climb. What was Mucum on about? But then the ladder began to vibrate and understanding slammed into Ark's brain. "Oh . . . ," he whimpered.

"We're in the squit!" Mucum screeched.

They both clung to the thin rungs of the ladder. Not that it would make any difference.

The tide was on the turn and two insignificant sewage workers were perched directly in its path.

15 · BRIBERY OR EXECUTION

"Isn't it past your bedtime?" Petronio couldn't resist crowing. He licked off the cold, midnight dew that had formed on his upper lip and wiped his face with his sleeve as Mercury ambled along.

Flinty ignored him as his boys led horse and rider down the rubbish-strewn woodway. The gang's black clothes merged into the fog, turning them into floating wraiths.

After half an hour, Petronio sensed a series of shapes behind the trees on his right, blurred by the fog. Lamps set into the interspersed trunks and regular posts along the woodway showed a set of low, squat buildings with blacked-out rectangles for windows, their straight edges in strict contrast to the curves of branch and leaf. As the gang moved on, Petronio saw that this settlement dwarfed the Court of King Quercus. Fenestra was right. This mission could be the turning point.

They skirted the edges of the barracks for a further twenty minutes before finally pulling up near a corner trunk. The walkway between acted as a drawbridge, currently open, the ropes on either side slack. The double doors beyond were sheathed in iron and shut fast. Embossed into the archway was a figure of a brown, overmuscled bear with its huge jaws clamped around a dying wild dog. They had finally arrived at their destination: the armories of Moss-side.

The stallion was nervous, his hooves skittering on the wood as Petronio pulled gently on the reins.

Suddenly, the hollow slits on either side of the doors were filled with pointing arrows.

A voice boomed into the darkness, "Who goes?"

Flinty was having none of it. Despite carrying no shield, he marched straight across the drawbridge and up to the right-hand slit, until the arrowheads were virtually resting against his chest. "Who goes? Who buddy goes? I do, mate!"

The voice from behind the slit faltered, but only momentarily. "What business do you have before I put more prickles in you than a hedgehog!"

"Look at my face!" Flinty ordered, without a hint of fear. "Recognize the family resemblance, by any chance?"

There was a huddled whispering, as if the hidden soldiers were in conference. A second voice came back rapidly. "Master Flint. I do apologize. Our duty officer, Tomo here, is new on the job and had no idea that the son of our esteemed commander had decided to pay a visit . . . at two thirty in the morning."

"Yeah, yeah, yeah. Got a guest. Wants to see me old man. Says it's urgent."

The slits were suddenly empty of arrows. There was a grinding noise of hidden cogs as the doors slowly drew open, pulled by massive chains.

"All yours now." Flinty stared at Petronio, hate in his eyes. "I'll see you later." It was either a promise or a threat. He stalked off down the woodway, his gang melting into the shadows.

"Come on, boy!" whispered Petronio, stroking Mercury's neck. "There might be some oats for you!" He walked the horse across the drawbridge and ducked his head under the archway. The doors closed behind him with an ominous clang. There was no going back now.

The soldier who stood in the courtyard to greet him wore a scowl in place of a welcome. Petronio wondered at the chain-mail skirt. Its wraparound features might protect your bits, but it was just too girlish for his liking. The sword strapped to the man's side was another matter. It certainly wasn't there for ceremony.

The man's eyes widened, taking in Petronio's ridiculously slashed doublet and cross-gartered stockings. "What dressed-up boy's prank is this?" His card game had been interrupted by an adolescent! A perfect hand—Ace of Trowels and King of Chestnuts. *Flipping stick!* A week's wages rode on the outcome.

Petronio forced his breathing to stay calm. "I don't see any little *prank*, sir!"

"Ya insolent piece of puffed-up puppy fat! Shall I ask my men to make sport wiv ya?" he snarled. "Target practice, p'raps?"

Petronio slid off his horse and stood facing the soldier, who towered over him. "Or perhaps you could take me to Julius Flint. I have a message for him."

Some of the other soldiers spilled out of the gatehouse, ready for some entertainment.

"By yer accent, I can see yer traveled far. Tell yer what!" The soldier walked around Petronio as if he was inspecting a cut of meat. "We'll keep yer horse, which I 'ave to admit is a rather fine specimen. Then we'll give yer a good beatin', 'n' after, when yer got the message, we might let yer wander back to whatever pompous hole yer crawled out of!"

A pack of hooligans was one thing. Highly trained soldiers were another. This would require a different form of persuasion. Petronio wished he could use his trump card. The son of High Councillor Grasp would be treated with instant defer-ence. However, his business had to stay secret. Any of these men could have mouths bigger than their brains. The sergeant had to be played carefully.

"You know, I think your superior would be most disappointed to learn that his guest had been treated in so rough a manner. Indeed, if Commander Flint were to later find out that a certain opportunity had been missed because"—he paused and stared straight into the man's pockmarked face—"an inferior officer had decided to act on his own initiative . . . well, I'd hate to be in your shoes, *sir*."

The sergeant came to a halt in front of Petronio, doubt clouding his face. It was enough. The seed was planted.

"Full of yourself, ain't yer?"

"No. But I suggest you wake him, just for safety's sake? Yours, not mine."

The sergeant had happily skewered a few radicals on the end of his sword over the years. Now a fourteen-year-old was giving him orders! What was the wood coming to?

"Fine. Let's wake Commander Flint out of his well-earned slumbers and see what he does with you!" The sergeant looked around. "And I dunno what you lot think this is. Get back on duty!" he barked.

The other soldiers grumbled as they drifted back to the gatehouse. Fighting was in their blood. All these years of peace were seriously bad for their health.

"Before I take yer to see me master, we need to do a little search! You can make it easier by 'andin' over any weapons, yer know, catapults and other toys. Wouldn't want the master attacked by a trained kiddie assassin, would we?" The sergeant had to have his moment of satisfaction.

"Absolutely!" said Petronio. One second, he was unarmed and the next, there was a knife in his hand that in no way resembled a toy. The move was so sudden, it forced the sergeant to step back. "I do understand. Can't be too careful these days!" The knife flipped over until its carved bone handle was offered to the sergeant.

"Yeah. Right. Well, then. Anything else?"

Petronio was loath to walk around this dangerous place without any backup, but he didn't fancy the sergeant's greasy hands dirtying his fine clothes. After a minute, the sergeant's hands held a small but deadly pile—throwing knives, a slingshot, and two sticks with a chain between that had garotted a few cats when Petronio had been practicing. The sergeant briefly disappeared into the gatehouse with the booty, then stepped back out.

"Why visit the armories? Ya *are* an armory! Boys shouldn't be tooled up like that!" The battle-hardened veteran shook his head, though part of him was wishing his cadets were this hard.

Petronio ignored his comments. As far as he could work out, what he carried was about average for Moss-side. "My horse?" he questioned.

"Yeah. He'll be taken care of." The sergeant hadn't signed up to play the dogsbody, but that's what he was now as he led the boy across the planked-out parade ground.

Petronio struggled to keep up as the sergeant strode straight into the fog. A minute later, a smooth trunk reared above them out of the gray blankness. A primitive set of stairs led up to a door in the bark. It was the only way in or out. There weren't even any windows. Every step creaked. It was Flint's warning system. The man was obviously paranoid, and probably with good reason.

Before they even reached the top, the door flew open. Petronio gasped. Standing before him was a legend come to life.

Commander Flint, leader of the northern armories, filled the doorway. His bronze breastplate glinted under the door's gas lamp, covering a broad chest. His large surcote was gray velvet with embroidered lapels and his knee-high boots were of soft black leather. The face was smooth-shaven and almost handsome, apart from the kinked nose. The stories said it was broken in the street brawls as the young Flint rose up through the gang ranks. By the time he joined the military, he was already well versed in the art of war. The Commander's hair was curly, the cut almost feminine. And the eyes, intense, darker than most Dendrans', took in the sight of a young apprentice with no surprise.

"Sir. Visitor to see you, sir," announced the sergeant. "Boy, sir. Says he has a message, sir. Told him where to go, sir. But he insisted!"

"Thank you, Sergeant." The voice was cultivated, all hint of its northern roots flattened and smoothed out like a branch-way. "You can now go back to your very important card game, hmmm?"

"Yes, sir. No cards at all, sir. On lookout, of course!"

"I wouldn't doubt it for a second!"

The sergeant hesitated, wanting to see what would happen to the loathsome youth.

Flint merely stared until the sergeant retreated reluctantly down the stairs.

The commander turned to Petronio. "I am so sorry for this rude welcome to our barracks. Please do come in." His graciousness was startling as he motioned the boy forward with a sweep of his hand.

Such politeness was unnerving. The apartment Petronio entered was spartan but comfortable. A camp bed, apparently unused, lay in the far corner. On the other side, underneath a map of the whole island of Arborium, was a desk covered in papers. The gas fire was turned down, murmuring in the background. In the center, there was a daybed and several seats around a sturdy wooden table.

"Come, you must be thirsty and hungry."

Before Petronio could object, a dark red wine was poured into a thin-stemmed glass and handed to him. He drank gratefully and eagerly munched on the sweet pickled walnuts that Flint slid across the table as they sat down.

"It is so difficult to find these first-growth nuts. But they are tenderest when picked early."

Petronio found this conversation harder than all previous threats. Flint's charm was disarming, though underneath it lay steel.

"I could wake the cook and have something hot ordered up?" inquired Flint.

"No, no. You are too kind." Petronio had seen his father in action. Two could play at diplomacy. "I have had sufficient."

"Perhaps you would like to rest? We could talk in the morning?"

And allow his pack to be searched? Who knows what could happen to him in the dead hours. "Thank you for your offer, but sleep can wait."

Flint sat back. The boy was precocious, that was for sure. He waited. If there was a message, it could now be delivered.

"Have you heard of Maw?"

"Ha! Very good!" Flint roared with laughter. "Our little island surrounded by a whole world of glass and steel, and you ask if I have heard of their empire? I am not entirely ignorant!"

"And I didn't mean to imply that, sir." Petronio was careful to keep the respect in his voice. This was Commander Flint, not a boy called Flinty. "Is your aim to defend the sovereignty of our kingdom against such usurpers?" He felt like he was talking out of a book. But somehow the language, carefully guarded like the fortress he was now in, suited the scene.

"Naturally. My duty is to the King. Even if he treats his beloved troops almost as exiles by stationing us up here. In his unchanging reign, there seems little required of us anymore. However, I swore on this sword, long ago." Flint patted the scabbarded blade as if it were a beloved pet, not a killing machine.

Petronio had one card to play. He laid it on the table, in the shape of a purse that spilled its contents across the smooth surface. The rectangular objects caught the gaslight, glinting yellow as they chinked against each other.

Flint's eyes were forced down, unable to hide their fascination. "If this is gold, it is in a currency I have never seen before!" Instead of the insignia of crown and leaf that stamped all of Arborium's coins, these ingots each bore a set of engraved windows, one fitting inside another like acorns in a cup.

"There's more. Much, much more." There. Petronio had spoken.

Two responses were possible. An offer to bribe the commander of the armories was the highest treason. Either negotiations would begin or he, as traitor to Quercus, would be hanged like a crow from a branch.

Petronio waited for the answer.

16 · FINDING YOUR ROOTS

"Help! I'm drowning . . . can't breathe . . ." Ark was surrounded by utter darkness, closing in on him too fast. Even his voice was swallowed, reduced to a whispering croak.

"Hush now, boyo. No need to fuss. Yow've slept fer hours, but yow safe now!" The voice was rich, almost feminine, with a lilting accent he couldn't quite place.

Hang on! That meant he was alive! Ark slowly surfaced from his dream. His sore hands, wrapped in a soft cloth, felt around him—rough surfaces, but comfortable. He opened his eyes. Both of them. Odd. The swelling in his right eye had almost vanished. "Where am I?" It felt warm and humid.

"More important, boyo, where did yow come from?" The man was sitting at the edge of what must have been a raised bed of moss and was, for now, Ark's sanctuary. At least Ark thought it was a man, though with the strangest features he had ever seen. The man's hairless skin was pale white, almost translucent, revealing a map of bluish veins running underneath. He wore a floppy white shift and loose linen britches, as if his skeletal frame had been wrapped in a sheet. His feet were bare and bony, whiter than any mushroom. The eyes, with magnified pupils that looked as though they were drawn by a child, stared back at Ark with concern.

"I was being chased." Ark knew there was something more important than telling his story. He tried to think, then suddenly sat up in panic. "Mucum. My friend. Is he . . . ?" He feared the worst.

"The big feller, with hair loike fire? Warghhh!" A grin cracked the man's face in two. "He be snorin' loike a good 'un! Let's leave 'im be!" The man suddenly leaned forward as if he was an eager child ready to hear a story. "Go orn, then. Yow was speakin'?"

The last thing Ark remembered was Mucum's cry and the shells quivering like a million dim gas lamps. "I was being chased by guards with swords. . . . I tried to warn the King, but they found me and . . ." Ark finally took in his surroundings. The room had to be deep in the heart of the tree. The walls and curved dome of the ceiling were gnarled and fissured. In the gaps, gaslights flickered, filling the space with a drowsy warmth. Ark could hear a constant background hum and an odd clanking noise coming from behind the only door.

"The King? Well, we don't have much to do with 'im down 'ere." The man talked about Quercus as if the court was in another country. "Anyways. Oi was just checkin' the valves before bed when Oi 'eard a scream. Now, Joe, Oi says to meself, oh, that's me name, boi the way!" Joe leaned over the bed and unraveled a long, stringy arm.

"Arktorious Malikum. Pleased to make your acquaintance." Ark felt unsure about shaking the thin, papery hand but found the grip strong and calmingly cool to the touch.

"Waarghhh . . . ," continued Joe, retrieving his hand. "That screech don't sound loike a ratty to me, I says: *What do yow think, Flo?*"

Ark looked puzzled for a second.

"Sorry, loike. That's moi daughter, Flo. Yow'll meet her soon enough. She came skitterin' along with me and we popped our old 'eads through the porthole. There yow were. A pair o' somewhat stinky boys, Oi must admit, clingin' to the ladder . . . tide about to turn. What's to do, eh?"

Ark looked at this tall, friendly creature with fascination.

"Couldn't leave yer! Oi says to Flo, *We'd better get goin'*. She gave me a smile that would melt a mushroom and we reached out quick to pluck the pair of yer free loike nice bits o' iron ore from the seam. It was a close run 'fing!" Joe shuddered, shutting his eyes for a second. "Your matey was a bit on the 'eavy side, but he warn't nothing compared to a good load o' rock. Mind yow, our little Flo was huffin' and puffin' like an enjin by the time she dropped him down. Yow were both out for the count boi then. Lot o' gas 'round 'ere, must've knocked yow out! Warghhh!"

Joe was a natural-born tale-teller, making near death by tidal wave sound like a jolly adventure. Ark smiled at the thought of Mucum being heaved over the shoulder by one of these slender creatures.

"As Oi slammed back the porthole and dumped yow in an 'eap on the ground, 'Er Majesty" — and the man swept his arms around to indicate the tree they were deep inside — "decided to blow. One second later and us lot would've been porridge."

"Thanks!" said Ark, blurred memories of being cradled by this thin giant flooding back into his brain. "We owe you our lives."

Joe sat back, an innocent smile crossing his face as he fiddled sheepishly with his hands. "Naw! Don't say that! Not every day we get visitors! Moind yow, yow war a bit scratched up loike. But our Flo sorted yow out with some salve. Them scratches on them hands were pretty nasty and yow eye was loike a slug!"

"It's been a rough couple of days," said Ark, making the understatement of the year. His legs ached from the long climb, his fingers felt sandpapered, and his butt was tenderized by the fall through the kirk roof. He looked around for his clothes. There they were, hung on a chair, clean and dry. His bag hung over the back along with his belt. He hoped the feather was safe inside.

"Toime to get some grub on," Joe announced. He stood and Ark's neck craned up in awe as he worked out that Joe was well over eight feet tall.

Joe closed the door, leaving Ark alone to get changed. A minute later, a second door that Ark hadn't noticed slammed open, and a tousle-haired Mucum stood in front of him, scratching his armpit, half asleep. "All right?"

"I think so. They saved us, you know."

Mucum nodded.

"Did you know about them?" Ark pointed his finger at the door as if Joe might come back in at any second.

"A bunch of bald stick insects! They give me the treebie-heebies!" Mucum shuddered, remembering the tales his dad had told him about tribes of root miners burrowing deep underground. "Still, I guess the gas and iron gotta come from somewhere. But as long as there's a good fire when I get home at night, and somefing in the pot, it don't bother me."

Ark looked around. "Home . . ." Even the word seemed foreign. He felt a sudden ache in his guts. "I miss Mom. . . ."

Mucum suddenly looked away.

Ark could have almost hit himself. "I'm sorry. I forgot."

Mucum barely nodded. "History," he muttered. Then his lips sealed tight.

There was an awkward silence while Ark tried to remember what Little Squirt had told him in confidence one day at work. There had been one last, small outbreak of the plague eleven years ago. Mucum's mother had been one of the unlucky ones, though rumors had said she was getting better before she was taken away by the Holly Woodsmen.

Ark tried to change the subject. "The guards will still be looking for us."

"They ain't gonna come down 'ere, are they?" Mucum snapped.

And we're farther than ever from the King, thought Ark as he unwrapped the bandages around his hands. He expected scabs at least, but there were only red marks.

Mucum walked around the room, peering into corners and prodding the moss bed. "Still, they can't help bein' ugly. . . ."

There was a polite cough. "Yow be wanting some vittles," said a voice from right behind him. Mucum turned, his face flaming red with embarrassment. The figure that held a tray bearing food was a smaller, very obviously female version of Joe, wearing a loose camisole that floated over her pearl-white skin.

"Th-thanks!" Mucum stuttered.

"Oi be Flo! And yow be that boy from far above what I held in moi arms!"

Mucum didn't know where to put himself. Her smile was stronger than any punch. Bald, yes. But ugly? Two pairs of fluttering eyelashes were having a strange effect on him. "Ta . . . much appreciated."

"It be moi pleasure! Oi says, *Pa, can't have the tide sweepin' them fine young boys away!* It was moi that washed yow . . . all over!" She stared at Mucum.

Mucum went even redder, as if his face was a firework about to explode.

"How old be yow?"

"Err . . ." Mucum's normal self-confidence had suddenly

vanished. What a stupid twig, forgetting your own age. "Oh! Fourteen."

It was as if all of Flo's birthdays had come at once. "Why, that be moi age, too. We be a right young pair!"

"Yeah . . . ," said Mucum. Same age, but she was at least a foot taller. The conversation was messing with his head.

Flo finally pointed to the tray. "Soup and shroom-bread. Moight not be what yow used to, but the warter is the freshest, deepest-root-seekinest stuff yow'll ever slip between yow lips!"

Mucum wished the girl would stop looking at him but was distracted by a salty, rather enticing smell.

"Yow lot from up top be somewhat little. Yow needs to get some good grub down. Then yow might grows a bit, and catch moi up, warghhh?"

Mucum had never been called little before, but as the towering girl finally bent over to put down the tray, he felt like he was back in nursery school.

"I be leavin' yow to it!" Flo bowed over and backed away, her eyes still filled with curiosity at the sight of these two tiny Dendrans — one in particular. A blink of her two hypnotizing eyes and she was gone.

"I think she likes you," said Ark, stating the obvious.

"Suppose it beats hangin' out in the sewers." Mucum wasn't going to admit to anything. He perched on the edge of the bed and grabbed one of the hot, steaming bowls. "Though I dunno what these lumps are!" He plucked one out of the broth with his spoon and studied it. "Eyeballs? Or worse . . ." Mucum's lips turned down in disgust. "They could be goat's —"

"Got it!" said Ark. "Mussels! That's the answer!"

"Yup!" said Mucum, bending his free arm to flex a bicep. "Can't help bein' a handsome hunk!"

"Not those muscles!" Ark sighed. "Freshwater mussels, glowing in the dark!" He remembered the shells, opening and closing like a million pairs of hands in the deep water shaft. Diana always provided, even down here.

"So, you can get 'em down yer? Yeah?"

"Yes, of course!" said Ark. He sat down next to Mucum and tucked in.

Mucum looked doubtful for a second, until his stomach got the better of him. After the first slurp of the nutty, briny liquid, he was won over, even forcing himself to chew the rubbery lumps. "This is a bit of all right!" he finally managed to say, dunking a lump of dark bread in the bowl to mop up the remnants. "In fact, I'm almost starting to feel like a Dendran again! Time for Plan B."

"The Councillor's men know I'm alive," said Ark. "That makes me a target. But they've never seen you."

"What, so you stay down 'ere livin' the easy life and I'll jes' climb back up and get myself a few arrows in the gut? Thanks, mate!"

There was a knock on the outer door and Joe came bustling in. "How did yow loike our Flo's hot pot?"

"Very nice. Thank you," said Ark. "Joe . . ." Ark didn't know where to start. Mucum was no help, avoiding his eyes. Ark tried again. "We're in trouble. Or rather, Arborium is in danger. Traitors are going to overthrow the King at the Harvest Festival and destroy the island. And we're the only ones who know."

Joe frowned for a second. But his bleached white face couldn't stay miserable for long. "Yas! There's always strange goings-on up top. Never really concerns the loikes of us when there's work to do!" He smiled again, as if all thoughts of revolution had dissolved into water. "I been prayin' for a couple of helpers for many a day and 'ere you are, landin' roight with us! Yow'll be joinin' me today, Oi think."

"But we have to leave."

"Leave! Leave! Yow must be kiddin'! Yow're a gift, eh, mira- cle boys?" The subject was dismissed. Joe held the door open. "Are yow comin' or what?"

Mucum shrugged his shoulders. If one of their treenage girls could pick him up as easy as a sack of potatoes, he wasn't going to argue.

Ark didn't know what to do. Either adults wanted to kill him because of what he knew, or they laughed off his concerns. The whole wood was going mad and it looked like they were both prisoners of the politest, strangest creatures he had ever come across.

17 · DIVING DEEPER

Joe bowed and gave his hands a fluttery flourish as he ushered the boys forward through the door. "Welcome to Joe's Divin' Station!"

The word stuck in Ark's brain. *Diving?* He always enjoyed his swims in the remote cruck pools hidden high in the canopy—there was a perfect spot where the water was cool and the fish ticklish on the toes. He often liked to venture there on his own, to spy out the darting kingfishers and share his lunch with the squirrels. But those days, filled with lazy sunshine filtering through green leaves, were long gone. He had a feeling that this was diving of a different sort.

Mucum had gone quiet, and Ark looked around him in awe. The station was a huge hollow cavern at least half a mile across, sides sloping in toward the roof way above. They must be near the bottom of the trunk, deep in the heart of the tree. Light was provided by various pools of what looked like water but had to be liquid gas. Flames danced and twisted on the shimmering surface, filling the cavern with an acrid smell. And throughout, a tangle of enormous tubes twisted out of the cavern floor and made its way up to the roof and beyond. A forest inside a tree.

Ark stared at the liquid, mesmerized. "We . . . we're not going to swim in those, are we?"

"Ah, no," chuckled Joe. "That be liquid gas! We be goin' down them pipes. "We call 'em *Xylem*. Oi found yow in one of 'em." He pointed at the boys, then back at the tubes as if Ark and Mucum were simply another product of mother nature. "Theys are part of 'Er Maj's plumbin' system! Water 'n' gas! The stuff of life! Yow lot up top have it easy. Weren't for us, yow wouldn't be livin' so snug!"

Mucum still stared. This was an unwoodly place. On the far side of the hall, partially obscured by the forest of Xylem and the single huge column of heartwood that supported the roof and the tree above, they could see and hear rumbling conveyer belts.

Joe explained the process that began with his fellow mineral miners reaching deep beneath the earth, led by the living tree roots to excavate rich seams of copper, lead, and iron-bearing lode. Once transported up into the station, the ores were separated out, using giant magnets, before their long trip by dumbwaiter and barge to the Blacksmith estates down south.

"Isn't the *earth*" — Ark almost whispered the word — "only on the other side of these walls?" His eyes scanned the cavern without seeing any doors. In his mind, he pictured a foggy mud-swamp punctuated by the rearing arrows of smooth-skinned trunks.

"That's as may be!" said Joe. "We don't bovver wiv the outside, and the outside don't bovver wiv us! We got mussels, motherwater, fishies, and all sorts of fungus and moss to eat. What more can an old boy like Joe 'ere want for? Anyways, there's lots to do. Those up top need their pots 'n' pans to cook their grub in, and their knives and swords for 'oo knows what. Us Rootshooters be the boys and girls for the job!"

As Joe spoke, his workers gathered around in the green-tinged light to view the two visitors. They were all as tall as Joe, stretched out like the tree roots they worked inside, and each with the same pale skin, bleached through lack of daylight.

With their loose white shifts, they could have stood in for a gathering of ghosts. Some of them wore goggle pieces that magnified already enlarged eyes.

"Wot's yow?" said one of them.

Ark gave his name.

"And wot be one of 'em?" It was a woman who spoke, curious, as if the boys were an entirely new species.

"Plumbers," said Mucum. It was bad enough when Flo looked down at him. Now they were surrounded by even taller adults.

"Awww!" she laughed. "Yow be one of us, then!" It seemed they passed the test.

Several bells went off at once.

"Kit up!" announced Joe, suddenly businesslike. "We got yow some kiddie-size ones, moight fit!" He vanished for a minute, reappearing in a black suit that stretched tight over his thin frame. The other Rootshooters were also reclothing themselves. "Give these out, our girl!"

Flo stepped forward to hand each of them a floppy rubber suit that resembled a deflated balloon.

"You really need our help?" Mucum took the suit reluctantly. As far as he knew, Plan B didn't involve going off exploring with a bunch of rubber-clad eels.

"Yas!" said Joe.

Mucum held up the way too short skin. "There's no way I'll get into this!"

"Oi'll 'elp yow," said Flo, stepping forward.

"Nah. Don't you worry yerself." Mucum blushed as he turned away and tried to squeeze himself into the suit.

Five minutes later, they were both zipped inside their clammy kit and walking with Joe toward a stepladder leaning against the side of one of the bigger Xylem.

"Yow looks wonderful! A bit on the small side maybe, but no matter!" said Flo to Mucum with an admiring stare.

His arms and legs stuck out like bare twigs. "It's very comfortable, ta." Mucum felt as if the rubber was trying to strangle his whole body.

"Oi wish I could be comin' with yow! Be careful, 'cos if yow come to 'arm, moi mossy heart's gonner break!" Flo clasped her two bony hands together as if in prayer.

The rest of the Rootshooters gave a murmured "Aahh!" in unison.

Mucum was more than worried as he tried to avoid Flo's moony eyes. "Yeah. Righto." He wished Joe would get a move on.

"Yow looks wonderful!" mimicked Ark with a whisper.

Mucum tried to dig his elbow into Ark's arm, but the smaller boy easily darted out of his reach, an impish smile on his face.

Before they ascended the ladder, Joe grabbed two long rubber tubes, connecting them to holes at the back of the boys' suits. Ark's gaze followed the line of the tubes to the other side of the Xylem, where a machine resembling a crude bellows was manned by two huge insectlike creatures walking around a well-trodden circle. In the dim glow of the liquid gas, they reminded him of something he'd seen before, but in a very different place and on a much smaller scale. He couldn't believe it! Surely they weren't giant water boatmen, like those that skittered across the cruck pools high in the canopy?

Once Joe was connected, he pointed at his mouth, making circular motions. Air supply. He climbed the ladder, and the boys followed. At the top, there was a small opening in the tube. Joe leaned through it and peered down into the Xylem before easing himself through and disappearing from sight.

Ark felt a tug on his air supply pipe, and Flo motioned that he should follow Joe. As he squeezed through the opening onto a small ledge inside the cool, slippery Xylem tube, a damp smell of rain and sky rose up through the darkness that dropped away sheer below. Ark gulped. There was no safety ladder, no gaslights to help them on their journey. The thought of all that empty space made his head spin.

Once Mucum had joined them, Joe attached a brass shield to the opening. The world closed off around them, except for a small hole for their air supply pipes.

"Yow might need these." Joe handed them two long pieces of thin, multicolored tubing with a trigger at the end. "Two between us should be plenty!"

"Amazing!" said Ark, admiring the way these strange objects shimmered like miniature rainbows.

"They be forged from fire opals, dug from the deep!"

Mucum peered in the hole at the top of one of the tubes.

"Do yow really want your head blown away?" shouted Joe, pushing the end of the tube away. "It's a gas harpoon!"

"Keep yer hair on!" said Mucum, before remembering that was probably not the best way to address a bald Rootshooter. "Wot's it for?"

Joe pointed over the edge of the hole and down into the blackness. "Worms!"

Mucum laughed. "Oh yeah. Sure!" There were sunny afternoons he'd skived off at the scaffields, watching farmers digging the soil. Those little wrigglers that turned up under the spade were hardly of the killer variety.

Joe grabbed Mucum's shoulder until the boy almost winced. "Mealworms! If yow see 'un, aim for the mouth and pray to yowr godly Diana that yow live to tell the tale!"

Both boys looked into Joe's fishlike eyes to see if he was joking. He wasn't.

One of the gang pulled out a watch piece and checked the time against the printed tide table next to the porthole.

Joe rested his hand against the slightly hairy outer surface of the Xylem. "Never forget, the Tree's alive, boyo. And She loikes a drink, just like yow and me. She goes reg'lar as clockwork. Tide's out now. Get it wrong and, well, Oi've lost a few of moi best that way. Yow were dead lucky last toime."

Ark remembered the night before, clinging to the ladder, feeling Mucum's quivering bulk above him, hearing the click of mussel shells amongst the whispering greenery, and behind that an ominous groaning from the depths, as if the tree itself was taking a breath before all holly let loose. Dead lucky.

Joe's colleague gave the thumbs-up. It was time.

"Geronimooooo!" Joe shouted, and vanished into the deep.

Although Mucum was terrified, he wasn't going to show it. "Right, Malikum. You went first last time. My go." He pushed hard off the edge and was instantly gone.

Ark turned to Flo. "I'm not feeling too well, actually. Maybe I can stay here and . . ."

Flo smiled back sympathetically. "Yow be fine, little 'un! Now off yow goes!"

Without warning, Ark felt a shove in his back and he, too, plummeted, trying to keep his feet below him but having no idea in this pitch-black free fall which way was up and which was down.

18 · A CUNNING WAY THROUGH

Gold was an interesting metal. Petronio realized that Maw must have its own version of the Rootshooters. But gold was gold, whoever dug it out of the dirty ground. And it was gold that had reflected back the glint in the Commander's eye the previous night. The word *more* also had magical appeal.

The fog had finally lifted and sunlight beamed down on the high woodway. Mercury picked up on Petronio's mood, galloping south along the reverberating planks and eating up the miles with sheer joy.

Petronio's mind still dwelled on his extraordinary meeting with Flint. Had it really happened? The most powerful man in the North discussing the future of the country with a fourteen-year-old boy?

The silence had been excruciating, the gold ingots that lay on the table stamped with the insignia of Maw unarguable evidence of treachery. Petronio's eyes had flicked around the room, trying to make out the man by his surroundings. The wall of books suggested that he read as well as he spoke. As he waited, Petronio noticed for the first time that the other walls were lined with swords and hauberks of every size, knives, crossbows, beautifully polished brass knuckle-dusters, whips, and bats studded with sharpened spikes. This was no display of antiques. The art of injury was Flint's business.

The Commander could have summoned his sergeant and had the boy marched off to the dungeons for a spot of light torture followed by a nice public hanging to literally kick-start the day. Instead, he spread his hands as if to say, *So?*

The tension in the room deflated. Petronio realized he'd been holding his breath. Now he saw that Fenestra's reading of politics was sharp. Though the King was good at talking about loyalty, the rewards were not so easy to determine. Without the army, the peace of many years would not have been achieved. Quercus seemed to have forgotten those who had given him their allegiance, maybe not deliberately, but the results were the same: Pay was atrocious, and the food for the rank and file not worthy of being turned into compost. Also, it was clear that the Commander had a weakness for the luxuries of life. Treachery was less of a risk and more of a done deal.

Now Petronio was invited to speak, to fill in the gaps around the edges of all that shimmering gold. Petronio's words had been committed to memory. Paper messages would have been a danger. Fenestra had told him the basics of the plan only. She'd said that too much information was dangerous. To whom? Didn't she trust him? All Petronio knew was that Flint was to assemble a band of his best men ready for the night of the Harvest Festival, five days hence. As long as they followed the Commander and not the King, all would be well. The details could then be worked out when Flint next came south.

"It's not long," said Flint.

"Long enough," Petronio answered.

"I have to work out which of my men I can trust. Some will stay loyal to their country, though low wages and even lower morale can play havoc with a sense of duty. My old *friend* Quercus has forgotten to whom he owes the years of self-satisfied peace."

Petronio could see where this was leading.

"And so," Flint continued, "I shall need further funds to facilitate proceedings."

"Of course. Lady Fenestra has instructed me to do all I can to help." With a flourish, a second purse was produced and tossed toward Flint, who caught it deftly with one hand.

"I don't know what magic you perform, boy. But as long as you pay, I don't care whether you were mothered by the Raven Queen herself."

At that, they both smiled. Grasp Senior would have taken the Commander's words as a compliment.

Petronio was no longer just a messenger boy. Flint offered him another drink and swept the ingots off the table and locked them carefully away in a chest.

The sergeant was summoned to give the boy a decent bed for what remained of the night. Somehow, this boy had wormed his way into the Commander's goodwill. Instinct told the sergeant that whatever message the boy brought, no good would come of it. His foul mood was made worse when he'd been instructed to return the boy's weapons.

And now, as Petronio sped south on the silver stallion, he was almost giddy with it all, secretly hoping that Fenestra would be impressed by his success.

It was evening when he arrived home, gaslight already compensating for the weakening twilight. Petronio was famished. But to business first.

As he handed the reins to the groom, he spotted Salix marching across the yard.

"Where's my father?"

Salix glared at him. He might be beholden to the Councillor, but not his useless offspring. "Busy. Not to be disturbed."

"You know, it might be in your favor to treat me better. . . ."

Salix had a good idea what sort of treatment he'd like to mete out to the pompous toad. It was this boy's fault in the first place that the plumber had got away. Now Salix was being blamed for yet another vanishing act. Better to keep his thoughts to himself. He strode off to find Alnus and round up the others. The search was not over yet.

The lack of greeting dampened Petronio's mood, but he wasn't going to be dismissed so easily. He ran up to his father's study and burst in.

"Good news, Father!" Maybe, just this once, he might be praised. One look at his father's face told him otherwise.

"Good news? I'm glad yours is." Grasp sounded bitter, exhausted. "The boy is on the loose again and you were the one to let him go!"

Petronio was confused. "What boy?" He thought of Flinty and his gang—surely his father didn't care about the fate of a northern squit?

"Malikum, you idiot! How your mother ever managed to produce such an imbecile!" Grasp sat at his desk, his pencil stabbing a sheet of paper as if it were a prisoner under questioning.

Petronio did a double take. "But he's—?"

"Dead? Not when I last clapped eyes on him, slipping down a soil pipe like the rat that he is. And while he lives, our plans, and whatever *good* news you might have brought, lie in jeopardy." The point of the pencil snapped.

Petronio noticed his father's bloodshot eyes and unshaven face. He wondered briefly if the Councillor was losing the plot. How could Ark be alive? Salix and Alnus had seen him fly off the edge of the branch. No one had ever fallen off Arborium and lived to tell the tale. If it was a trick, then Petronio was almost impressed. Maybe the little runt did have a few brain cells after all.

Petronio was still bursting to tell his father about the Commander but reined himself in. "So, what next?"

"What's next is that I've sent some of my men to protect the King and guard the sewers the boy seems so fond of. The last thing we need is him popping up and filling our monarch's ears with unnecessary alarm. Meanwhile, I have put word out of a rather large pecuniary reward for any noble citizen who reports the whereabouts of this dangerous radical. Money is always a useful tool!"

Petronio agreed. Flint had been convinced partly by resentment against his exile up north, but mainly by the cold reality of cash.

Grasp put the broken pencil to one side and began leafing through some papers. "The matter is in hand, so you might as well go and do something useful, like homework, for instance. Leave us to deal with the consequence of your inaction."

The put-down was a signal to leave.

Petronio felt his face go scarlet. He'd gone farther than he'd ever been in his life, faced down a gang of murderous treenagers, inveigled his way into the armories of Moss-side, and convinced one of the most ruthless soldiers in the country to take on their cause, and now he was being dismissed?

"Father, I—!"

Grasp did not even look up from his papers. "What? You wish to tell me you can find the boy and bring him to me? If so, then I shall be pleased. If not, you can go."

Petronio turned toward the balcony doors, not wanting his father to see the burning in his cheeks. But someone else saw.

There in the glass on the other side, a face, mixed with his own reflection.

The doors swung open. Grasp looked up, shocked, his hands instinctively reaching under the desk for the knife he had hidden in case of intruders.

"Do you consider me that dangerous, Councillor?" The voice, though quiet, was sharp enough in its intent.

Grasp removed his hand. "My lady, how did you . . . ?"

"Oh. I didn't want to trouble your guards, seeing as they are so tired from their labors. I thought I'd let myself in."

The Councillor tried to recover himself. "You are always welcome." The woman unnerved him.

"And you seem to have forgotten greater matters in your pursuit of a mere smidgen of sewage. Your son has traveled far and, if I'm not mistaken, succeeded in his mission. Am I right?"

Petronio felt relieved. At last there was someone to plead his cause. "My lady, I did as you said." Quickly, he related the events of the preceding night, leaving out his encounter with Flinty but stressing how well negotiations had gone.

When he'd finished, Fenestra turned to his father and waited.

"I suppose congratulations are in order." The words were reluctant, grudging.

"Would that you praised your son more highly!" Fenestra hissed. "He has parlayed on our behalf with a man who would happily have had your boy flayed alive if he didn't like the cut of his cloth! Trust me, I know what Julius Flint is made of!"

Petronio felt the warmth of her praise. This was more like it.

Lady Fenestra continued, "We have put out bait in the form of gleaming treasure, and your commander has stepped into the snare. He is ours now! The plan shall succeed. In five days, your little island country shall be utterly changed."

All thoughts of hunger fled from Petronio as an idea formed in his mind.

"May I speak further?" He didn't wait for an answer. "There might be a way to bring our sewer muck out from whatever infested rat hole he's hidden in." That was it. He had their attention now. Even his father couldn't help but look up at him.

Petronio surprised himself with the perfection of this solution. "My lady mentioned *bait*. The boy has a younger sister, whom he adores. Your men should arrest her."

"A four-year-old girl!" protested Grasp, with no clue as to which direction his son's mind was moving.

But Fenestra clapped her hands together. "On my word, young Petronio Grasp. That is—"

"Workable!" interrupted Petronio. "Firstly, it keeps the family quiet. There'll be no blabbing about plots against the King." He paused, relishing for a moment their rapt attention. "Then put the little girl in the cells beneath this house and wait for the worm to come out of its hole. When he does, promise me this, Father!" He was the one in control now, not asking but making a statement of final intent. "I let him go before. But this time, as the slimy squit wriggles on the hook, he's all mine!"

19 · DEEP DOWN

There was no point fighting gravity. As he shot through space, Ark could dimly make out the forms of Mucum and Joe ahead of him, plunging like helpless babies with only thin umbilical cords to connect them to the real world. While trying to quell the rising tide of nausea and panic, he thought of his family. Shiv and his mother and father were farther away than ever. He was going where few Dendrans had dared. And it wasn't where he was supposed to be!

He'd expected to remain in blackness, but the tube around him now glowed softly green, with brighter sparks flashing as he whistled past. Joe had mentioned a phosphorescent fungus that grew lower down along the walls of these massive, hollow tree roots. Ark was grateful even for this echo of the far sun. The fungus spread above him in yellow lines scribbling away at the shadows. Who would have thought lightning could be grown?

"This is serious!" whooped Mucum, as he zipped down the smooth-worn slope. He quickly worked out that his suit was engineered with this exact journey in mind. The trick was to go with it, bending your body into the curves, hitting the turns, and using your butt to bounce off and accelerate out and down.

There was a loud splash and all three of them were suddenly underwater.

Ark was last to crash into the gleaming pool. Every nerve in his body went taut and his lungs worked overtime, grabbing at the air. He was drowning, imprisoned in some contraption dreamed up by a species of underworld nutter. The visor in his helmet began to steam up as he hyperventilated.

"Help!" he screamed, the sound swallowed inside his suit.

Joe floated up to him and grabbed Ark by the shoulders. He moved his right hand up and down in the water in slow motion, his goggled eyes willing Ark to look.

Ark got the message. He tried to slow his breathing. Trust that the insect boatmen were working the bellows at the other end. Slowly, the mist cleared from his visor. Ark moved his hands forward experimentally. The rubber suit acted like warm grease, slipping him easily through the chilly depths. It was like being in an enormous cruck pool.

He realized this was the water table, where the tree drank its fill and nature pumped the liquid of life high into the estate. As he began to relax, Ark watched a shoal of shimmering red ovalfish glide by, thin as paper, with eyes on either side of their heads.

Joe beckoned the two boys to follow and swam toward what appeared to be a tunnel opening. They clambered through into a shallower pool, half filled with silt.

Above the trio's heads, a million fronds hung from the roof like frail curtains. They were way below the earth by now, a place of far tales. An occasional glint winked back at them from the roof of the giant root—evidence of ore, according to Joe.

There was a hiss of escaping air as Joe undid the seal on his helmet. Ark copied the Rootshooter's movements, glad to be able to breathe normally again. He heard the churning ripples of deep water and the constant plop of the dripping walls.

"We should be safe fer about an hour. Leave yow helmets and breathin' lines behind and follow me. Yas?" Joe was all business now, in his element.

Mucum beamed, full of himself as he plonked his helmet down. "That was . . . out of this wood! You know, I'd swap jobs with them lot any day."

Ark shook his head, incredulous.

"Glad you're having so much fun."

"If you've got any memory left in that bonce of yours, you might recall it was your idea to climb down that Diana-forsaken ladder in the first place."

"We had no choice. Anyhow, we're not exactly saving the country down here!"

"You sound like a moaning grandma sometimes. Lighten up!"

"Speakin' o' light," interrupted Joe, "these are fer yow." Joe handed each of the boys a cloudy glass bottle. "Shake 'em hard, but only if yow need to. We've enough to see by fer now." Joe set off up the phosphor-coated passage. "Follow me close and stay in the center."

The squidgy silt reminded Ark of . . . what was it? *Oh yeah* . . . the stuff they worked with every day. He sniffed. The smell was different, loamy. It made him think of fallen leaves and last year's mulch pile in the corner of the scaffields. They were a long way from the sunshine now. His eyes picked up the increasing glitter of the roof and floor. Copper? Tin? Iron? Ark had no idea.

Joe had explained about the natural seams that the roots of every tree sought out. All the miners had to do was follow.

"But this is just one root system?"

"Yas!"

Mucum's mind began to boggle, trying to work it out. "And there's like . . . thousands of trees!"

"Yas!"

"So, what? There are others like you?" The thought of endless women Rootshooters fluttering their eyes at him gave Mucum the horrors.

"Yas!" A slow smile spread across Joe's face. "This 'ere's just one way in the many. Them roots is tangled together like breathin' tubes, as if the trees war all one big family! If yow wants, you could cross the 'ole country without ever comin' up into a divin' station, let alone goin' up top! Why, Oi've got kin out west and south, all workin' diff'rent systems!"

As above, so below, thought Ark. Arborium had just got a lot bigger.

They continued down the main root. The plants overhead dripped with life, shocks of vibrant green in the fungal illumination. Every so often, side passages led off both left and right, bringing with them a cold chill that sent goose bumps marching up and down the boys' skin.

"Don't move," hissed Joe suddenly, his frame coming to a standstill.

The boys almost collided with him. What now?

"Up ahead . . . ," Joe whispered. "Slow now. Back up, quiet loike. I don't think we'll be mining any ore today. . . ."

Ark heard a soft scraping sound directly ahead and coming in their direction. He motioned to Mucum. They both did as Joe suggested, taking one step backward, then another, hoping not to trip up, trying to make out the source of the noise.

"Could be a little one. If yow get the chance, aim for the mouth." Joe had his harpoon raised.

"This ain't like some kinda game with yer Rootshooter buddies?" asked Mucum hopefully.

Joe threw back a sharp stare, all bumbling friendliness vanished in an instant.

"No. Right. Jes' askin'."

They retreated toward the nearest side passage as the slithering grew louder and the walls of the root began to shake.

Something big was coming their way. Ark's mind went into overtime. Maybe Joe was wrong. It sounded more like a roof collapse or even a tree fall. It happened occasionally despite all emergency engineering. Trees were alive. They grew old. They died. And when the massive trunk slammed down into the forest, Diana help any who had not made it out in time. Whole neighborhoods could vanish in seconds, leaving a gap in the map, a part of Arborium gone forever. If this tree fell, it would lift up the roots and anyone stuck inside them. They'd be tumbled about like fish in a cruck pool.

Joe ducked down into the side passage, motioning the boys to crouch. The sound filled the main tunnel now, booming into their ears, crunching, slithering, sliding.

"It's not a little one," said Joe, sighing. "It's trouble, all roight!" He took one of the cloudy glass bottles, shook it once, and threw it out into the main passage. There was a tinkling smash. Dim phosphor and shadows gave way to a bright swarm of intense light as a thousand glowflies relished their short-lived freedom.

Ark bit his tongue in shock, feeling the blood well into his mouth. Both he and Mucum looked up, and up again, trying to take in the scale of what they saw as their feet stuck like lichen to the spot.

A segmented monster with a bruised-purple pulsating skin squeezed and filled every inch of the tunnel, writhing and uncoiling toward them at high speed. On the end of what had to be its head was a mouth filled with gnashing teeth that wouldn't look out of place in a sawmill. It had as much relation to a compost-munching worm as a mountain did to a pebble.

The monster briefly stopped, rearing over the three tiny figures, sensing vibrations. Anything that moved down here in its territory was alive. If the monster had lips, it would have licked them in anticipation. True to its name, the mealworm was hungry.

"I hope yow know some good prayers, boys!" whispered Joe through chattering teeth. "'Cos otherwise, we're trowly out of luck!"

20 · A MEETING OF THE MINDS

Grandma Malikum, when she was still alive, loved to talk about death. "When you're gone, what the ravens won't take, the worms will have. Oh yes! They bury what's left of you in the scaffields and what fine compost your tiny bones will make!" As she cackled, her whole face one big wrinkle of crumpled paper, the younger Ark shivered by the hearth, his mind filled with wriggly, segmented nasties.

Nothing to laugh about now. The glowflies threw every detail of the tunnel into sharp relief, from the zigzag of metallic ore cutting across the walls to the root fronds dangling like pond-weed from the roof. And there in front of them, the mealworm, squeezing through the twenty-foot-high tube, a pulsating monster with rotating teeth about to pulverize a trio of rather tasty little morsels.

Joe was busy muttering to himself in the split second before eternity came knocking.

Mucum merely stood there, goggle-eyed. A weapon. That's what he needed. A dim memory suddenly made him reach down to the pouch on the left leg of his suit. Flipping fungus! His hands came up empty. The ride down must have loosened the flap. He turned to Ark.

Joe had had the same idea. "Give it over, boyo!" he shouted.

Ark obliged, ripping the harpoon from his rubber trouser leg and handing it over.

Mucum wondered if they were too late. The monster was

so close that he could see the gobbets of slime trickling from its teeth.

But Joe was fast and his sight was true. He raised the shining tube, tucking it into his shoulder as his fingers closed around the trigger. "Come 'ere, yow big baba! Come and taste something sharp! I 'ope it sticks in yow guts!" And as Joe focused, he pulled tight on the trigger.

Nothing. Or rather, only a click. "Hmm!" said Joe, as if it was a mere technical problem. "Could be the damp down 'ere. Ah well! That be that, then."

"You what?" shouted Mucum. He couldn't believe his ears. Their last chance gone and Joe was shrugging his shoulders. Death as an inconvenience. He was tempted to try and punch the creature's lights out. Maybe not. His fists would simply be swallowed in that giant maw. Time to beat a hasty retreat. Using legs to sprint very, very fast. Screaming was also an option, though Mucum didn't do screaming as a rule. This time, he'd make an exception. Only problem was that his legs were not cooperating, sticking him to the spot like a statue.

Ark thought of his family. He'd let them down. He'd let down the whole country, stuck here deep under the earth while an overgrown slug finished them off. He could smell the thing— a stink of earth and rot and dead rat.

He suddenly remembered the feather, but it was back by his warm moss bed in the Rootshooters' place. Could he do without it? Could he make them all invisible, somehow? An image of a dusty, stained-glass figure appeared in his mind. This time, the Raven Queen's eyes appeared to be alive, encouraging him to think of the impossible.

As the thought slithered through his mind, it was like a door opening to the brightest incandescent light.

By all rights, fleeing down the tunnel was the best option. But Ark did the opposite. He began to walk *toward* the monster, slowly, raising both arms as if in prayer.

For the mealworm, this was a novel reaction. A pair of globular eyes, on long thin stalks attached to the side of the head, swiveled around to study the two-legged creature stalking toward it. The boy held his hands out, palm upward to indicate the lack of weapons.

"What yow doin'?" Joe whispered, trying to pull Ark back. The boy was going to be guzzled!

"Ark!" cried Mucum, knowing he should grab his stupid fool of a friend but unable to even move.

Ark's hands inched closer. Any moment now. There! *Ark!* a voice called. Although this time he didn't think he heard it out loud. He shuddered as his fingers made contact. The surface of the worm was slimy, dripping, cold. But the boy did not recoil in disgust. Nor did that giant mouth open wide to suck him in. Time slowed to a slippery crawl, finally standing still. The boy and the beast were joined now, and a new sound emanated from the mealworm, filling the tunnel, reverberating into the darkness.

Joe was beyond surprised. "Why, boyo! Surely that ain't the sound of purring!"

Ark answered mechanically, through the fog of his pounding head. "I know." And he did. He was under the mealworm's skin, could feel its unending trawl through dark passages, its lonely days and nights, its dull diet of mineral and earth, and its constant suffering from the parasites that lived under its skin, sucking away its blood until it could only gnash its teeth in pain and fury. "I know!" he said soothingly, understanding all that monstrous suffering.

The eyes on stalks momentarily softened, revealing in their dark depths a hidden intelligence. The two Dendrans and their Rootshooter guide were no longer its enemies.

Ark pulled his hands away. As the glowflies danced their last and the shadows deepened in the tunnel, the monster slowly retreated, shuffling backward awkwardly as if it were a guest who had turned up for dinner on the wrong day. It was over. They were safe.

"Diggin' ore be dull compared to what yow just did!" Joe clapped Ark on the back.

"Did you see, Mucum? I did it!" The boy's feet jiggled on the spot as if his body were filled glowflies.

"Good one," said Mucum, unsure of what he'd just seen. "You . . . touched that thing?"

"Yes, and . . . I felt it! Everything! Every tunnel mapped out in that magnificent brain of hers. Dark, though. And lonely." Ark's face was a curious mix of smiles and tears. His voice ran at a hundred miles an hour. "We're quits now? Yes? You with the rats, and me talking to a mealworm! Well, thinking, anyway. And it worked! Well . . ." Ark paused, not sure whether he could say it was all his doing. "Let's go, eh. I'm starved!"

Joe, with his long legs, had to trot along to keep up with the new hero as Ark virtually leapt back along the passageway under the dim glow of the fungus.

"What's got into you?" puffed Mucum as he tried to keep up.

"No idea!" Ark's eyes were bright. "Lightening up!"

"Hmph," grunted Mucum. "We were gonna be munchkins! Cheers." Part of him felt grateful, part, jealous.

Ark was on a high. "I told you before, she really likes you! I can tell you that, thanks to my magical powers!" His eyes glittered with mischief.

"Yer what? Who you on about?"

"Flo!"

"Give it a rest, will yer?" Mucum growled.

"Never in a million years. 'A right young pair!' she said. I feel lurrvve in the air!" The thought of Flo's big staring eyes suddenly gave him the giggles. "I dare you to give her a kiss! As soon as we get back!"

Mucum looked like thunder. "Look, right. Fair's fair, you savin' me life and all that. But give the subject a rest before I head-butt that conkers brain right out of yer skull!" This new, bouncy, chatty Ark was beginning to get on his nerves.

"Lookee in 'ere. This is where we grow'm little 'uns!" Joe pointed down a side passage. The phosphor dimly revealed an earthy tunnel, the floor littered with white bulbous shapes.

Mucum was horrified. He knew the Rootshooters were weird. This explained it. He imagined the children with feet rooted in the subsoil like skinny sapling monsters. "Yeurghhh!" he exclaimed.

Joe frowned at Mucum's comment. "Whoi the funny face? They be right tasty! Yow wants to try one?"

Mucum stepped back, almost knocking Ark over. He wanted to whisper to him to run. "They're cannibals! They eat their own young!" he hissed, hoping Joe wouldn't hear. Unfortunately, Mucum missed his footing and fell with a dull *clump* straight onto the shining white . . . things. "Help!"

he squealed. "They've got sharp teeth. I'm being bitten!"

Ark had already figured out what was going on and was almost doubled up with laughter. "Those aren't teeth. They're thorns!"

"Yas!" said Joe. "Can't have dulberries without brambles! Let's pick a few fer the journey back. They be ever so sweet."

"You mean, they're not . . . babies?" Mucum said, hauling himself back onto his feet, his brain taking a while to catch up.

"Baybees? Is this how yow lot up top grow up? Oi always wondered what them scaffields were for!" Both Joe and Ark were sharing the joke now, their giggles echoing down the passage.

"Oh, ha-ha! Very funny! How was I to know?" He tore off one of the fruits and stuck it in his mouth to show them he wasn't afraid. It was sweet and earthy, like honey. "Not bad, I suppose."

"Not bad?" Joe was shocked. "This be treasure, moi boys, and wait 'til yow taste the brew it makes!"

The moment they reached the diving station and pulled off their helmets, Joe's whistle cut across the cavern. The sound was like a candle drawing moths. Within seconds, it seemed that all the Rootshooter kin within the huge trunk were gathered, pressing in an expectant circle around the trio.

Joe waited patiently, his hands on Ark's shoulders. "Yow not going to believe this!" he declared to all his colleagues. "This boy"—and he nodded his head downward—"made best mateys with a . . . wait for it . . . mealworm!"

The whole crowd gave an "Oooh!" in delight as Joe proceeded to fill them in. When his yarn-spinning reached the moment that Ark had joined with the great worm, every single

Rootshooter closed their eyes and they all swayed gently like a copse of skinny saplings in a breeze. The short silence didn't last as Joe carried on painting Ark as the man of the hour.

Ark stood at the center of it all, lit up by all the gazing eyes. He was suddenly tired. Had he really done anything? Maybe it was just sympathy. A sense of what others, including creatures, go through. The enthusiasm of the Rootshooters was overwhelming.

Standing to one side, Mucum felt like a spare wrench hanging on a belt. This wasn't helped by Flo's constant fluttering glances. He remembered Ark's words and looked away nervously.

After swallowing at least a gallon of hot soup, Ark felt exhaustion seep into his limbs. His legs threatened to give way and Joe quickly motioned two of the Rootshooters to carry him back to his room. He was laid down on a moss bed and covered with blankets, where he drifted off. Had he really listened to that dark creature? For a second, he'd felt there had been another down in that tunnel. Not Mucum or Joe. Someone, or something, else.

Later, much later, he woke to the sounds of music, feeling refreshed and wondering at the racket. The Rootshooters were celebrating, with Joe scraping on the fiddle and the others joining in throaty voices. One of the miners, his white skin streaked with circles and smears of coal, put a long hollow twig to his lips. The resonating drone echoed around the cavern, making the walls vibrate as his cheeks puffed in and out. Even Mucum, his face flushed red with drink, was beating on a drum as their newfound friends danced and sang, turning the tale of the boy and the mealworm into the stuff of myth and legend. When they saw Ark standing uncertainly at the door, they cheered again and plied him with a cup of hard cider.

"Yow be one of us now!" shouted Joe above the clamor. "Yow saved me life and that makes yow me kin-brother. I am at yowr service 'til the day Oi be dead, boyo!"

Ark was embarrassed, but he got the gist. He was their lucky mascot. If he could keep away the worms, then their one main predator was dealt with. But this ignored the fact of a far more dangerous predator that stalked their whole country. He needed to go; he'd realized it the moment he woke up. He was running out of time.

"I can't stay!" said Ark, but Joe didn't hear him in the din of celebration. This was a night for feasting. After all, what could possibly go wrong now?

21 · INFANT TERRORISM

"Your daughter is hereby charged with . . . umm . . . terrorist activity!"

Petronio hung back in the shadows as Alnus delivered the charge. The surgeon apprentice couldn't decide what he was enjoying more, the guard's evident unease about arresting a four-year-old girl or the look on Ark's mother's face as the truth dawned on her.

"Are you crazy?" said Mrs. Malikum, barring the doorway of her shanty home with a broom. "She's only a child!"

"Forgive me, ma'am!" And Alnus really meant it this time. "I'm only following orders."

"Orders! I'll give you orders!" She came at the skinny guard with the broom handle first, thrusting it like a spear, suddenly catching him off balance.

It was Salix who saved his colleague from toppling over the safety rope on the edge, grabbing at Alnus's arm and leaning back with all his weight. Once he checked that Alnus hadn't tried flying for real, Salix easily disarmed the distraught mother, tossing the broom over the branchway, where it twirled around and down, clacking and echoing against the trunk until it vanished from view. He pushed past her into the gloom of the one-room hovel and scooped up the child, who instantly began to scream at the top of her lungs while Mr. Malikum feebly tried to rise from his sickbed.

"Shut your trap, girly!" Salix snarled, and the child

instinctively knew this was no game, but danger. Little Shiv did as she was told.

"And as for you . . ." Salix leaned toward Mrs. Malikum until she could smell the sour beer on his breath. "Call this a security measure. As long as we have your daughter, you won't be running around telling the world about mad conspiracy plots that don't even exist." He paused, drilling her with a glint in his eyes. "That is, if you want to see her alive again!"

Shiv reached out an arm and grabbed hold of her mother's top. "Mommy!" she half sobbed, half whispered.

"Let her go!" It was a stationary tug of war as Mrs. Malikum tried to pull her child from the soldier's strong-armed grip.

Salix's arms folded over the girl like solid rock. A sneer spread over his lips as he leaned slowly backward to tear mother and daughter apart.

"You are a disgrace!" Mrs. Malikum hissed through tight lips. "Using my child in this shameful way." Her daughter's hand now only clung on to empty air as Salix stepped away. "How can you?" she implored.

"Not up to me." Salix shrugged his shoulders, feeling guilty despite himself.

Mrs. Malikum visibly slumped.

Salix delivered his speech. "That's better! Trust us, she'll be well fed and watered in Councillor Grasp's holding cell. All you have to do if asked is say that your daughter is infectious, under quarantine. Agree?"

She had no choice but to nod her head like a lowly servant. The pain in her heart was too much to bear. Only Diana knew what had become of their son. Now this.

"That's settled, then." Job done. With his bearlike arms

wrapped round the child, Salix stalked off, not even waiting for his colleague.

Alnus felt uneasy. It was one thing chasing treenage troublemakers with dangerous information in their heads. But incarcerating an innocent child? He backed away, leaving the mother sobbing and the father curled up in a cot-basket, impotent with fury and rage.

Good! It was exactly as Petronio had planned. He melted back into the leafscape as the mother wailed and collapsed on the floor of her hovel. Squit happens. The woman would get over it.

Anyhow, the plumber's apprentice had given them no end of trouble. Time to repay the favor, give him a taste of his own making. And the little girl was the perfect wriggling worm, the bait he hoped would draw the little canker out of whatever hidey-hole he'd bolted down. When Ark returned home, the boy's honor would make him try to rescue his little sister. Chivalry was overrated, but for once, it might help the outcome.

Maybe Grasp Senior would finally see the sense of it and approve of his son's actions. Never mind. The game was his now. It was time to sit and wait.

Grasp had other matters and, more important, his king to attend to. The meeting was going as well as could be expected. The room, deep in the heart of the palace, was not overlarge and was plainly furnished with good oak furniture, a table covered in scrolls and maps, and the two chairs they sat in. The walls were unadorned plank, with not a tapestry in sight. The plain wooden goblets they drank from contrasted with Grasp's own gold-leafed version. He was the King, for Diana's sake. All this so-called humility and "servant of the people" nonsense was seriously outdated! He really was ignorant of what went on beyond the palace gates. The truth was that society consisted of leaders and servants. It was the way of the wood. Feeding the poor with a feast once a year at harvest was not about to change that. Grasp and his Alder Councillors already controlled most of the wages in the country, skimming off the cream for themselves. Quercus really had no idea that he was effectively running the country in name only. This coup would put an end to his nonsensical ideas forever.

The flickering gaslight revealed a man of late middle age, strongly built, with a trimmed, graying beard, wide forehead, and hazel eyes that stared unwaveringly at Grasp. The King's green gown lay loose at the waist, revealing a shoulder sash embroidered with gold-threaded oak leaves. The silk doublet on his chest and fine suede boots on his feet were both dyed dark blue, a color that none but the King might wear. The dye, produced from fermented knotweed represented the only crown that the trees wore: blue sky. On either side of the chair stood the two obligatory royal guards, their eyes fixed impassively straight ahead, their oiled muscles glinting in the gaslight.

Grasp felt sure of himself, even now eyeing up the room and working out how it would be redecorated once he was in power. The King was droning on, as usual, and then stopped, as if waiting. Suddenly, Grasp worked out that an answer was required. He took a punt. "It is something to consider."

"But what about our borders? I fear for our little island. Do you think Maw is up to its old tricks again?"

Grasp cursed himself for stirring up the old man's fervor, but he was prepared for this one. "Commander Flint's patrols have met with no incursions. The gas that the trees have given off for generations is still doing its job."

The King scratched at his beard as if he might find a different answer in there. "Yes, I suppose you are right."

Grasp smiled placatingly. This was the King's favorite phrase these days and he never tired of hearing it.

"It's the technology I am concerned with," the King continued. "We are the last frontier, a tiny kingdom holding out against the odds. . . ."

"And doing very well at it, my lord!" Grasp interrupted.

"Yes, yes. I am aware of luxuries being smuggled in. The mud-pirates who live below must be tolerated while they are still able to bring goods that we cannot manufacture ourselves. Our scaffields have not yet cultivated a usable tea crop, and a cup of something warm is no threat."

"Indeed." If Grasp nodded any more, his head would fall off. The old fool didn't half go on.

"But what else can slip in, eh?" The King paused, his eyes resting on the Councillor.

For a second, the Councillor panicked as the silence deepened. He could not stop a flush from creeping across his face like poison ivy. The two bodyguards still looked dead ahead, but was that a sudden tightening of the grip on their weapons? Had he been found out? Was this a trap? "My l-lord!" he stammered. "Nothing . . . erm . . . that is, nothing would get past Flint. He is the best."

King Quercus waited before answering.

Maybe this was the moment. Any second, Grasp expected

the heavy hand on his shoulder, the accusation, the bodyguards springing to life like two life-threatening machines.

Finally, the King sighed. "Of course. You are right. I grew up with him, you know. In a fight, he's the one I would want by my side. I still wonder if Moss-side was the best place to put the armories."

The young Grasp had known full well how Flint had ended the uprising. The King's shame at such deeds in his name had been a spur for sudden inspiration. Supported by the other councillors, Grasp had suggested the general populace might feel less threatened, after the years of unrest, if their army was stationed out of sight. It also provided another benefit in that it had given Grasp more power in the capital city. This was his secret and the reason he had prospered as the King had gradually weakened. He hoped Flint would never find out.

The King's question meant that Quercus was not about to have Grasp arrested. The Councillor pulled out a handkerchief to wipe the sudden sweat from his brow. "They can always be summoned quickly enough if there is danger. . . ." He changed the subject. "Now, I trust the plans for the Harvest Festival are to your favor?"

"Oh please, Ambrosius, less of the formality. The plans are fine. It seems you have it all under control as usual: the music, food, security."

If only he knew. "Don't worry, my lord, my men are the best."

"Good, good. Maybe this is one night when we can celebrate what we hold dear in this little kingdom of ours. Who would dare attack us on such a holly occasion, hmmm?" It would be good for his subjects to have a night off: fresh, roast timber goat, maybe even the odd deepwood boar skewered on the spit, washed down with a little too much to drink.

"I am glad to have men such as you under my command. Come, let us leave these matters behind and share a sip of something stronger! The vines of the southern scaffields were a great success last year. Our Arborian wine is maturing well."

Grasp almost heaved a sigh of relief as he drained his cup. An hour or so of dull small talk was little price to pay. The date was soon approaching when the old man would finally be out of his way.

Several cups later, Grasp had to be lifted onto his horse. As the drink had flowed, Quercus's jokes had become raucous and rather hilarious. For a second, Grasp almost felt a prick of conscience. Then it was gone, dissolved by the thought of Fenestra's promises. This once visionary King had built little but castles in the air. It was time for something more substantial.

As the sure-footed horse plodded its way through the last of the evening light, Grasp felt a sense that history had a place reserved for him. In a few days, the halfhearted moon that rose palely in the sky would soon be shining on a very different country.

The horse suddenly reared up as a shadowy figure planted itself in the roadway. Who would dare to step out in front of the High Councillor? But his pride covered a deeper fear. Salix and Alnus were no doubt playing dice in the guardroom of the house around the corner. They were near, but not near enough. If it was a thief, Grasp's purse was heavy, and the drop to the stinking earth below, a long one.

"Who would block my way?" He tried to keep his voice from shaking.

A mass of clouds scudded across the sky, clearing for a second to reveal an excited face, pale as the moon itself. "It is I, Father."

"And why does my son need to crawl about in the night like a snake?" Relief gave way to fury.

But his son ignored the anger and the question. "Listen! We have succeeded! I have the girl!"

For a moment, Grasp's drink-addled head thought Petronio was talking about Fenestra. Then his mind cleared. This was welcome news. "Good . . . good."

"And where the girl is, the brother shall surely follow."

Grasp almost smiled. Loose ends were being tied up. "Take my horse. And ask the servants to bring me food. Immediately."

Petronio could think of several answers to his father's demands that would have got him in instant trouble. Why bother with servants when he, the son of the house, was treated no better? But this night was his. He wouldn't let it be ruined. He kept his mouth shut and led the horse away.

Grasp suddenly never felt more sober. He made sure that a serving woman was sent to keep the young child company, feed her, and soothe her to sleep. It would not do to have his evening interrupted by the screeching of a commoner. Salix and Alnus were summoned to keep careful watch and apprehend the boy if he should turn up. They were not to kill him, at least not until he had answered several questions. Then they could do what they liked.

As his father ascended the stairs, Petronio carefully made his way back through the courtyard, hugging the shadows and easily avoiding the two guards. He slipped quietly into the kitchens to make a flask of chicory coffee. The night ahead was going to be cold. He crept from the house, down the woodway along which any unexpected visitor would have to come. This was one part of the plan he had no intention of sharing with his father, let alone those two imbecilic guards.

Petronio chose his spot, where the branch had a natural kink and its curve created a hollow of deeper darkness. He sat carefully in the shadows, pulling the knife from his belt and sharpening it on a small whetstone. Spots of light rain began to tip-tap on the woodway. Perfect. If Ark turned up . . . when Ark turned up, Petronio would make sure that this time, he would not get away.

22 · FLIGHT AND FIGHT

The party was in full swing.

"Good stuff, eh? Get it down yer neck, mate!" Mucum shoved a rough-carved stone cup at Ark, almost splashing him. "S'not bad down 'ere, really." His eyes had already glazed over and his words were thick with the drink.

Ark held on to the cup without sipping. "They're good people" was his only response.

"The best!" Mucum was squeezed next to Flo on a dried-moss bed. Sitting down, they almost looked the same size. She'd changed into a flowing red skirt and green velvet bodice embroidered with patterns of curling roots, laced tight round the front. The effect was startling.

Mucum nudged Ark in the ribs and grabbed his friend's head with both hands to whisper in his ear. "I really like 'er, you know."

Ark struggled to free himself. "Yes. I got that."

"No, really, really," slurred Mucum, his eyes nervously flickering back to Flo, whose smile now rose above the noise of the party. "Secret, right, between you and me, us being buds and all?"

"Of course." Ark desperately tried to retreat, but Mucum's pudgy fingers gripped even tighter.

"I'd like to kiss her, but I've never snogged anyone before!"

It was Ark's turn to go red. It wasn't as if he was an expert in that area, either. "Right. Great. Go for it."

"Yer think so? Don't tell anyone; they all think I've kissed

loads of girls! Got a reputation to live up to, yer know." Mucum
let go of Ark, plucked up his courage, and slipped an arm around
Flo. She snuggled in closer to him in response.

Ark looked around at his newfound friends. There was good
food, lively music, and, above all, companionship here. But a
thought darker than any mealworm kept gnawing away at him.
Maw would not mine this earth gently. Their huge machines
could rip the very roots from their harbor. Joe and his kin
would become slave labor, if they even survived the assault on
their home.

Ark slowly edged away from the party until he was lost in
the shadows of the cavern. It was time to go. He thought about
Mucum and the adventures they'd had so far. But Mucum was
safe down here. If Ark could face a monster worm, surely he
could find a way to the King? He was alone again, like always.

"Where be yow off to?" Joe sprang up out of the shadows
like an elongated dream.

Ark nearly fell over with fright. "Oi be off to . . . explore."
Crazy. He was even starting to talk like them. "I mean, I'm
off to explore." The explanation sounded lame. He waited for
Joe to grab hold of him.

"Good for yow!" The quizzical look left Joe's huge, round
eyes. "If yow keep going arf in that direction, yow'll find the
ore cars! Plenty to see, and glad yow loike our humble home.
Yow're part of it now!" He patted Ark on the back and loped
off toward the music with a spring in his step.

Ark felt terrible. No one lied down here. It was a place of trust.
But if he told the truth, Joe wouldn't let him go, ever. "Thanks,"
he whispered at the departing figure, "for everything."

Ark quickly nipped into the room he'd slept in to retrieve
his bag and plumbing belt. Keeping to the darkest corners,

he headed away from the music and out toward the ore cars. All that crushed ore had to go somewhere. From down at the roots, that could only mean up. He spotted the train track and a few cars slowly trundling along with no driver in evidence. The train appeared to be heading toward a tunnel in the far side of the cavern.

Ark sprinted toward the last car and hopped onto the mineral express. No turning back now. Within seconds, he was enveloped in total darkness. The gloom soon faded as they arrived at a tipping station. Each car was balanced at either end on a huge axle. The cars ahead began to slowly tip over to the left, pulled by a giant magnet at the side, to spill their load into an overgrown box on the side of the track. This container was attached at each corner to a four-way hoist. When the box was full, the ropes went taut and the cargo began to lift. Box after box slid up in smooth transit and was swallowed by the blackness above. Although Ark strained his eyes, they couldn't pierce the shadows.

Never mind. This was a free ride and saved him having to take the stairs, all five thousand of them. His legs had never been so grateful. The only problem was how to avoid being flattened by a few hundred tons of industrial ore. Ark scrambled over to the right-hand side of the car and held tightly on to the edge as it began to lean over. Soon, as he gripped tight, his legs were dangling in the air and his nose filled with dust. He desperately tried not to sneeze, in case there were any Rootshooters around. At the very last moment, and with a quick prayer to Diana, he closed his eyes and let go.

There was a bump and Ark felt a piece of rock scrape his shin, hard. He tried not to cry out as he dared to open his eyes. He had made it, perched on top of the mound of ore, inside the box as it slowly rose up to the ceiling. There was an awful screeching noise and the ceiling split in two, like a pair of giant hinged trapdoors, filling the cavern with the smells of . . . earth. As the box swayed slightly from side to side and slowly slipped from the safety of the cavern, Ark crawled to the edge and peered over.

"Flipping fungus!" The familiar tree trunk on his left was not the reason why he nearly fell off in shock. He was horrified, then fascinated to see the ground itself, not thirty feet below him, spreading out from the roots like a soily brown scaffield. The Holly Woodsmen said that the earth was unclean. Nobody who left Arborium to climb down had ever returned to tell the tale. And yet this place didn't look dangerous. The smell was loamy, deep, and pleasant.

An animal, nibbling on vegetation, looked up to see a brown face staring back.

Ark would have expected deformed creatures born of ancient pollution, not this little snub-nosed, wide-eyed beauty, taking fright and vanishing on lithe legs into the twilit forest. He was hungry for the view, enraptured by a marching army of skyscraping trunks vanishing into the distance. Between them, the land seemed lush and healthy. Rays of evening light filtered through from far above, like exploring fingers.

And there, tucked like a bird's nest into the huge curl of a root, was a cottage, cobbled together from stone and moss. A single swirl of smoke curled from the leaning chimney. Any second now, the door would open. But it didn't. Was this one of the houses of the mud-pirates? How could they live so far from the sky? If only curiosity could knock and gain entrance, but the box rose too quickly, stealing his view.

Gradually he was carried farther and farther away from

the ground. The motion made him feel queasy. Was it only two days since he'd fled from the palace, slipping like a slug from the guards? The problem of what to do loomed large. As the box ascended, his homesickness began to abate. At a mile's height, branches began to snake out horizontally from the trunk, and these were adorned with the familiar additions of ropeways, scaffolding, plumbing pipes, and the messy business of Dendran civilization, held together with the iron that was smelted from the pile of stuff beneath his backside. It was familiar, safe.

As the box climbed higher, it swayed perilously close to an empty branchway. Ark had no time to even think as he bent his legs and leapt. *Twigs alive!* he mouthed as he landed in a heap on solid wood once again. He rolled over and stood up, looking around to make sure he wasn't observed. Feeling the wood beneath his feet again filled him with hope. And when he realized where he was, he felt that the Goddess was surely with him. The iron ore's journey had taken him not just up but westward as the series of cogs and giant wheels thrust the crushed rocks and Ark's container one step nearer the smelting districts. Home was only a half-hour walk. He wanted to kneel down and kiss the bark in gratitude.

As the dusk settled and shadows lengthened across the branchways, his sense of freedom vanished. Nothing had changed. His house was probably being watched. And what did he have to tell his mother? That he'd failed to get to the King? Maybe he should head straight to the castle. The clocking-off bells rang out through the forest, and the woodways would soon be filling up with tired Dendrans rushing to get home.

It was all right for them. Home meant the warm gas fire and

a steaming plate of food. But that was no longer an option for him. He slipped onto a smaller branch line and headed away from the crowds.

Five minutes later, his head peered around the door of the kirk. The inner sanctum looked empty. He crept toward the side chapel. Candles flickered in clay recesses as the polished wooden floor caught their reflections. At the altar, a familiar figure was kneeling on the floor. The silence spread out, unbreakable.

Ark had no choice. "Ahem," he coughed.

The figure remained, unmoving. "Come to pray, my Malikum?"

What good would that do now?

"I hear your doubt. Sit by me a while." Warden Goodwoody raised her head and motioned Ark to a nearby pew. She sniffed the air. "That smell you bring with you . . . I think I remember it. When I was young and still sighted, I used to explore all sorts of forbidden places. . . ." Her voice trailed off. "But speak to me, my Ark. They said you were dead. Then you weren't, and now there is quite the commotion about you."

Ark found himself trembling as he perched on the chair. "I did nearly die . . . a few times." And what else had he done? Vanished into a cloak of dark and touched a mealworm. He didn't know if it was his abilities or mere timing. He did know he was not the same boy who came to see the Warden for guidance two days ago. Too much had happened since then. It was ridiculous, but he felt older, more determined than ever.

"Yes, and I have a feeling the trees have been with you all this time. This is a place of wonders, but most Dendrans have forgotten that. Not you, though?"

Ark nodded, then realized she couldn't see his agreement. There was more hidden in the woods than he'd ever dreamed of. "The feather—"

"Is guiding you, yes. But you are not there yet. There is much to do. Perhaps too much." Goodwoody sighed.

She was right and he was an ivy-strewn fool. The King was as inaccessible as ever. "How's the roof?" he said, finally changing the subject.

"Oh, that!" The Warden smiled wryly. "The Woodsmen were most suspicious of my story, but I could have hardly climbed up there and made the hole myself."

"Is my family all right?"

The Warden paused. "Your mother and father are fine. I managed to smuggle out some food that would have rotted in the kirk otherwise. But . . . I don't know how to tell you this. . . ."

"What?"

"Your young sister . . ."

Ark felt his heart suddenly lurch. "Is she ill? Did she fall? I shouldn't have left!"

"No, my Ark. Your mother came to me a short while ago. She was in a bad way. The Councillor's men have arrested your sister on charges of terrorism." She shook her head. "The wood has gone mad."

Ark jumped up. This was ten times worse than a mere mealworm. "They can't have! How dare they?" He thumped his fist on the chair. "And it's wrong!" He burst into tears. "I overheard a plot that will destroy the whole of Arborium. I ran and they tried to kill me and I tried to warn the King but couldn't," he sobbed. "The feather only helped me escape, though I kept hearing this voice. And then we were down in the roots, and I knew I had to get back, and—"

"A voice?" the Warden interrupted.

"Yes. It keeps saying my name."

"It's Her! It's really Her!" A look of astonishment crossed Goodwoody's face. "She's calling you and your time is coming."

"What do you mean?" The Warden was riddling again.

"Diana knows best. All shall be well, though the journey is fraught with danger."

But at that moment, all Ark could think about was Shiv. He wiped away the tears with his sleeve and turned abruptly. "I have to go."

The Warden heard the change in his tone. "Diana was also enraged once. The Wood-Book talks about how She laid low the temple of the honeylenders! Trust that which lies within you!"

"Whatever that is!" shouted Ark. The door slammed and he was gone.

"Goddess speed you!" Goodwoody called out to the empty chapel. Her knees ached on the hard floor and she felt the worm of doubt inside. Capturing a child, destroying Arborium! Were her prayers any good in the face of such evil? And the voice that Ark mentioned — could it really be?

Ark sprinted from the kirk. He knew where he was going, but beyond that, nothing. He'd taken on a mealworm. The Warden was right. Time to stop doubting himself. The anger flowed through his veins like molten iron.

23 · A FRIEND IN NEED

Mucum never knew that a girl could have this effect on him. It was one thing bragging to your mates but another to have the real-life Flo snuggled up next to him, their bodies swaying to the rhythm of the music. He turned to look at her. Some hair on her head would be useful, but then his short crop was hardly different. In fact, apart from the height, skin color, and funny accent, they had plenty in common. And when she smiled at him, oh boy, his stomach flipped. If only he could pluck up the courage to kiss her! He was in serious danger of turning sloppy.

Mucum scanned the circle of faces around the fire. They were a good bunch, these Rootshooters. He looked again. Something missing. A face. Whose? It would come to him in a minute.

Joe came ambling back into the circle to sit down.

Mucum quickly moved away from his new girlfriend.

"Yow be fine, young boy!" Joe's eyes hadn't missed a thing. "It be good to see our Flo so 'appy!"

Mucum squirmed under the gaze of his big eyes.

"Don't think Oi didn't see!" Joe tapped his nose, every inch the proud father.

Mucum cleared his throat and cast about for a new subject. His mind began to work again. "Where's Ark?"

"Oh, don't yow worry about him. He's gone arf to explore, so he says!"

Mucum sat bolt upright, his head clearing in an instant. "No, he hasn't! How could I have been so stupid?" He'd taken his eye off the root ball. "I have to leave. Sorry."

His words fell into the crowd. The music faltered, stopped, as the other Rootshooters turned to stare at him.

Joe broke the silence. "What do yow mean?"

"He's not *exploring*. He's gone. Vamoosh! Run away!" Mucum shouted out the words, angry with himself. "And I should be with him."

"Gone, yow say? But he told me . . ."

"He lied, Joe!"

The whole crowd sighed as Flo grabbed his arm. "Whoi would he do such a thing?"

Mucum felt backed into a corner. "Ark tried to explain. You wouldn't listen. We ain't miracles. Us two didn't come here by some divine trickery. We were on the run." He expected Joe to sweep his hand away like he did before, but the old man's gaze stayed serious. "Our king, our country . . . your country. It's in trouble. The whole place will be destroyed if the coup against the King is successful. If yer love the trees and yer home, you should listen up!"

A few of the miners began to mutter about matters up top being of no interest to them, but Joe raised his arm and they fell silent. "Young Mucum, tell us all."

He did, right from the beginning when he bumped into a panicked Ark on the woodway that first afternoon that seemed so long ago. Could it really have been only two days ago? It was a story to beat all stories. The miners oohed and aahed with every event, shocked to hear of Dendrans who could fill their minds with treachery and lies. As Mucum described the encounter with the sewer rats, Flo's heart almost burst with admiration.

"So, when you pulled us out of that water pipe, we were a pair of cowards, running from big men with swords," Mucum finished, hanging his head down, unable to look at his friends.

It was Flo who leaned over and gently lifted his chin. "Yow see my kin 'ere? Warghh! I can promise yow that each of them thinks yow both be heroes! Am Oi right or not?"

Nobody spoke for a second, and Mucum knew he'd lost them.

"Am Oi right or not?" said Flo, and there was iron in her voice this time, unbending, willing a response.

"Yas!" said one of the Rootshooters. "Yas!" said another, and within seconds the whole crowd was shouting, then cheering.

Joe pointed a bony finger at the ceiling of the cavern high above and, one by one, his fellow miners fell silent. "Moi daughter is right. Old Joe 'ere has been a fuddy-buddy. What goes up" — and he lifted his eyes in the direction of his finger — "must come down. I still think yow were sent. Yowr Diana ain't known for makin' mistakes. Now, young Mucum, what do yow want from us?"

Mucum couldn't believe it. "I need to find him, quick, and then, we have to get to the King. The Harvest Festival is only a few days away and that's when the squit's gonna hit the fan, unless we do somefin' about it."

"Fine. First things first, let's trace him out. Jacko, George, be off with yow!" Two of the taller Rootshooters sprinted away, their huge strides eating up distance as they vanished into the gloom. Not a minute later they came back, barely out of breath.

"He be going out with the ore, Maister Joe!" said Jacko.

"Straight through the trapdoor, Oi reckon!" said George.

"Warghh! Yowr boy be clever!" Joe answered with an approving nod. He thought for a second. "It be a good way to go, but slow. If yow want to catch up, best take the lift."

Mucum found his bag plonked in his lap and Flo pulling on his hand and leading him toward one of the Xylem in the center of the cavern. Unlike the other hollow roots, this one went straight up to the roof like an arrow. Two double doors lay wide open and blackness beckoned beyond. Flo let go of his hand and worked a pulley at the side of the doorway. Slowly, a small open-sided compartment slid up into the space from below.

Joe was all business now, consulting his watch and some numbers carved into the wood frame. "A couple of minutes, yow got."

Mucum didn't like the look of the enclosed space. "You want me to get in that?"

"Yas!"

"But what is it?"

"The lift, dear one!" said Flo sadly. "Mighty quick it is, too. Yow don't think we use the ladder all the time?"

"Coulda told us that this morning. It took us hours to get down 'ere. My legs are still achin'!"

"Oi love it when yow complain! 'Tis mighty sweet, Oi think!"

Mucum squirmed. Any more niceness and he would explode.

"Now, see that belt?" She pointed to a seat inside the compartment with some kind of leather harness strewn across it. "That needs be strapped up tight. Come arn!" She gently led him into the compartment, sat him down, and began to tie him in.

Mucum looked up. There were tears in her eyes. "Hey. Don't worry. I'll come back!" Another lie. He didn't know if he would.

There was a far-off rumbling sound. The whole cavern began to vibrate. "Step out, our Flo!" shouted Joe.

Mucum felt a cold breeze whistle through the gaps in the planking. "Are you sure this is safe?"

"Yas!" said Flo as she bent over. Just as she was about to kiss him, a blast of wind rattled the cage and threw them apart.

The moment was gone. She looked sad. "Hold on tight."

He tried to look away but couldn't as Flo backed out of the cabin. "See yer!" he said, trying to sound casual, as strange feelings bubbled up inside him.

The vibrations grew louder and the whole cabin began to shake.

"When yow need us, we'll be there!"

Mucum knew that Joe meant every word. As the doors slammed shut, he had one last glimpse of Flo's face. Then darkness.

"All right, Diana. I'm not right sure if you exist," whispered Mucum, "but if you do, can I ask you a favor? Not dying would be a bit of all right . . . please?" His last words were drowned out as the tide turned and the thirsty tree decided to take a drink. The water shot up from the depths of the earth like a liquid arrow, slammed into the fragile wooden cabin, and accelerated a terrified Mucum from nought to one hundred miles an hour in under a couple of seconds.

He was falling, upward. A shooting star. He held on for dear life. Every bump and jolt threatened to smash the lift to smithereens, and his teeth clacked around in his mouth like a whole set of wooden spoons. If this was the way the Rootshooters visited the forest, they were welcome to it. For a few seconds Mucum forgot how to breathe, until there was a wood-shattering *BANG! Strapped up tight,* said Flo. She was right, though the leather belt bit hard into his skin as he was almost catapulted up through the flimsy roof.

Somewhere, a tiny bell chimed. Outside the lift, a pair of doors slid smoothly open. From down under to up top within sixty seconds! Mucum undid the harness and tried to stand up, dizzy with vertigo and drenched from the water that had leaked through every tiny gap in the lift. The open doors revealed a curtain of creeping vine, punctured by stray shards of cloudy evening light. He stepped across the gap in the shaft, pushing through the leafy barrier onto good, solid woodway. He'd made it! A wide, lunatic grin crossed his face until he remembered what he'd left behind. He turned back to see the entrance of the lift almost swallowed in the greenery, on a quiet offshoot of the main branchway.

A memory came to him from when he was younger. A school outing away from the city. One of the pupils suddenly shouted out, "Egghead!" They'd all looked up to see the strange outwoodish figure, striding past them. The clothes were obviously different: flowing, white, elegant compared to the practical stuff they wore in the forest. As the Rootshooter walked away, the rest of the class pointed fingers and burst into laughter. Anyone not Dendran was fair game. Mucum felt his face go hot with shame. No wonder they kept themselves to themselves.

There was no time to lose. Joe had told him where Ark was most likely to land. Mucum set off, trying to shake away that last look in Flo's eyes. His main problem now was Arktorious Malikum and then the small matter of saving their little island. Oh, for the easy life . . .

As he pounded the boards, trying to work out if he'd intercept his mate in time, a weeping face distracted him. It was a woman walking alone, her face streaked with tears.

"Mrs. Malikum?"

The face looked up, eyes drained, mouth looking as if it would never smile again. "Is that you, young Master Gladioli?"

Mucum winced. At work, his second name was forbidden territory. He was nobody's flower. This once, he'd make an exception.

"You appear to be wet. Have you been swimming?"

"Not really." There was no way he could tell her the truth. "Are you all right?"

"I'm . . . fine. Just been to kirk."

"Did you see Ark . . . Arktorious?"

"No. Yes. I mean, never mind. You go home. Save yourself." Her voice was high-pitched, almost hysterical.

"I don't understand."

"Neither do I. It's best. Good-bye!" She moved to brush past him.

"But wait. Don't you wanna know about the King and all that and what we tried to do?"

Mrs. Malikum didn't even react.

"Somefin's wrong 'ere. Where's Ark? Tell me!"

She paused, biting her bottom lip. "I've been told to say nothing. But I had to speak. I went to see the Warden and told her everything. She said that Ark would be fine and not to worry about Shiv, but I ask you. My little girl . . ." The woman was gabbling like a goose.

"Hang on a sec! Shiv? What's she got to do with it?"

Mrs. Malikum peered around Mucum's broad back, scanning the trees as if danger lurked in every knothole. "I was told to say that she's ill. But you've been with Ark, I can trust you. . . . She's my daughter and they took her. Grasp's men. For treason, they said." She dissolved then, almost collapsing into the boy's arms.

It was all wrong. Mothers were supposed to comfort kids, not the other way around. Mucum's head lit up like lightning. No wonder they took Shiv. Buddy clever, too. Ark's stupid sense of honor would lead him like a timber goat to fungus.

"Go home! You're only a child! You should never have become part of this," she sobbed.

"But I am part of it, and Ark needs my help." They'd come this far together. He wasn't going to let the stupid twig down now.

"But the Warden said Diana protects!"

"Good for her. I think I might jes' lend a helping hand, eh? Maybe you should get back to yer hubby? He's a good gaffer, by what Ark told me. I'll look after yer boy, but I need to go now."

Mrs. Malikum looked lost and uncertain, a small figure in the dusky treescape, as Mucum backed away. Then he turned and ran, hoping to catch Ark before he did something totally conkers.

24 · BAIT

The sun had long gone, leaving only drizzle and darkness. Petronio needed to keep sharp as he crouched behind a parasite laurel bush that sprouted from the side of the woodway. The flask of coffee helped: scalding and sweet, the way he liked it. As the chill of evening descended, he pulled his cloak around him and sipped silently, then sat back satisfied in the shadows.

This spot was perfect for an ambush. The boy would come. Petronio had no need of prayers; his plans were simply made to be fulfilled.

When Petronio felt the telltale vibrations on the branchway, he knew it wasn't a wild boar off for a midnight snuffle, but a boy driven by a sense of honor.

"Evening, Malikum. For a plumber's boy, you don't half cause a lot of trouble!"

The voice that came from behind the laurel was unmistakable. "Petronio!" it said. "I thought your family was low, but kidnapping my sister really scrapes the barrel!"

"Oh, does it? But it brought you here, didn't it?" There was a sharp sound as Petronio lit a candle lantern and placed it on the branch.

That was when Ark realized who had been the target. His sister was the worm used to catch the wriggling fish. "If it's me you want, then let her go!"

"Honestly, that's just the sort of sappy rubbish I'd expect from you. Of course it's you I want!" The blade that slipped out of the shadows gave his words an edge. "As for your sister, she can stay here to keep your family quiet."

"Where is she? If you've hurt her, believe me, I'll make you pay!"

A monster mealworm had better motives than this slimy, overfed brute. He'd dealt with one, now he'd sort out the other.

"Ha! Listen to you, sewer boy. Suddenly got magical powers, have we?"

Ark didn't know. Perhaps he had. Maybe if he grabbed hold of Petronio, the boy would fall still. "Answer my question! Where . . . is . . . she?" Each word shot out of his mouth, the force behind his voice making Petronio awkward for a second.

But only a second. "You think you can command me, sewer rat?" His knife glinted in the flickering lamplight. "Don't worry, killing little girls is not on the agenda, for now!"

"You'd sell your own family for gold!" Ark hissed as he launched himself at Petronio. There was a sudden silence in the forest as if every tree waited for the outcome. Ark saw his fist fly through the air. This wasn't about feathers or magical powers, only revenge. Whatever he'd felt down in the deeps was long gone.

Petronio's training was about defending himself against skillful opponents, not righteous treenagers going berserk. Before he knew what was happening, Ark had landed a punch that grazed the side of his face. Petronio's knife flew from his hand, skittering in spinning circles across the wood. He made to grab it, but Ark was all over him like a clinging vine scrabbling for purchase.

"Get off me, you squitty little bud!"

The drizzling rain had become a downpour. Ark hammered

away with his fists, forcing Petronio onto the ground, trying to
hold back his thick arm as it groped toward the fallen knife.
It was only inches away. If Petronio got it back, Ark might as
well jump now. There were no screams, only grunts and groans.
This was no playfight.

Petronio strained with all his might, his knees scraping on
the rough woodway. He could feel Ark's fingernails scratching
across his face like splinters. It was like wrestling with a bramble
bush. *Come on!* The knife was near now. With one last massive
effort, Petronio reared up and leapt for the blade, throwing Ark
off his back. He grabbed the handle, twisting round like a vine
snake as he lunged.

The knife did what it was forged to do, coming up and
slicing straight through Ark's leather jerkin and the thin shift
underneath to score a bloody furrow in his chest. Ark jerked
back with the intense pain, his body slamming onto the wet
woodway, almost slipping off the edge. His hand instinctively
reached up to check his wounds. The shift he wore clung to the
cut and the wetness spread across the cloth. At least his guts
weren't spilling out . . . yet.

"You'll have to do better than that, squit-for-brains!" taunted
Petronio. The constant drum of rain was now joined by the drip
of Ark's blood onto the road as he tried to stand up.

Ark felt his confidence drain away. He'd come all this way to
be killed by an overfed bully. "I'll—"

"You'll what? Plunge my toilet?" Petronio was finally in
control. Guards be hanged. There would be no dungeon for
this boy.

But as Petronio bent forward, his knife itching to bury itself
in Ark's neck, he heard a thrumming fill the night air. Petronio

paused, analyzing the sounds, taking in the iron scent of Ark's blood. "Ah! It looks like I won't need to finish you myself! It's very rare for anyone to be hungrier than me, but when it comes to hunters, I respectfully bow out. Have a good journey, Malikum. I guess we won't be seeing each other, ever again!" Petronio retreated, a smile of victory on his face.

Ark tried to move, but his body, heavy as dead wood, fought against him. He'd thought it was thundering up above. He was wrong. This was a different, far more dangerous tempest. With a wingspan wide as a roof, and eyes that glittered like diamonds, a huge raven came soaring from the darkness, drawn by the perfume of lifeblood, her claws ready to take the injured prey as it stood defeated and defenseless.

Mucum could only watch from a distance as the bird swooped low. He'd never run so fast in his life, his feet close to slipping on the wet woodways as he'd skidded around corners and sprinted over crossroads, aware that every second mattered. And now this.

Mucum had heard the telltale beat of wings overhead just as he'd caught sight of two figures ahead, one standing and crowing over the other. At that moment he knew Ark wasn't going to die like a warrior. To the ravens, summoned by the smell of blood, his friend was a morsel of meat. Nothing more. The Holly Woodsmen would call it a sacrifice, revering the dark bird. Stupid superstition!

In the dim light of their candle, the two figures appeared cut out, like silhouettes in a painting, frozen in time. And then the raven's shadow swallowed the scene whole. A moment later, one figure reappeared, the wrong one.

A roar reared up through Mucum's lungs and leapt from his mouth, shattering the night air. "Yer gonna pay fer this!" He charged toward Petronio like a battering ram, not caring if the birds took him, not giving a twig for his fear. Let them try it! Maybe this was finally Plan B—slam the surgeon's boy out of the way, scoop up Ark, and run for shelter.

Petronio looked up, his normal arrogance wiped away with shock as Mucum dived through the air, ready to fell him with one easy blow. Petronio's dagger had been wiped on a convenient lump of moss and put away. There was no time to ease it from the scabbard. His eyes met Mucum's, picked up on the hate that was far brighter than the limp candle lighting up the scene.

The punch, so close and packed with intent, never managed to land on Petronio's nose. Instead of the crack of broken cartilage and a spuming spray of blood, there was a sudden wash of wind that blew both Petronio and Mucum off their feet. The raven's wings beat like a hurricane, and a single screech nearly burst their eardrums.

"Mucum!" Ark cried out, helpless in the eye of this storm.

To Mucum's horror, a pair of claws reached down from the sky and plucked Ark from the forest, his home, all that was known to him. A second later, both boy and bird were gone, leaving only two dazed treenagers lying on the walkway.

Mucum lay for a second, anger blazing within. He took a deep breath and levered himself up. Whoever regained their senses quickest would win. "You buddy buzzard. Got my mate killed. I'll have you! I'll—" Before Petronio even had a chance to rise, Mucum was on him, leaning with all his weight into his rubber-soled shoe, pressing it hard into Petronio's neck.

"Please!" Petronio gasped. "I didn't mean to . . . it was an accident."

But Mucum was too far gone. "I saw you smile when the bird took him." Enough said. A couple of seconds and the boy's neck would snap like brittle ice. He'd never killed anyone before. What would it be like? He was about to find out.

25 · ONLY A BOY

Petronio's eyes bulged out as the pressure on his neck bore down. For the first, and possibly last time in his life, he was about to cry. How pathetic.

As Petronio's face began to turn blue, Mucum suddenly felt a thick arm snake around his neck from behind and the point of something very sharp press into his ribs.

"Easy now! Take your foot away, sir. Immediately. I wouldn't want my knife to slip, would I?" The voice was older and carried authority.

Mucum thought about ignoring the order. He was done for in any case. And maybe he could take at least one piece of vermin with him. But self-preservation kicked in. He lifted his foot off, aware of a strength that could easily snap his own neck. "All right. Doin' what you say . . ."

Petronio coughed loudly, then rolled over, retching his dinner all over his expensively embroidered shift. He almost said thanks. The guard had saved his life, after all. Then he remembered who he was. He wiped his mouth and stared up at his savior. "About buddy time, Salix. What took you so long?" Petronio felt the imprint of Mucum's shoe on his neck. There would be bruises later, but he'd live. He tried to stand up, swaying slightly and soaking wet as he regained his balance.

"Looks like we caught our last little loose end!" Petronio brushed mud and bits of dead leaf from his padded britches as he walked over to Mucum. "Your boss, Jobby Jones, sold you out for a couple of sovereigns. And what kind of sissy name is Gladioli?"

"Sod you!" Mucum should have killed him, but now he was stuck like a fly in the guard's muscly web. All he could do was spit into Petronio's face. The aim was good and he idly noticed that a decent gob now hung from the other boy's nose.

"Such insolence, from a nobody! Is that the best you can do?" Petronio pulled out a silk handkerchief and slowly wiped away the saliva. He was tempted to pull out his knife and stick the common oaf there and then. Instead, he slammed his fist into Mucum's stomach. "That, boy, is for dirtying my doublet. These clothes cost, you know!"

Salix pulled his knife away just in time, letting go of Mucum's other arm so that the boy doubled over in agony.

Petronio straightened up, pleased with the effect. "That was for starters. Take him to the dungeons. I'll deal with him later."

Mucum felt numb as he was pulled up and dragged away, no better than a bark-dog on a leash. Ark was dead. The country had gone to the logs and he was finished. As the guard prodded him forward with the point of his sword, he realized his promise to Flo was permanently broken. He wouldn't be back, ever.

After his prisoner had been taken away, Petronio lifted up the lamp, its flickering wash of weak color lighting up the pool of blood on the woodway. Why had he let the dumb bird have all the fun? He should have dealt out the slicing punch into the gut, a perfect disemboweling. Ark would have stared as his intestines slid out of his stomach like glistening worms.

Petronio's ability to deliver a killing blow had so far been limited to a safely trussed-up wild boar, squealing in terror as he hacked at its neck. Doing it to a Dendran was . . . for a moment he didn't know what it was.

Yet, when he informed Councillor Grasp of Ark's death twenty minutes later, he had almost received a smile in acknowledgment. Petronio left out the small fact that Salix had saved his life.

"You should have let my men deal with Malikum!" said Grasp, sighing. "But at least our work will no longer be impeded." It was the best Petronio could hope for. He was dismissed. He thought about calling on the little sister and telling her that her brother was dead, but even he had some limits. Let her sleep.

Later that night, when the rain finally ceased its soft rhythmic tapping on the cedar shingle roof, and the moon came pouring through the window, spilling silver over the floor, his door swung silently open.

Petronio was instantly awake, feeling for the blade under his bed.

"Shush!" came a soft voice. "You do not need to defend yourself against me!"

Petronio sat up. "My lady!"

"The Councillor hasn't appreciated your true capabilities!" The voice kept quiet as Fenestra silently slipped toward the edge of the bed and sat down.

"Well . . . ," said Petronio, unsure how to continue.

"Well, nothing. I admit to you that he is a useful pawn, but no more." The moon caught her eyes, daring him to defend his father.

Petronio was happy that at least one person in this miserable damp excuse of a city had the guts to stand up to Councillor Grasp. "I thought he'd be pleased, but all he could do was go on about the guards."

"My dear boy. You have what he lacks. Initiative. For one so young, your cunning is surprising!"

"Thank you!" Petronio was glad she could not see his blushing face. She was wearing some kind of perfume. It filled his nostrils like a drug.

"Oh, don't thank me. It was you who came up with the plan, then executed it. We do not have such giant birds in our country. These creatures are evolution's concept of a killing machine. In a way, I admire them. Are you sure they will not let him go?"

The question was pointed. "The religionists think the ravens are death's henchmen. Personally, I don't believe in that superstitious claptrap. But throwing away a free meal isn't in their nature."

"Good. Our little friend has proven to be somewhat slippery."

"Not this time," Petronio assured her, closing the subject. "What happens now?"

"The future, of course!" She was playing with him.

Petronio knew it and the thought made him bitter. "Right. Thanks for letting me know," he said with an edge in his voice.

Fenestra ignored the sarcasm. "And you have played your part well. Go to sleep now, my clever boy."

Boy. That's all he was to her. He wanted more. Much more. It was humiliating being left out. His father had recently met with Flint, but all the Commander did when he passed Petronio on the stairs was grunt an acknowledgment. He had changed from negotiator back to messenger boy in one blink of an eye. And now Fenestra was not letting him in on the details, despite her praise. He looked up and she was gone.

After that, sleep was impossible. There was only one thing that would relax him. Petronio quickly dressed and stole from the room. The whole house was in slumber now, the only sounds the creaking of wood in the wind as the house gently swayed. Fenestra had no doubt retreated to whatever hidey-hole she had made for herself.

Petronio crept downstairs, hoping his father's study door had been recently oiled. The hinges were on his side and within seconds, he stood by the Councillor's desk. There was the box that started it all. As he lifted the lid and sniffed the expensive cigars within, he realized that, thanks to him, the spy had been uncovered. Who said smoking was bad for your health? He lifted one of the cigars and rolled it between his stubby fingers. A little celebration.

He went to the balcony doors, undid the latch, and let himself out. The rain had long gone, leaving a chill in the air. The half-moon was lower now, the dawn not far away. Even the stars were losing their brightness. Petronio lit the cigar, dragging the fragrant smoke deep into his lungs and letting it stream out through his nose as he leaned on the edge of the wrought-iron railings. Below him, the crowns of the trees stirred in the breeze like a dark green cloud, already browning at the edges. Soon, all this would change.

As he reentered the study, a thought struck him. His father was meticulous when it came to paperwork. If there was a plan, he would have written it down, despite Fenestra's warning that paper was incriminating. Now, where to look? The desk was too obvious, as was the filing cabinet backed against the wall. Even Grasp wouldn't be stupid enough to file it under *T* for *Treason*. What did that leave? Maybe he'd secreted the files behind the tapestries?

The answer when it came was both obvious and unintelligent. Grasp had commissioned a portrait of himself from one of the best painters in Arborium. Petronio remembered the month of sittings. Woe betide anyone who interrupted the head

of the house as he posed. Petronio walked over to the painting, in which the Councillor sat on an ornate, jewel-bedecked
chair surrounded by hunting dogs. He wore a demigown
with long, hanging sleeves, the facings turned back to show
the inner white fox fur. Underneath, Grasp wore a black velvet cote over a pink satin doublet. The painter had created
a remarkable resemblance, turning the Councillor into the
pompous, preening bore that he really was. However, Petronio
was not searching the darkened study in order to improve his
appreciation of art. He carefully lifted the gilded frame off
its hook.

Yes! The vanity of it! The best place to hide your secrets?
Behind *yourself*, the great Councillor Grasp! In a hidden alcove
sat a thin, hinged box. Petronio quickly lifted it out of its hiding place. Inside lay a scroll. Petronio took the parchment over
to the windows and unrolled it, trying to decipher the script in
the predawn light. Fenestra had mentioned the future. Here it
was in black-and-white. Pure treason, enough inked evidence
for a spate of hangings all around. Petronio shuddered at the
thought of it.

The day was known already. Sunday. The Harvest Festival.
And here were the dark details. A population drunk on good
wine wouldn't know what hit them. As for King Quercus?
Petronio read on, appalled but delighted. Who would suspect
their very own army and its dearly trusted leader? At the peak
of celebration, in a country filled with the noise of feasting, the
King would be asked by his faithful bodyguards to leave
the feasting area, and all possible witnesses. Once the paid-off
men had the King where they wanted him, the deed would be
done. Time for the soldiers to move in. Virtually no blood
would be shed as the country changed hands. All that Fenestra

had done was offer the right amount of gold and whisper in a few ears.

As Petronio rolled the scroll up and placed it carefully back in the alcove, he heard footsteps coming toward the study. Loud footsteps of two people: It could only be Salix and Alnus. The picture still leaned against the wall. If anyone came in, it would be the first thing they noticed. There was no way out. Petronio shrank back into the shadows like a trapped rat. This time, there would be no sewage worker to blame, and the guards might choose to attack first, ask questions later.

26 · THE RAVENWOOD

❧

One second Ark was in the drenching mist of thick cloud. The next he was pulled up by beat of wing into the sudden space of stars and night. The moon looked as if it had been ripped in half by the same claws that now held him tight in a curved cage. Ark's teeth clattered in their sockets. His clothes were woven for Arborium, protected as it was by leaf and branch. Up here, the wind scoured his skin. Yet the cold was the least of his worries. The warning squawks of the raven might as well have been kirk bells ringing out his death.

He couldn't believe that Mucum had somehow managed to follow him. Why didn't he stay down in the roots with Flo? At least he would've been safe. Ark's last and fleeting hope was that Mucum gave Petronio what he deserved.

But all that had vanished, a long way behind him now, as he swooped over the forest, covering miles in minutes. Ark was dimly aware how rare this sight was, Arborium laid out like an undulating tapestry of leaf and shade. A real bird's-eye view. His mind recalled the map he'd seen on Jobby Jones's wall, and here it came alive, rising and falling beneath him. To the east, he could see the nighttime lamps encircling Hellebore, the castle at its center rising up like a budding flower. But they were flying west, where the lit-up roads and small platform villages soon petered out.

However, he wasn't a passenger out for a ride but a parcel of meat in transit. As soon as these claws let go, he was going to be ripped into very small gobbets of flesh. His father had always said to keep a lookout in the woods, in case he fell victim to the raven-gift. Well, that's what he was now. *Sugar and spice, gristle is nice.* A gift for some animal's guts. His goddess was a long way away now, and feebly whispered prayers, no protection.

Maybe he'd imagined the mealworm's purr. For a moment, he tried to feel his way into this other creature's mind. But all he saw was a shunning blackness. He even thought about the feather in his bag, but what good was a feather against a whole bird? His arms and legs were squeezed tight in this tiny cage. The stench of his captor was overwhelming, a foul animal stink of decomposing tissue that seeped into his nose.

The wound slashed across his chest began to throb.

The bird paused, hovered for a second.

Ark peered through the claws, his eyes trying to comprehend the sight ahead of them as the bird then began to climb. The trees had vanished, beaten back in a long straggly line. He could make out a rocky wilderness that sloped up and up again. Oh! A chill began to invade Ark's bones. Mountains! Great soaring crags that towered over the forest, curving away both north and west in a gigantic circle. They were bare places, treeless, like a Dendran without clothes! The raven's black wings carried him over ice- and snow-covered summits that looked sharper and more dangerous than any claws. Then, at last, they began to spiral downward, down out of the night and toward the forest on the other side.

Ark remembered the far tales from his childhood. The West was where the sun rested its head. If you didn't say your prayers, sleep would carry you there, to the land of nightmares. Once upon a time, there was a forest that the ravens returned to at night. A place of twisted trees, ruled over by a dark queen. The Ravenwood.

Then they were over the trees, descending so quickly, Ark only saw streaks of branch and leaf reaching up to him. He closed his eyes, waiting for the sharp stab of beaks, as the claws that held him retracted and he tumbled into what felt like the inside of a goose down bedstead. Feathers tickled his nose and he was unable to hold back a sneeze.

The sound of the bird's flapping wings vanished into the dark. Abandoned, he stood and stared around him. He had been dropped to the bottom of an enormous nest in the crown of a tree. Moonlight filtered through the massive leaves: The nest was empty except for a small scattering of bleached white bones. He had to get out of here! Ark tried to scramble up the sides, but the feathers lining the branch-built construction were slippery and the edge of the nest too high.

Suddenly, he heard a slithering sound followed by a soft hiss somewhere up above. His beating heart told him that this was a wild wood. Nothing known. Nothing safe. In panic, he burrowed under the feather lining, intending to pick a hole in the nest and wriggle through. Plumber's instincts. He pulled enough feathers out to see the structure of the nest. This was no flimsy pigeon roost. The branches were torn, bent around, and woven into ropes thicker than his arm. Without a saw, this open-air nest was a wicker prison and he was bait in waiting. But whatever it was that crawled along the branch up high must have lost interest. It slid away, its rough skin rasping against bark.

Ark breathed a sigh of relief. He looked up into the starry night. There was the familiar Plow, digging the furrows of the heavens, and Orion the hunter stared down at him. Ha! And he was the one hunted. He sat back in the nest, feeling lost. Why had he run straight to Grasp's place? He was in such a righteous rush to save his sister, he hadn't paused to think.

He should have smelled a trap! Now it was all over, or would be as soon as that raven returned with its cronies. But apart from the lonely call of a nightjar, the forest remained strangely silent. The softness of the feathers finally soothed him. It had been a long night. Had he really only left the Rootshooters a few hours ago? His eyelids were heavy and he began to drift off into strange dreams where eyes stared at him from the shadows.

A voice broke into his sleep. "Well, well, well, what have we here?"

Ark woke suddenly, aware of a sharp branch sticking into his back. His shift had dried and stuck to his wound and his whole body ached. The light had changed, night swapped for a cold, predawn mist. The hours had flown. Ark licked dew off his lips as he looked up, wondering for a second if rescue was at hand. However, the face that peered over the top of the nest did nothing to reassure him. Its owner was an old woman. Her skin was dark as if competing with night itself, but her eyes were as green as vivid moss. Her thin form reminded him of a snake. Was that what had slithered above him in the dark?

Suddenly, the woman slid over the edge to land feetfirst right in front of him. As she towered over him, Ark saw a body bent with age, clothed in a cloak of raven feathers and long black petticoats. A dead fox curled round her neck, perhaps waiting to wake up.

In total terror, he scrabbled away from her to the farthest part of the nest.

"I speak, and yet your mouth does not respond. I say again, what have we here?" The eyes stared, unblinking, like an owl's.

"Why do you care?" said Ark, as boldly as he could muster. He felt sure he had heard the voice before. And the eyes were strangely familiar, the way they bored into him.

Who was this shadow woman with her tumbledown nest of raven-black hair? Was he still dreaming? Perhaps the tales his mother had told him when he was little were true. Could this really be Her? Impossible! Stories didn't come to life.

A hand reached out and gripped him by his jerkin, pulling him up to eye level as if he weighed no more than a button. Her arms were bare, muscles tight as grasping tendrils. "It speaks." Now there was amusement in her eyes. "My children brought you to me. Not many survive. So once again I ask you what you are."

A rush of air raced around his system, his nerves spread like nettle rash across his body. Ark knew he was awake and that this was no normal Dendran. He stared at her in shock. The hand that held him suspended in midair was all wrong, fingers and fingernails fused together to make a honed set of sharpened claws. One swipe with her other hand and Ark was sure his head would be sliced from his body.

And what the holly did she mean about her children? Ark felt compelled to answer. "A boy."

"Yes. Indeed. And one who drops coins in shrines, trying to buy hope with mere metal."

He shivered. "How do you know that?"

The woman didn't bother answering, finally dropping Ark back onto the floor of the nest. "Tell me more, boy," she said.

"My name is Arktorious Malikum, a plumber's apprentice, son of Mr. Malikum." And here, up high in this strange tree, he was out of place. His panicked eyes briefly took in the wood that soared above the nest, still wreathed in dawn mist. The branches that crisscrossed the sky were gnarled and twisted like arthritic fingers, the leaves spotted as if autumn had already infected them.

"Your words cover up truth. You are a sewage worker, a delver in dark places. I thought I could smell something foul." The taunting tone reminded him of Petronio.

"It's a job." His hands clenched and unclenched.

"A job. Yes. That is what you are. A job now completed." The woman had obviously decided his fate. "My curiosity is dulled. You are a thin snack with too much gristle. Sometimes my birds bring me treasure. Sometimes they don't. I have too many important things on my plate to bother with the likes of you." The woman let her eyes slide away. "I have found you wanting, and the conversation tedious. My children are welcome to you." The woman snapped her fingers.

Out of the shadows and from the surrounding treetops, a thousand pairs of eyes suddenly winked at him. There were more ravens than he had seen in a lifetime, a city of feathered monsters. Ark looked again, and the woman had turned away, dismissing him as if he were a wearisome tick to be plucked from the folds of her wrinkled black skin.

The nest he crouched in was no more than a serving bowl. The birds clacked their beaks, screeching their dawn chorus as they prepared for a feast.

27 · CURIOSITY KILLS

The portrait on the floor, the big gap on the wall, Petronio shrunk into the shadows all spelled out one word: *Thief!* The footsteps paused outside the door.

"You checked this earlier?"

"Do I look stupid, Salix?" came a grunted reply.

"Yeah. Every shift I have to work with you!"

"Ha-buddy-ha!"

Petronio heard the sound of a cork being pulled out and then several glugs.

"Give us some of that before I die of boredom!"

If they knew who was on this side of the door, he'd be in trouble. But the footsteps faded away down the corridor.

"You fool!" Petronio whispered to himself, wiping a bead of sweat from his forehead. Salix and Alnus doing their rounds, dumb as clockwork, easily evaded. Crazy! He'd been more frightened of a couple of inept thugs than a Dendran-devouring raven. He hung the picture back up, making sure it wasn't crooked.

Five minutes later, he made his way, step-by-step, up the stairs, trying to avoid the creaking treads, falling at last into his bed and a deep, dreamless sleep.

The next morning came, fresh and clear after the dawn mist dissipated into the leaves. His hand was still sore from the punch he'd delivered to Mucum's guts. Though not as sore as the boy's stomach would be. He was tempted to go down to the dungeon for a bit of taunting. Maybe later. The boy, and Ark's sister, were right where he wanted them.

In class, the teacher droned on about the vein structure of the body—the transport system for blood. As Petronio sat at the back of the lecture room, he thought about Ark's blood spilling into soup for the ravens.

His mind fell back to the night before: the satisfaction of seeing Ark's terrified face as the claws plunged toward him. The whimpering scream as the boy was plucked from the branch like an insignificant weevil. But then came his father's unenthusiastic response, and worse, Fenestra's dismissal.

The sudden anger sharpened his mind. After the lecture, instead of joining the others, he decided to head for the woods. When he'd helped Fenestra with the injection that saved her life, there was one question that had remained unanswered. Where was she going? One way to find out. In his mind, he traced the path they had taken that afternoon and his feet quickly followed, soon leaving the crowds of Hellebore behind as he threaded the thinning byways. At last, he stood at a sign, which pompously read:

ROAD CLOSED DUE TO COUNCIL REPAIRS.
FINDING NEW WAYS TO KEEP THE COUNTRY ON THE MOVE!

Arborium was full of spots like this, filled with rusted cables and rotting plankways. They were signs of the old empire when the whole forest was filled with Dendrans, before the ancient black plagues reduced the population to an echo of history. Occasionally, the plague came back like a curse to remind the tree dwellers that Arborium was not impregnable. Eleven years before, there'd been a small outbreak, taking out a few sewer workers and their families before fading away in the coldest winter for generations. Nowadays, nobody thought twice about it, though this was the main reason why many had upped sticks and headed for a new life in Hellebore.

These abandoned, rural woodways had no profit in them. As long as they stuck up a sign, the Council could pretend that a repair team would eventually deal with the problem.

Petronio wasn't sure what he was looking for. He stepped over the sign and walked onto the spot where he'd first seen Fenestra in trouble. Luckily, the path beyond continued in one direction. He gingerly avoided the various holes in the road, trying not to look down at the mile drop below. If Fenestra had a hidey-hole, this was perfect. Other Dendrans wouldn't take the risk down here.

Petronio paused. What was that? He was sure he heard a slight shuffling noise. Probably a squirrel. He wished he had his catapult. There was no greater satisfaction than seeing one of those nosy little creatures slammed off the branch and tumbling through the air. The surface grew worse as he walked. Parasite plants—ferns and nettles—had been allowed to take hold. The path turned into a jungle sucking out the lifeblood of the trees. He stopped to look more closely. Various nettle stalks were bent out of place. Footsteps had been here before him.

He trod carefully and quietly, his ears tuned in to every rustle of the forest. He came to a clearing, a crossroads where two branchways intersected, supported in the middle by a massive hollowed-out trunk riddled with woodworm. Three possible directions. He entered the archway of the trunk, looked up to see the vaulted roof above him. Which route should he take?

A sunbeam provided the answer, as it shot through the leaves.

There! In one of the doorways, a shred of snagged material. Petronio bent to examine the tiny fragment of cloth. Some of the strands caught the light, as if woven from metal. This was no Dendran cloth. Petronio smiled and was about to stride through the archway when a sight stopped him in his tracks.

Thirty or forty yards away, a figure crouched behind a bush. The figure was clad head to foot in an outfit that appeared to absorb the color from the leaves around until it was hard to make out what was man and what was bush. Even more interesting was the weapon the man cradled expertly in his arms. Petronio had never seen anything like it and he made a point of knowing all things armorial. It was a transparent hollow tube with one end nestled into the man's shoulder; his finger appeared to be clamped on to a curve of silver halfway along the tube.

Petronio shivered. He had no desire to find out what the weapon could do. He had a feeling that his own dagger would be no competition. He'd reached his goal. This must be Fenestra's destination. This was a soldier from Maw. Despite the camouflage, everything about him screamed out foreignness. What was he doing here? Petronio calmed his breathing. It might be better if he retreated. Fenestra was right after all. He'd done his part.

But another part of him was curious, drinking in the sight. He even thought, madly, of walking up to the man and asking him about the shoulder stick. He had to find out more. The hollowed-out trunk gave him an idea. *Where there was wood, steps will follow* went the saying. He looked again and found a series of crumbling steps leading up and around. Petronio carefully placed a foot on the first stair, testing it for creaks, making his way up toward the sky and a better vantage point.

He felt it before he heard it. A slight reverberation in the wood. Then a breeze sprung up, filled with a muffled and rhythmic *thwack-thwack*. By this point, he was perched about a hundred feet higher up, having crawled through a hole where a branch had rotted. His eyes could make no sense of the sight. It wasn't a bird, unless birds were made of metal. And yet it hovered over the forest, matte black, almost silent. On top, four blades whirred around so fast, it made Petronio's eyes blur. The breeze had become a strong wind, almost pulling him off the tree.

"Seen enough, have we?" snarled a voice behind him.

Petronio could have punched himself. He'd been so caught up in the vision before him that his guard had been briefly let down.

"Don't speak another word. Unless you want your brains spattered over your nice green leaves!"

Petronio felt something cold press into the back of his head. He wanted to know what Mawish weapons could do. Now he would find out. The only thing he couldn't understand was how perfectly the voice mimicked the Dendran accent. Maybe that was part of their training: the Maw Army Language course: *Learn to speak like Dendrans and then kill them!* Complimenting the man's speech was hardly going to save his life.

"No one is supposed to know that we're here!" The voice paused as if coming to a conclusion. "Which makes you a liability."

The weapon pressed harder into Petronio's skull until his head throbbed with pain. He closed his eyes, unable to stop himself begging the Diana he didn't believe in for help, just this once.

28 · A SUDDEN DISCOVERY

For Ark, this was the last scaffield straw, feeding a spark deep within the exhausted boy. To be dismissed as nothing was somehow even worse than the knowledge of the ravens' hunger. The sun chose that moment to tip itself above the horizon. The first rays pierced the depths of the nest, gilding Ark's brown face, the hesitant warmth filling him with insane hope.

Without thinking, he drew out the raven feather from his bag, feeling the sharp prick of the quill. Would it work? It was almost as long as his forearm and felt heavy enough. *Hold the feather, grab the weather.* Ark pulled his arm back and heaved it with all his might. The feather, as if in memory of flight, shot like the wind straight toward the retreating woman's back.

The quill was as sharp as a throwing knife, soaring through the dawn with perfect aim. He knew with the certainty of the new day that the feather would penetrate cloak, puncture skin, and dig deep into her dark heart. Soon, the woman would cross the River Sticks to meet her own maker.

Sensing danger, the woman suddenly swiveled around. Her green eyes glittered with amusement. A hand shot out to pluck the speeding weapon from the air. It was over before it had even begun.

Ark slumped back, his last hope clutched tightly in the raven-woman's hand. There were a few seconds of tense silence. Ark was defeated, but if she was going to give the order to the mass of shifting birds, he would not act the coward. He held her gaze.

"Now that," she said, "*is* interesting. A boy who has mastered fear. The use of my gift was also well improvised."

Ark was confused. He expected death, not praise. Then he figured it out. "It was your voice, when I followed the squirrel, when I grabbed the feather, when I was hiding with Mucum. . . ."

"Yes. Note that the only way out of here is up." The woman grabbed Ark's jerkin again and tossed him easily to the top of the nest, where he landed in a heap. He felt like one of Shiv's play sticks, thrown around for the sheer holly of it. Managing to sit upright, he briefly swayed backward with tiredness, then pulled himself together, aware that if he fell, the drop would be brutal.

The woman scurried up the sheer wall of the nest below him like a spider, and walked off down the branch. She turned back briefly. "Come. If you have mastered your fear, then there is no reason to be afraid."

Ark saw that the nest was wedged between two forking branches. But these were not carved flat like the woodways of home. As he stepped off the nest, the way ahead turned into a treacherous and ankle-twisting path of pitted bark and slippery lichen. He reluctantly drew closer, staring up at the figure who towered over him. Despite her crookedness, he also saw for the first time her fierce and ageless beauty.

"I have been looking over your shoulder from the beginning. Forgive my little test. I had to see what you were made of. A cruel face is not the only one that I wear." The woman picked her way down the path, her figure flowing between pools of shade and light. "Walk with me now."

Ark tried to keep up as the branch climbed up and curled around, his eyes reeling with the strange sights of this new land. A butterfly bigger than a horse fluttered past, its iridescent blue wings an echo of the distant sky. The truth of the woman's words clicked in his head like a cog. Twilights where he wandered in the woods alone, feeling that he was being watched and dismissing it. "But why?"

"Later. At least let me introduce myself. You may call me —"

"Corwenna! The Raven Queen!" Ark's eyes went wide with recognition and fear.

"How delightful! I have not been addressed as 'queen' for years! Yes, I am sometimes known as the Raven Queen, but I am more than that, Ark, much more. I am the guardian of this created land. I, too, was grown like the trees. Sometimes, science and miracles come together." She stopped and bowed gracefully.

"I'm A-Ark, short for Arktorious," he stammered. A minute ago he was a potential murderer. Now they were making courtly introductions. "Umm . . . you're not going to eat me, are you?"

"Oh really. These nursery rhymes do exaggerate!" She studied him for a second with her vivid green eyes. Why did they look so familiar? It was unnerving.

Ark was in shock. Goodwoody talked about Dendrans ignoring the Raven Queen at their peril. Now she walked alongside him, living and breathing! "Hang on! Does that mean that Diana is here somewhere, too?" He peered around, terrified of meeting the target of his prayers.

"The mother of us all is long gone." Corwenna frowned.

"Did you . . . know her?" Ark couldn't stop the questions tumbling out. It was all too much to take in, just like this tangled treescape that confused his sense of direction. He longed for the familiar woodways that he knew like the back of his hand, the safety ropes that gave Dendrans their sense of security. Here, there were no ropes to steady the nerves, only a tortuous route that was keen to trip him up and pull him over the edge. The branch suddenly narrowed and Ark quailed. "I can't . . ." The woodway swayed in front of him, a skinny tight-rope of wood, no wider than the width of his foot.

Corwenna smiled as she strode confidently over. "You need to trust. The wild wood will never let you fall."

Ark wasn't so sure. These trees were tricky, treacherous. Finally, he tried to calm his breathing and carefully stepped forward, convinced he was about to slip. But somehow his feet found the right gripping points and he was over, scampering to keep up with his new guide.

"Well done!" said Corwenna as Ark at last caught up. "As for the answer to your earlier question. Oh yes. I knew her with all my heart and soul. But let us leave her in peace for now. Your curiosity does you credit. Dendrans are normally so dull, with their rituals and woodsmen and misguided prayers, but you, Ark, have always been different. You have the ability to understand nature's true power, something far greater than be-leaf alone. This is why you were made, foundling boy."

His body was a jangle of nerves, his mind racing to catch up with her words. They wrapped him around like the suffocating vines that crept up the trunks of this impenetrable forest. Could it really be true? He thought back to all that had happened. If she knew everything, why was she playing with him? Perhaps she was right. And perhaps the reason he had been brought to the Ravenwood was to meet Corwenna!

"Then help me save Arborium. My home is in trouble! If you are who you say you are, not just some crone from an old story, you'll know that already."

"Arborium is always in trouble!" Corwenna shrugged. "It is no longer my concern."

"When I was attacked by your raven, I was trying to warn

the King that Maw is about to overthrow the kingdom. Let me go, or if you're so powerful, why won't you help me?" She had to help him! But he must be careful. To taunt his captor was madness.

Corwenna was almost pushed back by the force of his words. She paused, looking down at the boy in a new light. "Well, Ark, it does seem as though my experiment has finally borne fruit. When my mother first brought the seeds of these trees to this once barren island many years ago, I knew the time to fight for the trees would come again." The coldness of her voice was replaced with a surprising tenderness. "Welcome to the Ravenwood, Ark. We need each other. It might well be that you are the first-ever visitor who will live to speak of us. Now come, you must be tired. I shall dress your wounds and feed you."

Ark was stunned. Is this what this strange woman had wanted all along? Was this a game to her?

The empty woods suddenly filled with the sound of wing-beats. Corwenna checked her stride. "Here we are."

Ark had no idea where they were, only that every branch in the tree above them was now speckled with watching eyes. A feathered bodyguard of thousands. The door set into the hollow trunk that reared up in front of them was covered in sigils and scratchings: strange symbols of the moon, and trees that were half trunk, half woman. One of the pictures, of a female figure with a bow and arrow hunting down a tree stag, disturbed him.

Corwenna swung the door open. Ark had no choice but to enter.

A fire was lit in an ornate iron grate covered in embossed ravens with eyes of precious stones. The room was sumptuously furnished and the flames reflected off endless jewels and shiny metal implements.

"The birds have a way with shimmering objects. Some useful, others mere glitter. But is it not so with Dendrans and their love of gold?"

Ark nodded. Councillor Grasp was well named.

"They have stolen me an imitation of wealthy Arborian life, but these baubles will never corrupt my heart." The woman poured from a flask, pushing a crystal glass over to Ark.

This was far from home. Ark looked into the fire, suddenly aware of skewers hanging over the flames. His mouth watered: The smell of roasting meat was pungent, overpowering. He had had visions of being forced to crunch raw squirrels and bugs on some nest-scrape filled with bird excrement.

"Raw flesh is fine for my feathered friends, but I prefer my meat cooked. Here, help yourself. And before you ask, it's goat."

It was a long time since Ark's last meal in the subterranean land of the Rootshooters. The meat was tender, seared on the outside, oozing and juicy as he bit into it. He finished the chunks of the first skewer and devoured a second, washing it down with a fiery juice that tasted of fermented black currant.

Corwenna picked at the meat on her plate, her sharp fingernails like delicate claws.

"So, goddesses eat food as well?"

She burst out laughing. "I suppose I could cook up a few well-meaning Dendran prayers, but that would be thin fare!"

Ark finally managed a smile.

"That's better! Now we have important matters to discuss. We know that Arborium is in danger. The country has been sick for a long time."

Ark nodded, thinking of the rich kids playing in the castle gardens and the hovel he called home.

"And now comes an interloper ready to pluck the fruit from the branch!"

"Maw?"

"My birds have eyes. It is they who tell me what is happening in the wide-wood. The woman you overheard encouraging Grasp to betray his own king—Lady Fenestra—is more dark goddess than I ever was! Maw has bred a perfect monster who would devour us all."

"But if you're the Raven Queen, can't you wave a wood-wand or something?" Ark still couldn't believe he was sitting opposite Her. If only his parents could see him now. "There's old shrines to you all over!"

"As I have said, Ark, what a few doddering Dendrans believe I am and what I actually am are two different creatures. It's time for you to hear the truth. But that begins with a question. Where are we?"

"Inside the trunk of a tree. In the Ravenwood. In the far west of Arborium."

"And what made the trees?"

"Why the school lesson?"

"Answer me!" Corwenna demanded.

"Um . . . the scientists of long ago. They followed a message borne from the Goddess, to create a world up in the sky, safe from the polluted earth and those who would harm us." This was the green ark that would shelter Dendrans from all the storms to come. It was a childhood tale that tree dwellers grew up with.

"In a way, that story is true. Long ago, there was a group of scientists and thinkers who could see that forests would soon become extinct. Land was valuable to build on. Nearly all the trees had been cut down to make way for cities of glass. And when the growth of saplings was outlawed to protect the value of the remaining timber, it was time to act. They were led by one woman. A woman with no message apart from the yearnings in her heart to stop the madness of the world."

"That's heresy!" Ark was shocked.

"Fact twists and turns like a growing branch over time. As the generations pass on their words, history is woven into far tales. This woman was strong and smart. In great secrecy and with the help of her colleagues, it was she who created the first seeds of the trees of Arborium. Others in her group found an uninhabited island in the middle of the ocean, one of the last few wild refuges. An island that somehow had been overlooked by the nation that would one day become the Mawish Empire."

Ark knew exactly which island Corwenna was talking about, but all that he believed in was being turned upside down.

"As leader, she was the one who made the final sacrifice. She faked her own death — easy enough for a great scientist. As she left the city she had grown up in, her heart was heavy for the family she had to abandon. How she arrived on the island is another tale, and who can say what went through her mind as she dug the seeds into the hostile earth? It was an experiment, which is a sort of prayer, I suppose. A dream to create new life when the rest of the earth was turning into great forests of glass and steel."

"She was real?" Ark dreaded the answer.

"As real as you and I sitting here tonight." Corwenna paused to look deep into Ark's eyes. "And I am a daughter of that real woman, that scientist whose faith made Arborium. That is the end of all fact. My precious birds whisper me tales about my mother, about how she sent herself to sleep, curled up in a shrouded ball for a thousand years as the seeds sprang up around her, but how true they are, I don't know. They tell, too, of the ravens of old, no more than three feet from wing tip to wing tip, that pecked at some of my mother's seeds. They were transformed, just like the trees. Science stretched their beaks, bulked out their bodies, made claws into scimitars and wings large enough to slice through clouds. But science only explains so much, for within those seeds, greater mysteries have unfolded than even I shall ever understand."

Ark could picture it then. A bleak place of moorland and heather, where only storms soared over the empty inland vastness. And out of that nothing, that stillness, the action of rain and sun on those first seeds had created Arborium. . . . "But the earth below us is dirty; that's why the trees grew so high! I don't believe you."

"The facts are not bothered by what you think." Corwenna allowed herself a small smile. "Only the earth beyond these shores was polluted. It's just that the story has twisted over time. And before you ask where the Dendrans came from, think."

"They could have come from Maw for all I know!"

"Not so stupid, are you? Yes, Ark, they were refugees. A boatload of them, braving strong winds and heaving oceans that tossed and swayed like treetops in a storm, praying to escape the march of the new world and find some peace, a land they could call their own—a land where trees still thrived."

Ark tried to imagine the scene. He'd never even come close to the sea.

"Such a rickety old boat, filled with desperate men, women, and children. Oh, to come across this green-gladed paradise—there was no poisonous gas, not yet—and its creator, who welcomed them with open arms." Corwenna smiled at the thought of it.

"And that's how we all came here?"

"It's a story for another time. But you don't think all those woodways were built by magic, do you? The boat carried not just dreams, but carpenters, engineers, bakers, and builders. They brought whole cities in their heads, but not the dark machines that filled the sky with clouds of filthy smoke. They only needed guidance to make sure the mistakes of Maw were not repeated."

Corwenna stood up. "It is late and you are in need of rest. I must finish." She sighed to herself. "You do know the woman's name, of course?"

Ark could see a word forming in his mind but would not believe it. He remembered the carving scratched into the wood outside Corwenna's home.

"Yes, Ark . . . Diana."

"Then, there is no . . . Goddess?" The words stumbled out as Ark's tongue recoiled from the idea that tripped off it.

"What is a goddess? What does that mean? You can understand the minds of animals, you can sense the trees, but does that mean we should worship *you*, young Ark?"

"No . . . I . . . that's not fair!" His mind raced. Was every prayer a waste of both breath and thought?

"Not necessarily. You are born both of science and the wood. The intention behind your whispered words to Diana was right. Perhaps that is part of what kept you going. You know I have always been watching and waiting for you. The ravens are your guardians. That is why they have never hurt you, however close you may have thought you were to death. The feather you found was plucked from the breast of my most precious bird. When the time comes, it will serve you again." She paused and her green eyes suddenly looked distant. "That day I placed you and your twin in the arms of the people whom you know as your mother and father, I was abandoning my own children." Corwenna stared down at him with unexpected tenderness.

Ark felt his heart almost burst. Suddenly, it made sense, even though he didn't want it to. "But my twin died. You didn't leave us in their arms, you left us in a nest in the cold!" he cried out.

"Yes, you're right, and though you understand it not, I ask your forgiveness. In the times to come, you will meet her again."

Before Ark could even think of a reply, Corwenna grabbed his hands. "There are even more important things at stake, Ark. This used to be my motherland. Now men rule the roost and have made a mess of it. I am old. It is up to you to act. As long as you know that, then there is hope. We must tend to your talent. Who knows what you are capable of?"

29 · ACTING SCARED

Petronio was seconds from death. Out of the corner of his eye, he'd glimpsed one end of the weapon. It was completely see-through, shiny and smooth. How did it work? No time to think, as the soldier pressed it hard into his skull. Funny how the ravens were going to get a feast out of him after all.

It wasn't like him to give up so easily. How was he going to save himself? Maybe prayers were the answer.

"I have to make my peace by kneeling," he mumbled. It was a risk. Either his head would be blown off or the soldier would find some tiny shred of conscience inside his breast.

"Get on with it, then, and no funny tricks."

Petronio could hear the man's impatience. It was a start. "And how would I learn to take on a fully armed soldier in school?" Petronio slowly backed out of the hole until they both stood inside the hollow trunk, balancing on a warped and rusting iron platform at the top of the steps. A shaft of midday light poured through the hole, filling the clammy gloom. A blossom bat flew past, protesting at being disturbed. At least the weapon had moved back a few inches and was no longer sticking into his skull. Good.

"Don't know and don't care."

"What, you don't care about killing a helpless kid?" Petronio made his voice frail and whiny, his whole body language that of a terrified child, as he slowly slid into a kneeling position. The man was behind him still, near enough for Petronio to smell his breath with its strange scent of mint.

"One less Dendran, as far as I'm concerned. Now get on with it. You've got thirty seconds."

He made one last effort to keep the conversation going, every word wavering. "I didn't see anything, honestly." Petronio could have kicked himself as he had a sudden brain wave. This man wasn't his enemy! It was all a misunderstanding. He simply had to prove it. "I'm on your side! I've been working for Lady Fenestra." Petronio heard a shocked gasp in response.

"Don't you dare say that name out loud!" The man sounded panicked for a second, ready to do anything.

"But—"

"But nothing. If you were on our side, why were you spying on us?" Brutal logic.

Petronio had no answer. *Curiosity* wouldn't be a good answer. He crouched on the wood, feeling the rough surface on his knees. This was ridiculous. He really was on their side. But mentioning the Mawish envoy had the opposite effect than he'd intended. Big mistake. There was only one way out now.

"You little rat," the soldier blustered. "What corner did you scurry from? You've heard too much. You need your mouth shut permanently, as I topple your overweight body off this stupid branch. Now pray!" This soldier was used to commanding his inferiors, and this bit of scum was running out of time.

Petronio bowed his head and began mouthing the words he'd learned in kirk. "Lay me down in sweet glades. Though I walk through the woods of the dead, thou art with me, thy stick and thy staff to comfort me. . . ." The words were by rote, but every part of Petronio's body was tensed up, ready for action. He heard a grating click and figured out that the man's weapon was ready. Then Petronio sensed him leaning closer and closer, intent on doing the job.

Now! Petronio's left leg kicked out like a horse's and made instant contact with the man's shin. There was a satisfying crunching sound as the shin shattered and the soldier collapsed on the ground, screaming, with his foot at an unnatural angle, white bone exposed to the air. At the same moment, Petronio heard a sound like a soft *swoosh* of feathers and felt an intense stinging pain in his ear. No time to think. He leapt up, wondering if Diana had answered his prayers after all. As he jumped over the man to head for the stairs, an arm shot up and grabbed his leg.

"You little—"

"Not so little after all!" said Petronio as he aimed a savage kick with his free leg, connecting with a part of the soldier that caused him to double up in further agony and begin piteously mewing like a kitten. The arm let go and Petronio began pounding down the stairs. The soldier he'd first spotted wasn't far away. Petronio was in serious danger. Maybe he should have snatched up the man's weapon, but he didn't know how it to use it. As far as he was concerned, it was a lump of strange glass that would slow him down.

A few seconds later, he reached the bottom of the stairs with four archways heading in different directions. He peered right, just in time to see the second soldier only yards away, pointing his transparent weapon.

By now, Petronio had figured out that whatever came out of the glass would be fast and lethal. He heard a second, almost silent *swoosh* and ducked. Part of the archway collapsed, showering him with splinters. Petronio turned and fled, hoping to find refuge among the parasite ferns that covered the route he'd used to get here. He might not be wearing camouflage, but given enough greenery, maybe he stood a chance.

He wished he could stop and talk some sense into the soldiers, tell them that without him, Fenestra would be nowhere. But it was too late for words. Projectiles whizzed past his head like demented swallows. Petronio dived for the first patch of ferns, rolling as he landed in the soft clump. The branchway was wide enough to support a whole colony of these annoying plants. For once, Petronio was glad of Council ineptitude. He crawled left, then right, squeezing his way like a scaffield mole deeper into the foliage.

There were spies here, too: sudden strands of nettles hidden until it was too late. Petronio tried to ignore their attacks. Better a few stings than sudden death. Petronio paused to catch his breath. He touched his stinging ear and his hand came away red. Maybe the ferns would disguise the smell. Otherwise, the ravens would be on him like maggots to a rotting corpse. This was not turning out to be a good day. Fenestra had told him he had done his part. He should have listened.

He picked up the sound of the soldier angrily kicking at the ferns.

"Where are you, you piece of foreign muck? One of my best men's down and I'm not gonna let you get away with it!"

Petronio felt righteous anger. Who was the foreigner here? Doubts about Fenestra and her promises to Grasp began creeping into his mind. With soldiers like these in her employ, maybe she'd simply massacre every living Dendran? Once they'd given her what she wanted, what use were they?

The nettles gave him an idea. To fight fire, you need fire. It was what his father's guards had always drilled into him ever since he'd picked up a kitchen knife and thrown it at a rat that was trying to raid the larders. The animal was skewered and a humble kitchen instrument revealed its darker side. Anything could be a weapon. The real talent came in using your brain to create opportunity out of despair.

Petronio gritted his teeth as he grabbed a clump of nettles in his fist and silently pulled them out. The roots had dug deep into rotten bark, but were no match for him. Ignoring the swelling in his fingers, Petronio began to double back. He needed to get behind the soldier, who had made his first elementary mistake. Stamping about and making a lot of noise meant that you couldn't hear what was going on around you.

Petronio took advantage, his bulk moving with considerable ease as he gently probed his way through the ferns until he was almost directly behind the soldier. He thought of different methods his education had afforded him: the kick into the small of the back and, as the enemy falls, the jump onto the neck followed by an easy *snap*; or the surprise throttle, strangulation from behind. Time to try out his improvised weapon.

"Show yourself, you sniveling excuse for a spy!" The man pointed his weapon into the jungle and several branches were splintered into jagged scars.

"Whatever you say!" shouted Petronio, leaping up and around as he smeared nettle leaves all over the soldier's face, rubbing them into his eyes and cheeks and nose, hard.

The effect was instant, and perfect. The soldier fell to his knees, scrabbling at his face as he screamed out in agony. Nothing like a natural weapon to save the day!

Petronio wondered about kicking the soldier over the edge. No. The man's head would balloon up to twice its normal size for a couple of days, but he'd live. And so would Petronio. It was time to get the holly out of here.

Petronio felt the buzz. Nothing beat a good fight and the adrenaline kick still surged its way pleasurably around his body.

Ten minutes ago, he'd nearly been killed, and now? He'd never felt more alive. He strolled away through the jungle, rubbing his swollen hands. As he replayed the action in slow motion in his mind, he heard a sudden, familiar *swoosh*. His gut felt as if it was splintering into thousands of pieces.

"What?" he groaned. So near and yet so far. As his mind began to cloud over, he realized that soldiers always have colleagues. He should have been more careful. He looked down to see what appeared to be a shard of glass sticking out of his chest. Blood instantly bloomed over his doublet. His eyes rolled up and he fell with an echoing thump onto the branchway.

30 · A REALLY BOARING LESSON

Ark slept through the morning and into the afternoon, in a side room as sumptuously furnished as Corwenna's. He had no doubt that the mattress was filled with raven feathers. His dreams were easily as dark. *There was a nest, high in the cruck of a tree, and two babies cradled within. One was crying for all his worth. But the other was coughing, a little body shivering all over as the wind swirled around them like a hungry hunter.* . . .

When Ark finally woke, it was to see Corwenna sitting at the end of the bed, studying him. "I must get back. Little Shiv . . . the King." He tried to sit up, to move away from this old crone who'd told him she was his mother! Perhaps it was just a terrible dream. He was still feeling so weak.

"Ark, this is about more than the King. You know that. In any case, what power does he truly hold? The rot is too deep for him to make a difference."

"I don't know what you expect from me," he said angrily. "You said it was up to me. What can I do against trained soldiers?"

"You do not think well of me!" Corwenna sighed.

"What do you expect? It's not every day the Raven Queen announces she's my mother!" His heart suddenly yearned for home. To be back with Shiv, to be chatting to his father in his cot. Mr. Malikum, a man who climbed a branch and found a pair of orphans. "Then who is my father?"

The green eyes looked away for a second. "One day I shall

explain. If I told you that every tree in this land would hold you in its curling branches like a father would, you might not believe me, yet."

He didn't. He couldn't. Instead, Arktorious Malikum, the foundling boy, son of Arborium, gave a great sob while his new mother held him tight. "And why did you leave me?"

"It was the will of the woods. If you hadn't grown up as a Dendran, you would not have known what to fight for. But the day that I swaddled you both in that cradle of twigs nearly broke my dark heart. And one day, I promise you will understand why your twin had to go on another, far more perilous journey."

Ark felt her hurt then. Corwenna was no longer a strange and powerful being but an old woman grieving for all that she had to lose.

"I'm sorry, but you have a greater purpose, Ark. Deep inside, you know it's the truth." She gently wiped the tears from his cheeks. "Destiny is sometimes hard as heartwood. You prayed for a way to make things right and perhaps Diana, mother of us all, has shown you the way. What is the point of worship if it doesn't bring results? I have been here almost since the wood began. Maybe I can reveal some of its mystery." Corwenna let go of her boy and stood up. "Come, there are clean clothes for you. Once you have taken some food, we shall start. You have to develop the skills that are inside you. You weren't let loose on the sewers without training, were you? You need a teacher."

And she was gone, her black petticoats swirling behind her.

Miserably, Ark stripped off his old sweaty and bloodstained clothes. The cut across his chest had begun to scab over. It was a score rather than a deep wound. He'd been lucky his grotty jerkin had been so thick. There was a zinc-lined basin in the corner, filled with clean-smelling rootwater. As he finished washing, he looked over the new clothes, laid out as if she'd known all along that he was coming.

He pulled on a pair of hose spun from dyed black wool, much less itchy than his old stockings. Over the top went his new britches, of padded black velvet. His shift tied up at the front with horn buttons and he cinched this in with a supple leather waistcote. The shoes were close fitting, far more comfortable than the old ones his father had passed down to him. He looked in the mirror that hung above the basin. *A raven on legs.* Is that what he was? He no longer knew.

Ark stood uncertainly at the threshold of his room. Corwenna had said that he could save Arborium. All at once, he hated her *and* knew she was the one who could help him do it. So far, he'd only felt the loneliness of a mealworm and thrown a feather through the air. It was hardly wood-shattering.

He took a deep breath and finally pulled open the door to a staggeringly bright day. The light punched its way through the canopy. The branchway ahead appeared empty. He looked out toward the mountains and home. He felt so alone. This place with its jungle of wrinkled trees all woven together was alien and yet eerily beautiful. Where was Corwenna? He looked all around at the deserted canopy. Today there were no eyes staring back at him from the trees.

Ark tentatively walked along the road, with each step soaking up the rays of sun that darted about the curving path. As the rays warmed his face, he felt strength returning to his body. After a few hundred yards, he saw a huge trunk looming upward. The way widened and began to shelve into a perfectly round cruck pool, its surface smooth like a giant eye reflecting the blue of the sky above. Only this pool appeared to be natural, untouched by Dendran saw or chisel. Instead of sluice gates and aqueducts to channel the rootwater from far below, this concave hollow where two giant branches met the rearing trunk must have been filled with rainwater. To one side, on a raised wooden platform, sat Corwenna, cross-legged, her eyes closed, her body still as stone.

Ark coughed lightly.

"Ah!" said Corwenna, opening her eyes. "Are you hungry? I'm starving."

"I don't know. Why?" The dawn meal suddenly seemed a long time ago.

Corwenna stood. The fingers of her left hand uncurled, beckoned to Ark from across the cruck pool. "If you are hungry, you will learn. Come."

"What? You want me to walk across the water?"

Corwenna frowned. "No. I think we'll leave that to the legends. This afternoon we go hunting. We haven't got much time."

Ark saw she was pointing out the path around the edge of the pool. He was still tired. If only he could plunge into those delicious depths, but Corwenna had already vanished into the trunk behind her. He ran to catch up, jumping down the stairs inside the trunk two at a time.

The Ravenwood felt different. Yes, there were hollow trunks and branchways. But there, the similarities ended. While Arborium was engineered, this place, hidden on the other side of the mountains, felt as if every part had been grown. Even the stairs he pounded down were higgledy-twiggledy. Perhaps the tree itself had decided to take up carpentry. Edges melted into each other, and the steps were concave hollows rather than carefully planed treads. As he caught up with Corwenna at the next level down, she paused by a hollow archway strewn with ivy. The branchway that led out ahead of them kinked and twisted as if it was a snake fossilized into wood. Instead of scaffolding and supports, the giant branch wriggled out from the trunk and fused into the branch of the next tree. The track that crossed between the trunks and over the great deeps below had been gouged and pressed into the bark by the hooves of unknown creatures.

"Where are we going?"

"In Arborium, everyone rushes. They talk about going *straight* to work. Or they say, 'I'll be there *straight*away.' When Arborium began, it was not meant to be thus and it is not so here, the one place Dendrans have not reached with their influence. My dream, and I hope it is yours, is that our whole wood can be made clean once again, if you play your part. Be careful and follow me close."

Corwenna turned away from him and plunged into the path. Ark tried to follow, even though the branchway supported its own living forest—a tangle of gigantic rhododendron, laurel, and clumps of hawthorn that sprung up from the path and scratched away the smartness of his new apparel. The scents and colors assailed him from all sides, disorienting and dazing him, flower petals the size of ravens' wings fluttering past his vision. As he tried to push through the bushes, he was aware of other movements and scurrying sounds. The worst that Arborium had to offer were bad-tempered wasps drunk on fermented apples. He didn't want to know what lay hidden in the shadows off these pathways. "Wait for me!" he shouted, turning a corner and almost bumping into his new teacher.

"Hush!" Corwenna put a finger to her lips. "Can you not hear them?"

Ark was itchy and hot. The only sound he could now hear was the occasional squawk of ravens high overhead.

"You remember when you were trapped in the sewers and the guard came to stare in at the porthole?" she whispered.

"Yes." He was no longer surprised that she seemed to know everything.

"The feather-gift was part of it. A raven does not shed his cloak lightly. It was a sacrifice for my Hedd to give up one of his breast feathers. He knew it would be used well. . . . But the other comes from what made you. You were born on wood. You come from the wood. Therefore you have inherited the skills of every tree. You simply have to discover them."

Corwenna fell silent, and then he heard it. A drumming in the distance, reverberating through the branch and into the soles of his feet.

"Quick now." She grabbed Ark tight around the shoulders, her sharp fingernails digging through his shift and into his skin. "This is a deadly test. You must be all ears. These trees, at their core, hold stillness dear. It is the reason why we always come back to the wood for our dark hearts' ease. Remember the guards!" With that, she let him go.

What the holly was she on about? The path was empty. Corwenna vanished as easily as the world he'd left behind.

The drumming sound grew louder. A few hawthorn leaves fell, as if some far-off giant had shaken its tiny, twisted branches. Whatever lay ahead of him on the path approached at speed.

Ark found his heartbeat speeding up as his eyes nervously tried to pierce the shadows. "Corwenna?" he croaked, dry-throated. His legs had the sudden urge to turn around the way they came and run holly-for-leather.

Too late. As the drumming grew into a roar, the thicket ahead of him suddenly gave up its secrets.

"Oh!" Ark gasped. When Corwenna had mentioned hunting, he had no idea she meant this.

A phalanx of wild boar thundered straight toward him along the path. They were only twenty feet away, closing fast.

Ark had seen the odd boar back at home. Occasionally, one found its way into town from the wilder parts of Arborium and everyone ran around screaming at what was basically an overgrown pig. Admittedly, the tusks might give you a bad cut if it charged you, but boar weren't terribly intelligent. Step out of the way and they would run on, leaving most Dendrans shaking but safe.

Corwenna had warned Ark about the Ravenwood. She was right. These beasts, like the trees around them, had been twisted and stretched out of all recognition. They were mountains of muscles on legs, with the addition of a pair of tusks that could easily impale a whole family on their sharpened lengths. One was enough to take your breath away and remember every prayer that had ever been thrown upon the wind. But a horde of them, shaking the very wood they thundered along? He didn't stand a chance.

Every word Corwenna had spoken instantly fled from his mind, except that it was obvious he was born from the trees. Ark was rooted to the spot in the center of the path. Like a sissy sapling, he was about to be snapped in half.

31 · HUNGER TO LIVE

If Mucum had been around, he would have made a joke about being boared to death. But there was no best mate to invent an instant plan of action. Instead, Ark faced a battalion of wild beasts. If the thundering of their hooves didn't shake him off the branch, then their tusks were guaranteed to punch daylight straight through his guts.

Corwenna said she was his mother! Would a mother really leave him to be trampled to death? Ark felt the sweat on his forehead. The boars were so close he could smell their scent, rank and strong. Their unblinking eyes were like bright coins. He was terrified.

Corwenna's last words suddenly came to him. *Remember the guards!* What had he done as he and Mucum were trapped behind the door? The boars were ten feet away now, their heads lowered, ready to scoop him from the path.

As Ark felt the lead animal's breath, as the monster's tusks were ready to plunge into his chest, every word Corwenna said fell into place. Now he had no raven feather to clutch. She had said that he came from the trees, and what did trees do best? They stood there throughout all seasons, holding out against driving rain and pummeling wind. Well, being "rooted to the spot" might not be such a bad idea. His heart filled with a crazy confidence. It was almost as reckless as jumping off the edge. He'd either live or die, two sides of a coin spinning through the air toward him.

At the last second, Ark looked down. If he was part of the

trees, the boars would ignore him. But to turn away from the oncoming horde felt like an act of folly. Every part of Ark's body tensed.

The animals did not check their stride. Instead, they flowed past Ark, their sides brushing against him as if he was a solid rock. In the space of one breath, the boars were gone, behind him, trampling bushes as they vanished down the highway.

Ark slowly unclenched himself, twisting his head around, unable to believe he'd done it. He was miraculously unmarked. All that remained was the faint smell already being borne away by the breeze.

A sound of clapping interrupted the silence. "A little bit last-minute, but it will do, I think." Corwenna glided out of the shadows, her feathered cloak flaring out behind her like a pair of wings.

"It'll do?" Ark's voice felt dried up. At least his feet were working again as he turned to face Corwenna, though there was a moment when the soles of his shoes almost stuck to the wooden surface. "I could have been killed!"

"Yes."

"And that's all you've got to say?"

"No. You could have, but you weren't. I believed in you, Ark." Corwenna's eyebrows arched in amusement. "But I'm still hungry."

"I'm sorry," said Ark. "Let me get this straight. I nearly died a few seconds ago and you're more concerned about your appetite?" Ark was usually meek and mild; he was changing, transforming into something else. Mucum was the one to get mouthy. What was happening to him?

"Yes. But don't worry. Our friends are coming back and this time we shall not let them go so easily."

"What do you mean?" As the branch began to quiver, he knew exactly what she meant. "Oh no, not again!" Lessons at school were never like this. At least you didn't risk life and limb.

"Now listen well. I shall not leave you this time. But you must do as I say."

Despite what he'd achieved, Ark felt the fear again. He wasn't ready for yet another encounter. Not this soon. His lips went dry and his heart began to slam against his ribs as if it were a bird trying to escape the bony cage. It was for the good of Arborium. "Fine. Tell me. All right." If worse came to worst, he could surely play statues one more time.

"If you are truly of the wood, then there is much to be discovered." She pulled out a small mirror and handed it to Ark. "You must reflect on this and always know that light is both friend to the leaves and yourself."

"A mirror?" he squealed. "But I don't need to comb my hair!"

"Don't be silly, young Ark. Use the light!"

The branch beneath them shuddered as the living, breathing, stinking mass of boars stampeded toward them. There were only seconds to spare.

A ray of sunlight hit the mirror and bounced off it, lighting up a small patch of the woods to the left of the path. "Oh!" said Ark, wondering if he had time. He swung his hand, trying to direct the small beam onto the way ahead. It wavered and bucked before he finally focused it on the lead boar now only a few feet away.

"Good!" whispered Corwenna in his ear.

Ark still had no idea whether it would work, until the mirror caught the lead boar's eyes. The effect was instant. The boar was blinded. It crashed headlong through the bushes that lined the woodway and slipped off the edge. The others in the herd played a brutal game of follow-my-leader, the sound of their high-pitched squeals excruciating as one after another toppled through the gap. Ark gasped with dismay. He hadn't intended a massacre.

But Corwenna had chosen her spot with care. The forest was particularly thick here, and the branches that radiated out beneath them a woven warren. Living high up in the canopy gave the boars agility. They tumbled and fell like airborne cats, each one managing to land upright on the thicket below, scrabbling for purchase on the bark, and then squealing off onto other paths into the deep woods.

All except one that still stood on the path in front of him. Maybe this tusked giant was a throwback or, like Ark, *different*. It was not fooled by the business with the mirror but more interested in attacking those responsible for nearly destroying its kin. It approached slowly, eyes consciously turned from the mirror, tusks lowered, ready to spear Ark to kingdom come.

"Well done, my boy!" called Corwenna.

Ark was surprised. He was about to be gored to death and Corwenna offered congratulations.

However, it was not him she addressed as Corwenna stepped out toward the lone boar. "We are impressed with your resolve." As she spoke, she held the animal's gaze.

Ark watched from the side as the boar stamped and snorted at its enemy. It stood its ground. Corwenna put up her hands as if showing the beast that she had no weapons and stared at it, unblinking. "There now. Easy." She coaxed the creature with her stare. It shuffled forward like a dog, drawn to heel.

Up close, Ark could see the creature was as frightened as he was.

Without moving, Corwenna hissed at Ark, "What are you waiting for? Find the blade in my belt. Use it."

Ark saw the hilt peeking out from her petticoats. "You want me to—?"

"The will of the woods. Eat or be eaten. Between the eyes is most merciful."

Ark found himself moving in slow motion, lifting the blade out as Corwenna kept control. He felt sickened by the Raven Queen's power.

"I can't!" he whimpered.

"If we turn away, this animal will happily deal with both of us. We need to eat. What is it to be?"

Ark made a decision. He raised the knife high above the boar's head. The forest stilled and Ark was aware of Corwenna suddenly dropping to her knees and murmuring:

> *"Enter thee into the dark,*
> *Honor to thy shape and spark!"*

Before he had a chance to question what Corwenna was doing, Ark's hand was free again, slamming down toward its target. He caught one last glimpse of the boar's eyes, flicking toward his in terror before the blade went in.

The boar gave a sigh, before slowly toppling over on its side. Ark pulled the blade out in disgust. Blood oozed slowly over the woodway. Mucum killed the sewer rat with ease, and Petronio would have happily skewered his former schoolmate. But any sense of victory eluded Ark. Killing went against all that the Warden spoke of.

"You are shocked. But his passage to the other side will be safe now."

"What . . . ?" The image of Goodwoody kneeling in kirk came into his head.

"Exactly," Corwenna answered. "Do you think we do not honor the dead?" She stood up, watching Ark closely. "Besides, it was a good lesson. You will need a strong stomach for what is to come, my child. And we only have a few days to prepare you."

Ark watched as a raven tumbled from the sky only a few feet away. The boy backed up. Maybe Corwenna did control the ravens, but those claws could easily rip him in half.

"This is Hedd!" said Corwenna.

A pair of dark, pupil-less eyes looked down at him. Was he expected to say hello?

"You can say what you want. But it might be good to temper your fear with admiration." Corwenna strolled toward Hedd and stroked the bird under his beak. He gave a deep, rumbling caw of pleasure. "These birds are the beating heart of this forest."

"Well, er . . . thanks for rescuing me from Petronio," Ark said, feeling rather stupid.

The bird inclined his head as if he understood, then plucked the dead boar from its resting place. With a flap of huge feathers, both bird and beast were gone into the green gloom.

"Come. Hedd shall carry our dinner ahead of us. This morning, I was not sure if you were up to the tasks I had set to you, but now I am forced to praise you!"

"Why? I stood still, worked out how to use a mirror, and stabbed a poor creature to death. That's not going to save the wood, is it?" Ark felt nauseous.

"Your Holly Woodsmen preach about be-leaf. Maybe you need some of that faith right now. You and your friends might become a force to be reckoned with."

Corwenna had a point, though Ark's hands felt dirty. "I suppose I did all right. It beats plunging toilets any day." Then he remembered the way the boar looked at him as the knife went in.

"If you are to succeed, you must become friends with death. That is what lies ahead of you, if you are willing."

"My best friend is probably dead. Isn't that enough for you?" He was sick of the fight, sick of the way Corwenna plucked thoughts from his mind like a scavenging crow. The afternoon's events were catching up on him. He felt his body tremble all over, as if his limbs were turning to jelly.

A few hours later, and with a bowl of boar stew sitting comfortably in his stomach, Ark lay back in bed.

Corwenna sat with him. It felt strange. His mother . . . his other mother was the one who normally came to sit by his bed.

"What do you mean about becoming friends with death?" The words twisted around his head, like this strange wood that now held him in its grip.

"You'll see. This training is not for nothing. It is part of a journey you have been destined to take since the day you were born. I hope you are up to it."

Ark didn't like the sound of that.

"I'm sure you don't. Ark, I am old and frail, and you are Arborium's future. Soon, all shall become clear." She nodded her head once and stood. "Whatever prayers you have, use them now before you sleep. I shall leave you." She swept out through the open door, which shut behind her as quickly as it blew open.

It was too much. At least the bed was warm. He had a new mother, he was supposedly the future for Arborium, and the people he loved were in terrible danger. And now, he found out that he'd been praying not to some far-off goddess all his life, but to his own grandmother. Ark hugged himself. Even though he was exhausted, his head would not leave him alone. He closed his eyes, but all he could see was his little sister with her impish grin; the smell of the smoky fire at home; Mucum blundering toward him, desperate to avenge his honor; Petronio's dismissive laugh; the gleam of the ore in the root tunnels down below; the faraway voices plotting destruction as their sounds filtered through the plumbing. It all washed over him like ripples until his body finally had enough and he drifted into a long, troubled sleep.

32 · DUNGEON DELIGHT

"Where in Diana's dim and inglorious name is my son?" Grasp sat behind his desk. If he had had any remaining hair, he would have been pulling it, hard. Instead, he took out his anger on the man in front of him.

"Don't know, sir. 'Aven't seen 'im." Since when was Salix responsible for that preening wood louse?

"You don't know, do you? That's your problem," hissed Grasp. "The people I employ tend to know nothing about nothing. It's a wonder I even bother to pay you!"

The guard fingered the stiletto in his belt, idly wondering how it would look plunged deep into his arrogant employer's eye. "Well, I could go and look for him, I suppose." The last thing Salix wanted to do was head out into the cold. He'd saved the boy's life once. As far as Bombax Salix was concerned, that was once too often.

Grasp paused, puffing out his chest hidden behind a ridiculously pink satin doublet. "He's probably out sucking the sap or some other such nonsense." The Councillor allowed himself a single, grim twitch of his lips. He'd been a hollyraiser when younger. And the boy was only fourteen after all . . . still, it was rather late. "Well, then. Let me know when he returns. You can send him to my quarters."

Salix turned to go.

"By the way, have you told the Malikum parents that their son is truly and finally dead?"

Salix nodded his head. The plumber's boy had got away from

them too many times. But to escape the clutch of the ravens? It had never been done, and Salix was not stupid enough to believe in miracles. The task of informing the parents had been the only satisfying part of his day. To see the once feisty mother reduced to a shambling wreck was pure pleasure, and the way the boy's father crumpled back into his pathetic cot brought a savage twinkle to the guard's eye.

"Good. We still have the girl as leverage, which should keep them quiet until our plans are accomplished. Leave me."

Salix knew that Grasp liked his minions to walk backward out of his office in some kind of pathetic deference. He did the opposite, swiftly turning and walking to the door. To slam or not to slam, that was the question. He decided that leaving the door slightly ajar was a small victory, especially when he heard Grasp heave himself up a few seconds later and stomp toward the door, swearing loudly.

"Buddy draft! Buddy incompetent nincompoops with squit for brains!" The slam, when it came, was particularly loud. Much as Grasp loathed his underlings, they were necessary for the dirty work of politics. Insolence would never result in getting the sack and Salix knew it as he whistled cheerfully all the way downstairs.

Three floors below, in a cell lined with planks and riveted with iron, Mucum paced up and down like a caged dog. His ribs ached and the point where Petronio's punch had driven home felt like one big bruise. The night before, the guard had given him a helpful shove.

"Welcome to your new home!" he'd said. "Oh, and would sir like a snack before bed?" Salix had paused briefly, savoring the moment, while not waiting for the answer. "Well, tough luck!"

The door had slammed, and the massive key scraped around the lock, leaving Mucum to both the dark and hours of sleepless regret.

If only he'd stopped Ark from leaving the Rootshooters' station. It was all his fault! And now his best mate was dead, ripped apart by the ravens. Suddenly, he missed his dad. The old geezer wasn't too bad, really, and he must have been tearing his hair out, wondering where his lad had got to. There would be tears at some point, but for now he was only focused on what lay in front of him. He knew his own chances weren't looking too good, either. At least he wasn't alone.

A high-pitched squeal brought him back to the present.

"It's an upside-down lady with funny eyes!"

Mucum lay on the excuse for a mattress, trying to get some sleep. He huddled farther into the corner, trying to escape the slicing wind that came through the gaps in the walls. "What are you on about, Shiv?" He'd never understand the minds of little kids. They were truly a few planks short of a cupboard.

"Upside down!" Ark's sister insisted.

"Yeah, right!" Mucum was surprised they'd stuck him in with her. For much of the night before, she'd sobbed her tiny heart out and for a while, as he tried to calm her down with a good cuddle, he had forgotten about his own problems. Instead, he thought about his earliest memory, being held in his mother's arms. Those days were long gone.

Shiv jumped up and down, disturbing the dust on the floor. "And she's blowin' a kissy. Oooh, she's blowin' it to you! Look, Moocum!"

"Please, Shiv, leave it out, eh! I've had a bit of a rough time and I'm not in the mood for yer games." He hadn't dared tell the little girl about her brother. What did it take for someone to imprison a four-year-old? "Now, when yer finished makin' fings up, how about we work out a plan to get us out of here, eh?" Mucum finally turned over and sat up.

A shaft of moonlight broke through the high-up, barred window frame. And there, as Shiv had told him over and over, was an upside-down face.

"Yow promised to come back and see me!" Her eyes twinkled like a pair of mischevious fireflies.

Mucum jumped up and ran to stand under the window. "Flo! What the holly are you doing here?"

"Thought Oi'd pop by for a visit. Ain't yow going to introduce me?" Flo was hanging the wrong way up, her legs wrapped around a length of rope, her pale white face filled with concern.

"Well . . . erm . . . This is little Shiv. Shiv, this is my friend Flo."

"Told you so!" said Shiv. She turned to the window and gave a little curtsy. "Pleased to meet you. Do you walk on your hands?"

"Only when moi feet are sore!"

Shiv giggled, peeking at those two enormous eyes through her interlaced fingers.

Mucum couldn't get over it. "You came all that way, just ter see me?"

"Warghh! Weren't that bad, with the lift 'n' all. Easy as . . . as pie! I hope yow missed me?"

"Course I did." Mucum was glad it was dark and no one could see him blushing.

"Oi be glad of that!" Flo smiled. "Now, Oi thought yow might want this." With much effort, the upside-down Flo reached a hand into her knapsack, which was threatening to fall into the forest depths below as it hung from around her neck.

Mucum was excited. If she'd brought a hacksaw, they could cut through the bars and be out of there.

"Thar we go!" She pushed a wrapped-up lump through the gap.

Mucum reached up and caught it. He pulled off the cloth. "What's this?" He frowned.

"Oi *brought* yow a pie!"

"Oh . . . thanks. A lot." Mucum couldn't believe it. Petronio would consider him a very overgrown loose end. There was no way the Councillor's son would let him out of here alive. And what had his girlfriend brought him? A pie!

"What am I supposed to do with this?"

Flo's eyes filled with tears. "Why, yow be eatin' it, moi handsome, and sharing it out with that little girly yow be lookin' after, that's what. Ain't it no good?"

"Oh. I'm sorry, Flo. It smells great." Mucum almost kicked himself. Her only thought had been of him all this time.

Flo instantly cheered up. "Yas! It be made of dulberries, but the taste is not dull at all!" She crinkled her nose at her own joke.

At that moment Mucum felt his heart cleave in half as if an ax had sliced through it. He remembered the dulberry patch growing deep in the hollow roots beneath the diving station. How could he have thought Rootshooters grew in the soil? This girl was flesh and blood. "Good on yer, Flo! What 'ave I done to deserve this?"

"Why, yow be an honorable boy. That be plenty! Don't give up hope yet! Boi the way, don't bite too sudden on that pie; thar be something sharp and useful hidden inside! Warghhh!"

Every time Mucum thought the Rootshooters were not quite all there, they proved him wrong. To survive down in the depths of the tree required brains. Flo had brought him everything he needed. Food, and a weapon for when the right moment came. Maybe he wouldn't die after all.

"Give us a kiss, then!"

Mucum was shocked. A kiss? "Err . . . Flo, not sure if you've noticed, but I'm kind of in prison here."

"That be no problem for a big boy loike yow! Now come 'ere!"

At work, no one told Mucum what to do. Even Jobby Jones phrased his commands in a way that suggested Mucum might be doing them all a favor. But when it came to girls, Mucum was out of his league. He hadn't had the courage at the Rootshooter party. It was now or never. He reached up the bars and strained, lifting his whole body off the floor. He pushed his mouth between the bars, feeling like a fool.

"Yuck!" said Shiv. "That's disgusting!"

But before their lips could touch, there was a sudden slam far off in the building and footsteps coming closer.

"Aww!" said Flo, pulling away. "Never yow mind! We be savin' that kissy for later."

Mucum did mind. Life definitely wasn't fair! He dropped back to the floor, aware of the danger.

"Oi'll be back in a few hours, Oi promise! Yow must get thee and the girl out before the night is done and then we shall meet up," Flo whispered.

"Wait, girl!" Mucum hissed. "How am I gonna —?"

There was no answer, only a tug on the rope. Flo's face rose up and away, vanishing as if she had been no more than a moony vision.

Mucum had no time to think. He put his fingers to his lips, shaking his head at Shiv to tell her to be quiet as he quickly hid the food and its lifesaving contents under the mattress. As the footsteps pulled to a halt outside the cell door, he hoped they hadn't been overheard. If they had, then a dulberry pie and a tiny knife would be no defense against the thrust of a well-aimed sword.

33 · THE MIRACLE OF TECHNOLOGY

"You had a very, very lucky escape."

Petronio heard the words as if they were muffled. He knew they were addressed to him and that the voice was female. He also worked out that his chest hurt, as if some buddy carpenter had mistaken it for a plank and been practicing with hammer and nails. At that moment, his eyes were still closed, but the voice was evidence enough that he was probably alive. He doubted that the boatman on the River Sticks would have such a feminine lilt. Anyhow, if he were dead, it would hardly be called "an escape."

What exactly had Petronio escaped from? It came flooding back as a groan of pain issued from his lips: his little spying expedition; the soldier ready to shoot him after he said his prayers; the nettles rubbed in the other soldier's face. Petronio flexed his fingers, feeling the swollen bumps where the stinging plants had exacted their revenge.

As he tried to open his eyes, the voice continued. "As for my men, it took a good deal of persuasion to stop them from stringing you up from the nearest branch, especially as one of them had a shattered tibia thanks to your efforts. Though as a surgeon's apprentice, I'm sure you knew what you were doing."

He could detect a grudging hint of admiration in the now comfortingly familiar voice.

"Here, drink."

Petronio felt his head lifted up as Lady Fenestra's face finally came swimming into view. "Ow! Lights too bright . . . ," he murmured. The drink was fizzy and sweet.

"Yes, well, this is a flypod surgery bay after all. The morphine has reduced the pain. The eight hours of sleep should have helped as well. How the glass bullet managed to miss your heart, I will never know. It might be worth thanking the quaint goddess you worship on this little island."

Petronio grunted with the effort as he tried to sit up. Fenestra obliged by putting more pillows behind his back to give support. Aside from the bed, it was as if he'd been transported into a fantasy land. There was some kind of clear tube running into his arm. And two discs rested on his bandaged chest, joined by wires to a square box on a trolley. A number blinked out of the box.

"Eighty-four bpm resting rate. Considering your internal injuries, your heart is doing remarkably well."

But as Petronio looked around, the number began to shoot up. He was surrounded by lights and levers lining the wall of some huge, metallic cocoon. There were too many straight lines for his liking. His first instinct was to rip all the wiring away and get out, quick. There was a window, and the glow of infernal machinery lit up the nighttime forest beyond. That was what he knew. Safe. Familiar. Maybe he could kick the glass out, squeeze through the frame? But his arms felt heavy and his legs wouldn't do what they were told.

"Calm yourself, young Grasp. You are protected here." Fenestra's usually cold eyes filled with concern. "If your own so-called doctors had experimented on you with their primitive bloodsucking leeches, you'd be dead meat. Our technology saved your life."

Petronio gasped. "Flypod, bullit . . . tek . . . no-log-y?" Every word sounded strange on his lips. But if he was alive and bandaged, then maybe Fenestra was speaking the truth. He hadn't been sucked into the belly of an alien beast but was convalescing in a cave of wonders. He took a deep breath, willing his stupid heart to follow orders and slow down. Next came curiosity, the part of Petronio that had gotten him into trouble in the first place. He was suddenly greedy for the meaning behind these strange words. All in good time. A sudden wave of sickness passed through his system. "Thank you," he finally muttered, before sinking back on the pillows.

"It was partly my fault," mused Fenestra. "You had done your duty, and done it well, convincing the Commander with a bag of somewhat valuable coins. But then I dismissed you. The way you found my trail was" — she paused briefly, looking at the pale boy on the bed — "enterprising. My men are highly trained. It is not easy to creep up on them, let alone take two of them down without a weapon in sight. Naturally, there are consequences to this. They have been demoted as punishment for letting a mere boy show them up."

"Wanted to know . . . ," Petronio whispered in his desperation to impress her with his initiative. "Found the plans and —" The drilling started up again in his chest. He felt the urge to scream, but clamped the agony down tight. "Had to see where you . . . were hiding."

"And you succeeded. We chose a part of the woods that was unlikely to be found, well away from the city. You are our first visitor, aside from a few curious goats. By the way, this is yours, I think." She handed him a long thin shard that resembled an icicle.

"What's this?"

"Your lucky charm. Shot from one of my men's g-guns at a thousand meters a second with the aim of slicing open your heart. My personal surgeon dug it out of you. You wanted to know what a bullet was. Here. You've earned it."

Petronio fingered the projectile, feeling its lethally honed edge. Glass belonged in windows. This took boring materials into a whole new dimension. Suddenly, arrows and knives were tedious and dull.

"Yes. I have grown used to the miraculous properties of fire-arms. In Maw, we take such things for granted."

Petronio was filled with awe. *Firearm* was the perfect description—like an extra invisible limb that could call forth instant flame. What he could do with one of these slung around his shoulder! The thought of stupid Dendrans begging for mercy under the gaze of such a weapon was more than appealing. The little island of Arborium suddenly seemed lacking in excitement.

Fenestra continued, "Naturally, we had to have a base, a place to prepare. My method of transport? You're sitting inside it."

Petronio's eyes flicked around again as he remembered what he'd seen the day before, hovering high over the forest. "The metal bird? I'm inside it?" He looked at the number on the blinking box again shooting up to 105, 106, 107. He was both terrified and excited. No wonder his heart was slamming away under his ribs. "You can fly!"

"Yes. We can. The skies and the rest of this planet belong to us. The only tiny, fetid green spot of resistance is right here. But yes, compared to your lumbering ravens, our machines are far superior."

Petronio detected her condescending tone. Arborium must feel so backward to her. But there was one thing that didn't make sense. "With all this tekni . . . er . . . teknologgy . . ."

"Technology," she corrected.

"Right. With all that . . . why didn't you . . . take out Quercus and . . . set up shop?" Petronio was still short of breath.

"Good thinking, young man, and believe me, we would. But the blasted trees appear to have their own powers. Do you remember injecting me?"

Petronio nodded. If he hadn't been curious in the first place, Fenestra would be dead.

"Indeed. If the trees had had their way, I would have been no more than a virus stamped out by their protective gas. I explained this to you before. Making the vaccine is an arduous process and our scientists have been unable to mass manufacture. Otherwise, the armies of Maw would have swamped this backwater long ago. As for dropping molt-bombs, why destroy this most valuable crop, complete with ready-made slaves on site to do our bidding?"

"Molt-bombs? What are they?"

"Superheated glass. Four hundred and sixteen thousand degrees centigrade, dropped from the sky to burn up everything in its path. You'll learn. This place is so backward."

"Still got soldiers."

"Some. We used up all of the last stocks immunizing them. Our researchers have told us the antibodies will only work for a further four days."

"Don't understand." She'd lost him again.

"To put it simply. If we don't pull this off within a few days, we'll fall down dead like your rather pretty leaves. So we'd better hope that Commander Flint earns his wages. Don't worry, though; every computer must have its backup, and so must every plan."

Each time Petronio felt he understood, Fenestra would leave him far behind. What was a backup? What lay behind the plan?

"And a computer is also what you are lying inside. Think of it as a machine with thoughts."

"Logical thoughts," interrupted a smooth, masculine voice.

Petronio nearly jumped out of bed. "Who the holly was that?"

"Only the onboard program," replied Fenestra. "Tell me, George, what is our escape trajectory?"

There was no pause as the voice answered. "All systems up and running within twenty-three seconds. Vertical ascent of three hundred meters will be achieved at fifty-four seconds. We shall then accelerate due west at a cruising speed of one thousand three hundred kilometers per hour, reaching the port of New Walk in five-point-six hours. Have a nice day."

"Thank you. Perimeter scan still clear?"

"There are no foreign elements within two hundred meters."

"Good," said Fenestra, still talking to thin air.

Petronio eyeballed the room. A voice without a body? Totally conkers! "How does it work?"

"Oh really, young Grasp. I am a politician, not a quantum engineer. Probably wave modulation using synthesized speech built into binary consciousness programming. The Dendrans are backward. To even call this a developing country would be an overstatement."

And that's what Petronio felt. More than out of the vine loop. It was like being back at school on his first day, with the older kids laughing because he didn't know where to hang up his cloak. In this room of clean lines, he felt sweaty and awkward.

Fenestra paused. "That sounded harsh. I am sorry. There are those among you who are eager to learn, yes?"

"Yes." She had taken him under her wing. It wasn't a bad place to be.

"That's settled, then. I have not forgotten that you once saved my life. Now I have repaid the favor. That makes us equals. In the coming times, you shall be of use to me, I have no doubt. But don't worry, I will never again treat you as a mere messenger."

Petronio soaked up the compliment and for a brief moment the pain in his chest subsided.

"Oh, your father has been informed of your 'accident' and that you are currently in my care."

"He won't like that. Wants to . . . keep me under his eye."

"Yes, I can see how hard he is on you. I have my own teenage girl. There is an art to looking after them that is lacking in the Councillor. But trust me, he will not argue with his future employer. You need to stay here and recuperate. If the wound heals well, I might be able to convince one of my men to show you the basics of marksmanship. Pulling the trigger of a g-gun is not as easy as it looks. Would you like that?" There was a glint in her eye, filled with temptation.

"I . . ." Petronio felt that he was stepping off the edge of the woodway with a vast drop below.

"If my daughter, Randall, were here, she'd turn you into a sharpshooter within days. But my men are more than up to the task. After you have rested further, you can start. What do you say?"

The nighttime sick bay no longer felt strange. Here was a feast of words, machines, and power, and he, Petronio, had been asked to sit at the top table. At that moment, he would have happily put his prize crossbow on the fire for kindling. The message was clear. She'd saved him for a reason. Those who could learn would profit. How did the old carpenter's saying go? *If you can't nail 'em, join 'em.*

"Yes," said Petronio. He was back in the game.

34 · ESCAPE AND BETRAYAL

Mucum was annoyed with Flo. Admittedly, the pie was tasty, the folded map of the Grasp residence wrapped around it quite useful. The hidden knife was also sharp enough to do the business. But the note she'd left only told him to escape the dungeon and meet her on the woodway as the sun rose.

"Wot am I supposed to do?" Perhaps the Rootshooters were a few roasted chestnuts short of a bagful after all.

"You could vanish!" said Shiv. "Like magic!"

"Yeah, we could do wiv some magic." Mucum's eyes went wide. "Hang on a sec, young lady." He scratched his head, hoping that the plan forming in his brain was worthy of his dead best mate. It was a matter of honor. As for vanishing, well, most cardsharps he met were masters not of magic but deception. "Any good at screaming, little Shiv?"

"Oh yes. I love making a big noisy!" She nodded, her curls tumbling over her shining brown cheeks.

"Good on yer. Think of it like a game. Do yer want to play?"

Shiv bounced up and down on the spot and clapped her hands. "Yes, please!"

"All right. Be ready to give us yer best scream, eh?" He then explained how it would work.

Shiv nodded again. Her beaming smile was thoroughly impish.

"Oakey-doakey! Let's do it!" The cell narrowed toward the single door, leaving a space about four feet wide above the door where the walls closed in. Mucum leaned against one of the walls and lifted his right leg up, planting his foot firmly on the opposite wall. He tensed his leg muscles, hoping they could take the weight as he lifted up his right leg and planted his rubber-soled shoe firmly on the other side. Good. The wall was rough, gripping his sheepskin cote and preventing him from sliding back down. An inch at a time he crabbed his way upward until his bent body was balanced directly over the door frame. By now, his armpits and his back were damp with sweat and he could already feel the ache in his thighs.

"About now would be good, Shiv."

"Now, what?" said Shiv, looking both evil and innocent.

"Oh, Diana help us. Now . . . please!" he said through gritted teeth.

"Oh goody!" said Shiv, opening her mouth impossibly wide and emitting a shriek that should have had Dendran mothers running to her aid from a ten-mile radius. There was a moment's silence followed by the clump of boots.

"Remember your words!" whispered Mucum, feeling his body start to go numb.

The door grate slid open, revealing a single staring eye behind it. "Wot you screamin about, you little brat? Better be good, 'cos you interrupted my kip!"

"He's gone!" wailed Shiv with a convincing touch of terror in her voice.

Hidden above the door, Mucum smiled. Ark's sister was a born actress.

"Gone? Who . . . where?" Alnus was taking a while to catch up.

"He was poorly and got thinner and thinner and thinner." She paused for effect, then began wailing again.

Alnus slammed his hand against the door. What was it

with children? "Can yer spell it out in simple Dendran?"

"Course I can!" Shiv sang. "He got so thin, he vanished. Just like that!" She threw up her arms to indicate the empty cell.

The single eye went wide as it roved around the empty space. Alnus got the message and did not like its contents. "Oh, that's not good, that is. I'm in trouble now!" The key grated in the lock, and the door swung open. "Sure he's not under the bed?"

Mucum wasn't. There was no room and Alnus knew it. What he didn't know was that the prisoner was about a foot above him, trying very hard not to breathe. A drop of sweat fell from his forehead and landed on the guard's tunic. Instinctively, Alnus moved his hand up to his shoulder to feel the patch of wet.

Don't look up! was the only thought in Mucum's head. That, and hoping his legs wouldn't unclamp themselves. If he fell, it would be straight into the welcoming arms of his jailor.

"Damp in 'ere" was the guard's only comment as he peered around the cell, trying to figure out what the holly was going on. "You say 'e got thinner. That don't make no sense!"

As the guard stalked toward the window to see if the lad had somehow wriggled through the bars, Shiv was already backing toward the wide-open door.

It was time for Mucum to make his move. If he could only slide silently to the floor and slip out of the cell, they'd be free. The plan had a few problems. With such a tiny room, any sound was amplified. Even as Mucum slowly lowered himself, a plank behind his back did what all planks do best. It creaked.

Alnus spun around, a look of genuine surprise plastered on his face. "Where'd you come from?" he sputtered. But the guard wasn't about to wait for the answer. He'd already pulled out his stiletto from its sheath and was advancing toward Mucum.

"Calm down, mate. I was jes' practicin' me climbin' skills. No 'arm done, eh?" Mucum retreated, Shiv cowering behind his knees.

"Thought you'd fool me? You're like all the others. Let's play a joke on Alnus, they say. He's always good for a laugh!" The look on the guard's face indicated that there were no fun and games to be had at this particular moment. "Well, I'm gonna make your disappearing act permanent!" Both blade and man leapt through the air, aiming for Mucum's chest, hoping for bloody impact.

Mucum saw the knife flying toward him. He wondered if he had time to pull out Flo's thoughtful gift, currently tucked into the inside flap of his cote. By the time he reached the blade, he'd be dead. Far better to play this the old-fashioned way. He'd been involved in some good fights with the local lads in his time, and the rule of the wood was simple: There were no rules, only survival.

At the last second, as the sharp blade was inches from his rib cage, Mucum leaned back on his left foot and stepped out of the way.

Alnus didn't have time to be surprised as his stiletto stabbed empty air. He was more than surprised, though, when he felt a very well-aimed kick connect between his legs and crush a particularly sensitive part of his anatomy. "Eeeeek!" he screeched in a ridiculously high-pitched voice as the knife tumbled from his hand and clattered onto the floor. It was shortly joined by a body as Alnus collapsed, both hands clutching himself and trying to contain the utter agony that quickly sent him toward unconsciousness.

"Don't be such a wimp!" snarled Mucum, standing over his victim. "My friend was far braver than you'll ever be!"

Shiv ran around and around the knocked-out guard, chanting, "Hit him in the hazelnuts, hazelnuts, hazelnuts, hit him in the hazelnuts, we all fall down!"

"What sorta nursery rhymes are they teachin' you kids these days?" Mucum grabbed her by the hand. "Come on, little Malikum, time to get you home. I need to visit a few old pals and deal with some squit!" Before leaving the cell, he bent over Alnus and took the keys from his belt, his fingers fumbling.

"Ow, me bits!" moaned Alnus as his eyelids fluttered.

"We will *be* in bits if I let you get up, matey!" Mucum delivered a good old crunching uppercut with his right fist. Alnus's head snapped back and almost bounced off the floor. Mucum paused for a second, listening for trouble. "Sleep well!" he said before heaving the guard's unconscious body onto the excuse for a bed and covering it with a blanket. It might buy them some time. Then he took Shiv by the hand and made for the doorway. He peered out nervously. All clear.

"Let's go!" Mucum said. "This way!" He pulled the dungeon door shut and locked it before turning right and hoping that the map of the building was accurate. If it was, then a certain plumbing trapdoor was going to make the perfect hidden exit.

Ten minutes later, they were out and well beyond the house, waiting at the crossroads, thick morning mist hovering just above their ankles. Mucum couldn't believe he'd done it. Maybe, with Flo's help, he'd get to the King after all.

Flo stepped out from behind a laurel bush. "Oi'm glad yow be safe," she whispered.

"Search parties gonna be on their way. We gotta make a move."

"Yas!" Flo seemed in an odd mood. She didn't come forward to embrace Mucum and her voice was uncertain.

Mucum was puzzled. Where was the kiss she promised?

"Let me take the girl and look after her, for now." She put her hands out to Shiv, who happily skipped across the woodway.

"Are we off on a nadventure?"

"Yas. Oi think so." Flo then pulled a blade out of her shift and advanced toward Mucum.

"Wot you doin'?" Mucum was shocked.

"It's for yowr own good, moi boyo!"

"Drop it, Flo. Ain't got time for muckin' about!"

Flo moved with surprising speed, her long legs closing the gap between them. Before he could even put his hands up in defense, she had slashed at his right arm, slicing the skin open.

"Are you an acorn nutter?" Mucum clutched his arm, watching in horror as the blood dripped down and all his faith in the Rootshooters leaked away with it. "Why help me escape and then sell me out?"

Shiv was crying, trying to run from Flo, who held the little girl tight.

Before Flo could answer, she felt a sudden breeze from above.

"Oh no!" Mucum cried, as a raven plunged out of the dew-drenched fog straight toward him. "How could you do this?"

"Oi be sorry!" shouted Flo above the noise of beating wings. "Oi had no choice!" she cried as the bird, drawn by the incense of blood, veered in toward its target.

35 · AN OLD FRIEND

When Ark first heard the voice, he thought he was dreaming.

"Geroff me, you weirdo!"

He sat up in his bed, suddenly awake after a long, deep sleep. He knew that grumbling moan from anywhere. Surely he'd imagined it?

But at that moment, the door to his bedroom slammed open.

"Don't wanna go in no more dungeons, lady. I've 'ad enough prisons to last me a lifetime, right... Hey!" A bulky figure was shoved inside none too gracefully.

"You read the wood as if all is against you. Use your eyes to see the truth!" Corwenna snapped.

Mucum looked up. "Ark! Is that you, old bud? You're supposed to be dead, or am I dreamin' 'ere?"

"No. You're awake. I think." A smile burst like a blossom over his face. The last time he'd seen Mucum, he was fighting for his life in the pouring rain in another country.

"Fair doo-doos!" said Mucum. "I fort the ravens 'ad you. Yer gettin' pretty good at dodgin' death, mate. I'm impressed. Now, can yer tell me 'oo's the crazy hazel-switch with the funny hairdo?" He motioned behind him with his thumb.

"Mucum, meet my m—" But Ark couldn't say it. Not yet. "Meet Corwenna, Queen of the Ravenwood."

The words stopped Mucum in his tracks. "Yer jokin', mate. This bag of wrinkles? I gave up believin' in all that oakey-croakey stuff years ago."

"Did you?" she asked, a hint of danger in her voice. She drew herself up until she suddenly towered over Mucum. Her dark skin shone like coal and her eyes were blinding in their intensity. "I am Corwenna," the voice boomed, carrying within it thunder and lightning, the decay of winter and the urge of spring. "All that is visible and hidden in these woods belongs to me!"

Mucum was convinced. "Oh my giddy tree goats!" He fell to his knees. "Forgive me insults!" He was trembling all over.

Corwenna softened, her figure shrinking to almost Dendran size again. "Oh, do get up! This shuffling around on knees is only for the dullest of pilgrims."

"Righty-ho." Mucum stood up and edged back toward the door. "I'm not dreamin' you or nuffin'?" For someone who didn't believe in all that mumbo jumbo, meeting a bona fide deity was a shock.

"I am as real as the wood you stand on."

"Yeah. Well . . ." His brain couldn't take it all in.

Ark jumped in. "But what happened with Petronio?"

"I was about to sort him out once and for all when one of Grasp's guards crept up behind me with a sword. After that, it was the dungeons. I escaped and then it all went wonky. Me girlfriend tried to cut me in half, and I got stuck in a cage of claws and nearly froze me bits off while a big birdie took me on a little trip over the mountains. And now I find you hangin' out with a . . . a goddess! It's been a holly of a ride!" He looked around the room with its fine furnishings. It might not be a prison, but he still wasn't sure what this place was.

"I hope you will forgive your Rootshooter friend," said Corwenna. "It was a necessary deception to bring you here."

"She weren't sellin' me down the woodway, then?"

"No. What I asked of her was difficult. Your religion preaches forgiveness. I hope you might consider it in her case."

Mucum's despair slowly lifted like a dawn mist. "She still likes me, then?"

"I hope you're only pretending to be stupid! Of course she does. Liking is the least of it. I have known and admired the Rootshooters since—well, we have no time for that now."

Mucum couldn't get over the living, breathing Ark. "Buddy 'eck, I fort you was dead wood!"

"Takes more than an apprentice surgeon to finish me off!"

"Yeah. We'll save 'im up for later." It was a promise.

All this time they'd been gabbling and Ark hadn't been able to ask about the most important person of all. "Shiv? You found her in the dungeons? Is she all right?"

"Sorry, mate, shoulda told yer first thing. We both escaped. Now that I know Flo ain't a total traitor, I reckon yer little sis is in good hands."

Ark felt hope spring up like sap. "Thank the trees!"

"And she's got a decent pair of lungs on 'er. You should've heard 'er scream to get the guard's attention. It's thanks to Shiv we got out in the first place."

"That's my girl!" Ark grinned. "But you think she'll be all right?"

"Yup. Them Rootshooters gonna be all over her. She'll be in hugs heaven!"

Corwenna backed toward the door. "You two catch up. There isn't much time. You'll be leaving tomorrow."

"I only jes' got 'ere!" Mucum groaned.

Ark smiled. If his friend was complaining, all was well. Then Corwenna's words hit him. "Leaving? Where?"

"Have you forgotten your purpose? You cannot stay here forever. Preparations must be made. The battle is coming. Soon you will be ready."

Ark felt the familiar knot of doubt tying up his stomach.

"Battle? What battle?" said Mucum. But his words floated on thin air and the room was suddenly empty. He shivered. "This Corwenna. It's really her?"

"Yes. She's taken me under her wing, so to speak." It was time to finally tell him, though the words wouldn't come easily. "She seems to think I'm her . . . son. Well, sort of . . ."

"Yer what? Fancy explainin' what the holly's goin' on?"

As Ark dressed himself, he filled Mucum in on the last two days. By the end, Mucum looked impressed. "A goddess for a mom. And yer tellin' me that yer grandma made this whole lot? Buddy dell!" Mucum suddenly frowned. "Hang on. This forest didn't grow in a few years. No way. Which means that the old bird Corwenna is seriously ancient!"

"I guess. Just like the trees. I still can't take it all in."

"Well, who'd 'ave thought it? Anyhow, if she rules the roost, and there is gonna be a fight, she might let us use the R.A.F."

"What?"

"Raven Air Force. Could be the ticket against Grasp and his thugs."

The door opened behind them, followed by a delicious smell. Corwenna proffered a wooden platter piled high with food. "Will boar-bacon sandwiches be acceptable to you young gentlemen?"

Mucum stood up. "I'll forgive anyone 'oo feeds me a bacon sarnie. Cheers!" Without waiting to be asked, he grabbed a couple and stuffed them down his gullet. "Phew," he said a few mouthfuls later, "I'm almost feelin' Dendran again."

"I now see why you chose him as a companion." Corwenna allowed a smile to cross her lips as she dabbed some salve onto Mucum's arm and wrapped it in a soft compress of comfrey leaves. Mucum gritted his teeth, but wouldn't show her it hurt.

"Yes," said Ark, remembering, "although I don't think I had a choice."

"Eat well. Take your rest. Then go and explore. Though if you hear a hissing sound, I would suggest you run, fast. The adders around here are huge and would happily squeeze the life from both of you and swallow you whole."

"Oh right. Thanks for that. Nuffin' like the thought of slitherin' snakes to make my day."

Corwenna ignored the boy's sarcasm. "And tomorrow, I shall give you a gift" — she paused and studied the boys with a sudden sadness — "a gift of death."

36 · DEADLY TRAINING

The bandages wrapped around Petronio's chest felt like a vine squeezing out his breath. It didn't help that the transparent g-gun 500 he cradled clumsily was as heavy as a lump of bog oak.

"Are you stupid, boy? Point the muzzle down; otherwise I could get hurt."

If this soldier patronized him anymore, Petronio would be tempted. How was he supposed to see it when it was completely see-through?

"Put your goggles on."

Petronio did as he was told, his nose wrinkling at the strange chemical smell as he pulled them over his forehead. The blue-tinted lenses made the outline of the gun suddenly as sharp as day. He studied the man's mottled uniform, browns and greens leaking into each other, his face a smeared makeup experiment gone wrong. As camouflage, though, it worked. And the gun itself was a miracle. Without the goggles, it simply melted into the background. No wonder the sniper had managed to take him down.

"You know I'd happily shoot you again, you arrogant piece of squit, if our high and mighty lady hadn't ordered me to look after you."

Fine. He was here to learn. Petronio pointed to a hollow tube in the side of the g-gun. "And this?"

"The chamber. Check it's empty before engaging the magazine."

Petronio was confused. He wasn't about to get married.

The soldier took a shiny block and shoved it under the rifle until there was a click. "Pull the charging handle, take the safety lever off, and you're ready."

Petronio didn't like feeling the fool. Give him a stiletto and he could confidently hit a man in the chest from thirty yards. But this? "Why doesn't it shatter?"

"Oh man. This ain't your normal old-school window glass! Them scientists went right down to the molecular level and made this stuff superstrong. That's why our shining cities tower over your tiny trees. This material is the future. And when you put it in a weapon, the only thing it's gonna shatter is anyone who gets in the way!"

Petronio was impressed, greedy to try it for himself.

"Now, shock suppression is built in," the man continued, "but this baby is still gonna buck you like a horse, with a good kick to the shoulder. Look through the sights and aim for that far branch there—and the juicy acorn hanging down. Man, it feels bad shootin' at trees. In Maw, even a splinter is worth more than gold."

For a second, Petronio tried to imagine it.

"No trees?"

"Nah, man. But we got skyscrapers like you wouldn't believe. Still, even with all those millions of people, it gets lonesome in the city sometimes. That's why I joined the army. It's good to be part of a crew. Anyhow, you're takin' your mind off the ball. Get to it, boy."

The target was a good hundred yards away. Petronio's left hand felt sweaty on the trigger. He focused his eyes and pulled. Even though he knew from experience that the gun was whisper quiet, he wasn't ready for the destruction it wrought. Branches to left and right splintered and cracked. He put the g-gun down as he'd been instructed, clicking the safety catch back on, and sauntered over to check his target. Despite the chaos around it, the acorn still swung in the breeze, taunting him.

"Thought so!" sneered the soldier, coming up behind him. "What does she see in some dumb bunch of DNA from out of town?"

He didn't understand the meaning of the insult, but the man's tone was clear. Petronio had a thin blade concealed in his belt. One flick of his hands, and the jeers would be cut short. "Give me a chance!" he said.

The man showed Petronio the balance of the weapon, how to account for wind and trajectories. By the time dusk came on, the acorn still hung like a tempting green jewel, and Petronio had taught his trainer every Dendran swear word in the twigtionary.

"One more go?" he asked.

"G-bullets don't grow on trees."

"You don't say!" Petronio hissed as he took aim. It was all about the calm before the storm, the emptying of the mind, total concentration. The target would be obliterated. All he had to have was faith. Even before his finger depressed the trigger, Petronio felt a fierce joy flood like sap through his veins. He knew, and because he knew, as the shot rang out, the acorn gave up its ghost, splintered into pulpy smithereens.

"Decent shot," the soldier said grudgingly. "The name's Heckler."

"Grasp. Petronio."

"Not sure if I can shake your hand, seeing as my colleague

will be hobbling for months thanks to your little shin kick."

Petronio smiled but felt lost when the gun was taken off him. To think what he could do with one of these beauts in his possession!

"You have progressed," Fenestra said to him later, as she came to sit by his bed. "Heckler thinks you have the makings of a marksman."

Petronio tried to hide the blush on his face. "It's amazing what guns can do."

"Yes, but a machine is only as good as the hands that guide it. I am sure there will be work for you when our plans are fulfilled. How is your chest?"

"Fine." If he admitted how much it hurt, she wouldn't let him continue training.

"You still need your rest. There is one further task for you to carry out." With that promise, she put out the light in the cot-bed, deep in the bowels of the flypod.

Petronio couldn't sleep. His new home gave off a constant hum, and tiny lights winked on and off like fireflies dancing across the panels above his head. He played the explosion of the acorn over and over in his mind. That g-gun easily beat his favorite throwing knife. So much power contained in such a tiny package. After an hour of trying to drift off, his eyes shot open. Would he even dare? Why not?

He knew where the armory cabinet lay, lined in an impenetrable alloy. The key was what mattered. As Fenestra had stooped over him before bed, he'd seen it glinting as it hung around her neck. He could hear the men's snores in the bunkroom down the corridor as he crept along toward Fenestra's quarters. His footsteps padded silently. One more advantage of Mawish technology. Metal didn't creak like wood.

The door swung open silently, and pale moonlight revealed Fenestra's sleeping form. He stopped for a second, looking at the curve of her lips, the smoothness of her skin. She had a beauty unlike any Dendran. It was off-putting. The key lay on the pillow, nestled in the tangle of the envoy's hair. If he pulled, she'd wake up. He knelt down, as if in prayer, hoping for inspiration.

Of course, the key was on a clip. If he moved quietly enough, he could unhook it. As he worked the clip, his fingers gently brushed a stray lock of her hair. It felt smooth as beech bark, tingling his skin. At least the envoy's breathing stayed regular, though his own was sharp and shallow. He was convinced that his heartbeat echoed around the chamber, but the woman never shifted.

Five minutes later, the key was turning in the lock and the cabinet spread its metal arms wide to reveal rack after rack of precision-made deadliness. A g-gun 500 was too obvious, too large, but a tumbled mound of smaller weapons was easy prey. They would never miss one from the top of the pile. He gripped a gun in his hand, felt the comfortable weight of it. It molded itself to his palm as if his hands were evolved for this very act. It would do. He slipped it into his doublet and closed the doors.

As he knelt by Fenestra's bed, trying to work the clip and return the key, she coughed suddenly. He stilled himself. If she opened her eyes, he'd be discovered: the trusted boy reduced to petty thief. There's no doubt she'd dismiss him, or worse.

His fingers froze into claws, the key dangling in front of him like evidence. What was he thinking? She trusted him and he repaid it with this!

But instead of shooting accusations from her lips, Fenestra gave a sleepy sigh and turned away from him toward the shadows. With relief, he retreated back to his room, cradling his newfound toy.

In the dark, with eyes wide open, Fenestra smiled.

37 · REUNION

The sun was bright as Mucum and Ark carefully picked their way along a meandering branch toward Corwenna's quarters the following afternoon.

"Yer know, this place ain't too bad!" said Mucum.

"Apart from the hornets the size of my fist?"

"Fair point, pal!" It was sheer luck they'd found a shimmering cruck pool and dived in as a stripy swarm buzzed by overhead. "Wot I'm tryin' to say is, it's kinda natural, not been messed with by a bunch of Dendrans, yeah?"

Ark looked around at this twisted forest that was almost beginning to feel like home. "Yes, I think I agree with you."

"Still. Don't like the sound of this gift."

Ark nodded. Training was one thing, but how could *death* be something that was given? The thought made him uneasy.

As they neared Corwenna's quarters, her door swung open and two unexpected figures rushed out.

Ark couldn't believe his eyes. Of all the miracles of the Ravenwood, he hadn't expected this. A tall, pale vision of beauty leading a little child by her hand.

"No way!" said Mucum.

"Will yow ever forgive me, moi luvvly-jubbly boy?" Flo's skin was pale, but her heart beat with a fierce, living joy. "Oi had to do it. Corwenna wanted yow and Oi had to take a message to the Rootshooters."

Mucum stared at her in surprise, lightly touching the scab on his arm.

Flo held back, doubt creasing her face, tears threatening to spill. Then Mucum smiled. "Come 'ere! Jes' promise me that next time yer tryin' to do a good deed, you won't use a knife?"

"Oi promise!" gushed Flo as she ran into his arms.

Mucum knew it was now or never. But with Ark and Shiv looking on? As Flo leaned forward with lips puckered, nerves got the better of him. He briefly brushed her cheek and tried to pretend it was all right by grabbing Flo in a massive hug and lifting her off her feet.

"Oi was so worried about yow!" she whispered in his ear. Her touch warmed him right through.

Ark scooped up Shiv and held her tight, a squealing bundle of happiness. "How's my little sis? I've missed you so much!" Her curls tickled his face, and anger at those who had imprisoned her rose up and threatened to spoil their reunion. But the smell of stew drifting from the open doorway comforted and calmed him.

"I'm a big girl now and I met all of Flosey's baldy friends. They've got no hair!" she said. "But they're very, very nice! And then we went on a nadventure and rode all the way here on the back of a huuuuge bird!"

"Are yow hungered? There's good tucker in 'ere," said Flo, taking Mucum by the hand and leading them inside.

A fire roared in the iron grate, the pot of stew bubbling in the flames. She took wooden bowls from a shelf and filled them to the brim. "Warghhh! Get that down yow!"

The boys dived into the delicious food until every last lump of tender meat was spooned away. Finally, they both sat back, soaking up the warmth of the room. Mucum stretched out his legs and gave a satisfied belch.

"What do you say?" demanded Shiv, with her hands on her hips.

Mucum's face went red. "Pardon me," he muttered.

Ark laughed for the first time in ages. "Well done, Shiv. Our parents did bring us up right!" Shiv smiled primly and snuggled up in Ark's arms.

A voice leapt from the shadows in the corner of the room. "Time is running out! The Harvest Festival draws near. This is why I have summoned you here."

They all jumped in their seats.

"Wish yer wouldn't do that. We'll get indigestion!" Mucum complained.

"Forgive me," said Corwenna, striding into the light. "I am an impatient woman, and old habits die hard. Follow me. I have something for you."

At the back of the living room was a door that Ark had never noticed.

Corwenna pulled it open to reveal a simple cave of hollowed-out wood. A small recess held a single candle. Ark sniffed once. There was a strange perfume soaked into the grain. The scent of roses. Suddenly, he felt overwhelmed with sadness.

"Is this . . ."

"The place it all began? You know that it is," said Corwenna.

Pictures seeped into Ark's mind. A fair-haired woman, curled up like a cat on the floor, wrapped in a blanket of cobwebs as she slept. Storms and seasons raging by outside. A pair of eyes suddenly shooting open, green as leaves, staring back at him across a thousand years with a look that could melt winter and bring spring to a barren land.

Tears tumbled down Ark's cheeks. "Can you feel it?" he said. But his companions merely shrugged their shoulders. Whatever message lay slumbering in this dark hole was for him alone.

"What's that shiny thing? Is it treasure?" Shiv's small finger pointed to the edge of the flickering shadows where a raven feather rested on the ground. Cradled within its curl lay a glass phial, threaded on a leather necklace.

"Treasure?" Corwenna sighed. "I'm afraid not, though this might be more valuable than life itself."

Corwenna crawled into the tiny hollow and carefully lifted the phial from its resting place. She shook the small bottle, the shadowy liquid within sparking under the dim light. "My brave Hedd traveled far to the north, to the Skylake at the edge of the Land of the Dead. There, Arktorious, he met with one you have dearly missed for so long. This dark gift is the result of his journey."

Whatever memories this wooden hollow once shrouded now fled, to be replaced with an icy coldness. Ark could feel the magnetic pull of the phial. And the Land of the Dead? He shuddered to even think of such a place. Too many questions. "What does the phial hold?"

"This substance is a foul creation. But it will be useful. The trees are truly amazing: They have many ways to arm themselves."

"But what does it do?" Ark suddenly wanted to grab the bottle and throw it into the fire, be free of it.

"I hope you never have to find out its true properties, though it might yet be the saving of you." Corwenna stared at Ark with piercing eyes. "If the time comes, you will know what use to make of it." She paused to look at each of them in turn. "For ones so young, you have journeyed far and achieved much." Her face was grave. "So, it must begin. Though my mind is strong, my body is weak. This fight is yours."

Mucum was the first to get Corwenna's point. "A bunch of kids against Grasp's guards and the spies of Maw. That's—"

"Impossible?" Corwenna spoke now with certainty. "Between you, you have tackled rabid rats, escaped guards, spoken with animals, and faced the wild boar of the Ravenwood. Surely a few soldiers and traitors should not be beyond your grasp." She addressed the last part to Ark, "As you are my son, I would expect no less!"

"But we're not even adults!" said Ark. "You expect too much of me."

"That is the point. The young are the future of this country. Think, plan, talk together. That's why you are here. Perhaps you can save Arborium from itself as well as from those who would destroy its trees!"

"Perhaps yer right," Mucum replied. "When yer put it like that, even I'm convinced we're great!"

"The odds may sound doubtful," Corwenna continued, "but if you pool all your skills, there may be hope yet. And there is this." She handed the phial to Ark and looked deep into his eyes. "Arktorious Malikum, you are flesh of my flesh, you have power greater than you know. Lead your companions, and bring hope back to Arborium. And for those who deal in treachery, make sure your mercy is swift and painful."

Ark felt everyone staring at him. "I—"

"Wait up a sec!" Mucum stuck his hands on his hips. "I've gotta foller a boy 'alf my size *and* he's younger than me?"

"By six months!" Corwenna laughed. "Does that amount of time make you a master of wisdom?"

"Nah. I was jes' sayin' . . ."

"And when the trees speak, even Corwenna obeys. It has been ordained since the day he was made. Think of it as the perfect combination of brains and brawn."

Flo squeezed Mucum's shoulder. What was the point in arguing? "And Oi can speak for all us Rootshooters to say we be on yowr side!"

"I'm not sure," said Ark. He'd never thought of himself as a leader before.

"Being certain of your ability would take half the fun out of it." Corwenna spoke lightly, even though she could see the dangers ahead. "And I have faith in you."

Strange, thought Ark. *That's just what Warden Goodwoody would have said.* A reverend and the Queen of the Ravens in agreement. The wood really was going topsy-treevy.

Corwenna nodded. "Maybe those prayers were heard. The answer lies not in miracles, but in action!"

Ark thought of how he'd lived a whole lifetime in the last few days alone. "Well. I've come this far. I'm not going to give up now."

Mucum finally gave in. "Oh, all right, then, count me in. Jes' don't expect me to call yer sir!"

"Now there's an idea," said Ark. "*Sir* has a rather lovely ring to it!"

Corwenna clapped her hands with glee. "The trees feed on light, and so have you, young Malikum. I do believe this intense young man is finally lightening up! Trust me, humor should be part of your armory."

"Flippin' fungus!" Mucum complained. "Not only is 'e gonna tell me what to do, but I also 'ave to laugh at 'is sappy jokes?"

"Sounds about right!" Ark grinned.

"I have grown fond of your stubbornness, young Master Gladioli, but I suggest you start thinking seriously about what lies ahead of you." The quiet menace in her tone was unmistakable.

Mucum got the message. "Righty-ho, Yer Maj! We finally gonna 'ave a proper fight?"

"Yes." Corwenna sighed, keeping her fears to herself. Ark was hers. Wasn't it a mother's duty to keep her child safe? But if the foundling boy could not face the ultimate danger, Arborium would be lost.

Ark tied the leather necklace around his throat to secure the phial. Where the bottle rested, his skin felt itchy and clammy. It was impossible. But so was everything that had happened since he'd overheard the plot.

Shiv jumped up and down with excitement. "Can we have a battle. A big one. Please?"

"Oh yeah!" said Mucum, crunching his knuckles. "About buddy time!"

38 · PRACTICE MAKES PERFECT

Fenestra's words echoed around Petronio's head. *I will never again treat you as a mere messenger.* Then what was he doing creeping home, every footstep accompanied by a nagging ache in his chest?

His recovery had been remarkable. In the School For Surgeons, he'd seen what happened with chest wounds; the gangrenous pus that oozed from the flesh bringing with it a stench unlike any other; the onset of fever; and the raving hallucinations as the patient was tied down. All perfect for students to observe the predictable rictus of death in all its glory. Few recovered, but the students passed their exams with distinction.

Instead, he'd been conscious within hours, fully functional the following day. The training with Fenestra's right-hand man, Heckler, had been a welcome distraction. Now he was almost on form again.

"It's all about money, young Grasp. Do you not agree?" Fenestra had teased him, dangling a leather bag filled with the *chink* of foreign gold. "And your father's men will play a crucial part. Make sure they receive it and they know what is required of them."

"I haven't let you down before, have I?"

"No. You are a most faithful" — Fenestra was about to use the word *servant* but realized it would not do — "ally. Guard it with your life. If they are not paid, they will see no reason to take up our modernizing cause. This" — she held up one of the ingots so that it caught and flashed in the sun——"is the only language that will reach inside and pluck my wishes from their bodies." She spoke as if it wasn't just wishes she wanted, but raw, bleeding hearts.

Fenestra had insisted he take no foreign weaponry. If he were to be stopped by a royal patrol, a simple body search would give the game away. He thought she had no idea of his night-time thievery. What nestled within his doublet was both wise and practical protection.

This morning, the world was turning brown beneath his feet, as if every leaf that grew was curling up to go to sleep. He was alone, or thought he was until he spotted two black blots hovering in a blue sky. He only glimpsed them out of the corner of his eye before one of the shapes resolved itself into a mass of charcoal-feathered muscle streaming toward him. The intention was plain.

Petronio only had time for the briefest of thoughts. *Ravens normally attack only when they scent blood.* Oh! Of course. He looked down to see his doublet had gained a new patch of color as he walked. One of the stitches must have given way. He was leak-ing, and this lonely spot on the abandoned outskirts of the city was far from safety and shelter.

The bird drew its wings back, slamming into reverse as its claws reached toward a nice, fleshy morsel of meat. The raven was confident and that was its undoing. Since when did a Dendran fight back? Such action would be sacrilege, a monstrous act in the eyes of the Holly Woodsmen.

Petronio didn't give a twig for fusty superstition. In one swift movement, he twisted around on the woodway to face his attacker. As the claws stretched out to rip into skin and bone, he snatched the g-gun 100 from his doublet, flicked the safety catch, and squeezed the trigger. The bird didn't even get a warning, as the tiny splinter of keen glass almost silently found its target. It traversed the air in a split second, burrowed through feathers, pierced skin, and smashed its way around several internal organs before exiting the bird's body.

The raven screeched. It was already dead, even though its brain had not yet received the message. The wings flapped out in an ungainly manner, all flight gone as the corpse plummeted toward the forest canopy.

Petronio heard sounds of cracking, several thumps. Then silence. He stared at the g-gun in his hand, marveling that a machine so small could dispense death on such a magnificent scale. Oh yes. The Empire of Maw had much to offer.

"Come on, then!" he shouted up at the sky where the other raven circled uncertainly. "I'll take the lot of you!"

The bird chose wisdom rather than death, wheeling away from the monster with blazing eyes and deadly treasure in its hands.

The boy laughed out loud. With the simple pressing of one finger, Petronio Grasp had killed a raven and made history. The tables were turning.

He stowed the g-gun, his mood immeasurably better. Who was lord of the forest now? The sun shone down in agreement as he strolled the autumnal byways, finally sneaking into the back entrance of what no longer felt like home.

He had no desire to bump into his father. The man would only scowl. Petronio headed for the dungeons.

"Halt? Who goes there?"

"Why are you squeaking, Alnus?"

Alnus coughed, wondering if he'd ever recover from Mucum's well-aimed kick between his legs. "I'm not. You can't go farther,

Master Grasp." If the boy or his father found out that Mucum had escaped, Alnus would be shortly walking the plank.

Petronio hadn't been called Master for a while, even though the words were tinged with sarcasm. "Why?"

"Err. The little girl and the boy. Ill. Very, very ill. Might be a bad case of color!"

"You mean cholera?"

"That's the one. They're under kworro . . . kworry . . ."

"Quarantine. Let's hope they don't die, eh?"

Alnus almost fainted with relief. The lie had saved him and Salix, for now.

Petronio was rather pleased. With Ark dead, and his trouble-maker mate sick, what could go wrong? "I've something for you." He pulled the purse out of his pocket and as Alnus leaned forward, he loosened the tie. He neglected to mention that the purse was not as heavy as when Fenestra had entrusted it to him.

"What's this for?" Alnus sniffed suspiciously as if gold had its own perfume.

"Tomorrow at the Harvest Festival, my father will make sure that the King's personal bodyguards are replaced by you and Salix. The rest is pretty obvious, if you get my drift."

Alnus normally didn't have time for Petronio, but the sight of all that glittering treasure was enough to make him forget all his resentments.

"You want us to . . . ?"

Petronio peered up and down the corridor anxiously. "Do I have to spell it out?"

Alnus shook his head.

"This is for now. There's more when the deed is done." Petronio explained the plan and finally handed over the purse. "And don't mention to my father that you saw me." Was this even his home anymore? He'd been treated more like a son by the envoy of Maw than he ever had by his dismissive father. When Fenestra left after the battle was won, Petronio was suddenly determined to go with her.

Alnus grinned. Seeing as Salix wasn't around, he wondered if there was a way to divide the spoils in his favor. Maybe it was time to move out of that hovel of his, get himself a girl, and settle down. With such rewards, he could even have his rotten teeth replaced. The future truly was golden!

39 · COMMUNION

Corwenna put her arm around Ark's shoulders and guided him to the door. She briefly turned her head back to look at the others. "Be patient. It is not quite time to leave yet."

The door opened and Corwenna disappeared. Ark was by himself on the woodway. But he wasn't alone. Above him, roosting in the branches and rising up in a thousand serried ranks, the guardians of the Ravenwood looked down at the boy. Glittering eyes bored into him, waiting.

Why had Corwenna pushed him out here? It was another of her tests, he was sure of that, but what to do?

Then it came to him. What had Mucum said? A Raven Air Force. Perhaps with their help they could really do this! But the ravens were creatures with minds of their own. He must convince them. That's what Corwenna was demanding of him.

Then, before he had a chance to speak, a thought came toward him, borne on the soft breeze. The words were stilted, as if formed by mouths that had no lips to shape them: *One of kin lost today. Boy Grasp. Spear of glass. Danger.*

With the words came pictures: A brave bird flying through the sky, aiming toward Petronio. The sudden shock as a shining shard shot through the air. And the pain felt by every single bird as one of their brethren plummeted down into the depths.

They were communicating with him.

Ark focused his mind and answered: *I am sorry for your loss. Together we can avenge your honor. I promise it.* Anger rose up inside him. Killing a sacred bird? Petronio had broken the oldest unwritten law.

Silence. Maybe the birds were studying a scrawny boy and seeing the hopeless nothing that he was. He felt the mass of them weighing the branches down, their brute force, the lure of the dark. Yet behind all this, a fierce, unwavering nobility.

It was up to him to ask the question, to tell them what he now was. He stared back at the shining, fathomless eyes, calming the tremor that ran through his body: *I am Arktorious Malikum, sewage worker. But I am also son of Corwenna, Ark of the trees. I have faced my fears. And will do so again. Will you help us fight the danger of Maw? Are you with me?*

Silence again. Ark wondered if he'd failed, if the ravens would dismiss his boldness as arrogance. A single bird bent its beak to its breast and plucked a parasitic tick the size of a clenched fist from deep within its feathers. The offending insect was crushed within its claws.

A screech shattered the still air. Ark turned. It was Hedd, elder of the flock, whose thoughts now spoke for all the raven brood. *Yes. Boy born of wood. We are with you. To the end.*

Relief washed over Ark. He bowed deeply, in gratitude.

Hedd continued: *Listen. We are eyes of Corwenna. We move like night. Better than night. We spy something that worries. Man of stone. Flint his name. Heart empty as hollow tree. His army is on move. He is traitor, boy of wood. Look.*

A white moth suddenly spiraled down through the air and landed in Ark's outstretched hands, where it unfolded into a sheet of creased vellum. Ark turned it over, excited fingers tracing out the scratching of ink-filled quills. It was a map of the castle and much, much more. Times, dates, schemes of dark deeds written out as plain as day.

Hedd screeched one more time. *Be brave. Be bold.* And with that, the sky suddenly darkened with feathers, and a furious wind pinned Ark to the woodway. He blinked his eyes and the Ravenwood was empty, its branches bare.

Ark studied the map and drank in the foul words inscribed on it. In his head, a plan began to unfurl like a spring leaf. Maybe, just maybe, it was possible after all.

The following day dawned gray and unpromising. As Ark, Mucum, and Shiv stood outside, a chill wind funneled through the forest, picking at their clothes with sharp fingers. Flo had returned a day earlier to prepare the Rootshooters.

Corwenna closed the door behind her. "Come. You have been fed. Here are provisions." She passed a bag to Mucum. "Ark, I return this to you." Corwenna handed over the feather that only a few days ago he'd tried to kill her with. "And little, brave Shiv, this gift might be small, but it is most useful."

"Candy!" she guessed, sniffing the tiny wrapper. "I like candy!"

"Naturally. I wouldn't want your throat to be sore at the wrong moment!" Corwenna smiled.

A dull light leaked through the leaves. Hedd stared down at them from his perch and made a clicking noise with his beak. Ark sensed the bird's thoughts. Fear for the future. But Hedd's oath to Ark was as strong as the branch that supported him. The raven turned his head sideways, a single glittering eye studying Ark.

It was time for yet more introductions.

"Hedd, Mucum. Mucum, Hedd," said Ark.

Mucum turned to the creature in question. How did he address a vicious monster? *Here, birdie, birdie* wasn't quite right under the circumstances. "Err . . . ?" He looked at Ark desperately.

Hedd continued staring at him.

Ark could feel the creature's enjoyment of Mucum's discomfort. "I think what Mucum is trying to say is, would you mind giving us a lift home?"

Mucum nodded. "What he said."

Corwenna crossed her arms. "He doesn't mind. Up you go."

Mucum tried to climb up the huge mound of the bird's back. After much slipping and inventive swearing, he managed to hook his legs over, but not before Hedd squawked a few times in protest. "Sorry, Mr. Raven! Didn't mean to kick yer in the guts. Yer know, I don't fink this is such a brill idea!" Mucum protested as he held on for dear life.

"Arktorious is right. You could win prizes for complaining!"

"Yeah, yeah." Mucum held his arm out and pulled Shiv, then Ark, up.

"By the way, hold on tight! And remember, the future lies in your hands now!" Tears threatened the edge of her eyes. But since when did a queen show her sorrows?

Corwenna swept up her left hand, giving the signal for takeoff. The bird flapped its huge wings, once, twice, three times.

"Up, up, and away!" screamed Shiv with delight as she burrowed down deep into the soft feathers.

Then they were airborne. Mucum nearly slid off as they rose up, his knees gripping the body like a horse.

"Grab me waist!" he screamed to Ark as the wind threatened to tear them away. At least Corwenna could have given them a pair of reins.

The bird screeched and wheeled off to the east, toward Hellebore and the unknown.

40 · PREPARATION IS THE KEY

❧

It was the day of the Harvest Festival and the sky was dark blue, hinting at the winter that lay ahead. Mucum and Shiv were on an errand, and even Mucum had to admit that Ark's plan was a good one. Already, the Ravenwood was a distant dream. It was time to stop running away.

Mucum lifted Shiv onto his shoulders. "Look, girl! The forest's on fire!"

Shiv squealed with delight, the bright afternoon sun adding to the color as every tree decked out its leaves in reds, browns, and glittering golds. Crowds were out, all off to Barkingham Palace for the festival. Adults waved about huge nets attached to bamboo canes, hoping to bag a few falling leaves, and children jumped into Council leaf piles stored up on the woodways. The mounds were ready to be recycled into paper, roofing material, and clothes. The cool autumn air filled with expectation and laughter. "Can we make a lantin?"

"Sorry, sweet pea. No can do. We're in a bit of a rush." The thought of missing the lantern parade was a killer. Like Shiv, he'd grown up learning to stitch the leftover leaves into the shapes of full moons, chariots, boats, and miniature trees. With candles on sticks inside, they turned the paths of Arborium into a glowing river of light as the dusk came on.

Tonight, the Harvest Festival wasn't about celebration, but danger. If they didn't get a move on, the King would be dead before the night was out, and tomorrow would dawn over an endangered land. The sewage station looked as rickety as ever. Mucum paused to sniff the air.

"It's stinky!" said Shiv, holding her nose.

Mucum nodded. How he'd missed the pong of honest poo! He pushed open the creaking door. Several faces swiveled in his direction. Mucum put his fingers to his lips as he stalked over to the raised corner of the room, gently putting Shiv down so he could attend to the job in hand.

Jobby Jones resembled a lump of quivering lard, wheezing snores erupting from his open mouth as his dreams took him far from the scent of raw sewage.

"Wakey, wakey, boss!" Mucum snarled as he took a bucket of yellow-colored liquid and poured it all over the fat man's face.

The effect was instant. Two jellylike eyes shot open. "What? What's going on? Call the fire brigade!" Jobby Jones leapt off his bed surprisingly quickly for someone of his size. As his pudgy hands tried to wipe the liquid filth from his face, he finally recognized Mucum. "How dare you! I'll have you reported for this!"

Mucum stood his ground, folding his arms. "Oh yeah? You already did."

The rest of the sewage workers stood and stared. Waking the gaffer with a bucket of Dendran's finest produce was not an everyday event.

Jones took in Shiv's face, split in half with a wide grin. "And infants are not allowed in here!" he screamed. "You lot, get back to work, unless you fancy having a day's pay docked from your wages!" Usually, the threat was enough. Today was different. This show was too good to miss. Nobody moved. The staring continued.

Jobby Jones floundered. His authority was being questioned!

"I'll deal with the rest of you later." A stubby finger pointed at Mucum. "But you should be in jail!"

"Shut it, Grandad. I was locked up, thanks to you. You know what we call Dendrans like you? Sap-sucking traitors. I hope the reward was worthwhile."

"No one talks to me like that." The man's face went purple as his eyeballs nearly burst from their sockets.

"I jes' did. Our little conversation is over." Mucum towered over Jobby Jones. The only thing that had ever held him back had been fear of losing his job. Too late to worry about that now. Mucum pulled his arm back and bunched his fist up. He was going to enjoy this.

The look of sudden terror on his boss's face was good, but the crunch as the boy's fist connected with that pompous nose was even better. The gristly sound was followed by a spray of poppy red blood soaking into the boss's once white shift. Jobby Jones fell backward like a sapling snapped in half by a hurricane. The thump as he hit the ground echoed around the chamber.

"That was for my friend Ark and also for all the lads you treated like squit for too long!" Mucum felt pleased with himself. Justified violence made him glow all over.

Shiv clapped and jumped up and down on the spot. A cheer went up around the sewage station and suddenly he was surrounded by his fellow workers.

"Buddy holly, we thought you was skivin' off," said one of the lads.

Little Squirt piped up. "The guards kept comin' round each day, givin' us the evil eye and askin' us where you and Ark both was. Real glad to find out he weren't a ghost! But I didn't say nothin', not to no one."

"All you lot, listen up. Ark and I need yer help," said Mucum, wiping his hand on his tunic. "The country's in danger and there's gonna be a fight . . ."

Ten sets of ears pricked up.

". . . a big one. Are you up for it?"

"Do boar squit in the woods?" said Little Squirt, speaking for them all.

"I fink they do!" Mucum responded with a smile. "That's settled, then. Phlegm and Biley, tie up the old gaffer. Shiv, can you be ready to scream again?"

"Shall I do it now?" Shiv opened her mouth to reveal a terrifying black hole. Every apprentice put their hands over their ears.

But before Shiv could let rip, Mucum grabbed her and gently put his hand over her lips. Who needed weapons with a pair of lungs like that? "Later, my little lovely. I'll tell you when. The rest of you gather around. We've only got a few hours. 'Ere's what we're gonna do. . . ."

Ark stopped on the woodway by the shrine, wondering if his coin still nestled in the watery depths. Then he was inside, enveloped by incense and musty shadows.

"I'd recognize those footsteps anywhere!" The Warden was praying. "Could it really be you?" Only two days before, she had conducted Ark's funeral, reading from the Wood-Book: *But a Dendran dieth, and is laid low: Yea, the Dendran giveth up the ghost, and where is he?* Her words had not taken one ounce of grief from the Malikums nor stemmed their rivers of tears. There had been no body, only a shroud filled with goat meat: a sacrifice for the ravens. The Holly Woodsmen had sneered at her request to lead the ceremony. Such archaic rituals were falling out of favor.

Ark walked across the kirk floor and knelt by the Warden,

allowing her gnarled fingers to read the map of his face. "You have cheated death once more!"

He thought of Petronio's confident attack, of ravens and boars. "I was lucky. The wood had work for me. But now I'm scared."

Though she was only an old, blind woman, the Warden could still give comfort. "The branch has led you this far. It will not drop you now. I promise. The good Goddess looks after Her own."

Ark nodded, wondering if he should tell her about Corwenna and who he really was. But now was not the time. "I have to fight for Arborium. Dendrans and others might die."

"And you want my advice?"

"I don't know what I want. At least tell my parents I'm alive, for now, and not to worry about Shiv." He got up to leave.

"Ark. Stop. I feel the anger in you and the evil that is abroad. If you let this hatred lead to murder, you will be no better than those who seek to defeat you."

Ark pulled away. "What? Let them maim and mutilate, while we turn the other cheek?" He felt the phial around his neck like a cold chill, urging him to destroy each and every traitor.

"I didn't say that. The taking of life is only for Diana."

Ark winced as he heard the word. Maybe it was all right to use his grandmother's name. She was the one who created this place from her dreams. It truly was a wood of wonders.

The Warden continued. "But as for fighting, the holly script is clearly on the side of the just!"

It was an answer, of sorts. Corwenna would happily wipe out every enemy with a smile on her face. But Ark was brought up as a Dendran. Years of kirk could not be so easily dismissed. "You might be right," he said, his heart unaccountably lighter, ideas beginning to whir like sycamore seeds.

"Be guided by your be-leaf!" whispered the Warden, though the door had already swung closed. Ark was gone.

Half an hour later, he met Flo at the top of the lift. "Time to make a quiet visit to the palace. Are you sure your crew is ready?"

"Oi be sure, moi good friend. We is about to have some fun, warghhh!"

Fun was not a weapon as far as Ark knew. All that Corwenna had given him before he left was a bag of juicy red apples and a whistle that apparently no Dendran could hear. What was he leading his friends into? The odds did not bear thinking about.

Soon, they were approaching the palace, weaving their way through the expectant crowds. The pleasure gardens surrounding the palace were normally closed to commoners. Now Dendrans from all woodwalks of life were leaning over the far parapets to take in the bird's-eye view of Hellebore. The outer courtyard of the castle was laden with tables, each piled high with the best that the harvest could offer, and much more besides from the King's own stores. Soon, the feast would begin. "Yow don't warnt to come in with me boi the back way?"

Flo could find her way through plumbing systems with her eyes closed. And there was plenty of kit to pick up once the rest of the Rootshooters arrived.

"No, thanks, Flo. I need to see if Corwenna's training works. See you there in half an hour."

"Yow'll be all right?"

"Absolutely!" Perhaps by sounding confident, he would be. Flo gave a last wink, then turned to join the throng. It was now or never. There were the steps up to the enormous oak doors guarded by the same sneering soldier. It was nearly dusk, the low light softening the air. The lantern parade was beginning. As the first lamps flickered, throwing trembling shadows across the ground, Ark stepped out from the crowd. He was in open territory. Corwenna had taught him to be still. How could you be still and move at the same time? There was only one way to find out.

The soldier was bored and annoyed that this evening he'd have to let the commoners inside. Surely he was there to keep the plebs out? There was a sudden breeze and the doors behind him blew open. "Buddy latch loose again!" he muttered. "I'll stick a twig up the royal carpenter's nose!" He slammed them shut.

Ark couldn't believe it. His every footstep had been lighter than air, his whole mind focused on keeping slow and unnoticed. Briefly, the soldier's eyes had trained directly on him. Ark knew he'd been spotted, until those same beer-stained eyes slid away and he was in! Amazing! From far off, he felt Corwenna whispering encouragement. But congratulations weren't in order yet.

He slipped unseen into the depths of the palace, using the memorized map to guide him, flattening himself against walls as servants rushed past, trays piled high with food in preparation for the feast a couple of hours hence. The map had shown where the King's personal guards would be positioned, and where the soldiers, brought down from Moss-side specially for the event, were on guard. Finally he followed the echoes of far-off music through the brightly lit passageways until he came to the right door. He peered up and down the corridor. Clear. He pushed the handle and crept in.

The high-ceilinged room was empty, apart from a set of

trestles set up along one wall, piled high with cutlery and clean platters. Looking down on the space was a small alcove set into the wall like a miniature minstrel's gallery, and straight ahead of Ark were wooden double doors. In a few hours the lords and ladies of Arborium would sit down to their own feast in the inner courtyard just on the other side.

"What think yow?" said Flo, suddenly stepping out from behind a curtain.

Ark stifled a shriek. "Apart from nearly giving me a heart attack, this space should work well." If Corwenna and her spying birds were right, they might stand a chance. "We haven't got much time."

"That be whoi Oi brought along a couple a good 'uns." Three more Rootshooters appeared as if from nowhere. In their long arms they held bundled lengths of heartwood.

"Will it be noisy?"

"Yow keep a lookout. All this music they be practicin' for the dancin' is makin' a right din. Don't think no one will worry about a few hammers and saws joinin' the orchestra!"

Flo was right. But worrying wasn't an easy habit to give up. "And the others have brought up the magnets?"

"Yas! They be already in place. Us Rootshooters never forgets. Do Oi look loike a dreamy girl?"

"No. You're right." Ark suddenly noticed that Flo had hair. "Is that a wig on your head?"

Flo laughed and the wig moved.

"Oh! It's alive!"

"Whoi, of course he is!" The wig suddenly sprouted eight legs and jumped off her head to land on the floor.

"Help! It's a spider! It's going to kill us all!" Ark backed into a corner. A mealworm might be bigger, but this *thing* made horrible clicking noises as it moved toward him. "Wahhhhhh!" he wailed.

"Quoiet down, yow scaredy-cat! He is nought but moi pet spoider, Harold. But yow can call him Harry. 'E is going to help us get on the web!" The spider gave a single disdainful look at Ark with its multiple eyes and then scuttled through a hole that one of the Rootshooters made by levering up a floorboard.

"I'm not going to call him anything," said Ark. "Just keep that *insect* away from me!" He was more than nervous. In two hours, the feast would begin. If they weren't ready, they might as well hand over their country on a wooden platter. As the Rootshooters began work, Ark cracked open the door and crouched down to wait.

Without thinking why, he took the raven feather and laid it before him. Then he reached around his neck to untie the leather strap holding the phial. His hand trembled as he reached toward the stopper. But there was no time for doubt, even when the stopper plopped from its end and a thin trail of vapor rose up.

He tried not to smell it, but his nostrils caught a stench that almost made him gag, his mind now choked with images of bursting boils, and pus, all things rank and decomposing. Quickly, before he lost the will to do it, he dipped the sharpened quill deep inside the phial until it sucked up several drops of shadow ink. It was done — the phial was back safely around his neck, the feather hidden deep inside his sleeve — though for what purpose, he still did not know. Ark prayed he would never have to find out.

They'd tested the engine half an hour earlier. Now the flypod stank with the nervous sweat of male bodies. Soldiers, attached by safety harnesses to the curving walls of the hold, checked their weapons carefully. A jammed breech could mean the difference between life and death. Lady Fenestra walked between them, gossip falling silent as she passed by.

She finally squeezed through a small hatch to the storeroom, where Petronio was resentfully taking stock of the equipment. "Not long now!" she said.

"And I'm stuck in here counting pairs of boots!" Petronio was furious.

"If all goes well, the Moss-siders will do all the work for us. Better a battle where you don't lose a single one of your men, but still win, hmmm?"

Petronio could see the logic of her words, but his heart burned for action.

"My men will provide backup if anything goes wrong. Now, you must promise me you won't do anything stupid!"

Petronio wondered if she could make out the bulge of the g-gun 100 in his doublet. "I promise," he said, his eyes meeting hers defiantly.

"Good. There will be much work for you when this is all over." She turned to go.

Petronio wasn't bothered about the far future, and as for his promise? Of course he wouldn't do anything stupid. But he might do something smart.

41 · ALL THE KING'S MEN

The work was done. Ark hoped Mucum and Shiv were ready. Now came the most dangerous test of his skills. They had all agreed that trying to convince the King at this stage was folly. Better to produce hard evidence. That was why he was now standing right outside the King's private chambers. A second ago, his breath shallow and his feet rooted in shadow, all the two guards had noticed was a slight smell of mustiness.

Their eyes went wide with recognition. It couldn't be! "Buddy holly! How did you get in 'ere, again?"

"The ravens 'ad you for a bite to eat!" the second soldier chimed in.

"And they spat me out," Ark snarled. "I don't taste so good these days! Now, I told you once before that the King is in grave danger."

And as before, the first soldier did what his training dictated. The left hook was fast, a clenched fist powering through the air. Explanations could come later. The King was in grave danger from an around-the-U-bend sewage worker.

"Please don't do that," asked Ark in a reasonable voice, his eyes connecting with his attacker the moment before the punch made contact.

Who could refuse such a reasonable request? Though it went against the grain, the soldier suddenly liked the boy's politeness.

"Have you gone hazelnuts?" shouted the second soldier at his befuddled colleague, as he lashed out with a kick that should have snapped several of the boy's ribs.

Ark neatly stepped to one side, watching a foot do no more than disturb a few particles of dust. "I mean the King no harm. It is Councillor Grasp you need to worry about."

Something in the voice, in the silky tones that delivered it, made both soldiers pause. Ark was suddenly glad of Corwenna's skills. Like mother, like son. If he slowed them down for a second, maybe he could tell them a story with more truth than the Councillor could ever guess.

Five minutes later, he'd won them over. Skeptical Dendrans were a tougher business than mealworms and boars. Such minds took a great deal of convincing. "The point is," he concluded, "are you with me and with Arborium?"

"When you put it like that." A short while before, the first soldier's instinct was to put down the interloper. Now he hung on his every word.

Ark was flabbergasted. Perhaps truth was the simplest weapon. It was how you applied it that mattered. Before the boy left, one of the soldiers actually shook his hand, though the other still cast suspicious glances up the corridor as Ark strode away.

"You don't think it's a bunch of make-be-leaf?"

"Nah. I heard Grasp talking to one of his inside men the other day. He shut up quick when he saw me. Didn't think about it at the time. Makes sense now."

"So you're sayin' we put our lives on the line for a treenage squit shoveler."

"Basically, yeah. This job ain't up to much, but I kinda like livin' in the trees. I've heard horror stories about Maw and I don't want that lot takin' over 'ere, thank you very much!"

Two hours later Ark stood quietly on a balcony overlooking the main inner courtyard of the castle. The moon was finally full, filling the space below with pale light. For some, it was a silver coin that would fill their coffers when the night was done. But for Ark, it was a staring eye of truth, unblinking and bright, soon to uncover dark deeds.

He studied the scene. A long damask-covered table ran around the square, the oak-leaf pattern spilling across the white cloth. Laid on top was the best that Arborium had to offer: great sides of oak-smoked boar and wooden bowls of apple sauce jostled with pitchers of first-flush wine and moon-shaped crusty loaves baked from scaffield wheat. At the courtyard's heart, a tall, copper-clad fountain sprouted sprays of water from its many sculpted branches as courtier children, young princes and petticoated princesses squealed and splashed each other.

At the four corners of the high battlements that surrounded the castle, great lengths of string dived into the sky, held taut by gilded leaf-kites riding the stream of wind currents far above. The kites symbolized the ideal of Arborium, bound to the earth yet dreaming of the heavens above.

The great and the good were assembled, paying homage to their king and raising endless toasts to the successful harvest. Among such jollity, it was hard to imagine that the future of their world hung in the balance. With every duke and earl and their armed retinues well on the way to drunkenness, the timing couldn't be better. The King looked at ease, laughing at one of Grasp's jokes. The Councillor sat on his left, with Commander Flint on his right. Quercus was surrounded by death dressed up as loyalty.

Ark's eyes focused in on the two bodyguards right behind the King, the same ones he'd talked to earlier. He hoped they believed him. If not, the plan was already doomed.

There was an explosion and the sky above was suddenly filled with bangs and flashes. The noise made the perfect signal. Ark remembered Corwenna's words. He hoped the trees were listening. It was the best fireworks display in years. Ark retreated from the balcony and worked his way back through the corridors.

At the same time, one of the bodyguards whispered urgently into the King's ear. Whatever the man said appeared to have an effect as the King rose to follow, striding straight toward the nearest door, which opened directly into the empty serving room. Every face in the courtyard was turned up to the sky in childish glee. Every single one of them had missed the tiny fact that the King was leaving the party, except for Grasp. The second bodyguard walked behind, turning once to wink at the Councillor. Grasp was reassured. So this was how Fenestra intended to act! He could now sit back and play the appalled witness when the time came.

Ark was already in the serving room, hidden in the shifting shadows. He felt the stillness circle around him like tree rings, remembering the first time he'd hidden with Mucum.

"You talked of the threat to my life and that we had to immediately retreat. But why couldn't we tell my head of security?" The King suddenly felt uneasy in this gloomy place, out of sight of all the court. His instincts told him that the guard's actions did not add up. "I demand to know—"

One of the King's so-called protectors grabbed him from behind in a bear hug, while the other stuffed a cloth napkin into Quercus's mouth before expertly tying a gag around it, fast.

The men were following their orders to the letter as they dragged him to the back of the room and straight up the stairs to the alcove. There a lull in the fireworks, giving the Dendrans time to raise their cups in defiance of the coming winter. A few seconds later, the final part of the display began.

If anything, the sound was louder than before, each rocket showering the palace in golden sparks, the walls shaking to every boom.

Another door to the serving room silently opened and in stepped two men with sharp stiletto blades drawn and ready.

"Bodyguards first. Then the old man, right?" whispered the big one, with a scar that zigzagged across his scalp as if a drunk had attacked him with a razor.

"I know. You don't have to keep going on at me."

"Yes, I do. You'd forget to put yer clothes on in the mornin' if I didn't tell yer!"

"Good evening, gentlemen!" Ark stepped out from the shadows, his hands empty of all weapons.

Salix took a second to recognize the former sewage apprentice. It couldn't be! "Wha—?" His shock turned to a sneer. "All dressed up, are we? Black looks pretty good on you."

"Thank you."

The clothes were different but the face was almost the same. "And there's somefin' different about you. . . ."

Ark stood his ground. "Yes. Quite a lot, actually. You'll find out."

"You've got bottle. I'll give you that, you little runt!" Salix said, almost admiringly.

Yes, Ark did have bottle. It nestled like a hornet around his neck. But now was not the time to find out what it could do.

"I . . . f-fort the ravens had 'im!" stuttered Alnus.

"Don't look like it, does it?" Salix smirked. "I guess we get to sort the sewer boy as a warm-up exercise. I'll slit his throat and you can stick him in the guts. It's what I call a fair division of labor. 'Ow does that sound to you?"

Alnus nodded gleefully.

"I don't know 'ow you escaped death, *again*, but I promise you'll be keepin' yer appointment now!" Salix advanced with his knife in his hand. The boy was too slippery for his liking. But where could he run to now?

"You don't really want to do that, do you?" Ark leaned on one leg and rubbed his vine-creeper shoe on the back of his calf, trying to get the shine back on the leather.

"Wot you got to be so confident about?" said Alnus.

"Let's just say, it's finally over for you two."

The boy should be pleading for his life, not making threats. Alnus was puzzled.

Salix was impatient, though. "Game's over, squithead. We do you, then the two bodyguards, and before the last firework blasts into the sky, old King Quercus will be dining on a belly-ful of steel."

"And your boss will reward you?"

"That's the whole point. Councillor Grasp, the King's most trusted advisor, is gonna give us plenty of readies after this! He'll be the main man running this place once Maw takes over. And the Commander's men can 'appily deal with the bunch of pompous ponces out there!" Salix flicked his thumb toward the double doors.

"I'm so glad you explained what you're up to." Ark briefly let his eyes flicker toward the high roof and the alcove hidden in the beams above. "It means I can now deal with you."

"Oh please, give it a rest." Salix had had enough banter. He rushed at Ark, blade held low. If the boy tried any countermoves, he'd be ready.

42 · PAYBACK

As the soldier grabbed him from behind, the King knew he'd been betrayed. But by whom? He'd fully expected one of the bodyguards to slip the knife in, now that they were away from the crowds. Instead, he'd been roughly manhandled up a set of winding stairs, then pushed through an open doorway. So that's what they had in mind! In front of Quercus, two pillars held up a small alcove that looked out over the serving room below. One push and he'd have been over the edge. A broken neck would cut the King's reign short.

One of the guards had shoved Quercus toward the edge. At the last second, he'd pulled the King back and grabbed his head, turning it so that the King was forced to look at the guard's face. For some odd reason, the man had made the sign of the Woodsman Cross, then put his fingers to his lips, indicating for the King to stay quiet. The whole wide-wood had gone mad. Why all this playacting? Better to have the deed done. His would-be assassin had then pointed his finger, swiveling the King's body so that he'd been forced to look down.

At that moment the back door had opened to Salix and Alnus, their blades ready and eager. As the hands gripped him tight, the King had watched the scene unfold in creeping horror. It was like being the only audience member in a play about himself. The treenage boy dressed in black finery did not look like any kind of match for the men. He'd recognized the scar on the taller one's scalp. But the words that crawled out of their lips like foul cockroaches had been worse than any stab wound.

They were out to commit regicide, choosing the fireworks for their cover. When they revealed that his most trusted advisors were behind the plan, the King had sagged at the knees, an old man let down by those he loved. He was a parcel, ready to be delivered up to whoever paid the highest.

And now Quercus tried to wriggle free, but the other guard stepped in, wrapping his arms around his chest like a rope. Again, the King saw the finger raised to lips, silently pleading for him to stay calm.

The boy below was to be admired. Both crazy and courageous. Would that all Dendrans defended their King so! It would be no battle. Quercus bridled at the dishonor of two trained men killing an unarmed boy.

"X marks the spot," a voice commanded. The King could only stare in horror.

At the sound of the voice, Salix paused in his attack, turning back to his companion just in time to see him look down.

"What are you on about?" Alnus could see the huge X marked on the floor beneath his feet.

"This!" said Ark, pulling a lever attached to the wall.

Before Alnus could even think—not that he ever did much thinking—a pair of trapdoors opened beneath his feet and he was taking his first flying lesson.

"Heeeelllllp!" screamed Alnus as he plunged down toward certain death, only to bounce back up a moment later as the giant spiderweb beneath the trapdoors buoyed up. But the second time he fell, the sticky web caught him and held him tight.

The King couldn't help smiling. If there hadn't been a hand clamped tight over his lips, he would have shouted *Bravo!*

"One down, one to go!" said Ark.

"Very clever, boyo!" snarled Salix. "But your treenage tricks ain't gonna stop me sticking this in your chest!" He came at Ark slow and steady, eyes roving around the floor to check for any more hidden hindrances.

From the hole in the floor, Alnus whimpered like a child, "Help us get out of here, Salix!"

"Sorry, mate. Got some killing to do! We're running out of time!" Salix fixed his eyes on the impudent boy.

Ark stood his ground. "I've had enough of you chasing me, threatening my mother. Worst of all, you took my sister! That is unforgivable. In the Ravenwood, they would have killed you. But Warden Goodwoody pleaded for your miserable little lives."

The King wondered what on wood the boy was going on about. The Ravenwood? That was the stuff of far tales, surely?

Salix felt his confidence returning. One more step and his knife would cut short the boy's confidence. "If I'd had the order, I'd have happily garotted the little screaming brat. Time to take you on a journey to the River Sticks!"

His weapon hand reached out and—

A girl appeared from behind a curtain. She was taller than everyone in the room and as bald as a raven's egg. "Moi turn now!" she said. "Yippee! Our stupid friend be standin' in the roight place. Do it, boys!"

Before Salix could even wonder who the strange girl was,

before he could plunge his blade into the boy's body, he felt an intense pain shoot through his right foot.

The King could only marvel at the engineering involved. Through twelve small holes in the floor, a circle of long heartwood staves plunged upward, creating an instant circular cage, surrounding every part of Salix. Except for a limb that unfortunately stood in the way.

"Arrghhhhhh!" he screamed, watching in disbelief as the sharpened pole shot up, right through the middle of his foot. "I'm in agony!"

"Then you shouldn't have put your foot in it, in the first place!" countered Ark.

"Oi be shocked!" joined in Flo. "Be that another joke from the most serious Master Malikum?"

"I think it was!" said Ark. Maybe Corwenna was right. Humor could achieve victory after all. Mucum had been onto something from the go. Ark felt giddy with joy. They'd done it!

By now, a pool of blood had spread around Salix's legs. The strong man crumbled. "I'm gonna die!" he wailed.

"Stop whining!" said Ark. "It's a scratch. I'm sure the King will want you to live long enough to face justice. After that, I wouldn't fancy your chances!" He suddenly looked up at the alcove. "Let him go."

The King was freed, the gag pulled from his mouth. The bodyguards gently guided him down the twisting stairs, helping him as he stumbled.

The two loyal bodyguards stepped away as the boy bowed deeply. "Your Majesty! Sorry I had to put you through this! It was the only way I could provide evidence of the traitors surrounding you."

Quercus was both amazed and saddened. Only five minutes ago, he had been enjoying the feast, feeling glad that he could give back to his people some small reward after a summer of hard work in the scaffields. His right-hand man had assured him that the country was safe. Every word was like bark stripped from a branch to reveal a different, starker truth underneath. "Who are you? How did you find out about this plot?"

"I am one of your subjects, my lord. You should see for yourself how we live, clinging to the edge of Hellebore. A sewage worker's lot is a hard one."

The boy had lost his respectful tone. But Quercus could hardly complain. His life had just been saved. "I'll never criticize a plumber again. The way you took on those two" — he paused — "common criminals was ingenious!"

The two bodyguards watched in awe as the wooden cage suddenly withdrew into the floor again, leaving Salix unconscious on the ground. Flo had already taken a pile of the cloth napkins from the table to try and staunch the flow of blood, though Salix didn't deserve her care.

Ark didn't have time for compliments. "I was working on a clogged toilet at the Councillor's house when I overheard Grasp talking with the secret envoy of Maw. They would take this country of Arborium and reduce it to a slave factory for wood and gas."

Shock was piled on shock. Quercus ran his fingers through his gray hair, pacing up and down. The boasting of Alnus and Salix suddenly made appalling sense. "This is terrible news. You must tell me everything."

Ark looked to the outer doors as if he expected trouble. "There is no time for explanation. Your failed assassins were dogsbodies, but they are backed up by great force. As you have already heard, your commander is no longer loyal to you. Your rule has let the country fall into disarray."

"How dare you?" said the King, his cheeks suffusing with anger.

Ark's green eyes turned cold. "I have stared into the heart of a mealworm, ridden on the back of a raven, and slipped past your guards like a ghost. I do dare." A chill descended into the room as Ark's words rang out. "Something true has been lost. Are you willing to fight to regain it?"

The King stroked his beard. When strange wisdom sprouted from the lips of boys, it might be wise to take heed. "I have been stuck in the palace for too long. Perhaps I have forgotten what the wood means to us all. I have been too complacent, ceding to others' words and priorities for too long." Quercus took himself in hand. "But I cannot put things right if all is lost this night. What do you propose?"

The bodyguards almost protested. The King was seeking guidance from a mere lad!

Ark had no such qualms. "You must summon those who are true to you and do it now!"

"How?"

"With all the authority your word used to command. The fireworks are done and a massacre is about to take place if we do not prevent it!" Quercus was the best leader they had. It was up to him.

The King was old, but new energy suddenly surged like sap through his veins. "We are Dendrans, yes?"

"In your service, my liege!" said each bodyguard.

This was more like it. "Now I am yours to serve, sire!" Ark joined in. It might be his plan, but without Quercus, all good intentions would crumple like fallen leaves.

"Moi, too!" said Flo, pulling out her other companions. "Us Rootshooters from the deeps be loyal to the last."

There was a pride in Quercus's breast that he had not felt in years. He drew his sword from his scabbard and strode toward the doors. "To the fight, then!"

43 · TO BATTLE

As King Quercus pulled open the double doors to the inner courtyard, the scene that greeted him filled his heart with confusion. The celebration continued unaware. Lords, ladies, dukes, and duchesses happily chatting away, feasting on all that the forest and harvest had to offer. Why should they worry when they were surrounded by well-armed protectors, brought back to the castle from the armories of Moss-side? Those same protecters, the King now saw, had weapons drawn and ready to cut laughter off at the roots.

The fireworks were finally over. It was the King's only chance. Would his people still trust him? "To arms!" Quercus shouted out across the square as a hundred puzzled faces turned toward him. "To arms! Arborium is betrayed!" Friends he'd grown up with took in the King's red face, his ceremonial sword never before unsheathed except to pass out knighthoods. This was no pleasing harvest play.

Grasp crawled under a table, hoping to avoid any personal injury, and Flint, annoyed at discovery, melted into the shadows to remind his soldiers they were no longer bodyguards but butchers in the making.

The assembled guests turned around toward the colonnade surrounding the courtyard. There were gasps at the sudden appearance of blades reflecting back the full moon. A new harvest, of blood, was about to be taken. But Quercus's rallying call momentarily checked their advance out of the shadows. The element of surprise had been taken from Flint though the odds were surely on his side?

The Marquis De-Gall, with a mustache that curled above his lip like creeper vines, and hair whiter than any shimmering cobweb, decided that imminent death was not on the menu. He suddenly swiveled around in his chair, pulling out a dress sword that had not touched action in thirty years. "For the King!" he shouted back. "For Quercus and Arborium!"

Ladies who were normally more concerned with nose powdering pulled dainty, jeweled stilettos from handbags and stood their ground. They might be surrounded, but they were proudly part of the hunting brigade, happily able to leap across broken branches to seek out timber foxes. Cowardice was not in their nature.

There was a moment of silence as the two groups faced each other. A young princess, with blond curls bright as sunbeams and a teddy boar firmly clutched to her chest, began to cry. The soldiers were trained to keep conscience at bay. A child's weeping wouldn't stop them. As the first raised his sword to strike, and as Ark prepared to give his own secret signal, a strident voice rang out.

"Stay your weapons!" Commander Flint stepped forth from the shadows directly in front of the King and his companions. His bronzed chain mail gleamed in the light of the gas table lamps and his visor was raised, revealing hard cheekbones and cold eyes. "My lord!" He bowed. "Forgive this intrusion."

"I forgive nothing, Flint. You were my trusted friend once. Have you really sold us out to Maw?"

"There is change in the air, Your *Majesty!*" Flint spat the final word. "The little people cannot bow before you forever. Safe in your castle, you do not see what is really happening in the wide-wood. We both know the price paid for the last twenty years of peace. And how is such loyalty rewarded? Poor wages and being banished to a cold billet in the armories!"

First the boy with his sharp criticisms. Now Flint, nagging his conscience like a sore tooth. Quercus shook his head, the visions of a happy harvest threshed to dust. Had he really lost touch?

Flint continued, laying out precisely what his intentions were, "We must make our future where we find it, in the new Republic of Arborium."

"You would pretend your cause is just? Gold has eaten all your common sense, man." Quercus was furious. How many years did the two of them go back? "Do you honestly think that Maw will keep its promises to you? Trust me: Like these trees, they will cut you down."

"Empty woods, empty words," Flint countered. "I do apologize for the way matters have turned out. However, if you surrender, I promise that my men will spare your friends here."

"Otherwise you would dispense with all of us, including the children?"

"War is as hard as heartwood, my lord. You and I know that."

Quercus looked for a second as if he was really considering this offer. "I cannot agree to your demand, whatever the cost. My dignity, and that of my people, will not allow it."

"Yes. I thought that might be your answer, old man. Fare you all well, then." Flint's visor dropped with a clang as he pulled out his sword.

It was the signal. As Flint dived toward the King, his men ran forward, poised to strike.

Ark felt hopeless. Children slashed and gored? He'd never

intended it. He pulled the lever hidden in the nearest wall. Would it work?

It did. Flint's blade was plucked from his hand like a feather as the sword flew toward the wall, landing with a great clatter. A hundred pairs of eyes were momentarily distracted.

"Dell and darnation!" shouted Flint.

From the shadows, Ark almost let out a whoop of joy. Maybe Goodwoody was right and the battle could be won without a single drop of blood shed! The phial of dark liquid might never need to be called upon. The hidden magnet was a good start.

But Flint was a hardened battle veteran. Setbacks, however miraculous, would not hinder the Commander. Despite his confusion, he instantly pulled a bone knife from an ankle holster. The instinct was good. Magnetized iron had no hold over this weapon.

Ark watched hopelessly as Flint advanced toward the King. However, Flint had not reckoned with the courtiers. They might be old, but the sap still flowed in their veins. They loved the trees like their own kin.

"I taught you when you were no more than a whippersapling!" said one of them, a retired major, blocking the way while the King retreated, holding up his weapon with obvious effort.

The Commander smiled. "Yes, you did, old man! Much appreciated." Flint swung his knife in a single savage arc, severing veins in the old man's arms. Blood blossomed and the offending sword dropped. "No hard feelings, eh?" he said with a stabbing motion deep into the chest that broke the man's defense, and his life. The body collapsed to the ground, the first casualty that night.

Ark realized how stupid he'd been. There were other magnets hidden around the courtyard, but they would remove weapons from both sides of the fight. So much for preparation. And where had Flo gone? He felt outnumbered and overwhelmed.

The battle was begun and it was one-sided from the start. The ancient Marquis De-Gall did his best, parrying and foiling his attacker, and one of the ladies cried with delight as her little blade somehow slashed the neck of a surprised soldier. The man dropped his sword and clutched at his throat, trying to catch the lifeblood that leaked through his hands. But these were isolated incidents as Flint's men trod through the smashed plates, swiping and stabbing both young and old.

All this time, Ark did his best. His handheld mirror was useful and cunning, harvesting light from the full moon above as he ran among the chaos, blinding one soldier after another with careful aim until the courtiers had time to knock them out. The Warden had talked about the sacredness of life, but Ark was still powerless to stop the carnage. He wondered briefly about the commoners feasting beyond the walls. Among the noise of their party, would they even hear the screams from deep within the castle as Arborium was stolen from under their feet?

Bodies fell, blood mingling with the wine from spilled pitchers. It was more than unequal. Those who survived scrambled over the tables toward the fountain at the center of the courtyard. The King was among their number, protected for now. But they were outflanked, surrounded by soldiers who closed in, eager as timber wolves for the final feast.

"All roight, me boyos?" The sound, light and tinkling like a bell, was enough to stop the soldiers for a brief second.

"Joe?" Ark shouted.

"Yas! My little Malikum. Yow saved me once. Oi'm just returnin' the favor!" The leader of the Rootshooters stood on

the high battlements, his white shift and long body turning him
into a spectral apparition.

As he spoke, other white-clad figures popped up. "Them
mealworms ain't nearly as nasty as yow lot!"

"Yow tell 'em, Dad!" said Flo, popping up by her father's
side.

Flint paused, wiping the blood from his knife on a convenient napkin. "A bunch of foreigner Rootshooters! Oh gosh, we
are terrified. Shouldn't you lot be out nibbling mushrooms, or
whatever else it is you ore monkeys do down there?"

"Oi be glad yow're scared!" shouted Joe. "Aim up, lads!"
Harpoons suddenly appeared, pulled from their loose white
shifts. "Take 'im first." Joe pointed at one of the soldiers standing on the ruins of the feast about to cut his way into the crowd
around the fountain.

There was a hissing sound and the man clutched his shoulder
where a tethered spike had suddenly impaled itself.

The man gave a wood-rending scream before collapsing to
the ground, unconscious.

"Now for the rest of yow sun-fed turnips!" Joe roared.
His intention had been to scare the growing daylights out of
Flint's men.

It almost worked. The soldiers wavered in their ranks, frightened of the white, haunting presences up above, shocked to see
their colleague cut down so easily. But Flint had fought his way
up through the woodways, where the unexpected was meat and
drink.

"Bowmen!" he shouted, his voice like the snap of a branch.

And before the Rootshooters could even pull the rest of the
harpoon triggers, arrows sped out from the shadowed cloisters
with deadly accuracy. The Rootshooters' height was for once a

disadvantage, presenting large, outlined silhouettes. The perfect target for trained archers.

Ark had no time to act, so instead he sent an impossible thought out to the trees. Could these sharpened splinters remember that they were once alive, once part of the living heart of a tree? His mind strained at the idea.

"Let fall!" he whispered, sending his words like whispering wings straight toward the deathly volley.

Deep inside the dead grain, a spark moved. And the arrows wavered in their intent. If it was a prayer, the answer had come.

Ark concentrated with all his heart. He would not have his friends cut down like scaffield corn! The arrows agreed, plummeting away from their course, ignoring the wishes of the bowmen who strung them. All except one that was too close to its target, too sure of its aim.

"Noooo!" screamed Ark, finally coming to his senses as his old friend staggered slightly, an instant, sharp branch sticking out from his skin. "No!" he cried again. Ark of the wood, trained by Corwenna, unable to stop a mere sliver of arrow when it mattered most.

"Oi be hurt!" croaked Joe with a puzzled grin as he toppled forward headfirst, his white shift turning red. He plunged straight down, dying as his last words fled his lips.

44 · DEATH OF A ROOTSHOOTER

❧

Petronio had heard the distant *thump-thump* of the rotor blades starting up. Echoes of boots clanged around the inner chamber, deep in the heart of the flypod. He'd wondered what was going on. All had been quiet for hours although the feast should have begun. Fenestra had kept him busy in the storeroom, asking him to check the figures once again, burying him out of the way. But he'd managed to filch a spare earpiece and tuned it to the right frequency. Using all this new technology already felt ingrained.

He could hear the panic in Fenestra's voice as she put her forces on alert. Their transport was already accelerating toward its target. Had the coup gone wrong? Outside this sealed chamber, the men were getting ready and once again he was stuck on the sidelines.

Heckler popped his head around the door. "I told her it wouldn't work. Man, these Dendrans are crazy! I knew it was gonna come to this."

Petronio noticed a twig sticking out of the man's tunic. "What's that?"

Heckler's face turned red. He looked around nervously as he tucked the twig out of sight. "Don't tell the Lady, but that beautiful little stick is worth more than my pension. Every man's got to look after himself, hey?" He winked at Petronio.

"Indeed!" said Petronio with sudden inspiration. Look after himself: That was exactly what he was about to do. "Something's going wrong with the inoculation reserves." He had to get Heckler's attention. If those reserves ran out, every Mawish soldier was a dead man walking.

"Here!" said Heckler, ducking his head through the hatch as he clambered in. "Let me check it out."

Petronio stepped out of the way to let the man inspect the glass-fronted freezer. He quietly lifted a shiny backup hard disk from a shelf.

Heckler bent over. "It seems all right to me!"

"And it will be all right!" said Petronio, slamming the sharp-edged hard disk onto Hecker's head.

The man groaned once, then slumped onto the floor.

"Sorry!" said Petronio. "No hard feelings." They were on the same side after all, even though the guy had once shot him. The choice of Heckler was opportune. The man liked his Buds. How strange that Maw named a drink after part of a tree! And he had a beer belly to match Petronio's. The black one-piece zoot suit wouldn't be a perfect fit, but he hoped no one would notice. After stripping the unconscious body, he gagged the mouth and tied the soldier up.

Five minutes later, what appeared to be one of Fenestra's men quietly locked the chamber behind him and adjusted the infra-red goggles on his face.

"We land in two minutes. Get strapped in, you fool!" snarled a voice behind him.

Petronio nearly jumped out of his disguise. But all that Fenestra saw was a combat-ready minion, ready to do her bidding. And that, after all, was his only intention. Adrenaline coursed like sap through his veins. At last, all his training had a purpose.

Ark ran toward the falling body, knowing it was too late. There was a dreadful irony, the master forger dying by the metal arrowhead he had dug from the deep roots. What power could bring the dead to life? Corwenna had shared dark secrets, but none for this tragedy.

Where was Flo? His eyes scanned the battlements as he ran, desperate for a sign. Loud sobs suddenly cascaded across the court as Flo threw her long arms over the battlements, trying to reach out for a life that was gone.

"Get down!" Ark shouted. "They'll kill you, too!" As Ark spoke, another phalanx of arrows slipped through the air. Ark had no strength left to stop them.

Despite her grief, Flo ducked down at the last second, the arrows sparking against solid stone. The remaining Rootshooters had learned a fatal lesson. Adding to the body count would achieve nothing.

Ark now stood over Joe's body, collapsed onto the ground, his eyes frantically searching for any sign of life. He knelt down, reaching out his hands, feeling only the warmth that was gradually leaving his old friend's body. Joe's eyes stared wide like a saint's, that same crinkly smile on the Rootshooter's face passing on a message that a good death was never to be feared. Ark grabbed a tablecloth, scattering goblets and glasses, then gently placed it over the body to make a shroud.

But battles do not wait on a single death. Before the next volley of arrows could fly, the Rootshooters took matters into their own hands. Working in teams, they launched a pile of leaves straight down into the courtyards. At least, they looked like a pile of leaves. But the soldiers' amusement turned to horror when they realized that these leaves had been cleverly stitched together. Each double-winged construction supported the weight of a single Rootshooter. Those who lived in the depths of the tree now flew down toward the courtyard with only revenge on their minds and deadly iron spitting from the mouths of their harpoons.

"For Joe!" they screamed. "Our kith and kin!"

Flint's men began to drop like plague victims. The Commander was furious. He rounded on the boy who was obviously responsible for this turning of the trunk tide. "Children and Rootshooters? You think you'll beat the Armories of the North?"

"Yes!" answered Ark, turning away from Joe. "And now it's my turn to deal with you!"

"Threatened by a boy who can't even grow a beard. How very droll." The commander crooked his fingers at two of his nearby men. "Kill him."

When Ark first came to the Ravenwood, Corwenna also tried to dismiss him. Then, he was a frightened boy. Now, he was angry, a true child of nature, tooth and claw.

Two soldiers circled him. "Don't really like it, you talkin' to our gaffer like that!" snarled the first.

"It's disrespectful-like," said the second.

"And those 'oo disrespect our boss need to be punished!"

Ark looked around. The battle was in full swing. He saw the King backed against the fountain, sweat pouring from his face, his eyes gleaming. Bodies were strewn around the floor like straw. Rootshooters dipped and dived like sap swallows, some hit by arrows, fluttering over the edge to fall into the forest, and others crashing into the massed ranks of bowmen, causing devastation.

He had his own fight to wage. The men closed in, ready to finish off the arrogant apple-pipsqueak.

"Spring is coming," said Ark.

It was a warning the men should have heeded. "It's fall!" said one of them, confused.

"No. Spring is here right now!" Ark stamped hard on the floor in front of him. His words and the Rootshooters' engineering were both accurate as a trapdoor slammed up, powered by a compressed spring. Unfortunately for the two soldiers, they were standing right on top of it. Like the Rootshooters, they flew. Unlike the Rootshooters, they didn't have the benefit of wings as they slammed with an awful crunch into the side of the battlements.

"Sorry about the lack of a beard!" said Ark as he turned and stalked toward Flint.

The Commander looked worried for the first time. But then he smiled. "You're clever, boy. I'll give you that. And your friends appear to have the upper hand. However, you never know what's behind you." Flint helpfully pointed past Ark's shoulder.

While all eyes had been focused on Ark's trick with the spring, one of the soldiers had slithered like a snake through the mounds of bodies, under the table, and straight toward the fountain. The soldier sprang up now, dispatching the King's closest bodyguard with a strike-punch to his Adam's apple, cutting off the windpipe and effectively strangling him. Then a knife shone out of nowhere. One calloused hand held the King's crowned head, the other a blade that rested easily against Quercus's neck.

"It seems we have a draw!" said Flint. "The slimy Rootshooters might win, but if your precious Majesty is dispatched, everyone loses."

Ark was flummoxed. One Dendran death against the whole of Arborium? Quercus might not have been the best of kings, but he was the symbol they were all fighting for. And that one Dendran's life was now in his hands.

"Glad to see you're thinking it over. Tell your friends to stop now, and we will let Quercus go into exile. I am a man of reason. I might even be able to persuade my colleagues not to butcher any more of the court's posh little brats."

Ark looked over Flint's shoulders and saw the princess with the golden curls lying on the ground as if sleeping. Her teddy boar was ripped open, its stuffing spilling across her dress. Flint was loathsome, his followers a poison fungus.

"Ignore every word!" the King spluttered as the knife nicked at his neck and a thin stream of blood trickled down. "My life means nothing. It is this kingdom that matters."

"Shut it!" snarled the soldier.

"No, Sergeant. His words have a rather noble ring to them. Nothing like a lost cause to make one feel nostalgic." Flint turned to Ark. "Come, boy, I need an answer. My time is precious."

A sudden scream that was designed to detonate eardrums distracted them all. Ark was shocked. He'd recognize the mouth that formed that horrendous sound anywhere. After all, he'd grown up with it. Normally, it was the harbinger of tantrums, but today it was a siren song of hope.

The scream came to screeching halt. All eyes turned toward its source, hidden behind a pair of double doors in the corner of the courtyard. As the echo died away, the doors burst open and a stinking fusillade erupted from them, aimed straight at the fountain.

"You could scream for Arborium, Shiv. Well done! That's it, Phlegm! Good aim, Biley!" came a familiar voice as the stream of unadulterated sewage hit the soldier threatening the King, squarely in the face.

"Urrgggh!" he spluttered, losing the grip on his knife and slipping in the muck before slamming onto the wooden boards headfirst. Unfortunately, the splatter effect meant that the King and his last brave defenders were no longer dressed in silk and velvet. Their cotes were now a fetching shade of sprinkled brown.

The King took advantage of the surprise, snatching the soldier's falling knife and standing none too gently on the would-be assassin's neck to stop him rearing up again.

Flint's eyes nearly popped out, his brain trying to formulate a reaction.

"Am I too late?" the welcome voice boomed out.

Ark almost burst out laughing. "Mucum, you're always late, but very, very welcome. Is Shiv all right?"

"You heard her."

"We all did!" shouted the Marquis De-Gall.

"Anyhow. Thought you lot might be in the squit. Now you are! The smell ain't too healthy, but a boy's gotta do what he's gotta doo-doo!" Mucum pushed hard and the massive squit cannon trundled into view, manned on either side by Ark's old colleagues. "I figured the scaffields 'ad enough fertilizer. These childish thugs could do with a bit o' growin' up, if you see what I mean!"

"That be moi boyo!" sang a voice from the parapets. "Oi always know'd yow be the bravest!"

Mucum couldn't help grinning. As he'd come in, the sight of Joe laid out on the ground had almost stalled him. He'd quickly checked the faces of the other dead Rootshooters splayed around the yard, feeling guilt at the relief when the one he searched for wasn't there. "Flo! I'm finally gonna kiss your socks off when we're done!"

"That be so romarrnnntic!" she said with a heaving sigh. "Yow'd better get on now. See yow later, Oi pray!"

"It's a promise!" This time, he'd keep it.

Flint felt ashamed of being defeated by a bunch of common boys. "What do you think you are doing?" he roared at his men. First they had to deal with weirdo white grubs thinking they could fly, then a boy who flung his men into the air. Now the very sewers had risen against them. To top it all, the few who had any hearts left beneath their chain mail nearly sighed at the exchange between Mucum and Flo.

Flint knew he was about to lose command. All that he had left was the loyalty of his men and their pride. "Would you be defeated by mere children?"

Their leader was right. They were armory born and bred. Their job was to maim and murder for whoever paid them the most. Flint shouted, "I want every one of them dead!" It was an order they understood.

But Flint's wish was not about to be easily granted. As his men let their blades lead them back into the fray, Mucum took control of his tiny but effective band. Little Squirt operated the rotating tracker on the cannon, turning a wheel that fired a constant jet of liquid like a geyser, spraying around the cloisters to take out the bowmen one by one. Mucum was hit in the arm by an arrow, but he simply snapped off the shaft and continued shouting instructions.

The remaining Rootshooters landed in the middle of the action and stripped off their wings, kneeling down to send a deadly spiderweb of threaded harpoons into the few archers who hadn't been washed off their feet by the force of the cannon.

Ark watched in amazement. He was humbled by his friends' risking all. With their help, the fighting might be quelled.

The King had regained his youth, deciding that mercy was not in the cards for the soldier trapped beneath his foot. He stamped down, snapping the man's neck, then jumped forward, roaring like a bear, his blade swiping and clawing at any unfortunate solider who got too close.

It was a rout. Flint backed away like a wounded animal, watching all his best-laid plans go amiss. Where was that coward Grasp? And would Maw abandon this coup so easily?

The squit cannon dripped dry, the tank that fed it beneath the castle now empty. Mucum was not bothered by this change in circumstances. "Come on, boys, let's clean up the last of this mess!" And with only meaty fists as weapons, he waded into the battle, swinging his big arms like a pair of broadswords. Even Little Squirt showed no fear, darting around like a squirrel to trip up Flint's men so that they fell directly into the path of stabbing harpoons or Mucum's bone-crushing punches.

Finally, a sick silence fell into the yard. Every one of Flint's men lay dead or groaning on the ground. The archer's bows lay scattered around the cloisters like fallen leaves, fingers that would never string up again now curled in a rictus of death.

Ark stood directly in front of Flint. "I will finish with you now."

Flint towered over the boy, the last traitor standing. "You have no weapon. I have no fear."

"But my words might convince you," said Ark. "Kneel!" The command was soft. He'd learned his true mother's lessons well. And mothers would fight to the death to protect their territory.

"You would have me bow down? I think not!" The arrogance still played around Flint's features—the jut of his jaw, the defiance in his gray eyes.

"Kneel!" said Ark, who would not be brooked. As their eyes met, the power of the forest flowed between them, enveloping Flint's body, forcing it to stagger as every ounce of willpower was put into resistance. However, given time, a tree will crack stone as easily as a chisel. Despite himself, the Commander's knees bent and he collapsed onto the floor.

The King watched, appalled at the ease with which Ark bent this once proud man into a bundle of shaking muscles. "Must you do this?" He stepped forward, trying to intervene. "We shall expose his deceit by trial. This is the way of the Dendrans."

"I am sorry, Your Majesty. But the moment your *trusted* colleague agreed to have you killed, his path was set." Ark remembered a nervous sewer apprentice running away from danger like a rabbit. That young Malikum was no more than a misty memory. "Now I will give the Commander one last chance for mercy."

All this time, Flint crouched on all fours on the bloody ground like a wounded animal. His lips tried to form words, but Ark's hypnotic hold stopped any response.

"You will ask the forgiveness of your king and the people who trusted you to protect them!" Each word was like an acorn dropped and instantly rooted in the dark soil of Flint's mind. Flint, surrounded by a cohort of corpses, bit down hard on his lips until the blood flowed freely down his chin. If he spoke up and admitted his wrongs, the mad boy would let him live. But that was not the way of a leader. He would not submit.

Ark knew exactly what the man's response would be. "You . . . will . . . do . . . as the forest desires!" And now it was Ark towering over Flint, every syllable hammering into the man's brain.

Flint's eyes rolled up inside his skull. He was losing everything. In his mind, gold ingots fell over the edge like leaves, forever too far from his failing grasp. It had all seemed so easy, so long ago. His lips parted as his mind finally snapped. "Not . . . King . . . Arborium . . . Mfffff." The next few words were gibberish. A string of frothing dribble unraveled down the side of his mouth.

Ark turned away and inclined his head toward Quercus. "Death is a great friend compared to the companions that will accompany this traitor's mind for the rest of his days." But despite the strength of his speech, Ark was trembling all over. He could taste the bile rising up into his throat, feel the twisting of snakes in his stomach. It took every remaining ounce of strength not to throw up there and then.

The King could not speak, though his hands clenched the hilt of a bloody sword dug into the wood. How could he judge a boy who had saved both his life and the country?

Two of Quercus's men tiptoed in fear around Ark, grabbing the body that was once Commander Flint and tying the hands behind the defeated man's back.

"It's finished," said Ark, his heart filling like a cruck well as he surveyed the courtyard carpeted in corpses. A terrible tiredness overtook him. He had done as the Warden asked, killing none himself, though he could not stop the Rootshooters exacting their revenge. But to bend a man's mind like a sapling and then snap it? If this was what leadership required, he wanted none of it. He felt as empty as the dark scene that confronted them all.

The battle was over, but it was the bleakest of victories.

45 · A SUDDEN TURN

A sound filled the night air, echoing around the wreckage of the courtyard.

Somewhere up above, a giant woodpecker hammered at invisible branches in a repetitive rhythm. The noise was so loud that all the survivors put their hands over their ears to block it out. At the same time, a fierce wind blew down, tugging at cotes, riffling through the hair of prone bodies, and blurring the eyes of those who dared look up. A thin black line hissed down from the sky. At its end came what looked like a fully garbed Holly Woodsman, descending at an impossible pace. Before the King could even speak, the figure landed and pulled back the hood.

"My lord. I don't think I have had the honor?" Despite the noise overhead, the voice cut through as clear as glass.

It was brave, Ark thought. All was decided, but her arrogance had lost none of its unnatural shine.

Quercus studied the woman who stood before him, fur-clad boots resting on the blood-spattered boards. "Lady Fenestra!" he shouted above the din of the rotor blades. "Envoy of Maw, I presume? Have you come to surrender now that you are surrounded?"

The sharp set of her smile was disturbingly confident. "Oh, let me assure you, if you look through the glass darkly, you will see that matters are the other way around, my dear little weak king!"

All stood spellbound by her performance. Was she mad? But the clouds cleared, revealing the source of that pounding rhythm. A black shape blotted out the sky, and from its belly, more dark lines spun out like instant spiderwebs. Each carried a figure cloaked in black, cradling shimmering danger in its arms. Red dots suddenly appeared like little fireflies hovering over the chests of the King's men.

Ark instinctively knew what was about to happen. All he could do was watch in utter horror.

"I think that now would be as good a moment as any? But please, spare the King." The envoy snapped her fingers and several simultaneous cracks echoed around the trees. The shining red wavering dots bloomed like sick roses. The scent of blood hit their noses as, one by one, good Dendrans collapsed on the ground, instantly stabbed by shards of modified glass, their life force pooling and spilling out of the courtyard and over the edge of the great trees to drop to the earth far below in dark, red, unnatural waterfalls.

Ark took in several sights at once. Up above, on the battlements, another feminine cry rang out as Flo was punched back by a single blast. Down in the yard, Mucum had ducked behind the squit cannon as g-bullets shattered harmlessly against the side of its barrel. Little Squirt was not so lucky. How could a tiny projectile lift a whole person off the floor? There was a gasp and the young sewer apprentice tumbled backward in a heap.

As all this happened, Ark was aware of the heat in his own chest. He glanced down to see his own, bright red buzzing dot. But Corwenna had trained him well. As the bullet came toward him, he watched its trajectory, dividing it up into milliseconds. It was a simple matter of telling this speeding product of Maw that he was no longer in its way. He stepped to one side, allowing all the rifle's projectile force to fall harmlessly, plowing into the far wooden wall.

The surprise lay on the face of the shooter. Petronio! Like a demon that would never give up, his chubby face leered toward him.

"Son of a beech!" was the only curse that came from his lips. "I thought the ravens had you!" It was rare for Petronio to be puzzled.

Ark had no time for personal grievance. The slaughter had to be stopped. Is that what the thin hollow whistle tucked in his cote was for? Petronio's words were a sudden gift.

Ark lifted the whistle to his lips and blew a note of total silence. But far behind the peaks of ice, and wrapped in branches that wriggled and twisted like snakes, sat a woman deep in the hollow of a tree who heard the note, as did every creature she cared for.

"Help us!" murmured Ark, at the same time aware of shining splinters eating up the distance toward intended targets.

Look through the glass darkly, said Fenestra. She hadn't looked hard enough. By allowing such alien weapons into the conflict, the envoy had lost honor and thereby brought on darker consequences.

All this, in the gap between one breath and the next. Maw was here and its troops were about to meet all that the Ravenwood could offer in return.

Ark's head turned to the west. They were coming as they had always promised. Now! The moon was blotted out as the sky suddenly filled with screeching shadows. A beating, flapping mass of black, far louder than the single, suddenly vulnerable flypod. And they were led by one bird, soaring through the slipstream.

Every eye turned upward.

"Blimming heck! It's Hedd and his gang!" shouted Mucum.

With all that blood, it was a wonder they hadn't come before. But would the perfume drive them wild? No one knew if they were friend or foe.

Ark had no time to worry about Dendran fears. The ravens of Arborium still needed his guidance. The boy reached out to Hedd, felt the keenness of that savage but noble mind, saw his intent but worried for the consequences. He pleaded with Hedd to ignore all instinct. The lead raven had to convince the rest of his furious flock. For once, they must not go for the injured, but for those who caused the injuries. As if in answer, the flock wheeled and turned.

For a brief moment, there was panic in the soldiers' eyes. With their armored vests and infrared visors, all they saw was a bunch of oversize birds flying toward them. Feathers against high-velocity rounds. Easy!

They turned their transparent weapons to the skies and let off a volley that would have cut a regiment of Dendrans in half.

And indeed, many of the brave birds fell at that first assault. Ark felt each death like a body blow. He saw the dimming of their eyes and even worse, the memories of their long, airborne lives spilling into the cold air around them. But their companions continued to fly, sharp and precise, their claws turned out to rip these interlopers into bite-size gobbets of flesh.

Weapons, far more advanced than anything Arborium had ever seen, clattered onto branch lines and plummeted toward the ground, spinning around in circles like the useless lumps of forged glass that they were.

And as for the Mawish force? They had been inoculated against gas. But there was no protection from razor beak and scything claw.

"My men!" the envoy screamed, clutching at a table in shock, forced to watch as her handpicked elite became meat. Victory was literally snatched away.

One of the birds came at Petronio, its beady eyes well aware that this prize was precious.

Petronio had finally met his match. No cunning would free him from this encounter. He turned to face the bird. *So be it.*

Grasp Senior had kept himself out of the action so far. He was currently cowering under a table nearby, able to see with awful clarity what was about to happen. Ignoring years of selfishness, he scuttled out from behind his cover and dived toward Petronio. "My son!" he shouted.

All these years, the boy had only wanted his father's approval. Is this what it took? Petronio's brain calculated the possibilities and came up with one rather excellent outcome. He would not be crossing the River Sticks today. Petronio opened his arms to welcome his father's saving embrace. But, at the very last second, he shoved hard, eyes locking onto the raven's. "Take this lump of overpriced fat! You're welcome to it!"

The incoming bird was presented with an even juicier morsel. Animal instincts took over. As Petronio ducked under the table to save himself, his father gave one last, gurgling scream. Councillor Grasp had committed the only selfless act of his greed-driven life. His reward was a claw that pierced his neck and instantly severed his windpipe. Its task done, the bird flew off to support its brethren as Grasp slowly fell to his knees, then thumped onto the boards.

Ark looked up. One of the ravens had veered away. Ark recognized the pattern of feathers around the neck. It was Hedd. What was he up to? Oh no! The bird was flying straight toward the only other creature that dared to travel the sky. However, this enemy had wings of steel. What could a raven do against such technical superiority? The answer was obvious.

Don't! Ark called, silently and desperately.

Hedd flicked back one last glance that contained only sadness. *Am with you to the end, boy of woods. Again we shall meet. Raven promise.*

Ark could do nothing more. No prayer, no sleight of hand, no begging to the trees would stop this bird's intent. He watched in horror as Hedd gave a single, screeching *crark*. The *thwack-thwack* of the flypod faltered in its beat. Hedd had flown straight into the blades.

Ark gave a single, powerless cry as the tears rolled down his cheeks.

And then the brave bird was gone, leaving only a drizzle of honest blood cascading to the forest floor. Ark clenched his fist tight at the unfairness of it all. Why did doing what was right hurt so much?

The metal monster was fatally wounded, listing to one side as it veered off into the trees to the east. There was a crash, a *whoomph* of flame that flared into the night and died away as the trees swallowed up the evidence.

It was over before it was begun. Ark stood at the center, numbed by such courage, surrounded by a storm of falling feathers.

As Mucum crawled out from under the wreckage of the cannon, and the last few Rootshooters tended to the wounded; as the King looked around in utter confusion, the grief of ages gouged into his face; as Little Squirt flopped onto his side and threw up great gouts of blood; as a child hugged his dead mother and cried a cruck pool of tears; as surviving ravens flew to nearby roosts to feed on Mawish flesh; as the envoy stood, surprisingly uninjured among the groans and rasping cries around her, Petronio took his chance.

He leapt up from under the table straight at his most hated enemy. "You! Why won't you die?" he snarled.

Ark saw his childhood foe in front of him, eyes fired up with the heat of the battle.

Petronio was not content with words. His eyes flicked briefly toward the man who was once Commander Flint. He grabbed Ark's right shoulder with one hand. The other plunged deep into Ark's stomach, searching for dark treasure. "Not so magic now, are you?" he sneered, stepping back to admire his handiwork, hearing the satisfying crunch as the blade bit.

Ark staggered back, clutching at the dagger dug deep into his guts as if it was a gift. All was expected, dealt with. But not this.

46 · THE LAST GRASP

Ark wondered why he wasn't in pain. Was dying really this easy? Then he burst out laughing. "Corwenna said that fruit was good for me!" he shrieked hysterically.

Petronio was thrown. After all, he'd just stabbed the skinny twig! "Have you gone mad? You should say a few prayers before you meet your maker."

"I did already, and they were answered!" Ark slid the knife from his body as if it was merely a blade in a butcher's block, dropping it out of Petronio's reach. So *that* was what the bag of apples was for! How did Corwenna know? Maybe miracles did grow on trees!

Ark's hand shot out and grabbed Petronio's wrist. "I don't think my Diana's forgiveness will do for you. Forgive those who tramp all over us? It's a good ideal. But not this time. And especially not for my sister's sake." Ark finally knew what the raven-gift was for. He hoped that Hedd would be proud.

"Ow!" squeaked Petronio, feeling a sudden pinprick in his palm.

The phial had been needed after all. Corwenna had talked about a gift of *death*. Now all was clear. The raven feather hidden up his sleeve served up its awful purpose. It had delivered a single drop of a liquid now eager for living veins of blood. "I learned much in the school of the wood. You presume that the trees are dumb. But they are not."

Petronio tried to release Ark's grip, but the fingers were like leeches. What gibberish was the boy talking? Too much time in the sewers had turned his mind to muck. Why couldn't the King's soldiers get him away from this maniac? He was happy to be arrested, to plead the bad influence of his father in court. The sudden tingling in his hand distracted him.

"I was warned about the misuse of power," Ark continued. "But there's a time and a place. This is both." His eyes also fell onto Petronio's hand, watching as the fat fingertips began first to darken, then to wrinkle. Corwenna had said the trees had armed themselves. Now he knew how.

"Hey! Let go of me!" screamed Petronio as a feeling of intense, sustained agony began to creep up his fingers, as if they were being sandpapered from the inside.

"It will be over soon!" The wrinkles crept up over Petronio's palm and up his wrist. He tried to move, but Ark's grip was tighter still.

Petronio felt fear then. Real fear for the first time. His bladder gave way and a warm trickle ran down his leg. "It looks like . . . bark!" he screeched.

"Oh, good boy. They taught you well!" Ark hissed. This was what the phial truly held: the living essence of every Arborian tree. The seed contained within this liquid was unstoppable.

Petronio's lower arm was turning to wood. He could even see beetles and ants crawling over what was left of his hand and tiny buds forming at his former fingertips. Soon, it would reach over his shoulder, toward his heart. And then . . .

"And then," said Ark, "at least you'll be of some use. Maybe a nice chair. Or a couple of planks. Good-bye, Petronio!" Ark knew he was now no better than this conscience-free thug. But the boy was a parasite endangering all the wild places of the heart. Ark had no choice.

"Deluded Dendrans! We are not beaten yet!" Fenestra

suddenly shouted. What could she possibly do now? Her forces were decimated and their leader a gibbering wreck. She turned toward Ark.

"I shall have your head displayed in a cube of glass. What you did to the Commander was unforgivable!"

Ark was no longer frightened of the envoy. "No, my lady. It was the Commander who broke all bonds of trust. As for your threat, I look forward to the attempt." This was ridiculous, parrying words with a defeated woman.

Good. Ark's mind was now concentrated elsewhere. Even as his arm was turning solid, Petronio felt the breeze of opportunity, hoped the envoy could keep Ark talking. By his feet lay a discarded sword. The fingers that lay curled around the hilt would no longer need it in this world or the next. But he did. Petronio suddenly leaned forward and grabbed at the sword with his free hand.

The bark had crept beyond Petronio's elbow, freezing all that was below into a gnarled wooden carving. It felt like his tendons were being torn in half, then remade into grain and splinter. A slight moan escaped his lips. He was terrified, not of dying but from knowing what he had to do next. The sword felt unfamiliar, wrong-handed.

"You will kill me again?" Ark asked.

"No!" screamed Petronio, the adrenaline flying through his veins. Did he have the courage? Only one way to find out as the sword swung up and around in a swift arc, straight toward his arm. "No!" screamed Petronio again as the well-honed blade did as it was told, snicking at skin, severing tendons and shearing through bone until all that Ark held in his hands was a half-wooden, half-bleeding limb that had once belonged to Petronio Grasp.

It was hard to tell who was more shocked. Petronio swayed on the spot, the sword in his remaining hand challenging anyone nearby as blood poured from the stump of his upper arm. He retreated toward Fenestra. "Stay away!" he snarled to his enemies.

The other soldiers stepped back, half admiring the mad courage of a lad who was willing to hack off his own arm to save his life.

Now it was the envoy's turn to act. She was standing right by the trapdoor that had sprung two soldiers into the air. A breeze blew through the gap, sweetening the already stale scent of blood. She reached toward the boy and wrapped him almost tenderly in her long arms.

She paused briefly. "Mark my words. Maw will crush your tiny country! This is but the beginning!" With that, she stepped out into the hole made by the trapdoor spring. Then they were gone.

Mucum ran forward, but the hole had swallowed them almost as if they had never been. The other soldiers were already clustered around, annoyed that the figurehead of the invasion had so easily escaped them.

"Nothing would survive that fall!" one of them muttered.

Ark strode over, his sharp eyes peering down. Below lay a sheer drop, broken only by the odd branches radiating out like spokes on a wagon wheel. In the dark, he could not be sure, but was that the envoy's cloak flaring out around her as they plummeted down? Never mind. They were no threat now.

"Are you all right, mate?" Mucum was breathing heavily, trying not to take in the destruction all around them.

"I think so. How's Little Squirt?"

Mucum had already carried his groaning friend over to where

the King's surgeon had gathered the injured. "'E'll live, and wiv a great scar to prove he's a good 'un."

"I am glad."

"Good to see you're *well armed!*"

Ark looked down at the object still held in his hands. He let the remains of the limb clatter to the ground. "That is possibly one of the worst jokes I have ever heard!" he grimaced.

"Well. You gotta laugh, really. Jes' a bit of *'armless* fun!"

"Please. Stop now, or I might have to kill you!"

A sudden panicked look entered Mucum's eyes. "Oh no. In all the rush, I didn't even think about her. Flo?" His eyes frantically searched around.

"I saw . . . I mean . . . she was hit."

Mucum's face crumpled.

Ark pointed and his friend ran toward the edge of the cloisters just as the doors burst open and several Rootshooters entered, carrying a prone figure between them.

"Flo!" cried Mucum, skidding on blood and feathers and squit as he ran over.

The Rootshooters gently laid the figure down and that was when Mucum got the surprise of his life.

The deathly pale girl opened one eye and winked at him. "Yow worry too much!" she whispered, obviously in pain.

"You're alive!" he said, kneeling down to take her hand.

"That be a most obvious conclusion!" said Flo. "Oi thought that us ironworkers moight be doin' with makin' some body shields. Whoi, yow'd thought they'd never 'eard of such things. What a malarkey, tryin' to get them to forge something out of their ken. If only a few more of moi mates had worn 'em . . ."

"What are you on about?" said Mucum. Big fat tears ran freely down his face.

"Come here, silly. Look yow!" Flo lifted up her white shift.

"Erm," said Mucum, going bright red. "Are you sure this is the right place and time?"

"Oh. Yow Dendrans are somewhat stupid sometimes! Look yow!" she insisted, lifting out a rectangle of iron from beneath her clothes with a very obvious dent in the middle. "Them strange sticks of glass didn't stand a chance!"

"Thank Diana!" He wasn't normally one for prayers to Diana, and maybe she *was* Ark's long-dead grandma. But his heart's longing had been answered.

"Oi am somewhat bruised, though! But look at yowr arm! There's an arrow stuck in there! Yow needs medical attention."

Mucum looked down at the broken-off shaft. In the heat of battle, he'd forgotten all about the pain. Now it came roaring back.

"But before them surgeons take yow off, will yow grant me one toiny request?"

"Anything!" said Mucum, gritting his teeth to ignore the throbbing.

"Yow made us a promise."

"I did?" Mucum looked confused.

"Oh Goddess save us! Do Oi 'ave to spell it out?"

"Err. I fink so. . . ." What was she talking about?

"That kiss yow were goin' to give me!"

"Oh. Right. That. Yeah." Mucum was aware that everyone was staring at them. "Do I have to?"

Flo's face dropped. "Only if yow want to," she said quietly.

"Go on!" said a soldier nearby. "Otherwise we'll have to kill you for being really stupid."

"Fair enough!" Even though he stank and was sweaty and

his arm was about to drop off, he leaned over, feeling her lips growing ever closer.

"At last!" said Ark.

"Yuck!" Shiv shouted as she ran out from the shadows to cling on to her brave brother.

Taking on rabid rats was a doddle compared to this. But finally, when his lips met Flo's, Mucum thought they were softer than any down-deep mushroom.

The kiss was honest, true, and very squelchy. A cheer went up, spreading out from the Rootshooters to the soldiers. Even the King, conferring with Ark, managed a smile.

As Ark looked on, he found a whole strange broth of feelings mixed up in his breast. He should be glad for them both, but there was a tiny twinge of jealousy, though he'd never admit it.

Flo finally broke off in more of a sob than a gasp of joy. "Oh! Oi am a fungus-eating, selfish tunnel bore!" she suddenly wailed. "All Oi wants is a bit of 'appiness. Silly, silly me!" She beat at her breast as she turned toward the floor where a figure lay. A figure who would never wink, nor joke, nor tell her off again. "Moi daddy was not so lucky! Woe is 'ere rooted in moi shriveled-up heart!"

Mucum grabbed the girl and held her tight in his big, rocking arms. She was right. There were many more families that night that would begin the dark passage of grief. And all because of the greed of a distant empire that was never satisfied.

47 · AN UNEXPECTED VISITOR

Ark was good at holding his breath. Sometimes, there were clams to be had at the bottom of his local cruck pool. It was a boyhood competition. Who could dive the twenty feet to the bottom off the slippery moss edge and stay down the longest? The pool, high up in the trees, was fed by the roots a mile below, and when the water filtered up, it carried with it the spores of these tasty creatures. The trick was to scoop at the embedded clams, using your fingers like a comb before pushing them into a net bag. Once he reached the surface again, heaving air into his lungs, it was time to count the catch. The most clams won and Ark was still unbeaten.

Today, the sun shone down as he broke the surface, dappling the water. There were already bare patches in the trees where the leaves had fallen. Those that remained were golden, almost see-through. And there were pockets of frost where frills of ice gilded the shadows. It was all change.

"You're mad!" said Mucum, sitting at the side of the pool and munching the last of the blackberries. "Cold water gives me the shivers!"

"That's the whole point!" Ark tingled all over, feeling the burn on his skin. Nothing would ever take away the stench of battle, the pitiful look in the Commander's eyes as Ark crushed the man's will. Had he done right?

He suddenly heard a reassuring voice. "No. What you did was forged with necessary justice."

Ark looked around, to see a high-hare perched on a nearby branch, head cocked to one side as it studied the boy in the pool. Its brown ears quivered like a pair of antennae, then it bounded off and vanished into the forest. Ark grinned. He must be imagining things! But as he trod water, he felt cleansed, buoyed up by the trees, his eyes taking in the rich blue of sky above him.

The fire pit was already up and running, stones lining a circular indentation at the edge of the pool. There'd been enough drama the last few weeks without setting fire to the forest. Ark threw the wet bag to Mucum and continued treading water. "Are you coming in, Shiv?"

Shiv dabbled her toes at the edge and gave a resounding screech. "It's chilly. Very chilly. My feet don't like that horrid water!" Since the battle, and every time she saw Mucum, she followed him around like a scaffield lamb. Mucum had never had an honorary little sister before, and despite her regular tantrums, he felt decidedly tender toward the little twig.

Flo looked up from chopping root mushrooms. "Oi think Oi'm getting used to all this daylight. 'Tis quite nice on moi skin, Oi thinks."

"You look as gorgeous as ever!" said Mucum.

"Whoi, Oi love a good compliment. 'Tis the best food of all!" She suddenly fell silent as the shadow of her father clouded the scene.

"Yer dad would've wanted you to be happy, eh?" Mucum did his best, but a bundle of words wouldn't take away what was in her heart.

She nodded, wiping a quick tear away. "Anyways, we be frying up a good feast of shrooms and clams. It's gonna be a tasty one. Yow all hungry?"

"Starving!" they chorused.

"Ow!" cried Flo as the knife slipped.

Ark saw a bright bead of blood gather at the tip of her thumb. For some reason, it made him feel uneasy, bringing back memories of the battle.

Seconds later, as he finally climbed out of the pool and sat down by the edge to dry himself off, he saw the water ripple out and felt a breeze ruffle his hair.

Then the sun was eclipsed by a black, feathered shadow.

"Oh no!" cried Ark as a huge raven, claws extended, descended directly toward them. History was repeating itself. He didn't even have time to send out his thoughts, to try and deflect this too swift, instinctive threat.

As Shiv opened her mouth to scream and Flo put up her arms in defense and Mucum dived toward his girlfriend to protect her, the bird closed in.

Ark shut his eyes, unwilling to see his friend snatched from the branch.

Instead of a scream, there was a flutter of wings, then silence. Ark peeked through his fingers to see a raven balanced on the branchway near the fire pit. It was preening its already glossy black feathers.

"Is this the kind of welcome I receive?"

Four shocked faces took in the figure sliding off the back of the raven. Black clothes and dark skin made the perfect camouflage. It was as if part of the raven had peeled away and come to life.

"Corwenna?" said Ark. He still couldn't call her Mother. That was a step too far. But why had she left the Ravenwood?

"I think I still have that name!" she replied.

There was an awkward silence between them. But suddenly, Corwenna knew she could not hide behind her usual haughtiness. She bent over and grabbed Ark to hug him tight. "Well done, my Ark!" she whispered for his ears only. "I knew you could do it."

Ark melted into arms that had held their land together for so long. It felt safe but too, too brief.

A few seconds later, she gently pushed him away and drew herself up to once again become Corwenna, Queen of the Ravens. "I can smell good food in the making. May I join you?"

"You frightened my girl!" said Mucum.

"Ah. Feisty to the last. It could only be you, companion of Arktorious."

"Yeah. Well. Could've let us know you were turnin' up!"

"I am sorry. So much has happened and there was my feathered family to attend to."

The ravens had been decimated. It was a dark memory for all of them.

Corwenna put on a brave smile. "But they live and they will breed again, though I miss my Hedd deeply."

Ark felt the wrench in his guts. When Hedd first plucked him from Petronio, the raven had been an enemy. By the end, he was much more than a respected companion. Ark still wondered what Hedd had meant about meeting again.

"You will find out," Corwenna whispered in answer to his thoughts.

"Hedd was a good 'un," said Mucum. "Took some guts to take on that flyin' machine."

"Yes!" Corwenna sighed. "It did. By the way, this is Hedd, son of Hedd."

The bird looked down on them and then locked eyes with Ark. Ark instantly felt the raven's pain and pride in his father.

Ark's thoughts went out with silent thanks for Hedd's fatal bravery.

Corwenna looked around. "I have not left what you Dendrans call the Ravenwood for many years. A week ago, I could not have made the journey, but my strength is returning. I think, thanks to you, this country beyond my nest feels different, less polluted with traitors' thoughts." She stared at the reflection of trees and sky in the water, then studied each of them in turn. "How are you all?" She sat cross-legged on the wood, her black petticoats spread out around her, making their own pool of feathers.

Ark spoke up. "The King's been pretty good, especially now that he's seen how the other half lives and the rot that lay at the heart of Arborium. My dad . . ." He paused. Mr. Malikum had looked after him since he was little. It was right to call him that. "My dad has got some decent medicine for the first time. Quercus offered us an apartment near the court in the upper canopy, but I like the smell of my home for now. It's good to be with my family again."

His mother had been overwhelmed with pride when she found out his role in saving Arborium. He couldn't bear to tell her the truth about his origins, though he suspected she guessed more than she was letting on.

When the tale was done, instead of treating him like a hero, Mrs. Malikum had brought him down to the wood with a bump. She'd slapped his face so hard the whole house shook, and shouted at him to never put himself in such danger again. Ark found himself smiling at the memory.

"So, how did you know about the apples?" he asked Corwenna. "Was it luck that Petronio stabbed me where he did?"

"Luck or the gift of the wood!"

They all fell silent for a second, listening to the soft hiss of autumn leaves.

"And now a question for my brave young warrior. Did the arrows really listen to you?"

"I couldn't believe it!" said Ark proudly.

"Nor could I foresee such ingenuity! I said to you once that the trees hold deeper mysteries that science can only guess at."

But Ark had stopped listening, remembering the one arrow that got away, that killed his friend's father. If only he could have stopped it. Flo had said several times that she didn't blame him. It didn't make it any easier. He changed the subject. "And that phial you gave me." Ark remembered the look on his tormentor's face as his arm turned to cold, dead wood. "Goodwoody warned me about murder, but Petronio had gone too far."

"Though I have never met your Warden, she is right. But so were you when you grabbed that boy of shadows by his hand and held on tight! He deserved all that the trees could offer!"

It was an answer, of sorts, though Ark still felt queasy at the thought of it, the ease with which his dark deed was enacted.

"D'yer fink Petronio's still alive?" Mucum piped in.

"I spoke to an acquaintance of mine, a certain mud-pirate who told me categorically that no bodies matching the description of the envoy or the Grasp boy were found at the base of the palace trees."

Ark didn't want to think about it anymore. For now, they were gone. He took the bag of clams and emptied it by the water's edge to give them a good scrub.

Corwenna continued. "The events of the Harvest Festival were only a skirmish. Even if that foul boy passed over to the other side, there are many more hungry for profitable change. Maw won't give up the prize so easily!"

She is right, thought Ark, suddenly tired despite the sun. They had merely stung the hide of a great beast. A brown, curled-up leaf slowly drifted down in front of him. He felt something stir deep within the roots of his soul. If he was of the trees, if their sap truly flowed through him, what was he capable of? The thought both excited and terrified him.

"If they come back again, whoi, Oi'll be the first to greet them all with moi harpoon!" Flo said.

"And that is why I still hold hope for the Ravenwood and this whole raised-up dream of Arborium. With such words and courage, they will have a fight on their hands."

"And I can scream them all away!" butted in Shiv.

"Sure you can, little one!" said Mucum.

"I heard that you wielded a certain sewage cannon with great skill, Mucum!" Corwenna laughed.

Mucum blushed. Having started off listening to his colleague gabbling about plots against the King, he'd come a long way. "I reckon we did oakay."

"And to think I missed the sight of Rootshooters in flight!"

"It was smelting good, warghhh! Moi brothers and sisters forgin' those leaves into shapes loike feathers that the wind found pleasin'!" Flo beamed at the thought of it and the frightened look on the faces of Flint's men. Maybe the Rootshooters had been down in the deeps too long. A bit of fresh air was no bad thing.

"Your father gave his life so that all of us could be here today. We are free because of him." Corwenna's words were an arrow of kindness, hitting Flo in the weakest of places.

"Yow be too kind. It ain't fair, though." Sudden tears trickled down her cheeks.

"No," said Corwenna, "it isn't. But his deeds will live on in books and tales. Trust me on this." She leaned forward to kiss Flo on her forehead.

Ark was surprised. Warden Goodwoody was normally the one for blessings.

"As for the rest of you, I hope the King has recognized your actions!"

"Too right 'e did!" said Mucum. "Some snooty vice commander from the armories came ridin' in jes' as the battle was over, demanding to know what all these kids were doing. He called it 'interfering in matters of state.' Broadbeam was 'is name. The bloke was even bigger than me, and a proud budder if ever I met one. It was a laugh to see old Quercus nearly bite his head off. As the King pointed out, without us lot, Arborium would be no more. Even better, the soldier was forced to hand over his best sword so that Flo, Ark, and me could be knighted for services to the country."

"Oh, that is too rich!" Corwenna laughed. "Must I bow down and call you Sir Mucum?"

Mucum was offended. "That's me name now! Don't you forget it!"

"I would not dream of it! Well, my lords and ladies, is it possible we could eat now? I have traveled farther than I've been in a hundred years. It does make one hungry, hmmm?"

"Yes," said Ark, "I'm *raven*-ous!"

Everyone groaned and even Hedd, son of Hedd, looked down, most unamused.

And they all sat in the afternoon sun, the first chill of winter on their skin, digging into the gifts that Arborium had to offer, as the raven guarded them with bright, unblinking eyes. There was more laughter and tears and toasts raised to Joe, the bravest of Rootshooters, and those who had fallen to protect this land that dreamed of sky.

ABOUT THE AUTHOR

Andrew Peters, who also publishes under the name Andrew Fusek Peters, has written extensively for readers of all ages, often in collaboration with his wife, Polly. Their work includes poetry collections, picture books, anthologies, plays, and graphic novels. *Ravenwood*, an epic fantasy set in a vast treescape, is Andrew's most prominent novel to date, and the first in a planned series. In addition to the original English-language edition, *Ravenwood* will be translated for publication in Germany, Switzerland, and Austria, Spain, France, the Netherlands, Poland, Lithuania, Turkey, Russia, China, and Brazil. As acclaimed publisher Barry Cunningham of the Chicken House describes it, "Andrew has created a world to match the best in classic fantasy. *Ravenwood* is breathtaking in its imaginative detail, gripping in scope, with real characters embarking on the biggest adventure of their lives with daredevil courage and always a sense of humor."

Andrew's school visits are renowned for their dramatic performances, infectious enthusiasm, and elaborate props. For *Ravenwood*, Andrew and his creative team crafted an incredible costume fashioned from real feathers, with a light-up velvet waistcoat! Check out YouTube for a sneak peek at Andrew's *Ravenwood* tour, and follow him on Twitter and friend him on Facebook at RavenwoodNovel.

Opposite and overleaf: Andrew Peters in his Ravenwood *tour costume, photos © Rosalind Peters.*